—— THE WAR OF ——

ORDINARY FOLK

VOLUME II
Exploits of a World War II MP

——— THE WAR OF ———
ORDINARY FOLK

SAUL LEBOW

The War of Ordinary Folk
Volume II: Exploits of a WWII MP

© 2024 Saul Lebow

All rights reserved. No part of this book may be reproduced in whole or in part, stored in a retrieval system, or transmitted in any form, or by any means, electronic, mechanical, photocopying, recording, or otherwise, without prior written permission of the author, except in the case of brief quotations embodied in critical articles or reviews.

ISBN VOL I: 979-8-9879768-5-2
ISBN VOL II: 979-8-9879768-6-9

First Edition
Published in the United States
Lebow Books

For more information or to contact the author, please write to lebowbooks@gmail.com.

Military insignia from the US Army Institute Of Heraldry is in the public domain and reproduced under the fair use doctrine. The appearance of the insignias does not imply or constitute endorsement by U.S. Department of Defense or any of its components.

This book is a work of fiction inspired by true stories and real events drawn from a variety of sources. Most names, characters, events, and incidents are the products of the author's imagination or used in a fictitious manner. In some instances, events, locales, and people have been re-created to enhance the story. To maintain anonymity of others, the names of individuals and places and the details of events have been changed. In any other cases, resemblance to actual persons, living or dead, is purely coincidental. The opinions expressed are those of the characters and not necessarily those of the author.

*To my Uncle Rubin,
and those who fought in World War II.*

Contents

Preface — 9

Part I: Four GIs in a Jeep — 13

Part II: The Ghost Among Us — 63

Part III: The Dark Side of the Holidays — 103

Part IV: The Light at the End of the Tunnel — 179

Part V: The Truth Be Told — 229

Part VI: Homeward Bound — 287

Epilogue — 339

Suggested Readings — 357

Acknowledgments — 359

About the Author — 362

Preface

HAVING TAUGHT AMERICAN HISTORY FOR ALMOST three decades in two high schools in Washington, D.C., and on reaching retirement age, I could work on a project that I always wanted to attempt but never had the time to complete. I desired to write a historical novel as my final contribution to the teaching profession and my former students. Not until the Covid crisis shut down my normal routine had I considered topics for writing a novel. Almost by chance, while rummaging in the closet for a book, I found a box with fifteen letters my Uncle Rube wrote to his pen pal during World War II. Although the letters were censored because of security concerns, they briefly outlined his activities and what he observed. From talking to my uncle, memories of my own of the Nation's Capital during the 1940s, and the knowledge I obtained collecting WWII material for teaching my students, I developed my main character, Rube Goldfarb. Arriving at Omaha Beach almost two months after the American invasion began, he served as a medic in *The War of Ordinary Folk, Volume I*.

Adding to the mix of the daily consequences of war, I include in the story, details about a long-distance romance and the impact of antisemitism and racism on the life of a scared, twenty-two-year-old medic. But despite all the trials and tribulations Corporal Goldfarb encounters both on and off the battlefield, his devotion to his fellow soldiers, girlfriend, family, friends, religion, and country never falters. However, for Rube, one of his biggest challenges will be adjusting to the adult world, which includes love, hate, survival, and death. He repeatedly grapples with his conscience.

Most war stories embellish the same themes seen through the eyes of presidents, generals, and diplomats. This book is written from a different perspective and allows the reader to experience war as viewed by mostly enlisted and drafted GIs. Among those who served, each has a story.

In Volume II, Rube Goldfarb unexpectedly must join a military police unit. With his training complete in Le Mans, Rube and his companions become part of numerous combat missions, including the Battle of the Bulge and other smaller encounters. After being assigned to provide security for the railroad transportation lines between Antwerp and Brussels, Rube must overcome the dangers created by a new enemy, black marketeers. The MPs, wearing the double cross pistol insignias on their shirts, would play an important role in securing the road to final victory.

Although fictional, the story is sprinkled with true impactful events that altered the course of history. When the American way of life was threatened, a nation, determined to remain free, joined together working in military factories at the home front, and fighting and dying on the battlefield, in the pursuit of victory over evil and tyranny.

After the reader finishes reading this page, my final history lesson continues.

PART I:

FOUR GIs IN A JEEP

One

Spectacular could only describe the view from the sky. Even though he was flying about seventy miles an hour, Corporal Rube Goldfarb, felt like time had stopped. The earth seemed motionless as different colors from the world below streamed by in a dance of rainbows. Somewhere over the rainbow, miles away, Le Mans, France and training to be a military policeman awaited.

As the small Piper Cub aircraft flew along the northern coast of France, Rube marveled at the October sky and wondered if he would still be alive as 1944 would be replaced by the new year. So far, he had conquered his fear of flying but Rube remained unhappy about leaving his medical buddies in Brest. At least this time, he would become part of a military unit and no longer surplus to be shipped back to some replacement center.

Seated behind pilot Roy Meltzer, Rube reminisced about his experiences in the past ten weeks as a medic. Amazingly, he still was alive. Having dodged death in a trench on the battlefield, and being wounded by an artillery shell, made this present flight even more miraculous. He had faced danger and seen plenty of death. What was left to frighten him? Even the uncertainty of being an MP would no longer impede his quest to return to civilian life.

One thing concerned him — the feeling that his girlfriend might be dating someone else while he was overseas. He felt helpless about her, but what options did he have? He hoped he was wrong, but she hadn't written to him in over a month. At least he had a pen pal writing to him. Nonetheless, in a few hours, a new chapter in Rube Goldfarb's military life was about to begin.

Having been so engrossed with the experience of flying and his private thoughts, Rube had hardly spoken to the pilot. After flying for half an hour, Rube finally felt confident enough to question the pilot. "Have you ever been fired upon while flying the Piper Cub?"

The pilot calmly answered, "Twice. The mission of this small plane is mainly to spot the enemy and radio their location to our artillery positions."

"Wouldn't that make this plane an easy target for the Germans?" Rube queried.

"You're right. Since we fly slow and low enough, the enemy, if they so choose, could score a direct hit. The main reason the Germans don't fire on our planes is it would give away their camouflaged locations."

"Do you have any weapons aboard?"

"I don't, but one pilot assembled six Bazookas on the wings of his plane and even destroyed several German tanks."

"No kidding!"

"Look, I have to check out a few places, so I'm going to fly the plane lower."

"You're not going to land?"

"No, just take a peek."

"What do you expect to see?"

"Do you see that farmhouse and the barn?"

"Yup."

"The Germans often hide tanks in places like that."

"What signs can you identify if that's true?"

"First, I look for tank tracks."

"Do you see any?"

"Not yet, but I'm going to check the outhouse."

"What?"

"Sometimes, you might see soldiers waiting in line."

"That's a new one on me!"

"If I don't see anyone, I look at the door of the outhouse."

"Isn't that somewhat kinky?"

"No, because if the door is closed, it usually means a family is living there, but if it's open, it might be because the air is stale inside, especially if many soldiers are using it."

"I don't know how you came up with that, but it makes sense."

"No sign of that this time."

Upon sighting a column of smoke, the pilot flew in that direction only to find an Allied plane had crashed. He quickly called headquarters with the location, and Rube interrupted and hollered, "I see a parachute on the ground."

A little while later, the Piper Cub flew over a wooded area. "Rube, hold on, I'm taking this baby down to just above the treetops."

The pilot then arched the plane back up. "Did you see anything?" asked Rube.

"I think so. But I want another look," he said as he pulled into another dive and quickly pulled up again.

"Change your mind?"

"Yes."

"Why?"

"Did you see those light flashes coming up from the ground?"

"No, but I heard something hit the plane."

"You wanna guess what that was?"

"Doesn't sound good."

Meltzer then called in the location of where a congregation of enemy troops had fired on his plane. Minutes later, the two-person crew heard explosions coming from the area the Piper Cub had just evacuated. Meltzer turned to Rube and said, "I think that enemy target won't give us any further difficulties."

Two

After landing in Le Mans, France, Meltzer checked the fuselage of the cub and discovered three holes. "That ride is something I will always remember," Rube told his pilot.

"Just another routine trip. Glad I could help you out. Good luck with your MP assignment."

Rube reported to MP headquarters and spent his first night at Le Mans in an old wood-framed barracks among other newly-arrived soldiers. The former medic was so exhausted that he barely reached the top bunk before falling asleep.

As gunshots echoed in the hall behind him, Rube jumped out of bed. He could hear the thud of mortar shells crashing into the building's exterior. A small crew of GIs had spent most of the morning placing injured soldiers into Red Cross vehicles. By noon the enemy attackers had overwhelmed the U.S. defense and easily advanced on the lightly defended living quarters. Rube and the GIs were well armed with grenades, M1 rifles, and a few Thompson machine guns but greatly outnumbered.

Once explosions ripped open the front door, all the defenders inside could do was fight a delaying action. Rube hoped the stairwells would provide an exit route for the outnumbered soldiers. Battles in the hallways slowed the German advance, but Rube and the GIs ran out of ammunition. Those GIs still holding out told Rube to move toward the steps that led to the escape door on the first floor. He didn't want to desert his fellow GIs, but they insisted, as they wanted to give the medic a chance to escape. Rube climbed a few steps and heard explosions from the floor above. Either the

Germans suffered more casualties, or all his buddies were dead. He flew down the steps. Suddenly, the door he had just exited sprang ajar, and several enemy figures appeared. With only his 45-caliber pistol, Rube opened fire, and the Germans pulled back, but an explosion at the escape door stopped Rube. Because he was out of ammunition, he reached for his Bowie knife as an enemy soldier rushed down the steps. Now the medic knew how Davy Crockett felt at the Alamo. With his knife ready to strike the German in the neck, Rube felt something suddenly hit him in the stomach. He lost all sense of movement and began rolling down to the exit platform. Sprawled on the floor, Rube growled.

He heard a voice say, "Are you alright, soldier?"

With sweat dripping from his armpits and around his neck, it took a few moments for Rube to realize he had just dreamed about his death. "I must have had a bad dream," answered the former medic.

"That happens a lot around here."

Regaining his composure, Rube looked around and saw other men in their bunks looking at him. "Sorry to wake you, men; everything that has happened to me over the last several weeks must have caught up with me."

Another GI, with a New-York-sounding accent, remarked, "Forget about it!"

After breakfast, Rube went to meet Major Phillip Greenwald, the newly appointed commander of the 96th Military Police Division. With some apprehension, Rube smartly saluted as he entered the commander's office. The first thing Rube noticed was that the commander was short, maybe only five foot three. Greenwald's first comment to Rube caused him to think quickly.

"What do you think of me?" asked Greenwald.

Rube hesitated and said, "My first thoughts compared you to an old high school teacher I had. She was about your size, but no one, I mean no one, would mess with her." Rube could see a small smile edge on the officer's face.

"Continue!"

"This gal might have been small, but she was tough as nails, and you'd better complete your homework. No excuses except for health and family problems. I'd say I learned more from her than any other teacher."

"Well, I must say your observation of your teacher fits my personality perfectly."

"May I ask a question?"

"Go ahead."

"I was told before I left the 136th that my promotion to sergeant would come once I joined the MPs. Have you heard anything about that?"

"I'll check on it."

Thank you, sir."

"I expect all my men to give me their best, just like your teacher, and from our talk, I'm sure you won't let me and the Army down."

"Absolutely, sir."

"I understand you have had combat experience."

"Yes, sir, I was in several missions while in the bocage and during the Brest campaign."

"You did this as a medic, correct?"

Rube nodded and said, "Yes."

"I also learned that you actively engaged the enemy occasionally."

"That is also true."

"Looks like we have a good match. Glad to have you aboard as a member of the 96th MPs."

As Rube left the commander's office, he heard him say to his aide, "The kid has a good mind, shows toughness, and has balls, an excellent combination."

So started Rube's career as an MP. It took several days to organize the various companies of MPs and wait for the instructors to arrive. During that time, Rube wrote to his brother, Sam.

October 2, 1944

Dear Sam,

A major event has occurred. I've been transferred to a Military

Police unit, not as a medic, but as a trainee. I'm unhappy about it, but I had no choice due to bureaucratic red tape. One positive is that I should see far less combat action. I will be stationed in Le Mans, France, for a month or more. So, when you write your next letter, use the address on this envelope. From what I've seen, the camp has been one of the best since I arrived in Europe. I'm about to meet the three men who will be my partners as we travel in our Jeep to perform various assignments.

A rumor has it that upon graduation, we will be able to visit Paris. I hope that's true. Tomorrow, I visit a tailor who will measure me for my uniform. What do you think about that?

Hope all is well back home. Please write.
Love to all of you,
Rube

Rube wrote basically the same letter to his pen pal and girlfriend.

On a cool day in early October, Rube began training with a thousand other MPs.

Driving a Jeep became one of the tasks all MPs had to master. It took a while, but Rube learned to shift gears and maneuver the Jeep. The medic, now turned Military Policeman, enjoyed driving a vehicle. Back home, most of his transportation was by streetcar or bus.

Learning the different parts of a Jeep and how to replace parts of the vehicle became one challenge he had to master during his training. During that time, he changed at least five tires. Some MPs were even allowed to ride motorcycles through obstacle courses. Everyone had to be proficient in traffic control and filing various legal forms. The MPs also spent much time becoming proficient at firing certain weapons. Since Rube had already fired a Thompson machine gun and a grenade launcher, he honed his skill at firing the M1 rifle. According to Rube, having the opportunity and experience of firing weapons proved to be the most important aspect of MP training. Still, nothing could re-create the atmosphere of firing a weapon under stress in combat.

Rube used his medical expertise to help MPs injured in accidents. One of the toughest activities came with learning hand-to-hand combat strategies. Being thrown, stomped on, or using holds to incapacitate the enemy left most GIs exhausted.

As the final days of the four-week session ended, four-person teams were selected to ride in assigned Jeeps. More like a social gathering than a military-sponsored class, the members of the different teams shared the opportunity to greet each other. Rube met his crew in a tent. First impressions made Rube understand the term "melting pot." Each of the three men he would be associated with and responsible for protecting, came from a different background.

Al Wise, from New Hampshire, was an only child and didn't have a lot of friends. But when the winter snows came, he excelled on skis and could even skate a little. He had almost received his biology degree from the University of Minnesota before war interrupted his career. Al looked the part of a scientist. Due to his wide forehead and bushy hair, along with bifocal glasses and a voice only a teacher had, made anyone who talked to him feel below his standards. Al also exhibited disdain for the life he now endured; he seemed like he'd much rather be reading Shakespeare than carrying an M1 rifle.

Jordan Turner could have entered any muscleman contest and be described as "buff." A farm boy from Oklahoma, he knew everything about farm animals and would answer any questions about cows, hogs, chickens, or horses, but who wanted to talk about these animals? So, Jordan didn't say much, but he'd always volunteer when a job was to be done. None of the crew could match his muscles and stamina. Jordan, one of six children, knew how to survive, and his team felt safer with the farm boy around. At nineteen, the "Okie" joined the Army, and his six-foot-five-inch frame made him noticeable everywhere he went. It took only one fight before every MP knew, "Don't mess with Jordan."

Will Ramsey came from Texas and delayed being drafted until he turned twenty-four because he was a Dallas cop. Will was a no-nonsense guy, who rarely smiled, but after a few beers could be the life of the party. Being tough and excellent with a rifle or pistol made him a welcome part of the team. Will had married, but it lasted only a year. He claimed to trace his heritage back to famous gunfighters like Joe Horn. No one challenged him about his family history. Will loved to gamble and always found out when and where a party was held. He had two brothers and a sister who lived in Houston but rarely saw them. His parents operated a gun shop, and one thing Will loved to do was to hunt. The Army presented him with the ideal situation to do just that.

A few days before the end of training in Le Mans, Rabbi Solomon Baruch made a surprise visit to the camp and held a *Shabbos* evening prayer session for Jewish GIs. Rube had arrived early at the tent where the service was to be held. Numerous chairs were available, although a few GIs were already seated. The corporal, soon to become a sergeant, found a seat near the front of the *bimah*. While waiting for the service to begin, Rube heard someone say his name. As he turned around, his mouth dropped. Standing beside him was Dan Silverstein, an old dance buddy from D.C.

"I don't believe it!" exclaimed Rube.

"What the hell are you doing here?" asked Dan.

"Same as you, praying to stay alive."

"Are you an MP?"

"Not officially until we graduate. When did you arrive?" questioned Rube.

"About a month ago."

"I see you already have the formal MP uniform. You look great."

With a pat on Rube's shoulder, Dan said, "You will soon have a date with the tailor. Using his tape, he takes down measurements and several days later you will be called back for a final fitting."

"I wish my dad could construct a suit that quickly."

"Oh, that's right, your dad is a tailor!"

"One sure thing, the tailors here do a great job."

"No doubt, the uniform makes for an impressive picture, but according to the Army, it's not the uniform that makes the military man."

"I understand what they're talking about. By the way, have you received your orders?"

"Not yet."

"Did you ever marry that girl you danced with?"

"I did, but only spent two days with her and left her standing at Union Station."

"What a shame!"

"Originally, I didn't want to get married as I felt my death would be extremely difficult for her to handle. But because of the health benefits and my insurance, she talked me into it."

"That really must have been a tough choice."

Dan asked, "Are you still dating Sylvia?"

"Only through the mail!"

"That must be very difficult."

"Before you joined the service, weren't you still working at the Archives building?"

"You bet," said Dan, with a smile.

"I always looked at you as a guy who preserved history, not made it."

"I didn't have much choice this time."

The two friends silenced their conversation as the rabbi entered the tent. He called upon a female nurse to light the *Shabbos* candles. As everyone in the tent recited the opening prayer, Rube remembered how his stepmother Mary would light the candles on *Shabbos*. First, she extended her arms out and seemed to gather the air around her and then placed her hands over her face and softly recited her prayer. A melancholy feeling spread over Rube's body as the rabbi started the service with a shocking opening.

"*Shabbat Shalom*! It's customary that a rabbi gives his sermon in the middle of the service, but on this occasion, I feel I must speak to you expeditiously with words of the present and thoughts of the past.

"I need not give you a sermon about war; you bear witness every day to its calamity. Yet we must continue to fight even though we know there are no true winners. In war, everyone suffers, especially the innocent, the young and the old. But we must go on, not because of pride and glory, but to challenge the oppressor so that civilized societies can continue to thrive. Hopefully, in the future, because of your sacrifices and what you accomplish, our grandchildren won't be taken from their peaceful lives and secured dwellings to be sent to a foreign land to fight. As we pray, men are dying because a man and his country wish to rule the globe. Their barbaric behavior only unites us further to continue the fight to eliminate this evil.

"I can't tell you how much I admire all of you and all the military servicemen and women who have the unenviable task of challenging the enemy. Our fighting forces everywhere will eventually win this war. I pray for your safety every month, every week, every day, and every second. Many tyrants have tried since the beginning of human life to wipe out the Jewish people, and they will fail again because of you. When we are victorious, finally, peace will return to the earth."

After the rabbi's speech, unlike at home, the GIs applauded and cheered. Rube had heard many speeches from outstanding rabbis, but to keep the decorum at the synagogue, the congregation didn't clap, but now, with the war going on, the atmosphere was different.

The service concluded with everyone singing the spirited poem, *"Adom Olam."* Afterward, the Jewish servicemen and women walked to a different tent where the mess hall staff had a cake, cookies, and coffee waiting. Dan had to leave because he had guard duty but took a few cookies. Rube remained and met with some of the other Jewish GIs.

Of all the men he talked with, Maury Rosen stood out the most. Maury, the son of Orthodox Jewish parents, lived in Fort Lauderdale, Florida, and had worked for a kosher food company before the war. At twenty, he would run early each morning to keep in shape. His body attracted many women as he had a phone book full of numbers.

As they talked, Maury told Rube about his first hours in combat. His company landed at Omaha Beach early on D-day. Before advancing beyond the water, enemy fire riddled the wave of soldiers as they advanced toward the beach. Maury remembered the shock of witnessing the death of some of his fellow soldiers. The GI continued running on the beach toward his ninety-foot cliff destination when a powerful blast hurled his body into the air. The impact of hitting the sand on the beach left him breathless. Even worse, he panicked as smoke drifted off the back of his shirt. After tasting particles of sand in his mouth, Maury tried to lift his face out of the sand without success. Fortunately, a medic arrived and, after ripping the shirt off his back, gave him a shot. With the assault still in progress, he removed a few pieces of shrapnel embedded in Maury's back. The medic then told the wounded GI that he couldn't provide any more help, and his choices were remaining on the beach that was still under fire or completing his mission of scaling the cliff. Seeing the numerous ropes that hung from the top of the overlook swaying in the air, shirtless, Maury began the climb to the top. Using only his fingers, knife, and strength, Maury, with his weapon covering the bandages on his back, pulled himself over the top of the edge of the cliff. Not even having a second to view the chaos on the beach, he ran to a trench where eight other GIs were encountering the enemy.

With only a few men, they realized that advancing farther would be difficult. But despite being outnumbered, this small group of soldiers attacked a nearby machine gun nest. After eliminating it from further action, Maury led an assault on a mortar position. Firing his Thompson machine gun, he provided cover for other soldiers while they launched their grenades. After taking over the enemy's position, the nine men, in a life-and-death struggle, stopped a German counterattack. With little ammunition remaining, the survivors of D-Day held their position until reinforcements arrived. Maury recalled when the replacements noticed his blood-soaked uniform, they thought he had been seriously injured.

Rube told Maury about his first encounter as a medic under fire and how his uniform was covered in so much blood that he had to burn it. After hearing Rube's stories, the two GIs, who each suffered wounds during combat, related how fear, anger, pain, and discipline learned in military training increased their motivation to stay alive. They couldn't agree whether it was luck or another force that both were surviving and wearing the U.S. Army uniform.

Three

Like fall in the states, the seasons changed rapidly in Le Mans, France. Not only had the temperature dropped over twenty-five degrees, but most foliage on the trees had disappeared. On a very crisp autumn day companies of MPs marched on the parade field wearing their formal uniforms. At noon on October 27, 1944, almost 1,600 men stood at attention and listened to General Wilson Hoover give the graduation speech.

"At ease, men. You have just completed your coursework to become MPs; now, the real test begins. The question is, will you be able to put into practice what you learned, and perform the duties of an MP? Some think our job is easy. As most of you know, the military has no easy duties. Your biggest challenge will come when you make split-second decisions. In our case, decisions often have life-and-death implications. So, we must know our location, available information, and population before making a split-second decision.

"Your training should allow you to complete your duties at the highest level, without any mistakes, and with a consistency that brings pride and respect to the entire MP division. Hopefully, by doing our part, we will help shorten the war. Godspeed."

The men cheered and applauded but when Major Harvey Warmick made his remarks, he received an even greater response. "Gentlemen, I will inform you about the schedule for the coming days. At 1800 on Sunday, all MPs will receive a four-day pass to visit Paris."

As Rube and other GIs struggled to pack enough clothes for their brief vacation to Paris, they listened to music on the radio while they cheerfully talked of plans, real and imaginary, upon arriving in the French city. A few hummed the song, "How Ya Gonna Keep 'em Down on the Farm (After They've Seen Paree)?" Suddenly the musical interlude was interrupted by a news broadcast, certainly nothing unusual for the men as news bulletins had become routine during the war. However, this news announcement was a rebroadcast from Germany. War correspondent James Cassidy announced, "Today, the National Broadcasting Company brings its listeners a program of a historic moment. This is the first direct broadcast of a Jewish religious service from German soil since Adolph Hitler and his Nazis began destroying not only the Jewish religion but all religions more than a decade ago."

Chills flashed through Rube's body as he listened to the fifteen-minute service led by Army Chaplain Sidney Lefkowitz. Toward the end of the service, the fifty-one Jewish soldiers present, together in unison, said, "Thank you, God, for allowing us to reach this day." With tears in his eyes, Rube repeated these same words.

As the day ended, the Le Mans base became a ghost town. Thankfully, for the hundreds of GIs, the extensively bomb-damaged French railroad system had been repaired so that the rail lines between Le Mans and Versailles, just south of Paris, were in operation.

Rube boarded the train to Paris with the other three team members. Once in Paris, he realized that the city, only a little more than two months since being abandoned by the Germans, had yet to return to normalcy. While most businesses and museums had reopened, and a strong Allied presence was on every block, the charm of this great city seemed to be missing.

Rube and his new companions decided not to remain together, as each soldier had his area of the city he wanted to visit. The Louvre and other museums attracted Al Wise. Jordan Turner wanted to walk up the Eiffel Tower if they let him. If not, he wanted to take photographs of the city with his camera. Will Ramsey would visit the restaurants and bars. Rube, at first, wanted to shop for gifts for his folks and girlfriend Sylvia. With little money, Rube had to be frugal about what places he visited. At least the Army had reserved places for GIs to sleep. Many natives of the city were outraged by the large number of buildings and facilities reserved for use by the Allies.

One of the stores Rube visited was a boutique with women's clothing. He saw a beautiful hat that he thought would look lovely on Sylvia, and despite its cost, he purchased it.

After finding one of the billets to stay in while on his four-day pass, Rube walked the streets of Paris. At times he felt like he was back home as the streets were filled with American soldiers from every branch of service. Some of the guys searched for open bars, dancehalls and, of course, the brothels. Others just took in the sights of the city they had heard so much about. It was a thrill for Rube to sit at an outdoor cafe and watch all the street activity.

While eating, the former medic spotted Dan Silverstein strolling down the street. He shouted, "Dan, this isn't Georgia Avenue!"

As the MP turned and saw Rube, with a big smile, Dan asked, "I see you have an empty chair at your table. Should I join you?"

"Absolutely."

After the initial greetings, the two men discussed their military experiences. Each had stories, some true, others somewhat exaggerated, but one question seemed to come up the most — "Have you encountered any antisemitism within the ranks?" questioned Dan.

Rube responded, "Not so much from the men, but certain officers have shown disdain for me. I'm unsure if it's my performance or our religion."

"So far, I've been lucky. I've felt little, if any, outward hostility aimed at me or other Jews. No one cares about your religion when the bullets start flying among the soldiers."

"I hear you, but who can forget how many in my community referred to Roosevelt High, where I went to school, as "Jewsvelt," because the school had ten to fifteen percent Jewish students .… Did you have many incidents of antisemitism at your school?"

"Nothing major, as far as conflicts among the student body. I can only think of one minor incident, more a joke than an insult. Something else played a role in keeping antisemitism at bay in the school."

"Let's hear it."

Dan began, "Students, teachers, and administrators were aware of a student in school who was the leader of a criminal gang. No one, and I mean nobody, messed with the kid. Troublemaker couldn't describe him. Outlaw was a better word. He was always in trouble, and downtown officials knew of his encounters with the police. One thing I didn't mention — he was Jewish. He clarified one thing as he walked through the school halls with his gang. Don't mess with the Jewish kids. School officials cheered, clapped, and danced when he graduated, but the Jewish students wondered if the once pleasant atmosphere between the different ethnic groups at school might change for the worse."

Rube responded, "Granted, the incidents of antisemitism during our high school days were mild compared to what was reported on the radio and in the newspapers. It hurts to hear American voices over the airwaves supporting Hitler's war against the Jews."

"I agree, especially those broadcasts back home that come from a priest who trashes our religion without rebuttal."

"What about those hateful diatribes by automobile magnate Henry Ford, who published his newspaper that blamed the Jews for the world's problems."

"Rube, the best we can do now is to do what we are doing. Continue to support the cause of freedom and fight against the Nazi menace, and maybe when this curse against humanity is destroyed, those who are antisemitic will see a different Jew and gradually change their opinion of us."

"Dan, I like your positivity, but I'm more realistic and expect little change."

"Let me end with this. Have you seen how the local Paris citizens pay back those who collaborated with the Nazis?"

"Yes, it's ugly but deserved," commented Rube.

"Maybe, if we win the war, there will be a new reckoning among the citizens about how regimes like the Nazis are a danger to all religions and freedom."

"I get the picture loud and clear, but will the politicians, economic leaders, and the general public?"

"That's the unanswered question," Dan concluded.

After paying the bill for their meal, the two talked about what they wanted to see in this newly liberated city. Both wanted to avoid the catacombs under the city, once used as a sewer and now the resting place for those who had passed away centuries ago.

One place they wanted to visit was the entertainment district, but neither knew if establishments remained open, but they would check. Rube also wanted to visit the artists' community, while Dan desired to travel a few miles away to Versailles. Rube asked Dan, "What's so important about Versailles?"

Dan responded, "That's where World War II started."

"Wait, I thought World War II started with the invasion of Poland by the Germans."

"Not exactly."

Both guys walked the Hall of Mirrors inside the Palace at Versailles the next day. As they walked through this magnificent mansion, Dan said, "If I had a wish, I would bring back those who wrote the treaty to end World War I. Then, I would have them stand before these mirrors. Instead of seeing themselves, they would see the images we see daily on the battlefield."

"I see your point, but I doubt it would make any difference in preventing the war," said Rube.

"You're probably right because the roots of World War I started between royal families that controlled territory throughout Europe."

"I never knew that."

"Here's what I learned from some of the archives I researched while working. Royalty in Europe often increased its power through marriage. With one powerful family joining another, empires could emerge as countries and municipalities formed alliances. Let me give you a make-believe American example of what I'm talking about. Suppose the Roosevelt family had two daughters. One married into the Rockefellers, and the other married into the Carnegie family. What would be the impact?"

"They would control most of the wealth and economic power of the nation."

"Exactly, that's what happened in Europe early in the 20th century. Royal families who influenced and controlled massive economic and political bases set the agenda for many European countries. Like many times among large families, disagreements arise, sometimes over money, broken promises, and the desire to be the most powerful. These disagreements led to angry disputes that brought about violence."

"Like, the assassination of Archduke Ferdinand."

"Correct, and all these countries and municipalities had alliances. So, when a violent incident broke out, all the different alliances suddenly were caught in a web of war. It was almost impossible for countries to break out of the alliances, and since each had pledged to protect the other, war was the only way out. Just like centuries ago, when kings and queens wanted to grow more powerful, they instituted wars. With knights as captains and lieutenants, they gathered the peasants and serfs to fight their battles.

"In this century, the same mentality existed, and the royal families had built their armies and used loyalty to the throne to secure the little people to fight against their enemies. Before long, England became involved, and when the German U-boats began sinking American ships, the United States had no choice but to go to war. The Versailles treaty, which ended WWI, set the stage for WWII as it blamed Germany for starting the war and made them pay extensive damages. Hitler used the treaty and antisemitism to seek revenge against those countries who signed the treaty."

Four

After returning to Paris, both men searched for a place to dance. They didn't have far to look as they arrived at *La Jupe De Danse*, "The Dancing Skirt." Neither was sure what was happening beyond the door, but they hoped only dancing. Once they heard the music, they entered and found GIs and young girls dancing up a storm. In Rube's own words, "Paris girls are special." He liked the way they dressed, talked, and danced. Soon Rube and Dan were dancing to swing music with beautiful girls. The young ladies enjoyed it when the soldiers swung them between their legs. Rube remembered how his friend Stuart taught him this move, but he never expected to have so much fun doing it, especially with attractive French girls.

Near 2300 hours, Rube said to Dan, "What's next?" When some young ladies began leaving, Dan and Rube offered to walk them home. They accepted. Normally, walking the streets of Paris would be no big deal, but most citizens were still jittery from recent events. Many retaliations against pro-Nazi individuals and numerous muggings occurred at night, making a simple walk home dangerous. Of course, the GIs weren't considering that when they accompanied the girls home. Near the girls' home, the group of five saw two headlights following them as they walked. One of the young ladies said, "I don't want any trouble."

Dan calmly said, "Neither do we." As the headlights came closer, Dan muttered, "I wish I had my pistol with me."

Another set of headlights was coming down the street directly in front of them. A voice in English shouted, "Are you girls, okay?"

They answered, "We are just fine." Then a flashlight shone on the faces of the group. Rube had to squint but could make out that the men were riding in a Jeep.

Dan followed with, "You wouldn't be MPs."

The answer came back "Affirmative."

Rube exclaimed, "You should know we are members of a newly formed 381st MP company."

"Do you have any identification?" retorted the MP.

"Yes, sir," replied Rube.

"Slowly reach into your pocket and give it to my assistant. Sorry to interrupt. We've had several robberies around here. You are probably unaware that a citywide curfew begins in forty minutes, so we will gladly bring you back to your billet."

Rube and Dan looked disappointed until each girl came over, kissed them, and said they hoped to see them again tomorrow. When the girls entered their home, an MP said, "We screwed up your evening, but we have to follow orders and protect the citizens of Paris." Without objections, both men climbed into the Jeep and, for once, could honestly say they could look forward to tomorrow.

The next day, the two MPs, tired yet exhilarated after touring parts of the pristine and beautiful city, had enough energy to return to The Dancing Skirt for another fun evening. As they walked toward the dance hall, Rube noticed something was wrong. The two soldiers had to dodge large pools of water, and this seemed strange as it hadn't rained in Paris since they arrived. As the two men approached The Dancing Skirt, they noticed two uniformed MPs standing before the entrance. Then they saw the building had been damaged by fire. Rube anxiously asked the MPs, "What happened?"

The taller one explained, "Someone threw a Molotov cocktail at the place and set it on fire."

"Anyone hurt?" asked Dan.

"Some, but not by the fire."

"I don't understand."

"The fire created a panic among the soldiers and dancers, and for a while, they were trapped inside until they smashed out the back door."

"Why couldn't they just open the door?"

"Someone had blocked it with a bunch of tires,"

"Unbelievable!"

Rube asked, "Did they catch the person?"

"Not yet."

"Damn," remarked Dan. "Maybe we should go over to where the girls live to see if they're alright."

"Do you think we can find it?" asked Rube. "You know it was night when we walked them home."

"Let's give it a try," answered Dan.

It took almost half an hour and a couple of wrong turns before they stood in front of the girls' building, a modest structure with five apartments within its walls.

"Do you remember which apartment the girls live in?" asked Rube.

"The only one I remember was Molly, who lived in apartment number five."

Walking up two flights of steps, the two MPs knocked on her door. An older woman cautiously opened the door.

"Is Molly home?" Dan inquired.

The old woman said, "Yes, but she's very sick."

"Sick or hurt?" asked Rube.

"Do you know what happened?" the old lady questioned.

"Yes, I think so," responded Rube.

"I can't stop her from crying. I think she must be hurt."

Rube asked, "Can we see her?"

"Tell her the two American soldiers she danced with yesterday are here to see how she's feeling," pleaded Dan.

The old woman, probably Molly's aunt, grandmother or mother, opened her bedroom door. Both GIs could hear her crying. After a few minutes, Molly appeared, and Rube said, "If you are hurt, we can take you to a doctor, or I was a medic, and I might be able to see what's the problem."

Molly said, "I'm not injured; I wasn't inside the dance hall."

"So, why are you so upset?" questioned Dan.

Dan's comments caused Molly to burst into tears again. Both GIs asked the old lady if she could make tea to help Molly get herself together. It took a while before Molly decided to talk to both men.

"So, what happened?" asked Dan.

Molly seemed like she didn't want to answer the question, but after a long pause said, "I saw who threw the Molotov cocktail at the building."

A surprised Dan remarked, "You said you weren't there!"

"I wasn't inside and had to stay late for my job; it was almost seven o'clock when I arrived at the dance hall. I saw this individual light something in his hand with a match and throw it. Suddenly a bottle crashed into the wall near the entrance and exploded into a ball of fire."

"Did you get a look at the person?" asked Rube.

"Yes."

"Did you recognize the person?"

No answer came from Molly as she ran into her room crying.

"Somehow, we have to get her to give us that name," Dan responded.

Rube thought for a minute and came up with an idea. "Why don't we tell her there is a reward for information leading to an arrest of the firebomber."

"Great idea. Now where does the money come from?"

"Good question," answered Rube.

"You can see these people are really poor."

"Did Molly say anything about her parents?"

"No, but her friend told me the Germans killed her father, and her mother died in a rocket attack."

"The old woman must be her grandmother."

"How much money can Molly make with a part-time job!"

"What if we miss a meal or two? We can always eat at one of our mess halls. I have eighteen, American," said Rube.

"Let me check my wallet. I have thirty-three, American," added Dan.

The two GIs agreed to offer twenty-five dollars in reward money if she gave them the name.

Fortunately, Grandma understood enough English so that she went into Molly's room to explain the GI's offer. When Grandma came out, she said, "Molly fears for her life and can't do it."

The two frustrated soldiers were about to give up when Molly withdrew from her room. With tears running down her cheeks, she told the GIs that the guy was a bully and had friends who could do bodily harm to her. Rube asked if he had ever threatened her.

"I don't know what you mean about threatening me, but he once tried to rape me."

Dan jumped in and said, "Molly, we have an entire army that can deal with him if you give us the name."

"What if someone tells him who ratted on him?"

"That won't happen. If you put his name on a piece of paper, we will take care of the rest, and we won't use your name."

Rube then took out a pad of paper that he used to write to Sylvia and asked for the name and address of the suspect. Reluctantly, Molly wrote down the name of Marcel LeSue. Rube again asked, "Are you sure this is the name of the person who torched the dance hall with a Molotov cocktail?"

Molly nodded, "Yes."

Grandma, who didn't know the exact address of the assailant but knew the street, told Rube, "He lives on Lafayette Street. The house is the only one that has a flagpole attached to it. Before the Germans left, a Nazi flag flew on the flagpole. The family, except for the son, fled with the Germans." Rube then placed the name in an envelope without any other identifiers on the top.

Grandma and Molly cried when Dan and Rube left, but each had enough money to keep them going until the city returned to normal and more jobs became available.

Both MPs briefly stopped at the apartment of the other two girls and listened to their story. Their mother offered strudel to both GIs as the girls gave a first-hand account of what happened inside the dance club. Both agreed that Molly had been lucky to miss the entire incident.

Less than an hour later, Rube and Dan entered the Army's headquarters. They asked to see the security officer on duty. A young woman wearing a WAC uniform pointed to the desk of the night officer who had stepped out for a moment. Dan dropped the envelope on his desk containing the culprit's name. The words "Very Important" were written on the front of the envelope.

Both were surprised when the officer arrived. He had stripes but no bars on his uniform. Sergeant Gerald Watson stood about five-foot-ten, and his large body made his face look small. Because he weighed near 300 pounds, he moved slowly. "What can I do for you?"

Dan said, "We are here to protest the price-gouging by some of the cafe owners."

"You're not the first." Then he noticed the letter. "Where did this come from?"

Both Dan and Rube shrugged. Rube replied, "We just got here."

"I wonder why it says important," remarked the sergeant.

"Maybe it's a secret admirer," answered Dan with a smile.

"I doubt it. I usually throw letters like this out unless it has 'U.S. Army' on it. But this time, there might be something important written inside. Excuse me while I look at it."

It took only seconds for the big man to push back his chair and rush past both soldiers. "Gentlemen, I have to go now," he said as the two MPs watched him waddle down the hall calling for a lieutenant.

The next day after the early breakfast, both men returned to the headquarters. This time they found a lieutenant who looked rather haggard. Dan asked, "Do you know anything about the transportation of the MPs back to the departure site?"

The officer replied, "Damn it; I forgot we are supposed to provide security for the convoy leaving at 1600." He continued, "I've been up all night. Incidentally, did both of you hear about the fire-bombing at the dance hall?"

"Yes," both answered. Rube added, "Actually, we danced there the day before."

"Well, we captured the assailant at 0300 this morning at his home."

"No kidding!" said Dan.

"I've been there since an hour ago. We found a bomb-making lab in his basement."

"Really!"

"I'm waiting for the French police to pick him up."

Rube responded, "I hear some of the French police force were working with the German Gestapo."

"I heard that too, but with French resistance people now in charge, if this guy escapes, anyone involved would be committing suicide. The resistance people don't play; they are the judge and jury for most of those who supported the Nazis." Before the lieutenant could continue to talk, he had to deal with another crisis and departed.

"Busy man," said Dan. "I guess the rest of the day belongs to us."

As Rube and Dan were about to depart headquarters, the WAC at the information desk informed them that for one time only, there was a free show at noon for the American troops at the Folies Bergère.

Before the performance, the two MPs stopped back at Molly's apartment. Only Grandma was at home. After inviting both men inside, she asked if they wanted some tea, and both men declined since they only had a few minutes to spare. Rube then whispered in her ear, "Tell Molly her problem has gone away." Grandma gave both men a big hug and kiss.

As the two men walked away, Dan said, "You know, the twenty-five dollars we spent might be the best money we ever will spend because it might have saved hundreds of lives."

Rube nodded and said, "I didn't mind her kissing me, but her kisses were like my stepmother's, wet and messy."

Dan chuckled and said, "Her kisses were much like what I get from my dog. Do you have a dog?"

"No, a cat."

"Well, their kisses aren't as wet as dogs'!"

"Our cat is more known for something else."

"What's that?"

"Every time the Jewish New Year comes around, she presents us with a new litter."

Both guys laughed, and Rube said, "I enjoyed spending the four days with you."

"Me too; time went fast."

"I won't forget some of the girls we met. I would give them a big *'oh là là.'*"

"I wish we had spent more time with those young girls."

"Watch it, Dan; remember you're married!"

With a sigh, each MP made preparations to report for the trip back to the camp near Le Mans, and they pledged to keep in touch with each other.

With some free time, Rube wrote four short letters to his parents, his brother Sam's family, his girlfriend Sylvia, and his pen pal Roberta.

October 30, 1944

Dear Roberta,

They call Paris the city of love. I can see why it has this reputation. The streets, buildings, and the pace of the city creates an atmosphere that encompasses the soul. I enjoyed staying in the city and visiting the historical sites and cafes rivaling Washington's. I even found a place to dance. The city is slowly returning to normal but violent incidents continue to plague the population daily. If I should make it home, I'll show you some of the pictures I took. Until that happens, stay safe.

Greetings from the city of love.

Your pal,

Rube

October 30, 1944

Dear Sylvia,

I am now returning from Paris. What a beautiful place. Thankfully, the Germans didn't destroy the city like they did in other places. I took some pictures; if I ever come home, they will be part of my scrapbook. The city would be great for a honeymoon or visit. Hopefully, if I return, I won't be wearing a uniform.

Much love,
Rube

October 30, 1944

Dear Pop and Mary,

I can't believe I just visited Paris. The city is still recovering from the German occupation but maintains its beauty. When I return home, I'll share my pictures with the family.

Yesterday we visited the Eiffel Tower and Versailles. I even danced at a club that played swing music. Please tell Stuart's parents so they can tell their soldier boy!

Your son,
Rube

October 30, 1944

Dear Sam, Marie, and Bernie,

I always loved Washington, but Paris has that special charm that makes you want to stay longer. All the sites, museums, cafes, and theatres make for a wonderful vacation place. Of course, I'm here for a different reason, and I expect to receive my new orders when we return to our base.

Love,
Rube

The truck trip back to camp proved to be long but uneventful. Most GIs slept off hangovers or caught up on their missed sleep. Once the convoy completed its journey and the men jumped from their vehicles, they immediately became confused, and wondered if they were in the wrong location. One GI said, "I think I'm back in Jersey."

Rube recalled seeing something like this scene while thinking about buying a car. Standing before them was the unbelievable sight of thirteen rows of twelve brand-new Jeeps, neatly parked on the exercise field that knocked all the MPs for a loop. "This can't be," echoed a soldier. The American automobile industry couldn't have displayed the vehicles better if parked at an auto dealership.

After the soldiers had time to mill around and inspect some of the Jeeps, the division leader, Albert Eichorn, addressed the newly formed MP units. "Gentlemen, this is our moment. This is when we will do our role to end the war. These vehicles before you will take you to areas all over Europe. You will be the 'poster boys' of the American military. Your uniform will signify the power that will eventually destroy the Axis alliance. But our glory will be determined by your behavior and ability to enforce laws without harming the freedom of those you swore to protect. That will be the deciding factor in how successful our mission will be. From what I've seen so far, you are our finest representatives. We will win this war, and you will help fill the void of governments abolished due to the war.

"Whatever time it takes, you will be the force that will allow recovery to occur. In some ways, this task could compare to the difficult mission our military has undertaken in defeating the Axis powers. I have no doubt we can complete the job of saving Europe and beyond. You might think we are glorified cops, but you are saviors to those who suffered under four years of German rule. So it shall be, we accept the challenge, and we will, despite our lack of size, become a giant in changing the course of history."

After hearing Eichorn's speech, Rube remarked, "It sounded like my old football coach rallying his players before a game."

Over the next ten days, Jeeps were placed on the backs of flatbed rail cars that would take them and their crews back to Versailles. This city would become the starting point for each MP team. Rube and his crew would be heading into the unknown but anxiously awaited the itinerary for the first trip in the new Jeep.

Five

Even if Rube's team had the opportunity to plan a vacation trip, it couldn't have been any better than the Army's version of their travel plans. After Versailles, the plan called for a pleasant ride to Reims, where the MPs would take two days to visit several interesting places. Then off to Metz. Although fighting continued nearby, the city had recently been secured from the Germans. After three days in Metz, the newly formed team of MPs would travel to Luxembourg to await new orders. The best part of the trip, according to Rube, was that Uncle Sam fully paid for it. There was only one catch; you had to survive the trip.

On November 11, the anniversary of the end of World War I, Rube's team of four prepared to leave Versailles for their trip to Reims. Since their new Jeep had no major storage area, one duffel bag contained everything the soldiers needed. Also stuffed aboard were several duffel bags filled with mail for the GIs. Each MP would drive an hour and then switch at the wheel. After leaving Versailles, it didn't take long before each soldier talked about their adventures in Paris.

Jordan Turner, the kid from Oklahoma, told his story first. He left the city the first day and, with another friend, who had obtained a Jeep, visited two farms restocking animals and repairing damage caused by the Germans to their agriculture facilities. Coming upon an old mill, the Okie and his buddy spent several hours investigating the machinery that operated the plant.

Will Ramsey, the former cop, bragged about how he spent two days with a beautiful French woman. He even described, in explicit detail, the type of sex they had.

Al Wise, the biologist, explored the city's various museums and visited several art galleries. He even toured a hospital in Paris.

When it came to Rube, he wasn't sure what to say. If he told the truth, no one would have believed him. So, the new MP pontificated about two historical theaters he visited, the Cabaret Music Hall and the Folies Bergères. "Several noted American performers played in these theaters. One of the most notable was the Colored American entertainer, Josephine Baker. Known for her dance routines and outlandish costumes, Josephine refused to accept discriminatory laws against Negroes in America.

"She couldn't tolerate traveling in separate train cars. She was disgusted that Negroes were unable to watch her perform in 'White' theaters. Most of all, she hated the segregated bathrooms. So, she decided to leave the United States and perform in Europe, where these restrictions did not exist.

"At the Cabaret Music Hall, built in 1869, Josephine danced with a string of bananas around her naked body." With the other three men listening intently, Rube heightened and enhanced the story to the point that it became untruthful, but the men hung on each word. He revealed that Josephine tore off a banana one night, opened it up, started licking it, and stuffed it in her mouth.

"No, she didn't," said Al.

"Oh, yes, she did," said Rube.

Jordan said, "I wish I were in the audience."

"Me too," said Rube with a smile. "But Josephine last played in the theater in the year 1936."

Al concluded, "She would never get away with a performance like that in America."

Will, whose sexual weekend left him limp, suddenly became interested in this story. Having the last word, he said with a chuckle, "As a cop, arresting her would have been no big deal, but bringing charges would be difficult, especially if she gave me a private performance!"

Midway through the trip to Reims, the four new MPs became involved in a spirited fight about choosing a nickname for each other. They threw around the usual goofball names until they became serious about selecting a fitting name. Rube's name was the easiest to agree upon, either because of his golden arm as a high school quarterback, which may have been exaggerated, or his last name. "Goldy" became his name.

Next in line for an obvious nickname was Jordan Turner, who came from Oklahoma and received the name "Okie."

Finding a name for Al Wise proved difficult, but after a heated debate, the crew settled upon "Chip" because his last name, Wise, was also the name of a company that produced potato chips, thus the name "Chip."

Will Ramsey never wanted a nickname but seemed delighted with his name. Because of Will's profession as a cop, who solved many crimes, he became known as "Will the Thrill" or "The Thrill."

All this banter led to a battle over what to name their Jeep. Like pilots who gave their planes a name that usually had an image of a woman with little clothes drawn on the side, the four MPs wanted something similar for their Jeep. With the trip almost over, the Jeep's crew hadn't come up with a name they all could agree upon.

Okie, driving then, mentioned that he thought the Jeep drove well and traveling in it wasn't a bad experience. Goldy gave a thumbs up to the assessment, but The Thrill said, "If it weren't for the mailbags that took away a lot of foot space, I would agree." Then he said, "What does the Army think we are, the Pony Express?" Bingo, Pony Express became the name of the Jeep.

The first successful mission accomplished by the "Pony Express" and its crew was the delivery of mail to the U.S. troops. The sight of a mail bag among the troops almost always acted like a magnet, and crowds of troopers appeared faster than at a fifty percent sale at Macy's department store. The worst part of any mail delivery comes when the last name has been called. For those who didn't receive any mail, it brings instant depression and a feeling of loneliness that lasts for hours and sometimes days. Every soldier has experienced this feeling, but the "GI Blues" could never compare to losing a buddy in combat.

The rest of the day, the crew hoped to sightsee in beautiful Reims. Once they arrived in the town, all their plans changed. Reims wasn't beautiful any longer as it had been mainly reduced to rubble from continuous bombing. This historic small town, now a casualty of the war, still had two sites untouched by the fighting. Dismayed by what happened to the town, the Pony Express crew eventually came upon what looked like a Roman arch. They later learned that this part of the arch had been built in 200 A.D. At that time, it extended thirty-three meters in length and was the largest Roman structure in the world.

Stopping in front of a church built in honor of the Virgin Mary, the Pony Express guys viewed The Lady of Reims Cathedral, one of the few buildings without major damage. This religious edifice took over three centuries to build and was completed in the fifteenth century. Under its high Gothic architecture, French kings held their coronations. Because of the recent fighting, the church remained closed to visitors, but from the foyer, the crew viewed the splendor of its interior.

A rumor that The Thrill wanted to check out dealt with one of the products that made the town of Reims famous, its champagne. According to The Thrill, GIs could buy a bottle at a certain hour and a particular place at a reasonable price. The Jeep and crew arrived early, and the MPs waited to see if this champagne promise were true. The boys drank the bubbly liquid that night and celebrated that they were still alive.

The next day while talking to some of the surviving residents of Reims, the team learned that if the Allies were victorious, the treaty signing to end the war would occur in this once small and beautiful town.

The day after, each man went on a scavenger hunt, a way of acquiring items that might be needed in the future for their survival. Goldy took the opportunity to visit an Army hospital in a mansion that was once a museum.

About a mile from the hospital, Rube spotted a shadow moving against the wall. At first, he thought it might be a sniper but instantly noticed the figure of a child about six or seven years old. Unable to speak many English words, she pointed to her mouth and said, "Food." Rube reached into his pocket and pulled out a chocolate candy bar but realized the girl needed much more help. Rube pointed to the girl and asked her name. "Petra Mylosh," she responded. Rube attempted to converse with Petra but had limited success because of the language barrier. Rube pointed to himself, "I'm Rube Goldfarb." Using pantomime, the young girl pointed to a collapsed building where she lived. Petra curling her hands in front of her eyes as if crying helped Rube understand that she was talking about her mother. She then motioned to herself and started moving her mouth as if eating. Without further comment, Rube asked the girl to take him to her mother. A block away, Rube found what was left of a human soul. Rube, seeing a pair of scared eyes and a lifeless body, turned to Petra and asked, "Is that your mother?" Petra nodded, covered one hand over her heart, and pointed a finger at her eye as she uttered, "Mama ... I ... help." She then rubbed her stomach, pointed to her mouth, and held up three fingers, indicating the days they hadn't had any food.

"Enough." Rube pointed to the Jeep, and it only took a few minutes to drive Petra and her mother to the hospital entrance.

Unlike the triage tents, the hospital's main objective was to give special care to soldiers who sustained serious injuries in France and Belgium. On occasion, the hospital at Palace du Column accepted a few civilians.

Rube had witnessed hundreds of downtrodden refugees, but in the light of the hospital, he observed two forms that once were human figures and now looked like skeletons. With only the clothes on their backs that hung like leaves on a tree, and an odor from their bodies that pinched Rube's nose, Petra and Rube listened to the mother cry while waiting to see the doctors. Attempting to console her mother, Petra kept repeating in a foreign language, words of support.

Petra's efforts and the mother's cry resonated in Rube's soul and activated something so bizarre that he couldn't believe it. Without remorse, from his wrist, he pulled the bracelet that his girlfriend Sylvia had given him before leaving for Europe and placed it on the arm of the young girl. Her arm was so thin that it fell off. Grabbing the bracelet, Rube asked Petra to give it to her mother, and it barely fit but remained on her mother's arm. For the first time, Rube saw a tinge of a smile on Mama's face. Tears came to Petra's eyes as, for the first time in over a month, she hoped their lives would be better one day. Mama stopped crying as the two were taken into the doctor's examination room, leaving Rube alone on the bench.

After seeing the desire to live in the lifeless faces of Petra and her mother, Rube waited for the voice in his mind to say, *what in the world did you do?* There was none. There was only Rube's wish to provide these poor souls the opportunity to sell the bracelet on the black market for a considerable amount of money. His doing a *mitzvah*, a good deed, might have influenced his decision to depart with Sylvia's bracelet, but for the first time, Rube began to realize that other factors took precedence over a long-distance relationship with his girlfriend.

Without guilt from his actions, the former medic, with his identification cards, orders, and the helmet liner he kept, checked in with the hospital personnel staff. Carrying his two medical bags and provided with a third bag, Rube asked staff members to assist him in acquiring items like bandages, morphine shots, tourniquets, alcohol, tape, and even operating instruments. As if a kid in a candy shop, Goldy stuffed as many medical supplies as he could into his satchels. If his stepmother had been with him, she would have said, "You are acting like a *chazer*." This Yiddish word was used around his house when he ate more food than necessary. Because the hospital had a surplus of medical supplies, Rube joyfully went on a Halloween-like "trick or treat" expedition and walked out of the hospital with bags bulging at the seams.

Okie found a farm where he picked up bags of powdered wheat, corn, sugar, and a metal bowl. He would later purchase a glass jar and a dozen eggs. After breaking eggs into the jar, he placed a top on it. He thought the mixture would make biscuits when they arrived back at camp.

The Thrill didn't bring anything back but discovered the site of the armory where additional weapons were stored.

Six

When the three men returned to camp, they saw Chip had purchased three paint cans, including red, white, and blue. The MP, now turned painter, proudly showed off brushes that he would use in painting the "Pony Express" symbol on the side of the Jeep. Chip would soon place a recognizable image on the naked Jeep.

Goldy watched as Chip painted a large H on the side of the vehicle. To Goldy, the H looked more like a football goalpost. Nonetheless, Chip drew a line from the top of the left goalpost almost to the right one. He filled in the space with the neck and head of a horse. Using the two poles at the bottom of the H, he turned them into the legs of the animal. He completed his horse by putting a tail on the left-hand side of the top goalpost. He then curved off the different corners of the horse, and from the letter H, Chip created a picture that fit perfectly on the side of the Jeep. Goldy looked at the object up and down but couldn't decide the animal's identity as a horse, but it had the color of the Lone Ranger's stallion, Silver. The white horse then had a figure on top of it that was supposed to be the mail carrier.

Chip had trouble painting the face, but the rider wore blue jeans and a red shirt. Somehow his white hat covered most of his face, so it was easy to mistake the rider's brim for the nose of the rider. Chip did better in painting the name, Pony Express, on the Jeep. When Chip completed the emblem, he gathered the group together. "What do you think?" he proudly questioned.

Surprisingly, everyone shared something positive. The Thrill summed up everything by saying, "I couldn't have done a better job." Of course, The Thrill never lifted a paintbrush.

Okie gave a better assessment a few hours later when he said, "It looks like Pinocchio riding a llama."

Before leaving Reims, the team went to the armory to select weapons more powerful than their pistols. Somehow, they managed to stuff a Thompson machine gun, an M-l rifle, a grenade launcher, ammo, and another bag of mail, into the Jeep before leaving Reims for Metz.

Goldy's team traveled half of the trip to Metz relatively easily, as the roads had little traffic. Then everything came to a grinding halt. All types of military vehicles stood dormant on the roads. The Thrill commented, "This is worse traffic than in the heart of Manhattan." For almost an hour, nothing moved.

Chip, who was at the wheel, said, "This is bullshit."

Finally, Okie said, "Why are we sitting here?"

"We are MPs," answered Goldy. Chip pulled the Pony Express to the side of the road to find out what was causing the hold-up at the four-road intersection. Walking the distance of no more than a few city blocks, the four MPs witnessed complete chaos. Soldiers were arguing, and tanks, trucks, and Jeeps stretched for miles. The acrimony stopped with the arrival of the MPs. "What the hell is going on here?" bellowed The Thrill.

Within minutes, the MPs took over positions that allowed them to alternate traffic every ninety seconds. Once the logjams were broken, traffic began to move. The slow and consistent movement continued before a Jeep with a small flag stopped in the middle of the intersection. Seated in the Jeep were three high-ranking officers. One said, "What unit are you from?"

Goldy replied, "We are MPs from the 381st Battalion, and we were stranded in line much like you, sir. It was us that decided to take control of this mess."

"Excellent," answered the officer. "I guarantee you this won't happen tomorrow." For almost five hours, the team directed military traffic through the intersection.

It was near 2200 when the team of MPs arrived at their destination in Metz. With the sounds of war all around them, the four exhausted MPs reported. The officer in charge was sympathetic to their ordeal with the crowded roads and proclaimed, "This has become the norm with all the military traffic coming into the area."

They were told where to bunk. The men weren't hungry, thanks to Okie, who baked some biscuits before leaving Reims, but Goldy wanted a cup of coffee. "Two tents down on your right," offered a soldier.

Sipping his hot coffee, Goldy relaxed and watched as another GI entered the tent. He wore a medical apron over his uniform, and Goldy presumed the soldier worked in the medical tent.

Goldy inquired, "Are you a doctor or a medic?"

"A doctor."

"I was a medic."

"What happened?"

"It's a long story, but now I'm an MP."

"What's your name?"

"I'm Rube Goldfarb but my guys call me Goldy."

"I'm Doctor Peter Andrews. I'm just finishing up a real tough day."

"I just spent hours managing traffic jams on narrow crossroads."

"I guess that's where our medical supplies are, but they haven't reached us yet. At this moment, the cupboard is bare."

"Hopefully, that convoy will get here tomorrow." Goldy finished his coffee and asked the doctor, "Will you be returning to the hospital tent?"

"I'll be there all night."

"Maybe, I should go with you to see your location."

"Sure, follow me."

As they walked and approached Goldy's tent, he said, "Could you wait a minute? I have to go inside and get something."

Within a minute, Goldy reappeared carrying three bags. "That didn't take long," said the doctor.

"I just had to tell my men I would go to the medical tent."

"What's in the bags?" inquired Andrews.

"Everything you want." Under a light strung over a walkway, Goldy opened the satchels and showed the doctor its contents.

"Where did you get all this?"

Goldy told him about acquiring medical supplies from a hospital in Reims. "It's all yours with one caveat — when your supplies arrive, you refill the bags."

"Deal," said a grateful Dr. Andrews.

"How many injured soldiers are under your supervision?"

"Far too many."

"Hopefully, these medical supplies will ease your present situation."

"I don't know what to say to my staff. I went out for coffee and came back with lifesavers."

"Tell them, like when manna fell from heaven, no one asked questions about the unexpected arrival," said Rube with a smile.

"Great answer, Goldy."

While in the hospital tent, Goldy heard the doctor say the same thing to one of his nurses. Goldy saw a man suffering from severe weight loss as he walked among the wounded. When the MP spotted a nurse, he asked, "What caused this soldier's condition?"

"Oh, she said, "He's not a soldier, but he fought with the French resistance. We have had a difficult time with him because he speaks a foreign language."

"You mean French?"

"No, it sounds like German, but we can't exactly tell what it is." Goldy went to the man and asked the nurse if she could say something to him. "He won't understand," she said, "and he won't speak to you in English." When the man spoke, Goldy instantly realized the man was speaking Yiddish.

Twenty minutes later, an Intel officer, Tom Abbott, joined Goldy at the bedside of Jacob Horowitz. Although not proficient in speaking Yiddish, Goldy had picked up enough words from his father and stepmother to converse. As Jacob spoke Yiddish, Rube translated it into English for Tom Abbott.

Jacob's story started in a small town in eastern Poland. When he turned thirteen, his parents moved to Warsaw. In 1939, when Hitler's army invaded

Poland, he had just turned nineteen. His parents, who were too old to leave, gave him much of their savings, and he fled with a group of young people. For the next four years, he lived like a nomad in many countries of Europe. While in Belgium, he joined an underground group that fought the Nazis. Fighting and survival were nothing new to Jacob. He first killed a German soldier by dropping a large piece of cement wall on his head and removing his weapons and uniform. From that point, he would do anything to stay alive, including stealing, robbing, and killing. One by one, the members of his resistance fighters were caught or killed. Somehow, he made it to France, where he joined the remnants of a French underground unit. For two years, his group sabotaged military targets, destroyed important facilities, and killed many Nazis.

With the invasion on D-day, his gang assisted the American troops. Because of his ability to understand some German, he became a listening post for the resistance movement. He arrived in the Metz area before the fighting began and sent valuable information to the Allies about the position of the German army and its size. Jacob believed the enemy had four divisions in the Metz area.

Three weeks later, Jacob was on patrol with eight of his fighters when they were ambushed. He and three other prisoners were taken to Fort de Mete. The Germans used the fort to hold French resistance fighters. The invaders told the citizens of Metz that Fort de Mete would serve as a prison and was not considered a concentration camp, but most of its population eventually went to the death camps.

After being beaten, Jacob convinced the Germans he had suffered a brain wound while fighting against the French in combat, and that is why he spoke German in such a weird way. Once the fighting started around Metz, security at the fort became lax, giving Jacob and three other prisoners a chance to escape. With broken German, he explained to the guards that his group of four had been ordered to repair damage to the fort's exterior due to Allied shells. While at the damaged wall, they found a spot where rain had made the ground below soft. All four men jumped down ten feet to freedom. Jacob found a hiding place in the attic of an abandoned home. Once the American forces entered Metz, they discovered him, and he hadn't eaten in two days.

The Intel officer continued his interrogation, and Goldy, who continued to translate, didn't return to his tent until 0200.

At 0600, he was awakened and told they were returning to the intersection to direct traffic as a new convoy of trucks would arrive at 1000. At least this time, they were given walkie-talkies to communicate, enabling them to avoid confusion on the roads. Six hours later, Goldy and the team returned to camp. When Rube found his cot in the tent, he went to sleep.

———•———

Seven

THE NEXT DAY AFTER MEETING WITH the commanding officer, the Pony Express members expected to perform the same routine. Their new orders couldn't have been more different. As they listened, the team realized this assignment would be much more dangerous.

"Gentlemen," Colonel Artie Spencer stated, "I'm not going to give you a lot of bull. This is a tough assignment. I understand you have been attempting to avert the daily breakdowns in our transportation network. This is happening because the major road we would like to take to move supplies directly to the front has been closed because of enemy shelling. Therefore, we take alternate routes to the front, which takes much more time and causes more traffic jams. Instead of using this roundabout route and digging out vehicles stuck in soft dirt or mud, I plan to recapture a highway the Germans currently control. If we accomplish this mission, moving our weapons, troops, and tanks into the combat zone, we would most likely tilt the fighting balance in our favor.

"To do this, I'm ordering four of our newly heavily armored Sherman tanks to move down the road leading to the front. They will take fire but should be able to get through, but we still need to get trucks and other vehicles past the enemy fire. I have used hundreds of eyes to discover where the enemy releases the barrage of shells that ravage our convoys, without success. I desperately need to take out those artillery pieces, and that's where you men come into the picture. Isn't it true all of you have combat experience?"

All four of the Pony Express crew answered with thumbs up.

The colonel continued, "I hope that by using a small number of men, the enemy will overlook your position and reveal the gunfire site. So, I decided to try one more time to silence the fire from the German artillery. With a limited force available, I have chosen you boys for this assignment. You will be properly armed with semi-automatic weapons, radios, binoculars, and camouflaged uniforms. Moving along the left side of the tanks should give you enough protection from any fire coming at the tanks. After 200 to 300 yards, you will see piles of rubble along the road — the remains of homes destroyed during the battle. We were hoping you could use the debris as a hiding place, and from there, you should be able to identify the location of the enemy fire. Every time we hit them with our firepower, we think they are finished. But they keep returning. There must be tunnels or underground placements protecting them from our artillery.

"One last recommendation, you must continue to move your position because, eventually, they will target your location with their shells. Once we can eliminate the enemy fire, victory is ours. Any questions?"

In unison, the foursome answered, "Let's get going."

Exactly at 1000, the Shermans moved onto the main road and, after a short distance, began to take fire. The four MPs moved along with the tanks until they spotted piles of rubble and hid behind the debris. As the steel monsters moved along the road, they fired at the enemy positions. When the tanks passed the MPs' position, the men focused on where the fire had originated. The American tanks and artillery pounded the German location but failed to silence their weapons.

The Thrill suddenly shouted, "Incoming, incoming," as mortar shells crashed near their position.

"Move, move," called Chip. Okie found a new location, and the crew continued to observe the enemy. The information from the MPs helped the artillery to pinpoint the area of enemy fire, but again they failed to knock out the enemy barrage.

Goldy watched a shell explode closer to the team's hideaway and said, "I think it's time to move again." As the crew departed their location, a mortar shell landed where they had been conducting surveillance. Okie again led the team to a new spot. As they moved among the piles of debris, Rube saw the tops of German helmets. He turned to his buddies and silently pointed to a large pile of the remains of homes. He motioned with his hands for the group to take two different positions. Without moving a muscle, the team waited until six armed Germans appeared.

Within seconds it was over. Before the smoke from their weapons settled, the MPs had moved to another spot. With their binoculars, they noticed a crevice or a trench where blasts of light emerged. Again, after notifying the artillery, a stream of shells appeared to make a direct hit on the location. One explosion after another continued.

Over the radio, Goldy heard the order for the convoy of American vehicles to move forward. Motors roared, wheels screeched, and the convoy darted into the valley of death in one fluid motion.

The four MPs charged closer to the advancing convoy as the first vehicles barreled down the once-impregnable road. The MPs waved the military parade of vehicles forward. With the trucks and other vehicles no longer being decimated by enemy fire, the Pony Express crew watched the last vehicle storm to safety.

With the mission complete, all four MPs congratulated each other for a well-done job. With the convoy on the way to the front, they hoped that this would be the backbreaker for the German forces, and they would either surrender or retreat.

On November 21st, the battle for Metz reached a crescendo as battling armies clashed. With Patton's Third Army leading the way, the remaining German forces surrendered the next day.

With Thanksgiving only two days away, for many of the American combatants, November 23 would not only include the traditional turkey day celebration but would be part of a victory celebration. In addition, the cessation of fighting would provide hundreds of GIs time to read the mail delivered by the Pony Express.

While the victors pampered themselves with a day off, the four members of the Pony Express were preparing to take the final leg of their journey from Le Mans to Luxembourg. They had one last obligation before they left — to report to Colonel Spencer.

"Outstanding work the other day," offered the colonel.

"Thank you, sir," the four men responded.

"I learned of your orders last night and thought we'd better talk. I'm sure you are aware of the surrender of most of the Germans in the Metz area. However, the city still has pockets of resistance, especially at a few forts. In addition, many of the roads out of town still haven't been cleared of mines. Also, some German soldiers escaped and could be anywhere outside of Metz. So, it would be extremely dangerous for you to travel to Luxembourg now. Maybe in two or three days, we will give the green light. If we are sure the roads are safe by then, I plan to send a convoy to Luxembourg, which you could join. Is there any special reason you must be there by the twenty-fourth?"

Each man looked at the other, and Goldy answered, "Not to our knowledge."

"Well then, why not celebrate Thanksgiving with some victorious troops?"

Thanksgiving Day, 1944, was one holiday the soldiers at Metz would always remember. The most important aspect of the day to the GIs was that they had survived the battle, and many thanked God and prayed for the recovery of the wounded soldiers. Even though other battles would be fought in the future, each soldier couldn't help thinking about "home."

The Army did a wonderful job and served a Thanksgiving dinner with all the trimmings. Goldy's crew was pleasantly surprised by how wonderful the food tasted. Yes, there was little ambiance around where the meals had to be served. Some soldiers ate in trucks, others in abandoned homes, and some ate their Thanksgiving meal at a battered table. For some soldiers, this was their first social gathering in months. The joy of talking to other GIs made the event even more special. But with weapons stacked around the table, everyone knew the reality of their life. Even if their feeling of warmth proved to be temporary, the men appreciated the effort of the Army to bring a slice of home life to the GIs. But as one soldier stated, "Nothing could top being at home." Each man hoped that next year would be entirely different and they could enjoy a Thanksgiving meal with their families.

Meanwhile, the war continued.

Part II:
The Ghost Among Us

Eight

On the morning of November 27, a convoy of trucks carrying troops and supplies, along with escorts from three armored carriers and two Jeeps, moved slowly toward Luxembourg. "I just don't get it; I don't," said The Thrill from the back of the Pony Express. With his feet on top of a mailbag, the former cop noted that they were headed to an area with more security than he saw in Paris.

"Why do you say that?" asked Chip. "You know that young Lieutenant, Alan Thomas. He showed me some aerial photos of the region around Luxembourg. You wouldn't believe the number of planes and tanks around the city, and you would think they could have sent some down to Metz while the fighting was ongoing."

"Maybe they were afraid it might weaken the city's defense," uttered Goldy.

"I don't think so."

Okie jumped into the conversation with an observation. "It seems sometimes the Army is short of everything and other times they are oversupplied."

"That's true," offered The Thrill.

Within an hour, the convoy covered the twenty miles to Luxembourg. Like many in Europe, the city had a long history, and most homes from a bygone era needed to be repaired. The homes were in poor condition, whether due to war, weather, or time. The once charming city desperately needed a makeover.

The crew of the Pony Express reported to headquarters along with a bag of mail. A disinterested sergeant put the mail aside, glanced at the letter written by officers explaining why the four men had reported late, and said, "Very well." Finally, he looked at the MPs standing across from his desk and said, "Everything is calm, not much activity anywhere, but we had a sabotage incident three days ago. Many of the citizens of this town continue to support the Nazis. Maybe that explains why they abandoned the city without a shot."

"What did they hit?" asked Chip.

"They blew up part of a bridge."

"Anyone hurt?"

"No, investigating the incident will be one of your jobs, and another will be to patrol the streets during daylight hours. Any time a convoy comes through town, your team will direct traffic. Also, your team will operate this security branch one night a week."

"What does that involve?" inquired Goldy.

"Mainly handling any calls, arrests, or citizen complaints."

"I suppose this is an all-night affair."

"You're correct."

The sergeant called for a private to show the new MPs their quarters. For a change, the GIs felt the new facilities were better than expected. "This is where we're going to live?" asked Okie.

"Yep," said the private.

"This house wouldn't be my choice back home, but it has running water and heat."

"This one has an outhouse, but some have indoor bathrooms."

"No doubt the officers live in those," The Thrill commented.

The next day the Pony Express crew visited the damaged bridge. The engineers had almost brought the bridge back into operation. One notified the MPs that, most likely, the saboteurs tied together some artillery shells left by the Germans and placed a timing mechanism to set it off. "Hopefully, this is a one-time event, but don't count on it," said another engineer.

Outside of some citizens shouting obscenities at the Jeep occupants, the team had an uneventful day. They even had a chance to retire early and get a good night's sleep.

"Get out of bed," were the first words the MPs heard as they awoke.

Chip screamed, "What time is it?"

After looking at his watch, The Thrill shouted, "0400."

"What?" said Goldy.

"Are we under attack or is this a drill?" mumbled a tired Okie.

"This is no drill. Get dressed and be at your Jeep in five minutes," an officer demanded.

As the crew made its way outside, they expected to be greeted by darkness. Instead, it was light as day.

"Holy cow!" a startled Goldy screeched. Sparkles flew under the light of flames.

"What's going on?" asked Chip.

Lieutenant Ron Steel explained, "The saboteurs struck again. Those flames are from fuel tanks that had been blown up."

"Jesus," said Okie.

"Anyone killed?" asked The Thrill.

"We're not sure. The fire unit hasn't put the flames out yet." said the lieutenant.

The crew spent the next five hours looking for clues about the oil tank facility. Outside of some tire tracks, they didn't find anything that would provide a clue about the identity of the perpetrators. Even trained dogs brought to the site couldn't discover a sniff of anything incriminating.

Back at their house, the crew attempted to establish some chronological order in which the saboteurs operated. Goldy noted, "The first attack occurred on November 24, and the attack on the oil tanks happened four days later. Also, we confirmed from the tire marks that the attackers were carried to the site in a large vehicle."

Chip said, "I think the next thing we must do is to interview some of the Luxembourg citizens to allow us to see if any organized pro-Nazi group still exists in the city."

Very few Luxembourg citizens agreed to talk to the MPs. One woman refused to give her name and told Chip, "I saw how they treated the Jews. The Germans and their Luxembourg allies are nothing more than thugs and animals, and if I give you any information, I might end up like the Jews."

"No doubt that a cell of saboteurs shares responsibility for the two incidents," said Goldy.

"The big question remains. How do we find them?" Okie asked.

"I guess we plan for the next attack, wherever that will occur," replied Goldy.

Four days later, the saboteurs struck again. They blew up several trucks and damaged four Jeeps at the military motor pool. And this time, they did something even more disturbing. They killed two soldiers guarding the facility.

From the American general down to the private, everyone felt the pressure to find the killers. The Pony Express crew used a map to locate the sites of the attacks. With pins on the map, they noticed that the first attack was in the western part of Luxembourg, and the second occurred on the opposite side, in the city's eastern part. You could draw a line between where the two attacks took place. The explosion at the oil tanks happened early in the morning like the others, but its location was off the grid to the north.

"So, where does this leave us?" asked Okie.

"I don't know," said Goldy. They put another pin in the map and continued to search for clues. The crew, frustrated and tired, had another task to endure on December 4. They were responsible for the overnight shift.

Surprisingly, Luxembourg had a quiet evening, but inside the headquarters, a large disagreement broke out between Okie and Goldy. It would be easy to understand feuds breaking out about politics, common military decisions, and comments about a family or personalities but a major disagreement "over a dance step" doesn't happen. But it did. Both Goldy and Okie did some dancing. Goldy enjoyed swing dancing to songs like "One O'clock Jump." Okie favored country western dances like the two-step or "Cotton-Eyed Joe." Chip and The Thrill enjoyed the banter between the two on who was a better dancer. But an argument erupted over how to do one step called a jazz box, and Okie firmly believed the step was just a box step. Okie moved a step to the right, then a step forward, to the left, and finally, a step backward.

Goldy said, "That's just a box step. I'll show you a jazz box step." He crossed his right leg over his left, stepped back on the left, and moved the right foot back. Okie disagreed. It wasn't long before both guys were screaming at each other. So, Goldy did the box step, but Okie couldn't do the jazz box step. Nonetheless, the argument continued until Goldy said, "I think you might have it."

"I told you so," a joyful Okie noted.

"I'm not talking about the dance step; I'm thinking about the saboteurs." That comment got everybody's attention.

All four men went to the map and inserted pins where the three incidents occurred. The pins almost fit the description of the box step. So, to make a box, they put a pin to finish it. As the MPs looked closely at the pin's location, somewhat shocked, the spot on the map identified the new airfield. The group then looked at the calendar. The next day was exactly four days after the motor pool attack. The sabotage of the fuel tanks and the bridge occurred four days apart. "I can't guarantee it will take place at the airfield, but certainly, there will be an attack somewhere," said Goldy. "What do you guys think?"

"That's good police work," said The Thrill.

"I'm not sure I agree, but it could happen," Chip agreed.

"I don't buy all that jazz, but I would bring in the lieutenant and hear his thoughts," answered Okie.

They all nodded in agreement, made phone calls, and held a meeting at 0200 hours. By sunrise, the camp became a mixture of dancing feet, speeding bodies, and the confluence of trucks, Jeeps, and armored vehicles that were spinning out of control as they navigated the camp. The MPs realized that if their theory proved wrong, they would be doing kitchen police duty for at least six months.

"I think the entire camp must be positioned near the air base," said Chip.

"They are sure protecting that airfield. I've been told only a few people are allowed inside the fence," replied Goldy.

"I heard they're working on some new type of plane," retorted The Thrill.

By 2300, everyone was in place for the expected assault on the airfield. Then the waiting began. Midnight passed without an incident, then 0100 and 0200 exited quietly. At 0230, the Pony Express crew began to panic. At 0330, the only thing moving near the field was a lone biker who peddled near the airfield without stopping. Okie said, "He might be a milkman going to a farm for his delivery." At 0345, the same biker drove by the air base again.

"I think something might be up," noted The Thrill. At 0357, the biker made his third appearance and stopped near the field. Using a flashlight, he waved it into the air. A minute later, two army transport carriers arrived, and four men from each vehicle jumped out carrying anti-tank weapons, machine guns, and grenades. A dozen floodlights illuminated the entire area as they moved toward the fence near the airfield entrance. Caught wearing American uniforms, the saboteurs could have surrendered but instead chose to fight. A crescendo of gunfire ripped the air. All eight men dropped. The lookout tried to escape but only pedaled a few hundred feet before being caught. A crowd of soldiers gathered around the eight bodies. Two were still alive and placed in an Army ambulance.

At that moment, a bottle of French wine appeared before the Pony Express crew. From their lookout post, Goldy asked, "Where did this bottle come from?"

"Like magic," said Okie.

"Who cares?" questioned The Thrill. Chip offered a toast, and the four MPs ended the early morning with relief.

With little sleep, the Pony Express crew attended numerous debriefings early on December 6. In the afternoon, the crew spent many hours reviewing different locations on maps of the area around Luxembourg. Before ending this extremely long day, Rube's team was informed of a meeting in the colonel's house at 0900 the next day.

The Pony Express crew arrived five minutes early at the colonel's house, which served as his office. The colonel appeared in the doorway before Chip could turn off the motor.

"Gentlemen, thank you for coming early. Do you have space for me in your Jeep?"

"Absolutely. Where to?" replied Chip.

"Keep on driving, and I'll tell you … turn left at the corner."

"What next?"

"Pull over in that alley." Goldy thought maybe the colonel had to take a piss. "Right here will be fine."

"Should we get out?" queried Okie.

"No, we have to talk, and I want you to listen very carefully."

Colonel Ron Gilmore heightened the mystery surrounding the meeting in the empty alley. "I must receive a unanimous answer if we are to continue. Gentlemen, what you see or hear in the next ninety minutes must never be told to anyone. That means you can't reveal anything to your family, friends, girlfriend or especially the enemy. Do all of you agree?"

All four GIs answered, "Yes!"

"Drive onto the airfield," demanded the colonel.

Upon arriving at the base, the five men were greeted by several MPs. Goldy did not recognize a single soldier, but all the men wore the same uniform. The MPs escorted the men into a rectangular, wooden building and departed. About fifteen chairs were set up in a small narrow room for the four MPs. The colonel said, "This is where our pilots meet before going on a mission. Please have a seat. Again, I must interject that talking about what you see or hear beyond this building is off-limits. Is that clear? Very shortly, you will be granted the privilege of being among the few that know about this secret project. From this moment, we must follow the old proverb, 'Know nothing, hear nothing, see nothing.'"

Nine

An MP standing by the exit leading to the landing strips and hangars saluted as the colonel's team approached. He said to the colonel, "Are these fellows aware?"

"Not yet," answered the colonel.

The MP swung open the gate, and the men entered the airfield. Nothing seemed unusual; Piper Cub planes and a few P-51 fighters were scattered around the airfield runway. "Would you like to examine the planes?" questioned the colonel.

All the men answered enthusiastically. As the MPs approached the planes, something seemed strange about the aircraft. After knocking their fists on the planes, The Thrill said, "I think these planes are made of plywood or some type of rubber." The group looked at the colonel, and he said nothing.

As they walked toward the field hangars, they noticed other planes protruding out of the entrance. But when they looked inside, the rest of the plane was missing. When they went to the larger hangar, they were astonished to see dozens of tanks parked inside. The colonel walked up to one and pushed it over. He looked at the stunned men and said, "The Army has a way of making you stronger." With a smile on his face, he said, "Rubber."

In the room where the pilots met, the colonel explained to the Pony Express crew what they just witnessed. "The other three hangars that we did not visit are occupied by some of the 1,000 men who are part of this military unit and are creating different deceptions."

"I'm still confused. What's this all about?" questioned Okie.

"You should be," answered the colonel. "Welcome to the world of the

Ghost Army.

"What you just visited was a make-believe air base with planes and tanks made of rubber. The whole operation has four major components, and its major goal is to deceive the enemy using sound effects, visual sightings, radio broadcasts, and special effects. Later I will provide more information about these special areas."

Chip interrupted. "Is this for some Christmas display?"

"I like that one," commented the colonel.

"Is this a game?" asked The Thrill.

"No," replied the colonel. "If you were flying in a plane over the base and photographed the airfield below, you would think you were watching an operational air base. Even the tracks of the tanks are false and made by bulldozers. When the tanks are placed around the field, it creates the impression of a heavily armed air base protecting Luxembourg. It's all about deception."

"Do any of the people who create these false planes and tanks go beyond the air base?" asked Chip.

"Absolutely, we have about a hundred members of the deception unit presently located southwest of St. Vith in the Commanster village. You will meet them shortly."

"Is that all they do is build dummy tanks and planes?"

"No, they create the sounds of war with their equipment. If they choose, they can send the sound of a tank fifteen miles."

"How did they accomplish that?"

"They use high-tech speakers, the size used on aircraft carriers."

"The enemy has no idea whether these sounds are real or fake," concluded Chip.

"Exactly. On one occasion General Patton used the Ghost Army for a week to deceive the German forces. I bet you didn't know the Ghost Army performed one of their shows near Fort Montbarey during the Battle of Brest."

"Unbelievable …! You said we would meet some of these guys."

"Your next assignment will be to escort their ten-truck convoy back to Luxembourg."

Goldy questioned, "Why do they need an escort? You said the unit has about 1,000 men. Why don't they do it?"

"Great question," said the colonel. "They have weapons, but to my knowledge, only once have they fired a machine gun at a plane for ten seconds."

"What?"

"I'm telling you, these men mainly come from the engineering, entertainment, and art fields. About half of the Ghost Army have artistic skills. Some are Hollywood writers, and others are Broadway set directors. Some are actors, radio announcers, artists, camouflage experts, and museum managers. And there are various architects, as well. They set the stage for the battle without firing a shot. Although they're not real soldiers, they perform very important tasks."

Chip commented, "So, you want MPs with combat experience to provide security to them and their equipment. Any danger involved?"

"This should be a cupcake assignment. With winter approaching and the German army retreating, everything has been relatively quiet at the front."

"When do we leave?"

"They are finalizing an assignment near an area known as Losheim Gap and will be moving southward to a new location around December 15. You can start packing your gear around the 13th. Over the next nine days, the citizens of Luxembourg could benefit from the services you provide as numerous convoys pass through the town daily. Any more questions?"

"Whoever came up with this idea must have been bombed, but I admit it's brilliant. Who authorized it?" The Thrill asked.

"Congress."

"Now, that makes sense."

"Anyone else have a question?"

"Yes," commented Rube. "Why haven't we seen the MPs at the air base before?"

"They are stationed here and on rare occasions leave the airfield."

"Why?"

"This city has some German sympathizers, and we can't slip up with someone saying something that blows the whole organization."

"What do these soldiers do for entertainment?"

"They perform."

"Come again, sir?"

"In civilian or military attire, selected MPs often spend a day eating and drinking at restaurants and cafes. There they spread disinformation and hope that German sympathizers would eventually provide rumors they heard to the enemy. The Ghost Army actors even go so far as to pretend to be drunk at the bar while passing false intelligence to those listening."

"I could live with that," commented The Thrill.

"Anything else?"

"Oh, I just thought of one last question," said Rube.

"Go ahead."

"Are we fighting a war or running one big con operation?"

"Both!"

Just then, the room door burst open, and an MP urged the officer to come out to the runway. The soldiers followed and were shocked to see a P-51 fighter plane landing. The pilot managed to land safely with part of its wing damaged. He climbed from the cockpit and told the welcoming crew, "Good thing I saw the airfield because I doubt my plane could have reached my home base. I didn't realize there was an airbase at this location."

"You are correct; this isn't a regular air base," said the colonel.

"How can that be? I observed at least ten planes around the runway."

"What outfit are you from?"

"The Army Air Corps."

"Great, I think we have to talk." Turning to the Pony Express crew, he concluded, "Sometimes we just can't cover all the bases."

While the colonel met with the pilot, the Pony Express crew had an interesting conference with Captain Noah Holtz, who presented them with their new orders. "Ever heard of a place called Commanster?"

"I think Colonel Gilmore mentioned it. But we know nothing about it," responded Goldy.

"It's northeast of Wiltz, near the Our River, which flows into Luxembourg. You couldn't find a more perfect site to conduct a secret operation. With a limited civilian population in town, and the 106th infantry stationed near the German border, the Ghost Army can operate without fear of an enemy attack. You can make the sixty-mile trip in a day if the weather permits. It will be cold, but no snow is in the forecast. On December 14, after leaving Luxembourg, your MP crew will complete the first phase of your trip by stopping at Wiltz. Early the next morning, you will start the thirty-mile drive to Commanster. The Ghost Army should be ready to move its ten-truck convoy and two Jeeps back to Luxembourg. The routes you will take are in your orders. Any questions …? Good luck."

Ten

Despite some rough and muddy roads and after crossing the bridge on the Clef River, the trip was uneventful until the Jeep Okie drove almost struck a woman standing in the middle of the road. After a volley of obscenities aimed at the person, the crew watched the woman fall to her knees. At first, fearing an ambush, the four MPs drew their weapons as they approached the woman. Immediately, they realized she was in bad shape. When she told them she had come from Bitburg, Germany, the entire demeanor of the MPs changed. Before any other words were exchanged, Chip was on the radio to the Intel division of the 28th Infantry, stationed southwest of Clervaux. It was only a few miles away, and it took less than ten minutes for the Jeep, now carrying five people, to arrive at checkpoints controlled by the 28th. As the woman departed the Jeep, she asked, "Are you boys heading to St. Vith?"

"Not that far," answered The Thrill.

"I must warn you, from what I witnessed in Bitburg, the Germans are up to something. Stay alert."

She disappeared as fast as she appeared, and the Pony Express crew was left to ponder her warning.

After arriving at Commanster, the members of the Ghost Army were making the finishing touches on breaking down their campsite. A few tents were still in place when the four MPs arrived.

"Right on time," said Captain Wilber Gray. "How was the trip?"

"Relatively easy," offered Okie.

"Any traffic jams?"

"Only minor stuff."

"Is this your entire crew?"

"Yes, sir."

"The mess tent will remain open for another hour, so if you want to take any food before we depart, by all means, go ahead."

"Thank you!"

"Also, check out the tent next door. I'm sure you will find it interesting."

All the MPs wanted something hot, and soup or coffee hit the spot. They were told not to bring food or drink inside as they walked to the next-door tent. Once the soldiers entered the tent, they understood the reasons for the regulation. For a moment, Goldy thought he had just arrived in an art gallery. Hanging from wires attached to the side of the tent were paintings done by various members of the Ghost Army. These paintings depicted the soldier's life and citizens living in a war zone. Goldy and the others were awed by the talent and quality of each painting, which had the artist's signature. Chip didn't recognize any names but thought each of them could have an excellent career in the art field. One painting that Goldy admired was a picture of an unsmiling boy holding a chocolate bar.

As Goldy and his team departed the tent, something struck them from the sky. Snowflakes came down so heavily that they could barely see Captain Holtz's tent. "I'll be damned," called Okie. "I've never seen snow like this before."

Captain Holtz's aide appeared through the snow and said, "I was afraid of this."

"You mean this happens often?" questioned The Thrill.

"Around here, if someone sneezes, we might get two inches. For some reason, we cannot predict weather conditions up in the mountains."

"Unreal!"

"Let me get the captain; we'll have to decide whether to leave now or wait until the snow stops."

"How long does snow last around here?"

"Sometimes ten minutes, maybe an hour, and occasionally, we have had storms last for ten hours."

"The weather reports in Luxembourg called for rain, not snow."

"In the mountains of the Ardennes, any precipitation can turn to snow if the temperatures are low enough. Here comes the captain, and whatever he decides usually ends up in a coin toss."

The captain's first words were, "Damned if I do; damned if I don't."

"Looks like another tough call, captain," responded the aide.

The captain remarked, "Gentlemen, any comments?"

Okie stated, "I think we should start moving out immediately."

"I would agree if I knew how long this would last."

The aide felt otherwise as he said, "I would hate to get stranded in the middle of the forest for twelve hours."

"I hear you," said the captain. "There is no good choice but lots of negatives."

"Lay it out, captain," requested Goldy.

"First, a lot depends on the snowfall. A small amount usually means the roads are icy and slippery. We could be delayed a few days if it turns into a major storm. Let's wait an hour; we will remain here tonight if it keeps snowing. In the meantime, I'll send out the bulldozers to smash the snow into a hard surface that will allow us to leave the forest area by 0500 tomorrow. Hopefully, there will be little traffic, allowing us to move onto better roadways. Once we are out of the forest, there will be a good chance we will only see rain. However, if the snow stops within the hour, I will give the order to start the engines of the convoy and head out."

After the captain left, the Pony Express crew debated the officer's decision. "I guess he knows the area better than us," stated the former botanist.

Being a city boy, The Thrill disagreed with the captain's decision. Quoting an old army adage, he said, "Don't delay to tomorrow what you can do today."

Okie loved the beauty of the snow covering the mountains and didn't mind staying an extra day.

Goldy pointed to a historical disaster in the Old West for his answer. "I don't remember the exact year, but many settlers were crossing the Rocky Mountains late at night, but half the company decided to move ahead despite the danger, while the other half agreed to leave the following morning. That night it snowed, and those who remained, spent the entire winter in the Rockies. Of course, they eventually ran out of food, and many died. To survive, those still alive did the unthinkable. They ate …"

Chip interrupted, "You don't have to finish the story, Goldy. I heard about the Donner Party."

The snow continued until 2300 hours, and the Pony Express crew spent a restful night sleeping on cots with the rest of the Ghost Army members in heated quarters of a building reserved for GIs. The silence of the forest created a surreal scene at 0400. The only sound that could be heard was the wind that swirled over the ice-covered Our River. As the men rose from a short winter's sleep, they had a quick breakfast of eggs and bacon and began warming up the motors of the ten trucks carrying the secret equipment the Ghost Army used. With over a foot of snow on the ground, Okie wished the Ghost Army and their escorts could spend an extra day at this winter wonderland, but like a disappearing ghost, the convoy departed at 0500 from Commanster. Thankfully, no enemy troops were in the area, as the sounds of vehicles cracking ice created an echo that could be heard miles away.

Even with the snow-filled roads in the Ardennes causing delays, the convoy traveled about twenty-five miles and arrived at the Township of Eschweiler. With the Pony Express vehicle at the head of the convoy, a bundled-up MP guard with frozen breath coming from his mouth asked, "I thought you were supposed to be here twenty-four hours ago."

The Thrill responded, "So did we, but Mother Nature decided something else."

"The road is clear ahead. Just be cautious on the curves and turns."

"Will do."

"Oh, one other thing, have you listened to the radio this morning?"

"Not yet," The Thrill answered.

"Be sure to turn it on. There was some chatter about a German assault around Losheim Gap. A small American force in Lanzrath is presently engaged in combat with the invading force."

"We just came from that region. It must be a German probing mission," answered Okie.

"That's possible, but keep an eye on it."

"Okay, we will check the reports."

"What's your next stop?" asked the frozen guard.

"According to the captain's directions, our next location is Wiltz."

The two-hour trip took much longer, not because of the snow but due to mechanical breakdowns of the two trucks. After almost an hour's delay, another obstacle confronted the convoy as a tree collapsed on the road. With a saw, and some explosives, members of the convoy cleared the road, but precious time had slipped away. During the hiatus, Okie listened to the radio and heard about a second point of confrontation on the border region of Germany. "Hey, Goldy, listen to this. What do you think?"

Goldy responded anxiously, "I'm not sure, but something is happening, and if you hear about another attack, let me know."

Ten minutes later, Okie told Goldy about another report of an attack underway at Hoscheid.

Rube reacted, "This looks bad. Has headquarters been notified?"

"I guess so, but they don't seem concerned."

"That's what happened at Pearl Harbor. They had warnings but chose to ignore them."

"Do we have some maps?"

"I don't, but the captain does."

"I'll drive our Jeep to the back of the convoy, and we can make the captain aware of this situation."

"Good idea," responded Rube.

Okie informed Captain Holtz about the radio broadcast. "Where did you say the last assault occurred?" asked the captain.

"Hoscheid," said Okie.

"Any word if the American lines are holding?"

"Not sure. Wait, here's the newest information. The attack on Hoscheid has been met with little resistance, and the enemy is heading toward Wiltz."

"I've heard enough. The Germans are launching a major offensive from the Ardennes against our northeast flank in Belgium. Damn it, have they finished clearing the road?"

Yes, but now they're working on a flat tire on another vehicle."

"How far are we from Wiltz?"

"Maybe less than ten kilometers."

"Holy hell! Get in touch with our units in Wiltz."

"Yes, sir."

"If we don't keep moving, those German forces could be on our tail in no time."

"More bad news, captain, said a radio operator," reported Okie.

"What?"

"A German assault is underway on our defenses in an area known as Skyline Drive. I hear our guys are putting up a stubborn defense, and thankfully a destroyed bridge on the River Our is slowing their advance."

"What direction are they moving toward?"

"Oh, my God, they're heading to Eschweiler, the place we just left."

"Move out, move out," shouted the captain. "If you can't change that tire in five minutes, we'll leave the truck."

As more and more accounts of an enemy assault became available, the Pony Express crew debated whether the words of the woman they had picked up on the road and dropped off at the 28th headquarters were a premonition or an accurate prediction.

From a position high in the Ardennes, the Ghost Army convoy watched a large dust and smoke cloud rising in the distance. Viewing with his binoculars, Captain Holtz ascertained that it must be coming from the advancing German army. "We are in big trouble," the concerned officer responded.

The race was on to get to Wiltz before the Germans, or else the Ghost Army convoy could be captured. Late afternoon, the convoy arrived in Wiltz.

The entire township seemed to be in a state of panic. Soldiers and citizens had already begun constructing defensive positions around the eastern part of the town.

After a twenty-minute phone call with headquarters in Luxembourg, Captain Holtz turned to a small group of soldiers and, with a stern face, said, "We are really in deep, and I don't know if we can get out." The captain's voice only heightened the tension of those present. Several Ghost Army and Pony Express crew members sat silently as the captain assessed the situation. "Men, we are trapped at Wiltz. What I learned from headquarters leaves us with few alternatives. Here's where we stand. Several German divisions are on the move throughout the Ardennes region. One of these divisions is headed directly toward Wiltz. To the north of Wiltz, another massive movement of German troops is conducting a scorched earth policy with everything in its path as it moves toward Bastogne. In case you have forgotten, that's the place where the only safe route to Luxembourg is still operational. Somehow, we must find a way to bring the Ghost Army convoy to this escape route with all its top-secret equipment. Add to this, the roads out of Wiltz are packed with civilians leaving the town and the reserve troops entering the place, so at this time, we are stuck here. Bluntly, we are up a creek without a paddle."

One of the Ghost Army crew asked, "Why can't we wait until morning and travel during the day to Bastogne?"

"We can't because a slow-moving convoy in open space during the day would make the convoy an easy target for German aircraft."

"So, how are we supposed to travel to Bastogne?" asked The Thrill.

"Anyone have an answer?" asked the captain.

The former cop asked, "When will the road be clear?"

"Not until late in the evening. Are there any other comments?"

"Why can't we travel at night?" questioned Rube.

"That's my plan, but that choice involves a lot of danger. Not so much being spotted by the Germans, but the weather and the slippery roads from the snow could cause the whole convoy to be isolated in unknown territory."

"How many miles do we have to travel to Bastogne?" asked Chip.

"At least twenty miles, maybe more."

"So, our only option is to move at night and hide during the day."

"That's the best I can come up with at this moment. I estimate that we might only travel five or six miles a day because the convoy will have to move at such a slow pace."

"Jesus, we are in a mess," concluded another member of the Ghost Army.

"Son, we will need a lot of praying and luck if we're going to pull this off."

"When do you think the German force driving toward Wiltz will arrive?" questioned Goldy.

"In a day or two! Whatever plan we adopt, we must move quickly. That includes all of us and the rest of our soldiers. Make sure every GI uses his time to eat, change socks, care for personal needs, and get some rest."

The captain called out the names of five soldiers who should remain, and Goldy's name was the last to be called. He told those five, "I would give us only about a twenty percent chance to succeed in this mission. Any suggestions you might have to help implement our plan?"

"Yes, these people who live in Wiltz are used to the cold weather like this. You would think they would have metal chains to use for their tires during the winter. Why not ask if we can use them when making our escape," offered Goldy.

"I like that, and those chains could stabilize our vehicles as we move through slippery spots. Any other thoughts?"

"Yes," a young lieutenant from the crew of the Ghost Army replied. "Why don't we paint a Red Cross on the side of the trucks to identify the convoy as a medical unit? This could clear a path for us if we come upon civilian traffic."

"Excellent. Who else?"

Chip expressed interest in finding this new type of tape that reflects light in the dark. "I think placing the tape on the rear of our trucks would help the driver identify vehicles moving in front of them, especially when we can only use the auxiliary lights instead of the main headlights. Also, be sure to acquire extra batteries for our flashlights."

The captain concluded, "I will see what I can obtain at the Wiltz headquarters. At 1730, I want all of you to report to the warehouse, and hopefully, I'll be able to provide you with our plan to escape Wiltz."

Later, in the atmosphere of the cold, damp, poorly lit warehouse, half a dozen men gathered among an assortment of trucks. A much more confident captain gave his troops a pep-talk and called upon each man to put forth a major effort as he said, "We have a lot of work to do in a short time."

Some men began refitting the trucks with paint, tape, and chains. As other GIs and the captain rummaged through boxes of deceptive devices, which the Ghost Army carried with them on their last mission, Okie held up an object that looked like an explosive mine.

"I hope that's not real," remarked Holtz. "How many of those fake mines did you find?"

"About a dozen."

"Bring the Jeep around. I think I can delay the Germans from entering Wiltz."

Using grenades to create holes in the road over the bridge, four MPs placed the fake mines in the newly made craters. "Be sure to leave a portion of the mine visible," demanded the captain. "We want the Germans to see them, and by the time they find out they are fakes, we will be long gone."

The five men returned to the town just as an engineering company prepared to leave. The captain recognized an officer he knew and spent a few minutes talking to him. Once Holtz returned, he had the MPs follow him to an abandoned house. There, hidden in the basement, were five live mines. The engineer told the captain they were lucky to spot them on the dirt road just before crossing the bridge to enter the town. Now they were going to put them back in the ground. Deliberately the engineers and MPs began placing the live mines into the town's main street.

Okie noted that the Germans would easily spot them, but Captain Holtz stated, "It doesn't matter because they will think they are fake like the ones on the bridge." All the civilians in the area were evacuated as the ten-truck convoy and a Jeep prepared to leave Wiltz. Only time would tell if the fake and live mines would delay the Germans enough to allow the convoy time to escape toward Bastogne.

Thirty minutes after midnight on December 18, the Ghost Army convoy slipped through the vacant streets of Wiltz and started the journey toward Bastogne. The convoy seemed to move in slow motion down the icy venues of the forest. Always looking for enemy scouts, the convoy maneuvered past excellent ambush locations without incident. Whether by luck or the falling temperatures, the enemy decided this was not the ideal climate for clashes. With Goldy at the wheel of the Pony Express, the vehicles performed much better with chains on the tires. He also found the tape significantly helped follow the trucks in front of the Jeep.

On occasions when the convoy had to stop because of an obstacle, the flashlights provided an excellent view of the surroundings. One stop had the entire convoy in awe. Suddenly out of the woods strolled a hump-back grizzly bear, and he ignored the convoy and continued his food search.

By the light of the day, the convoy had covered about ten miles. Goldy told his three buddies he had good and bad news about the trip. "What would you like to hear first, the good or the bad?" They all agreed on the good. "We are out of the forest area, and the roads are less likely to cause trouble for the trucks as the sun will eventually melt some of the ice."

"Okay, what's the bad news?" inquired Chip.

"The bad news is once the sun breaks through the clouds, it's only a matter of time before we run into groups of refugees on the road, which will slow our progress. But most concerning is, without the forest cover, how will the captain be able to hide the convoy from enemy planes?"

It was about 1300 when the convoy abruptly stopped as many refugees blocked any future movement. Seeing a kid carrying an American flag, Goldy stopped the Jeep and asked if he spoke English. "Yes," he answered.

"Are you aware if any of the refugees need medical assistance?"

The boy answered, "Absolutely. One woman is in labor and needs a doctor."

Goldy had never delivered a baby but knew the process and procedure.

Goldy then pulled the Jeep to the side of the road and slowly drove until he saw a group of adult women surrounding a person laying on a blanket. Stopping the Jeep, Goldy and two members of his team, along with the kid, jumped out. With his medicine bag, Goldy joined the circle. One of the ladies in the group said, "She's almost there." Goldy called The Thrill and Chip over, and after three tries, life emerged crying in the cold of the day. Goldy cut the umbilical cord and then wrapped the newborn in a blanket to the cheers of the circle of women.

After the baby was in the hands of the mother, Rube called the captain and asked him to peel back to the Pony Express location in the convoy as he might have some information for him. The captain responded, "What do you have?"

"Presently, I have a newborn and a young kid."

"What?"

"We just delivered a baby, but I have a kid who knows the area's geography."

"Be there in a few minutes."

Captain Holtz halted the convoy while he interviewed the kid. "Are there any hamlets or towns near here?" the officer asked.

"No," the boy responded.

"Are you aware of any bridges?"

"No," again was his answer.

"Any place where people might find shelter?"

"Yes."

"About where is this place?"

"The next dirt road is about three kilometers from here. Go right about one kilometer, and you'll see it."

"What is it?"

"I think it's some type of camp.

Eleven

Captain Holtz wanting more information about the camp, asked, "How many people are in the camp?"

The young kid thought briefly and said, "Several hundred."

"Is it for American prisoners?"

"No."

"Do you mean a prisoner of war (POW) camp housing German prisoners?"

"I think so."

Immediately, Captain Holtz thought this could be a game-changer.

Spotting Goldy's crew cooing over a baby, the captain said, "That's one assignment you never expected to perform." Everyone smiled. "We have a change in plans. Follow my Jeep, and if we can make the correct phone calls, we might be able to complete our mission of getting our friendly Ghosts back to their home base, with a little luck."

Riding in the Pony Express, the four men could only talk about the baby's birth. "Amazing," said Okie.

"It was one of my finest moments," remarked Chip. "That was beautiful; tops anything I've seen."

Goldy said, "All the blood, gore, and death we have witnessed can never blot out the beauty of life. We can only hope when the war is over, we will be able to see scenes of love and beauty instead of war and destruction."

In quite a contrast, these warriors, for a moment, became kind and gentle individuals that cared more about life than death. As the site of the POW camp appeared on the horizon, the men returned to the survival struggle they endured every minute of the day.

The POW camp consisted of a combination of tents and barracks. Barbed wire stretched around the ten-acre plot of land as dozens of guards watched 600 German prisoners.

Captain Ryan Douglas, the officer in charge of the camp, greeted Captain Holtz and the convoy. Then the two officers departed and prepared for serious discussions.

The first call went to headquarters in Luxembourg. Captain Fisher then called the Intel unit at a place called Spa. From there, calls went to Washington, New York, and London. They also spoke with officials from Paris, Le Mans, and Brussels. The main topic was the removal of 600 German POWs. No one could predict the results, but everyone had an opinion.

Captain Holtz and Captain Douglas agreed that the dire situation created by the German breakthrough would play a major role in the final decision on how to proceed. The time element proved to be another problem. The next morning the decision became known.

In a meeting in a small room at the POW camp, the day's activities became clearer. "Here's what's going on," stated Captain Holtz. "In approximately eighteen hours, German forces will overrun this compound. I'm sad to say that no Allied forces are currently strong enough to stop the German thrust. We have discussed various ways to handle the prisoners. Many of you would like to shoot them, but we don't play that game.

"On the other hand, we could abandon the camp and allow the Germans to free them. Not a chance. So, here's our next move. We plan to transfer them to another POW camp near Spa, about twenty miles north of Bastogne. We will use four of our trucks to carry one hundred prisoners. Those prisoners will switch every hour, with 500 walking at the convoy's head. This hourly replacement will continue until we reach Bastogne. The rest of the convoy will travel behind the POWs, allowing members of the Ghost Army to closely watch for any attempts at escape. Having 600 German prisoners walking down a major highway will cause traffic to part, like the Red Sea, which should eliminate any delays. Also, enemy planes wouldn't dare fire on their men. As for the U.S. planes, seeing the Red Cross painted on our trucks should deter any attacks. We should be on the outskirts of Bastogne by 2100. From there, the prisoners will board about twenty trucks to the POW camp near Spa. Any questions?"

"What if any of the POWs try to escape?" came a question from a truck driver.

"Pure and simple, the guards will have the authority to shoot anyone who tries to escape .... Are we good? Let's get this show on the road."

At 1300, "Move them out," shouted Captain Holtz, as the German prisoners' march began toward Bastogne. For the captured men, some feared the road untraveled might resemble the Bataan death march, where hundreds of American soldiers died early in WWII. Rube, however, conjured up the image of the old west cattle drive. In the 1870s, a major problem in such drives was maintaining control of cattle that wandered off the trail. In addition, the ever-present danger of an attack by rustlers or Indians hampered the progress of the cattle drive. For the members of the Ghost Army, play-acting as sheriffs became just another of the many roles this unit would accomplish in deceiving the enemy.

The perception shared by both warring parties proved wrong as no prisoner tried to escape, and no hostile forces attacked the column of prisoners. The trip took almost eight hours, not because of the weather, which was cold but not windy, but because the sheer number of men lengthened the time of the trip. Still, if prisoners or guards needed a rest, they could ride in a truck briefly. According to reports, no one on either side collapsed from exhaustion. By 2130, the prisoners were being transferred to trucks at a stop near Bastogne and eventually taken to the prison camp near Spa.

While the prisoner transfer was underway, Rube and the remainder of his team observed first-hand the mood of those preparing to defend the town of Bastogne. Immediately, Rube recognized the same panic they had seen on the faces of the citizens of Wiltz. No doubt that the German offensive created a massive cavity in the territory held by the Allies, and the Belgian town seemed to be the main target for the German war machine.

Since the Pony Express crew hadn't reported to the MP headquarters in Le Mans for almost four days, Rube tracked down a communication vehicle and received permission to contact his superiors.

A voice on the other end of the line answered the call and said, "I thought you were dead. Hold on, let me get Lieutenant Porterfield."

The surprised but relieved officer acknowledged that headquarters was about to place all four men on the missing-in-action list. He asked, "Did you complete the mission of bringing the Ghost Army back to Luxembourg?"

Rube reported, "The entire one hundred members of the Ghost Army and their equipment should be arriving in the city in the next two or three hours."

"Wonderful; we want a full written report on everything that happened."

"Absolutely!"

"Briefly, can you explain why you lost radio contact with us?"

"Mainly because of fear that the enemy would locate our position. In addition, we were transporting 600 German POWs."

"You were involved with that?"

"Yes, sir."

"No need to explain any further. What else?"

"Okay, here's what I have for you. We have been hit hard by the German attacks. Companies and units are scattered everywhere, and we are attempting to assemble a fighting force around Bastogne."

"Is that your present location?"

"We are close by."

"Great, we are assembling the remnants of different companies at a small hamlet named Marvie, just south of Bastogne. It's a strategic location where the Germans will strike before moving into Bastogne. Presently, our forces are preparing defense positions around there. Tomorrow, report to Marvie, provide as much assistance as possible, and await further orders."

"Anything else?"

"Just one thing, which hasn't been verified yet, but I want to make sure you're aware since you were without radio contact for a lengthy period. We have received information about a German parachute jump behind our lines.

What seems to be the most troubling is these paratroopers are dressed in American uniforms and can speak English. So, be extra cautious if you run into GIs and don't recognize the patches on their uniforms."

"Thanks for the info. We will be on the lookout for anything unusual."

In fifteen minutes, they arrived at the main road to Luxembourg. As the Ghost Army prepared to complete the final phase of their trip, Captain Holtz met with the Pony Express crew. He told them that he never expected to outrun the German forces. The officer thanked the four MPs for all their help and support, but he had one last request. Pointing to one of the trucks which carried his company's weapons and ammo, the captain noted that this slow-moving vehicle hampered the entire march.

"Of course, it did. You can't have ammo and grenades bouncing around in case you hit a rut in the road," replied Goldy.

"That's exactly why we can't take the ammo truck with us back to Luxembourg," said Captain Holtz. "In a few moments, I'll be stepping on the gas, and I want to hit top speed so we can arrive before sunrise. I think you boys will find a better way to use the truck and its contents. Not to worry, a few of my men still are armed with weapons, and I've been told that a military convoy, including tanks, will escort us even before we reach Luxembourg."

Goldy ended the conversation by adding, "Are you sure those vehicles and tanks aren't made of rubber?"

Everyone laughed.

The captain announced, "There's always one wise guy in the group."

With smiles, the men hugged and wished each other luck in the coming days.

Twelve

As the Pony Express crew watched the rear lights of the Ghost Army convoy disappear into the darkness, they realized the need to find a place to stay this night. The team split up as Goldy and The Thrill drove the ammo truck. Okie told his buddies, "Follow me; I think several farmhouses are in the Bastogne area."

"I'll circle and see what we can find," answered Chip, who was behind the wheel. In ten minutes, they found what seemed to be a deserted house and barn. After parking their vehicles behind the house so they couldn't be seen from the road, they checked the door and found it locked. So, Chip started walking to the barn.

"Hold it," shouted Goldy. "It's possible some German scouts might be inside the barn. You never know. Wait here while I go behind the house."

"What is he doing?" questioned Chip.

A moment later, Goldy returned and said, "The barn's occupied."

"Wait a minute. You go behind the house and tell us the barn is occupied?"

"Yes, I'm not sure if Americans or Germans are there, but someone is in the barn."

"That's it, and I will bet you a buck that no one is in the barn."

"I don't want to take your money."

"Don't worry about that. I want to know how you can say someone is in the barn."

"Enough; just be careful as we approach the barn."

Slowly the four men tiptoed to the barn. They found the barn door unlocked and slowly opened it. Only the light of the moon allowed them to spot six men. Both parties stood face to face with their rifles pointed at each other. One of Rube's crew lit a match, and Okie turned on his flashlight. All those in the barn were wearing the uniform of the U.S. Army. "Hold it," shouted one of the six men. "How do we know you're Americans? I hear the Germans have been seen in this area wearing the U.S. Army uniforms."

The Thrill replied, "How do we know you aren't Germans?"

"Look at our faces," answered a voice.

Flashing his light on the faces of the soldiers, Okie noticed all were Black.

"Is that good enough evidence?" countered one of the Black soldiers.

"Maybe you are Germans in blackface," implied Okie.

"Watch it, dude," came back the voice.

Goldy, seeing that dumb and stupid accusation had heightened the tension, told everyone to cut the bullshit. "Let's take turns and ask each group about the homeland."

"Go ahead," answered one of the Black troops.

"What unit are you from?" questioned The Thrill.

"The 333rd artillery."

"Isn't that an all-Negro outfit?" asked Chip.

"Yes," said the six-foot soldier.

"Why are you here?" asked Okie.

"The Germans overwhelmed our position."

"What the fuck happened?"

"We supported the 106th infantry, a newly arrived inexperienced unit, along the Ardennes when it seemed like the entire German army attacked. Stopping the assault proved futile. Even when our powerful 155 artillery pieces made direct hits on enemy targets, the Germans continued to advance and obliterated everything in their path. As the GIs from the 106th melted away, we kept firing until running out of shells. Then we retreated. We lost everything — men and weapons."

"Where are the rest of your men now?" queried Rube.

"You might be looking at the survivors."

"Jesus, you must be kidding."

"I wish that were the case, but from my last glimpse, I witnessed about a hundred men of the 333rd being herded along a road by their German captors."

"Where were they being taken?"

"I have no idea, but I saw an American plane attack the line of captive GIs and their German guards."

"What happened?"

"The attack allowed about ten or eleven men to escape. As for us, we ran our ass off and eventually came upon another retreating American unit moving toward the town of Bastogne and followed them."

"Damn, damn, damn, that's one escape even Houdini couldn't top."

"Okay, now it's our turn to ask you, White boys, some questions," said the tallest Black soldier. "Where were you stationed?"

"We're MPs on a mission in the Ardennes and fled the German onslaught. We just arrived from Wiltz, which we heard also had been overrun by the Germans," answered Okie.

After answering numerous questions, the Pony Express crew found themselves stumped on one question.

"What baseball team does Jackie Robinson play for?"

No one had the answer. "I've never heard about him," answered Chip.

"That's because he's unable to play baseball in the major leagues because of his skin color. What about Satchel Paige?"

"Oh, yeah, he pitches in the Negro Baseball League," proclaimed Chip. "I read about him in a baseball magazine."

"I think these guys are legit," said a short Black soldier.

Goldy said, "I think these fellows are from the states and I believe I recognize the one at the end of the line on the right."

Stunned, the Black soldiers had a curious look on their faces after that remark.

Goldy continued, "I'm going to move closer, so don't get trigger-happy."

"What are you talking about?" answered the soldier Rube was referring to.

"Yes, you're Terry Keys. I treated you at a hospital several months ago."

As the two soldiers moved closer, Terry remarked, "I'll be damned, you're Rube Goldfarb ... son of a gun!"

A perplexed heavy-set Black soldier said, "Terry Keys, are you a spy?"

"No, this guy helped me out in the hospital ... but Rube, weren't you a medic then?"

"You are right. But against my wishes, they placed me into an MP outfit. However, I still perform medic duties, if necessary." To help relieve the concerns of the Black troops, Rube offered all in the barn a sip of water with a mixture of booze in it.

"Hold it, Rube," an angry Thrill demanded. "When did you get that?"

"While the prisoners were being placed on the transport vehicles, I went to the medics' truck and showed them my credentials, and they gave me this flask."

"When has the Army given booze to anyone?" inquired The Thrill.

"This is mainly for any wounded soldier. Because of the frigid weather, this will prevent those injured from going into shock."

One of the Black soldiers then fell over like he was shot. He said with a little chuckle, "Save me from going into shock!"

With all the tension dissipating from the barn, the Black and White soldiers spent a memorable night in a barn only a few days before Christmas. Rube poured a very small amount of spiked water into each man's cup, and together each man drank and, for a moment, felt the warmth it created inside their bodies.

The men discussed different topics in the barn, but the question asked the most dealt with what part of the country they resided in before the war. Most Black soldiers came from southern states — the Carolinas, Georgia, and Mississippi, and one came from D.C. Rube asked the D.C. man where he lived, and he said, "In an alley."

Rube responded, "I thought they got rid of those places long ago."

He retorted, "Bullshit."

Before long, the group began to talk about Christmas and how they celebrated the holiday with their families. The Thrill stated that the barn was the closest he had ever come to spending time in what resembled a manger scene. Okie talked about feeding the animals on his farm during Christmas. Chip, who had a large family, recalled all the excitement of opening gifts. He described the holiday dinner and all the food and drinks served. Rube said, "I don't celebrate Christmas, but Hanukkah."

"You celebrate what? Han-do-cut?" asked the short Black soldier.

"No, it's pronounced Ha-new-kuh."

"Does Santa Claus come to your house and give you any gifts?"

"Not really, but we do exchange gifts."

"What type of gifts do you get?"

"Well, the holiday lasts eight days so I would get a gift a day. Sometimes it would be Hanukkah gelt — that's money — or a game. When I was a kid, one of the toys I liked the most was a set of Lincoln Logs. Other times it would be clothes I didn't like, but the best gifts were a football and a baseball glove."

One guy questioned if Rube didn't like Christmas. "That couldn't be further from the truth. I like any religion that attempts to guide the human spirit and provides comfort to those in need."

Chip changed the subject by asking the Black soldiers what gifts they received for Christmas. Everything from booze to stuffed animals was mentioned, but one stood out. The soldier from Mississippi described a gift he gave to his wife. He told all the GIs how poor they were then, so he didn't have much money to spend on a gift. Nonetheless, he bought her something and wrapped the package with colorful Christmas paper. The entire group anxiously waited for him to tell them what it was. "Well," he said. "It wasn't the usual gift you give to a woman, but it lit up our life and removed the darkness from our romance. It was a package of lightbulbs." Laughter erupted throughout the barn.

A smiley Okie said, "You gave your wife lightbulbs for Christmas?"

"Well, man, I was dirt poor. That's when I decided to flee my job at which I was spending ten hours a day in 'high cotton,' and joined the military."

"I have a question for Rube," declared Chip. "How in the hell did you know the barn had people in it?"

Rube chuckled and remarked, "I checked the outhouse, which was behind the house. The door was open, and there were footprints everywhere. Now, where's my buck?"

Much like kids at a sleepover, the men, for a couple of hours, enjoyed the friendship exhibited in the barn. Before going to sleep, the guys sang Christmas carols. Rube wondered, *would any goodwill shown among the Colored soldiers and the Pony Express crew continue when the war ended and everyone returned to civilian life?*

Very early in the morning, the two groups prepared to split. "Aren't you concerned about being discovered?" said Goldy.

"See, you White boys need to put that black stuff on your face, but we have natural camouflage. We will make it."

Each man wished the others luck at 0315. For a moment, the men who fought for freedom for all, experienced unity among themselves but once again would return to a "separate but equal" Army. At this time, Terry Keys and his five companions scurried off toward Bastogne, and the Pony Express crew drove to Marvie.

Part III:

THE DARK SIDE OF THE HOLIDAYS

Thirteen

Early on the morning of December 20, the Pony Express Jeep and the truck loaded with ammo and weapons arrived at the small village of Marvie. After parking in front of the house used as headquarters, the four MPs walked inside and unexpectedly found themselves in the middle of a major argument between two officers. With a razor-sharp stare, one of the officers shouted to the newcomers, "What the fuck do you all want?"

Rube explained how the Pony Express crew outran the German forces and brought a special convoy to safety. He then told the officers about the ammo truck. Suddenly their tone changed, and they wanted to learn more. As the discussion continued, each officer explained that they were between a rock and a hard place and desperately needed additional men and supplies. With the arrival of the ammo truck and weapons, the officers agreed that this provided them with additional weaponry that could be used in preparation for the coming enemy attack on Marvie.

After unloading the weapons and ammo from the truck, the Pony Express team was given a quick tour of the fortified positions around the village which included foxholes, trenches, and tunnels. However, reconnaissance remained a big problem as fog and snow reduced visibility to a point where identifying the location of the enemy became impossible. Even critical U.S. air drops of supplies and armaments into Bastogne missed the target zone, causing American artillery units to limit their fire at the enemy.

Later in the day, using the weather to conceal its tactical maneuvers, the enemy made its initial move against the town. The American forces from their strategic positions had no difficulties in repulsing the German probing mission. Scattered small engagements took place the next day, also with the same results of little troop movement.

On December 22, German artillery launched a barrage of fire against the Americans' fortified position. Rube, huddled in a dugout with his knees bent, somehow managed to isolate the terrifying sounds of weapons of war and, with trembling hands, attempted to write what he believed to be his last words before his death. As Rube prepared to put pen on paper, the ground shook violently from a nearby explosion, stopping him from completing his first word, *Dea ...*

The storm of shells continued unrelenting, leaving Rube eating dirt and grabbing his helmet. Within what seemed like an hour but was only a few minutes, the intensity of the ear-splitting Nebelwerfer rockets, called screaming meemies, came to a halt, as did Rube's romance with the "MP" on his steel helmet. With his uniform covered in dirt, the GI from D.C., obviously shaken but not deterred, wrote down his final thoughts.

December 22, 1944

Dear Roberta,

There are no holiday lights where I am now located. The only thing flashing are bombs exploding. I'm not sure if I'll be able to write again. I hope so, but if not, thanks for being my pen pal. Things are about to get rough here. All the chips are in. Someone will win, and someone will lose. For the winners, the cost might be great. Yet, those who survive must go on despite the pain of losses. No use in kidding you anymore. I'm at the front and can see the enemy. The next battle might determine who wins the war. I might not find the answer, but I did my best to combat this evil. I wish you all the best.

Your friend,
Rube

PART III: THE DARK SIDE OF THE HOLIDAYS

December 22, 1944

Dear Sylvia,

From Paris to the front lines, that's how quickly things change in war. This might be my last letter. I'm sorry I haven't been able to read more of your letters because of our screwed-up mail system. Let me say I will always remember our relationship. You made my life so much better, and I thank you for that. I wish our feelings for each other could stand forever. Over the next few days, many things can happen. I'm not sure what that will be. I wrote so many times about how much I miss you. Now, reality makes returning home by Christmas a pipe dream. I wish I had better news, but the outcome will impact many people's lives. Please pray for me and my men. I will always love you. I remain your devoted soldier.

Love always,
Rube

December 22, 1944

Dear Pop and Mary,

This might be the last letter you receive from me. Things are getting difficult here. Every day I'm still alive is a blessing. Please remember all the loving things we did together. I will always love you. Please don't forget me. I hope my brother Sam and his family will live in peace. I just came back from a long trip. God was with us. I hope He watches over me and my men in the coming days. Whatever happens, I did something to stop this menace threatening the world. Please let Sylvia know about any news. If those of us fighting under the stars and stripes can thwart the advancing enemy in the next few days, I think Hitler and his army are finished. One day he will pay for his crimes. These next few days will be critical in my life. Please pray for me, Papa. My time is short. Your loving son,

Rube

As Rube finished his letters, the darkness of the night receded, and a radio report helped lift the spirits of the soldiers on the front line. Despite being greatly outnumbered the 101st Airborne Division continued to control the town of Bastogne. The enemy seeing the gravity of the American situation, made a bold move. Four German soldiers arrived at Allied headquarters under a white flag. Unlike a nativity scene, they brought no gifts, but offered the Americans the opportunity to surrender. In response, Brigadier General Anthony McAuliffe, who attended Eastern High School less than two miles from the U.S. Capitol, replied, "Nuts." When a military officer explained what "Nuts" meant, the Germans quickly retreated to their lines.

By noon the next day, the weather had cleared enough that allowed a massive airdrop to be undertaken. For more than four hours, over 160 planes used parachutes to drop supplies and ammunition to the beleaguered troops trapped in the town.

With the improved weather conditions, the German ground attack commenced against Marvie. While on sentry duty, the Pony Express crew was first to spot six white-colored Panzer tanks and 500 German troopers heading toward Allied positions. The village's defenders watched as artillery shells created large holes in the lines of enemy attackers. Momentarily, the German advance halted as the enemy tank took a direct hit and exploded among the advancing troops.

With four Allied Bazooka teams firing from the front lines, their shells disabled other tanks. Some Bazooka shells bounced off their armor because of the extra steel on the German tanks. The U.S. soldiers in the trenches and foxholes didn't open fire until the enemy infantry came closer. It seemed to Rube that the German soldiers' outfits resembled those of Ku Klux Klan members. With their all-white uniforms, which matched the snow, the ground assault resumed. At first, spotting the enemy soldiers was difficult when lying on the ground, but they became excellent targets once they stood up. The Allied forces repulsed the first attack because the German infantry had less maneuverability.

A second wave of German troops supported by half-tracks and tanks managed to capture a hill overlooking the town. After a brief fight, the German soldiers fell back, but three of their tanks entered the town. Soon these steel monsters resembled the burning and destroyed buildings of Marvie.

According to Rube, stopping the German offensive would have been extremely doubtful without the contents of the Ghost Army truck and the fighting spirit of the GIs. Despite being outnumbered, the bravery of the American soldier continued to alter the outcome of the battle. On one occasion, Rube watched an American soldier hiding in a foxhole, place explosives under an enemy tank that reached the American lines. After the explosion, the top hatch opened, and before a crew member could begin firing his machine gun, The Thrill jumped aboard the tank and put a bullet into the head of the German. He then dropped a grenade into the tank before leaping to safety. The rest of the day, American soldiers huddled in their foxholes, hopeful that a German artillery shell wouldn't find its target.

By early evening, even with the arrival of reinforcements, it became obvious, with the casualties the Allied forces had taken and with little ammo, it would be too much to ask the men to carry on with the defense of Marvie. With the arrival of Army airplanes attacking the German positions, a much-needed hiatus occurred in the fighting, allowing for an orderly withdrawal of some American troops to the outskirts of the town. First, the wounded had to be moved and taken to triage centers. With much trepidation, the Pony Express crew permitted their Jeep to carry wounded soldiers back to Bastogne.

Along with the injured, the four MPs made certain that a duffel bag of letters written on an extremely dark day before the holiday would be delivered to the besieged town of Bastogne. It remained unclear if Rube's letters and those from other GIs in Marvie would ever reach stateside. If not, at least sending the mail provided the village's defenders with the satisfaction that their final words might one day be read by family, strangers, or historians.

As stars appeared over the battlefield, the Germans launched another assault on Marvie. To stop the assault the Army air force, using several P-47

American aircraft fighters, blasted the enemy's arrival into the town and halted the German advance. After an American counterattack, the shape of the town of Marvie became unrecognizable, and a strange configuration emerged, as each side controlled half of the town. The Germans responded with a heavy artillery bombardment, and by midnight the barrage had become so intense that the four MPs and seventeen other soldiers were forced to abandon their positions and retreat from the town.

All the GIs piled into the ammo truck left by the Ghost Army and fled as shells dropped around the vehicle. Rube had just told the driver to lower his window when a shell exploded nearby. The truck tilted to one side and regained balance, but the driver's door was blown out. The driver sustained some injuries, but by lowering the window, no one was injured by flying glass. Rube took over for the driver and got the truck to the railroad tracks west of Marvie, where the engine broke down.

The entire group of GIs then made their way on foot toward Sibret, the headquarters for an American division. Upon arriving at this very small enclave, Okie, using his binoculars, spotted Nazi flags flying from various locations. All the men's hearts sank. With their last escape route gone and no way to return to Bastogne as the German artillery continued its assault, the lost group of soldiers could only watch as U.S. planes ignored enemy fire to drop supplies into the town. Some landed in the town; some missed, and one landed about a thousand yards from where the men were located. It took all of five minutes for the group to discover the cargo that dropped from the sky. Just like finding a pot of gold at the end of a rainbow, over twenty soldiers cherish this unexpected Christmas gift of weapons, ammo, and K-rations.

Living in the woods in the middle of winter brought instant panic. The group agreed to find someplace to hide. But where? After trudging over snow and splashing over a creek, the men took a break. At Marvie, each soldier had acquired six pairs of socks — critical in keeping their feet from becoming frozen. The troops spent the night in a shallow gully; fortunately, it didn't snow. Despite the cold, the men made it through the night.

Somehow, before the sun appeared, the troops moved west of Bastogne and found a road running parallel to a railroad line. Moving up an embankment and standing on the railroad tracks, the GIs could see the skyline of Bastogne. Light flashes rimmed the buildings, and the sounds of explosions vibrated continuously. Certainly, it wasn't a place that Santa would visit in the coming hours. Up to this point, there was no contact with the enemy. But as the soldiers moved along the tracks, they saw what looked like human figures moving in their direction. Looking into the dark abyss before them, it became obvious they could no longer remain on the tracks if the men wanted to avoid being prisoners of war, or worse, dead GIs. All the soldiers cautiously moved down the embankment into the darkened woods. Silently they watched a German patrol on the railroad tracks pass over their location.

Fourteen

As the first sign of sunlight appeared, the GIs had luck on their side as they discovered a pathway farther into the dense cover of the trees. With visibility among the vegetation greatly limited, Okie spotted an opening that led the twenty-one escapees to an area where some B-17 planes had mistakenly dropped bombs. As the GIs navigated the debris and massive craters, suddenly, they heard rifles click, and someone shouted, "Don't move."

Rube thought that if the voice were German, it was all over. The voice directed the guys to the left, to a small creek. The person instructed them to follow the creek bed and raise their hands. The voice spoke again and warned the men that the land was mined on each side of the creek. Finally arriving at a small outpost, a dozen U.S. soldiers greeted the group of exhausted GIs. They questioned how the group found the outpost. Trying to control his temper, Chip finally lashed out and told the soldiers that his companions were tired, hungry, battered, and bruised. He continued, "If you plan to kill us, you should do it now; otherwise, offer us some food, water, and comfort." Lieutenant Rick Parker, the only officer at the outpost, listened as The Thrill rehashed their six-hour journey from Marvie. Somewhat reluctantly, the band of brothers finally accepted them.

Another soldier, who looked like he worked at a greasy spoon, offered the exhausted GIs some chicken soup he had just made on a makeshift stove. The soup was hot and tasty even though the soldiers drank it from a tin cup. Several of the men asked for an additional cup. "Only if my stepmother had been the cook would it have tasted better," said Rube.

While eating, Chip asked the lieutenant why his company didn't have more men. Parker explained that the remaining men were a combination of different companies that the German offensive had ravaged. He continued, "When Sibret fell to the Germans, an attempt was made to break through enemy lines, and its success or failure remains unclear. The GIs at this site represent the last remaining obstacle before the Germans completely encircle Bastogne."

Once the first light of day became visible on the horizon, the Pony Express crew, while touring the outpost's defensive network, were impressed with its strategic arrangement. With the proper number of men and arms, Rube's team believed it could hold off a much larger force.

Lieutenant Parker noted there was no shortage of weapons and ammo as those who attempted to escape earlier discarded much of their gear and weapons to travel light. While talking to Parker, The Thrill observed something happening on the railroad tracks; hundreds of troops were gathering instead of a few guards. From a distance, the five men could see the silhouettes of German soldiers parading along the railroad tracks. It looked to the lieutenant like they were about to have some visitors. Within a few minutes, the soldiers circled the lieutenant as he gave final instructions. "Warriors, it will get extremely loud in the next few hours, so listen closely."

The officer told his troops, "If this is a probing mission, I think we can handle it, but if it's an all-out attack and German tanks enter the battle, we're in big trouble. If this happens, evacuate the outpost." Parker's final comments to his soldiers made them aware of three signs he would use to inform them when to move toward the escape routes. "Either listen to the sound of my voice, or if you see me spinning my hands over my head, or upon hearing the booby traps exploding, get the hell out."

Rube and three other MPs entered the foxholes about sixty feet apart. With a BAR in the hands of Okie and Chip and with Rube and The Thrill possessing two Thompson machine guns, they hoped that would be enough to stop the enemy. The other GIs were scattered about fifteen yards behind a five-foot-tall timber wall built from the trees near the outpost.

On this day before Christmas, each man recognized the Germans weren't bearing any gifts, and if they survived, they'd never forget this memory. Rube later noticed a few soldiers peeing on their rifles even before the shooting started. The shocked MP shouted, "What in the hell are you guys doing?"

Nonchalantly, one said, "Our weapons are frozen, and this is a quick way to heat them."

Without warning, the Germans launched the attack. Simultaneously, gunfire from the railroad tracks and the outpost disrupted the silence of this day before Christmas. The accuracy of the gunfire from the outpost appeared to be on target as German soldiers collapsed and rolled down the embankment, much like little kids playing on a hill.

Still, the enemy continued to advance despite the casualties. With the launching of the grenades from the M1 Garand, the first wave of attackers melted away. The second wave also met heavy fire and pulled back before sharpshooters on the railroad tracks began reducing the number of GIs on the firing lines. It took the last soldier firing the grenade launcher to score a hit on the embankment that temporarily halted the devastating accuracy of the sharpshooters. Then came the noise that all those at the outpost feared, the tank motor. Chip first noticed an oblong structure appear at the top of the embankment. "Tank," screamed voices along the foxholes and trenches. The Bazooka team waited patiently until the tank reached the edge of the embankment, and an accurate shot struck its soft underbelly. Smoke came from underneath the tank and it slid down the embankment like a car with no brakes. The ground and the tank collided, creating a jolting impact the men felt in the foxholes and trenches guarding the outpost. Before the Bazooka crew could reload, two other tanks moved down the hill, followed by hundreds of Nazi troops. Again, the deadly fire from the outpost ripped apart the advancing lines, but this time the enemy's human resources and firepower proved stronger than the GIs could endure.

Lieutenant Parker yelled out, "One minute." As the German lines entered the mine location, Parker pushed a lever, and the ground shook violently with explosions. Before the debris had settled, less than two dozen GIs left their positions and headed for the woods.

The soldiers forced to turn their backs on the enemy endured a strange sensation. First, the feeling of defeat encompassed their minds; then their bodies reacted. They began to seek more air; their hearts beat faster, but the feeling that something was about to pierce their skin had the most impact. While running, Rube's chance of survival declined to a few seconds as a shell lobbed from a tank exploded, knocking him to the turf, and shrapnel flew over his body. Unable to rise, The Thrill and Chip yanked Rube to his feet. With bloody knees from the fall, Rube ran until another blast crashed among the fleeing troops. From that moment, Rube seemed in a daze as another shell exploded only twenty yards away. Like the end of a track race, as each soldier staggered across the finish line into the sheltering trees, relief and exhilaration temporarily gripped their exhausted bodies. Although one of the lucky ones to reach the safety of the woods, Rube somehow felt he missed something that happened while escaping from the tank fire. It took several days to recreate the scene in his mind, which he would never forget, a shell striking the ground where a couple of U.S. soldiers had been running. When the smoke cleared, Rube looked for a sign of life but could only see snow particles drifting in the air.

Out of breath, all the GIs split into small groups. The Pony Express crew remained together and tried to maneuver around trees, gullies, snow-covered holes, and fallen limbs. The biggest fear for the foursome was that a German soldier stood behind each tree. Thankfully, the woods were clear of the enemy's soldiers. Until dark, the soldiers from both sides played a game of "hide and seek." Unlike the kid's game, the four members of the Pony Express crew realized that as they searched for hiding places, their chances of survival dwindled.

The Thrill noticed the German troop movement in the woods on his left. Chip then pointed out snow particles floating in the air on the road in an area on his right. When Rube saw a fast-moving group of soldiers with dogs charging directly in front of the GIs, all seemed lost.

All the MPs agreed it would be impossible to outrun the dog team. The team moved quickly to continue in this deadly confrontation and found a gully between two small hills. Removing their helmets, the four men watched intently as the dogs broke loose from the clutches of their handlers. Rube was given the task of taking down the dogs.

It happened so fast. The dogs dashed over the ravine where the GIs made what might be their last stand. Everything else became a mixture of sounds that vibrated around their isolated position. When the smoke cleared, the shooting stopped, and several dead bodies lay before the GIs. Rube never fired at the dogs as they kept running once the shooting started.

"Damn," shouted The Thrill. "Anyone hit?" For a moment, no one answered.

Then, all three men answered one at a time, "No injuries to report."

"Okay, then, let's get the hell out of Dodge."

Before leaving, Okie fired two grenades from a grenade launcher he secured before leaving the outpost. The grenades landed near the German forces on the left that had been closing in on the fleeing Americans. The explosions caused those Germans to mistakenly think the grenade had been fired by GIs who were escaping on the road, but only Nazi soldiers were on that road. The result — German troops began firing on each other, which helped hasten the MPs' exodus as they used the distraction to move to a new location.

With only one direction available, the four GIs withdrew toward Lake Bison. An area with many trails and tree cover, the lake provided a temporary hiding place for the fleeing MPs. With the hope of finding a small craft they could use to cross the lake, a remote possibility, the team searched for a miracle in their quest to escape the Nazis.

Only hours away from the beginning of Christmas, the crew, under the cover of darkness, explored the edges of the lake area. At first, they couldn't believe it when they saw the outline of a small boat. Excited, the men sprinted to the vessel only to find a huge hole in its midsection.

Resigned to defeat, the Pony Express crew used the wood from the damaged boat to build a fire that they hoped would keep them from freezing to death. As the night hours passed, the men contemplated what would happen to them once the sun rose on Christmas day, if somehow, they survived the cold of the night.

By morning, the wind had ceased, and the crew spent time talking about what they had hoped to do with the rest of their lives. But all accepted the reality of what lay ahead.

Fifteen

If the four MPs were in Washington, they would have been thrilled to see snowflakes dropping from the sky on Christmas morning. Instead, the Pony Express crew languished on the edge of Lake Bison, waiting for German soldiers to end their misery. Despite their dreadful situation, the GIs wished each other a Merry Christmas, as they waited for the Germans to arrive. Still unsure about surrendering, the men debated the decision, but whatever action they agreed upon, they would do it together.

Whether by choice or the Germans wanted to show some reverence for the holiday, not much stirred during morning hours except a field mouse that ran past the location where the Pony Express crew remained. As the noon hour passed, it was unclear if the enemy had proclaimed a day of peace or decided to wait until the next day to finish the job.

For much of the day, small amounts of snow covered the frozen ground as the crew members wondered if this Christmas would be their last. To quell their nerves, a few walked along the frozen lake. Rube warned Okie not to go far in the lake to take a piss, and as usual, he didn't listen. When he returned, he told his buddies the lake was frozen solid.

Okie's description of the ice caused Rube to envision skating to freedom. Of course, the nearest pair of skates might have been in Holland. Chip ended all speculation about any escape by saying, "I think the final nail has been hammered into our coffin."

Rube felt the same way but kept thinking about something that happened when he was around nine or ten. So, to pass the time, he related the story to his buddies. "From a window in my apartment, off Thomas Circle in

Washington, D.C., I could see a statue of a Civil War general riding his horse. My dad worked as a tailor and never had a lot of money. But he took a small amount of cash each week to deposit in the bank. One of the banks that didn't collapse during the Depression was Riggs National Bank, located on F Street. My dad and I sometimes walked or rode the streetcar to the bank. My father, Abe, told me the money he saved would pay for my brother Sam's college education, and Abe promised to do the same for me. So much for that. But that's not the whole story. While walking to the bank, we passed a beggar on the street."

"You mean a bum?" questioned Okie.

"I wouldn't call him a bum, but a smart beggar."

"What was so special about him?"

"He had no legs."

"How did it happen?"

"I have no idea."

"Did you give him any money?"

"No, not him, but his friend."

"The beggar had a friend?"

"Yes, a monkey."

"Wait a minute, with no legs, how could he control a big monkey?"

"The monkey was small, and I remember it took my dime and placed it in a cigar box in front of the beggar."

"So, let me get this straight, the beggar with no legs had a monkey who collected money."

"Exactly!"

"If he had no legs, how did he get the monkey and himself to the street corner?"

"Great question. One day, my dad and I were walking down F street and saw him with the monkey coming down the same street."

"But you said he had no legs?"

"True, but he was riding on a board about the size of a two-foot square wooden slab with wheels on the bottom. He had a strap that linked the monkey to his belt, and he pushed the contraption with both hands."

"Wouldn't the cement damage his hands?"

"No, it looked like he had two small blocks of wood covered with leather that he used to push his way to wherever he was going."

"Well, Rube, what does this have to do with our present situation?"

"I'm not sure."

"So, why in the hell did you tell this story?"

"First, because it took my mind off our dilemma here, and it made me think how this man overcame so many difficulties."

"No doubt the man in your story is quite clever, but we don't have scooters to take us across the lake," said Chip.

Rube countered with, "True, but it gave me an idea. You know that tent I have been *shlepping* around since the battle at Marvie? What if we used our knives to cut four large pieces from the tent, folded them into two-foot square sections, and then with the extra pairs of gloves we have, we could go onto the ice? Then we would get down on our knees atop our newly cut tarp, push our hands backward, and see if this propels us forward on the ice."

"I don't know if it would work," said Chip with some doubt.

"Me neither, but what would we lose if we tried?"

"Wait a moment; that tent was supposed to protect us from the rains," offered Chip.

"I understand, but let's try, since we have zero options, and see what happens. I will only cut a small section of the tent, and we can give it a test run."

The Thrill interrupted with a major concern, "What if the ice cracks?"

Rube responded, "I don't want to go there, but if a 200-pound hockey player can skate on a thin piece of ice, why shouldn't we be able to cross a frozen lake?"

"I'm sure those ice rinks are constantly frozen, whereas a lake freezes and unfreezes."

Before attempting a trial run, Okie went onto the frozen lake and measured the ice's thickness to be almost three inches with his knife. After a short debate, Okie, with a piece of the tent under his knees, took the position that a college wrestler would take preparing for a match. The three MPs held their breath as Okie pushed off, only carrying his weapon on his back. In astonishment, the magic carpet traveled about forty feet.

Like kids on their first sleigh ride, four former Jeep riders exchanged their vehicle for a carpet ride they would remember forever. Using Rube's tape that gleamed in the night, the men could follow each other through the darkness of the night. As they cautiously moved over the ice, they listened intently for the sounds of ice fracturing, but only heard the cry of an owl somewhere in the woods. The men used their knives and bayonets to penetrate the ice to advance more quickly. With their sharp weapons firmly planted in the ice, the four MPs pushed forward, creating an additional source of power that allowed them to slide across the frozen lake. The MPs soon realized that this form of travel had a major impact on their arm muscles. The team took several breaks as the aches, pains, and bloody knees mounted. While they waited to regain more energy, their escape came to an abrupt halt as shouted Chip shouted, "Something ain't right."

"What's the matter?" asked Rube.

"There seems to be a gap in the ice. From what I can see, the ice appears higher in some areas than the others. I hate to do this, but I will use my flashlight to look ahead …. Oh, my God."

Ten feet from their location, Chip saw blackness but no ice. He pointed the flashlight to the left and viewed a fifteen-foot drop off to another lake level. This geographical trough extended for about a hundred yards. Many would view this awesome freak of nature as a picturesque scene, but four bitterly cold soldiers, could only look at the stars above with thankful and sincere prayers.

They could no longer glide on their knees due to the uneven territory that disappeared into the darkness. With no other choice, they had to stand up and use the flashlights, which placed them in increased danger of the Germans easily spotting them. Using the tent pieces around their bodies to protect them from the cold, the MPs moved slowly over the frozen lake. For the next hour, they carefully avoided the waterfalls, which posed a major hazard due to sudden drops in the level of the land.

With frozen bodies and icicles attached to their skin and tent cloths, the four MPs finally came within sight of the shoreline. Chip, who had lived in the north, informed the Pony Express crew of the danger awaiting them at the lake's edge. He told his buddies, about eighty feet from completing this unbelievable journey, that the ice could be thin and easily crack. Chip then lined the men up like the beginning of a track meet. He told the crew that when he signaled, they should drop the tent material and begin running toward the shore. "On my command," he said, "Slide like a runner stealing second base in a baseball game. When you slide, hold your weapon above your head. See you at the shoreline."

If a baseball umpire had been present, he would have called three GIs safe, and one would have made it due to interference. Only The Thrill's extra weight caused him to stop just before the shoreline, leaving the back of his pants wet.

On shore, the foursome hastily built a fire. As the warmth of the fire penetrated their skin, The Thrill confessed that he was one who never much believed in miracles, but what happened to the Pony Express crew on this Christmas day was indeed a miracle.

At sunrise, Rube volunteered to check on any activity on the ice. Much to his regret, he spotted German troops moving across the lake. Once again, the crew had to depart hastily. While running, Rube heard The Thrill say, "Where's Moses when you need him?"

Minutes after leaving the campsite, the team heard a horrifying sound. The ice cracked open, and simultaneously they heard the screams of surprise and fear from the panicked German soldiers. Rube turned to The Thrill and said, "I think Moses arrived a little late, but he made it!"

Sixteen

The Pony Express crew finally exited the woods with the Germans no longer in pursuit. Their sense of security lasted for only a few miles, as the four MPs observed a German Panzer tank when they entered an open field. For some reason, the occupants were abandoning the vehicle. Using his binoculars, Okie determined that three men were leaving the tank, carrying large cans. The other two hung around the vehicle. Okie and Chip assumed the tank was out of gasoline, and those crew members went somewhere to find fuel.

For the next twenty minutes, the MPs discussed the best way to take out the two tank crew members. Putting bullets into their bodies would have been easy, but that would alert the three other crew members. Killing them with firearms would be the last resort. According to The Thrill, they had to meet a silent death. When one of the tank crew went into the vehicle, Okie and Rube worked out a plan to take out the two Germans. With bayonets drawn, Rube told Okie that their necks offered the easiest targets. If necessary, a slash to the kidneys would also be effective. Both men crawled across the snow with a sick feeling in their stomachs. Rube had given a lot of injections as a medic, so he tried to convince himself this wouldn't be any different.

Rube wondered what Okie was thinking, but he, too, had experience taking farm animals' lives. He had no difficulty in killing livestock for food. But this certainly was a different experience. Both men soon realized there was no comparison between shooting someone far away and killing a human close-up with a long sharp blade.

Rube crept behind the German soldier who was smoking a cigarette and plunged the bayonet into his neck. He felt awful, but like when animals were killed in kosher food plants, death comes quickly and relatively painlessly when the artery in the neck is cut. Such was the case with the soldier. The GI then shouted something in Yiddish, which brought the other soldier out of the tank. Seeing Okie, he jumped down from the tank and struggled. Noticing that Okie was in trouble, Rube used his bayonet again to subdue the enemy soldier. Covered with the German's blood and his own vomit, a shaken Rube was barely able to stand as his knees and hands shook. Seeing Rube's condition, Okie asked his buddy, "Are you hurt?" but received no response. With Rube somewhat comatose, the rest of the Pony Express team escorted him behind the tank.

While Rube was drinking water, the MPs heard two shots. Acting quickly, Chip, The Thrill, and Okie dragged the bodies of the two soldiers away from the tank and waited in the overgrown weeds. Shortly after, the three other Germans approached. Not seeing the other two soldiers, they called their names. After the echoes from the MPs' rifle and machine gun fire died down, the next three German soldiers also lay dead among the weeds and snow.

Hearing the volley of shots seemed to bring Rube back to reality as he cautiously moved around the tank and saw his crew removing the weapons of the dead German soldiers. Before his team could ask about his health, Rube praised their performance and took command and ordered Okie to drop two grenades into the Panzer. With the German Panzer burning in the background, three GIs prepared to evacuate the field while Rube washed the bloody mess from his uniform and hands.

The foursome followed the trail taken by the Germans and came upon a farmhouse. In the distance, they saw a horse and a lamb inside a barn. As they moved closer, they heard someone sobbing. An older woman was standing over her fallen husband. Rube couldn't imagine how much pain this woman was now enduring. Seeing the crew, she hugged Chip, and all became emotional. She spoke both German and a dialect known in Belgium. Rube's Yiddish helped him communicate with her. Together the four MPs helped bury her husband. Rube admitted it was one of the saddest scenes he had endured.

They learned the woman's name, Anna, and the Pony Express crew tried to comfort her, but there was little consolation to offer her a day after Christmas. Despite the sincere feelings of the four GIs, only Anna had to deal with the trauma of losing her loved one which would last forever. Okie tried to converse with her and explain how her husband's killers had been eliminated. Still, the MPs felt the widow was hiding something else that heightened her gloom and doom, but none of the guys knew what it might be.

The calamity of the day left everyone spent. Rube and Okie had the opportunity to change from their blood-soaked uniforms into fresh, although wrinkled uniforms, they carried in their backpacks. Anna tried to decompress and reheated the evening meal she had made for her husband, but now shared with the four MPs. The GIs slept uneasily during the night, and Rube heard Anna crying and moving around the house. However, in the morning, Rube awoke to her scream and thought she was reliving the horrors of her husband's death, but soon he realized the reason for her screaming. A German officer's car had driven onto the farmyard. Half-awake, the foursome gathered their weapons and clothes, and she pushed the MPs toward a small trash chute that went into the basement. One by one, they slid down into a dark room. After a while, their eyes began to get used to the darkness and the smell of old waste, and they began moving around the enclosure.

Okie saw a light glitter from a crack within the walls, and as the four men moved around a pillar, Rube discovered a small opening that led to a sub-basement. Six eyes appeared to stare at him in the darkness as he looked inside. Before he could say anything, the MPs heard a shot ring out. At first, they thought the Germans had killed the old lady, but then the foursome heard her voice and a kettle hissing. The MPs figured the Germans, wanting something to eat, forced Anna to make a meal for them. What they couldn't figure out was why the Germans had taken so long to enter the house.

Once inside the old lady's home, the German officer and his entourage saw the woman working on a breakfast of eggs and biscuits. Anna welcomed them and explained that she saw them when they arrived and immediately started placing plates on the table and making their food. Anna said, "I don't have bacon, but I have lots of eggs." While Anna worked on the meal, the Germans quickly checked the house and noticed the trash chute. They questioned her about it, and she told them it went to the trash bin in the basement. They seemed satisfied with her answer and then sat down to eat.

In the basement, the now grounded Pony Express crew listened in horror as the Germans threatened Anna by telling her they would kill her if the foods weren't to their satisfaction. When the contingent of Nazi soldiers prepared to leave, one brought the lifeless body of the lamb they found in the barn and dropped it on the kitchen table. They demanded that she use this animal as a special dinner for them when they returned later.

Hearing the motor from the German vehicle start, Rube and the crew waited in silence and hoped the German officer hadn't left a guard behind. After twenty minutes and only hearing Anna sobbing, they crawled back up the garbage chute. She was distraught and could barely talk. With several dialects meshed-together, she managed to tell the men that the lamb had been with the family for years, and her granddaughter loved the animal and called it Jolly Lamb. Okie tried to comfort her but to no avail. Chip made some tea that helped her calm down. Rube offered, "We all feel horrible for you, but can you answer one question? Who are the people in your basement?"

Anna told us they were her neighbors. Somehow the Nazis found out they had some Jewish heritage in their family. They had killed the husband, but she and her two kids managed to escape. Anna and her husband had kept the mother, the boy who was twelve, and the girl who was ten, hidden for the past five months.

The GI crew went into the bedroom to discuss their next steps, which required life and death decisions. They talked about the danger confronting everyone in the farmhouse, and The Thrill mentioned they were trapped in a vise. The men realized they couldn't leave the civilians alone and yet couldn't travel with everyone, especially in this cold weather. Either way, they were screwed. To Rube, the best plan was to remain at the house until the soldiers returned. That would allow the crew to eliminate the officer and his aides and use their vehicle for escape. The four MPs concluded if the plan didn't work, at least they would go down fighting.

It took a lot of coaxing, but Anna agreed to cook the lamb meal, realizing it might save the lives of everyone in the house.

As Anna removed the lamb from the oven around 4:00, she heard a vehicle's motor approaching. The German officer and his crew returned without any other escorts. After using the outhouse, they entered the farmhouse and demanded their lamb meal. The German soldiers gluttonously ate the food while the four GIs huddled in a makeshift attic. When finished, one of the officers complained there was no dessert.

Anna explained she didn't have time to make any dessert. "Dumb bitch," shouted one of the Nazis; he then grabbed her arm, and another soldier leaped from his chair and screamed that the lamb was too tough and slapped her. As Anna fell to the floor, she reacted instantly and stood up and grabbed a frying pan from the sink. Another Nazi grabbed her hand and twisted the pan away, causing it to drop to the floor. The pan hitting the floor covered the noise of the four GIs coming down from the attic. Then a shot rang out before the MPs came down the stairs. Within a few seconds, the Germans had eaten their last supper. After a volley of gunfire came from the weapons of the four MPs, blood covered the kitchen everywhere. Broken dishes and wine glasses mixed with meal leftovers, and French wine dripped, dripped, dripped to the floor. Smoke still came from Rube's Thompson machine gun as he bent down to examine Anna's wound. Rube instantly knew she only had a short time to live. With glazed eyes, she mumbled something to him and grabbed his hand. She then shut her eyes for the last time.

fewer enemy soldiers. But at an intersection where several roads connected, everything changed. They viewed a German vehicle stretched across the road. A large light flashed on their faces, and machine guns pointed at their car. Gretchen rose and spoke in German, but it didn't seem to satisfy the four people in the vehicle. Chip slowly moved forward with the car as The Thrill slipped the pin from his grenade. A tap on Chip's shoulder signaled him to turn off his lights. Instantly, Okie fired one shot at the spotlight, and it exploded, and a second later, Chip threw the grenade and blew up the car blocking the road. Shots rang out as Chip floored the gas pedal, and the vehicle darted forward and crashed into the burning car. Sparks flew as the passengers were jolted, but Chip remained in control. Spinning the wheel like someone who hit an icy patch, he remained on the road as enemy fire riddled the fleeing vehicle. After driving from the checkpoint, Chip asked everyone if they were okay. All answered yes, except The Thrill.

A bullet had found its mark. Rube immediately dove over to the ex-cop. He had been hit, but not much blood appeared on his uniform. But with further examination, Rube found that the bullet had just missed the pancreas area but might have clipped the outer portion of his stomach. Grabbing his medic bag, he hastily administered preventive measures to stop the bleeding, but he realized the MP needed to be taken to a hospital immediately. To stop The Thrill from going into shock, Rube quickly used blankets to cover his entire body.

More trouble arose when Chip noticed the gas gauge dropping. A bullet had hit the gas tank as fuel leaked from the automobile. They all realized that soon the car would run out of gas, and they would have to continue their journey on foot. Once the gas ran out, they abandoned the car. Everyone battled the cold; some walked, and others carried The Thrill on a makeshift stretcher. Before leaving the German vehicle, Rube searched for a gasoline can, which he found. At first, the MP believed this would be their savior, but as Rube opened it, he only saw a small amount of gasoline. Still, he carried the gasoline can with him as they moved through the woods. Along the way, Okie discovered a crevice among some rocks that was a livable space for all seven individuals.

This is where the MPs and refugees would spend the cold, bitter night. With Gretchen leading the way with a flashlight, the group searched for branches and twigs to begin a fire. Chip poured what was left of the gasoline onto the wooden pile, and the fire provided enough warmth for their bodies that they managed to survive through the night.

The Thrill seemed to fade in and out, but the fire had relieved him from the cold. Rube knew The Thrill would grow weaker if he didn't get help soon. Chip and Okie said a prayer and asked God for help for their buddy. Rube repeated a Jewish prayer, *Mi Sheberach*, a call for healing the sick.

Near noon, Rube pulled four pairs of dry socks from his helmet liner and gave them to all the adults so that they could remove their wet socks and prevent their feet from freezing. Carrying The Thrill wasn't easy, but they managed to travel a few miles until stopping in a gully to rest and eat some K-rations. They listened as the wind whipped overhead. Rube checked the wounded man and realized that blood clots could become another problem. As the group sat on the cold ground, Rube leaned against a rock that moved. Everyone in the gully suddenly gasped as he jumped up, screaming. Okie thought Rube might have seen a snake, but he kept trying to push something off his body. "What is it?" hollered Okie.

"Bugs," answered Rube.

The former botanist, Chip, went to the rock and calmly identified the bugs. Then he said, "God has answered our prayers."

Rube couldn't believe what Chip said. *He had to be crazy to think that these gruesome-looking bugs were the gift from God that would save The Thrill's life.* Rube then thought Chip might have the same feeling about him, the way he was dancing around like he had some disease. When Chip mentioned that the bugs were called bloodsuckers, Rube began to understand what Chip had in mind. He should have realized that these bugs could be used to remove some of the bad blood forming in The Thrill's body. Chip clarified that the bugs wouldn't cure him, but it would give the fleeing group more time to get medical care for him.

PART III: THE DARK SIDE OF THE HOLIDAYS

All the Military Policemen but Rube put the insects around The Thrill's wound, and Rube covered him with blankets taken from Anna's house. After a two-hour hike, The Thrill opened his eyes and asked, "Where am I?"

Rube said, "You're still in hell with all of us." He smiled, and after a fifteen-minute break, Chip and Okie prepared to lift the stretcher, and out of nowhere, they heard a loud noise, and a motorcycle appeared around the corner. Soon, two other riders on their bikes with their weapons drawn joined the first motorcyclist. Rube shouted, "Don't shoot; we are Americans." One soldier who wore an MP uniform ordered the group, including the kids, to lie on the ground with hands spread out. Chip tried to convince the MP that all the men were also part of an MP unit but failed. Another MP said, "I don't know many MPs who wear German outerwear." Rube told him that the clothes came from dead Germans who they killed. Rube urged him to check the bullet holes in the jackets, which again was met with no response. The MPs then turned their attention to The Thrill and asked what was wrong with him. Rube told them that he had been shot and needed medical attention. After identifying Rube's unit to the MP, he still didn't believe them. He then demanded information about the woman and kids. The Washingtonian informed him that Gretchen's husband had been murdered, and both she and the kids were fleeing the Nazis. "Tell me more about your mission," one MP asked. Again, Rube told them they were originally supposed to escort a special company to Luxembourg, but the German blitz complicated their plans.

As the three MPs gathered to talk, a Jeep carrying a staff sergeant stopped in front of the crowd of MPs encircling the seven prostrate individuals. Rube was now on his feet with his hands behind his head and obeyed the order to turn around and talk to the sergeant. As he did, Rube stood paralyzed, looking into the eyes of the former quarterback for Roosevelt High School, Jerry Grayson.

―•―

Eighteen

Rube couldn't believe it. What were the odds of meeting a classmate in the middle of an armed conflict thousands of miles from home? To Rube seeing the former quarterback was exhilarating and somewhat awkward. He never really liked Grayson; he always had some wiseass answer, especially to younger kids. As usual, he started by telling Rube that the last time he heard about him, he was still a second-string quarterback. Of course, Rube didn't want to hear it, but it was true. He then hit his high school teammate with a comment that he never had the accuracy to be a first-string quarterback, which was also true. But Rube came at him with a knockout blow, "I'm doing a lot better here throwing grenades."

As the two talked further, Rube told Jerry about his escape with the Pony Express crew and Captain Holtz from Wiltz, Marvie, and Sibret. With new respect for each other, Rube learned that Grayson had worked with Holtz when the Germans nearly overran Luxembourg. The staff sergeant told Rube that Patton's Fourth Armored Division had broken through the German stronghold at Bastogne on December 26, and both men realized the magnitude of the events underway. Jerry then revealed to Rube that his MPs were leading the rear echelon of General Patton's Third Army into a region on the western edge of Bastogne. According to the staff sergeant, heavy fighting continued, and another armored division, the Tenth, joined the battle.

Seeing a truck with a red cross symbol moving up the road, Rube explained to Jerry that they needed medical help for one of their wounded soldiers. He immediately called for the ambulance to stop and care for the barely alive Will, The Thrill.

While The Thrill was being placed on a stretcher, Jerry asked, "Do you know anyone who might be familiar with the terrain of the area?" Rube instantly mentioned Gretchen and helped interpret a conversation that gave Grayson valuable information. Jerry seemed extremely excited about finding a quicker route to Bastogne.

As Doctor Mike Lavine and his team assisted The Thrill into the ambulance with the two kids, his staff was stunned to find bloated bloodsucker bugs over The Thrill's wound. At first, they panicked, thinking they were boils on his body, until Chip explained why the bugs were attached. Surprisingly, they gave Chip kudos for coming up with that idea. After a preliminary exam of The Thrill and checking his dog tag for blood type, a member of the medic team placed an IV in his arm. Once a new triage area became operational, The Thrill would be its first patient.

After looking at the malnourished kids, the doctor wanted to give them a complete examination. Gretchen reluctantly agreed after Jerry convinced her the doctor's caravan would follow his Jeep to a triage site. While the doctor's team set up the triage tents, Gretchen told Jerry about the shortcut to Bastogne.

Riding in a small convoy of Jeeps, Rube, Gretchen, and Jerry drove several miles down the dirt road before stopping at what appeared to be a cow pasture. Gretchen related that crossing over this flat area would cut the travel time to Bastogne in half. The convoy drove another twenty minutes and connected to a wide road that had a harder surface and enabled travel by heavier vehicles. Gretchen and Rube returned to the triage tent area while Jerry and his men marked the new route and searched for mines.

Upon Rube's arrival at the triage tent, he watched The Thrill enter an Army ambulance to transport him to a nearby airfield. Still conscious but shot full of different medications, he told Rube and the guys, "Carry on." After the ambulance departed, Dr. Lavine said he thought that The Thrill had a good chance to make it, and they would fly him to a hospital near Le Mans.

A little later, a Jeep carrying Jerry stopped at the newly built triage area. He picked up a hot coffee, and when seeing Gretchen and Rube, he came over and thanked them for providing such valuable information. "Is there anything else I can help you with?" Grayson's offer couldn't have come at a better time. Rube asked him if it would be possible to use a communication network to contact his MP headquarters in Le Mans, and Jerry said he'd arrange for that to happen after midnight. At 0033, a communication truck pulled into the triage area, and Rube was allowed to call the home base.

"Why is it you guys keep getting lost?" came a voice on the phone.

"Believe me; I wish that weren't always the case."

"What happened this time?"

"It's another long story."

"Wait, Lieutenant Gibson, I have the wandering Jew and his flock on the phone."

After talking to Gibson for almost a half hour, Rube finished with, "So, that's our story, and if you wish to verify it, call Sergeant Grayson."

"Not necessary," answered the lieutenant, "But that was a hell of a *bubbe meise*."

"What did you say?"

"My wife is Jewish, and she says that after hearing all my long stories."

"What a small world we live in," responded Rube.

"One last thing, since we could not verify your location, your name and those of your buddies might have been placed on a missing-in-action list. Would you like us to inform your family and the family members of your team to disregard any notice that might be sent to them?"

"Absolutely. Tell them I'm fine and disregard any message stating otherwise."

"Will do."

"Hold on; Sergeant Grayson wants to talk to you."

After speaking to Gibson, Jerry informed the Pony Express crew that they would stay with the Third Army until late-January, as Grayson's company was short of MPs and needed experienced combatants.

The next two days, Goldy, Chip, Okie, and other MP companies assisted in traffic control as troops and machinery from The Third Army made their way into the Bastogne region. Rube could only compare the Presidential Inauguration parade in Washington to what he now witnessed. The weather in D.C. always had a cold chill, and it took hours to complete the parade. In Belgium, the weather was colder, and the military parade lasted almost two days. In D.C., the commander-in-chief would ride along Pennsylvania Avenue in a new model automobile. In late December, General George Patton, in a Jeep, would lead his troops over a dirt road to fight the enemy.

While directing caravans of military vehicles and supplies, Rube heard soldiers cheering and quickly realized someone of importance might be passing his location. Instead of saluting, Rube, with a rigid arm movement, waved General Patton and those in his Jeep forward. As the general passed Goldy's position, an onlooker shouted, "Give 'em hell, general." That remark, for whatever reason, resonated in Rube's mind until he heard a slightly different version directed toward a politician some months later.

The sound of war could be heard everywhere around Bastogne. If one was oblivious to the events, he might have thought the town was celebrating the coming of the new year. As Rube watched the sky flash intermittently, it reminded him of the fireworks display he had seen at the mall in D.C. several years before. At one point, the artillery fire became so intense that those living in Luxembourg thought a thunderstorm had broken out somewhere north of the city.

On December 30, General Patton walked in the streets of Bastogne with his famous ivory-handled revolvers. In total disregard for being spotted by enemy snipers, he congratulated officers and men, took photographs with them, examined burned-out tanks, and visited battle sites. He even watched an artillery unit fire at an enemy tank, and when it struck the turret of its target, the general became very excited.

As the calendar turned to 1945, the MPs were removed from directing convoys of weapons, men, and vehicles to investigate a report, which had not been fully verified, but circulated, that about 5,000 German paratroopers had been dropped behind American lines in the area between Spa and Malmedy.

Chip stated, "We heard rumors about that several days ago, but we didn't know it involved so many Germans."

"Again, this report might not be accurate, but we must be aware of any groups of soldiers that don't meet the smell test," remarked Grayson.

With a smile, Chip remarked, "But Sarge, at this moment, we all smell!"

The hunt for the German intruders was temporarily suspended when a new combat zone emerged ten kilometers northeast of Bastogne. The town of Houffalize, captured during the German offensive, became a strategic military objective for both armies as it was the central crossroads leading in and out of the Ardennes. Despite heavy bombardments by Allied forces, the Germans held the town until the middle of January.

Rube and the Pony Express crew provided security while escorting war machinery and supply convoys as Allied forces encircled the beleaguered town. After establishing a checkpoint, the MPs had a close-up view of the combat. The vibrations coming from artillery fire and bombs crashing caused Rube to feel a sense of guilt. If still a medic, undoubtedly, his uniform would be coated with blood as he dodged bullets to save the lives of wounded GIs. From his perch at the checkpoint, he seemed more like an observer than a fighter. But once he considered the vulnerability of those engaged in combat, the former medic rationalized his horrific experiences during combat, and the guilt subsided.

For days, opposing armies battled around Houffalize, with neither side faltering. Unable to break through the enemy's defenses, the Allies launched a massive air assault against the town's occupants. While the bombing continued at the town unabated, the Pony Express members stood guard at a checkpoint. With a machine gun attached to the front of the Jeep, each MP performed guard duty as the battle continued. Rube was about to relinquish his guard time to Okie when he shouted, "Get ready. I think we are about to be attacked."

Okie and Chip gathered their weapons and watched German soldiers coming into view. First five, then ten, and the number continued to grow.

Okie screamed, "Don't shoot until they are closer."

Chip quickly called headquarters and reported, "German soldiers surround us." Chip's astonishing comment came next. "Oh, my God, they are dropping their weapons and surrendering. I can't believe what I am seeing. Over 150 just quit."

What happened at the checkpoint was repeated on the battlefield as thousands of German troops surrendered or retreated. Finally, on January 16, less than four weeks after being occupied, the Allies entered the town that no longer existed and learned that 189 civilians lost their lives in the German defeat.

By the end of January, the German offensive had collapsed, and almost all land lost during what was known as the Battle of the Bulge had been recaptured. The human cost in casualties from the battle that lasted from December 16 to January 20, was estimated at 75,000 men for the Allies and 120,000 for the enemy. The war was far from over as numerous other battles continued during the winter months, but with the failure of Hitler's greatest gamble, the German Army could only fight a delaying-action and retreated toward the homeland.

Nineteen

On January 8, 1945, Rube's letter from Marvie to his parents had arrived at their home at the corner of Allison Street and Georgia Avenue. During a phone call to his son Sam, Abe asked him if he could come over and read the letter. Sam replied, "Excellent idea. I'll bring along Marie and Bernie tomorrow."

Once the family gathered, Sam opened Rube's letter of December 22. He read aloud, "This might be the last letter you receive from me." Then he stopped and took off his glasses. Using some Kleenex, he wiped them off and returned to reading the letter. "Let me start again … 'This might be the last letter you receive from me for a while as I will be very busy in the coming days.'" Sam finished the letter using his own words. He didn't want his parents to hear the danger that threatened Rube and his men.

His dad might not have noticed Sam's anxiety. Marie knew something was wrong but didn't say anything. After spending several hours with Abe and Mary, the young couple and their son walked toward the streetcar on Georgia Avenue. Along the way, they spotted another couple across the street with a little girl. Both couples waved, and the man shouted, "Happy New Year."

Sam called back and said, "Let's hope the new year will bring peace."

After a brief conversation, the two couples departed, and then finally, Marie turned to Sam and asked, "Was there a problem with Rube's letter?"

A stoic Sam replied, "I think my brother is dead."

A Western Union telegram arrived at Sam Goldfarb's apartment a few days later. He had just returned from work, and his wife met him at the door holding an unopened telegram. Both knew what might be typed in the message. Sam thought about his father and how he would break the news. He could imagine Mary crying and how devastating the word of Rube's death would spread among the relatives. With trembling hands, he opened the Western Union telegram.

JANUARY 3, 1945

SAM, TELL POP AND MARY I'M OKAY. IF YOU RECEIVE ANY NOTIFICATION THAT I'M MISSING IN ACTION, THAT IS INCORRECT. WILL WRITE SHORTLY.

RUBE

With Allied forces again advancing toward the German border, the American psyche accepted the belief that the war would end soon. However, military officers stationed at Virginia's newly built Pentagon headquarters knew differently. Casualty reports offered a much more realistic picture. Not all casualties came from the enemy's weapons, but the bitter cold winter took its toll on Allied forces. Nonetheless, preparations were underway to launch attacks against the Germans' last line of defense, the Siegfried Line. Still, the possibility remained strong that the next few months would be critical in the Allied fight against the Axis powers.

The start of the new year brought a familiar foe to be reckoned with for many MP units. Once again, all units were placed on alert because English-speaking German paratroopers dressed in GI uniforms were reported to have infiltrated behind the American lines with a mission to create panic and havoc by changing direction signs, sabotaging Allied sites, and attacking the American supply chain of trucks and trains. Very little of the goals of this operation met success, but it had an enormous psychological effect on thousands of Allied troops and especially the military police who searched for their location. Almost every day, they would stop and ask soldiers questions that only an American could answer.

For Rube and his Pony Express buddies, who had returned from Houffalize, a similar threat confronted them. "You can't be serious; they are still searching for the invisible paratroopers," proclaimed Chip.

"Here we go again." An outraged Okie summed it up the best by saying, "We have hunted, searched, and discovered nothing. Do we still have to travel this road again?" Like a singer on stage who is about to finish a song and says, "One more time," so it was for the MPs. For the next few days, military police units would be responsible for finding the invisible enemy in an area the size of D.C.

"I can't take this crap anymore," cried a frustrated Chip. "I know ghosts when I see them. We sent an 'army of ghosts' through Belgium to Luxembourg, but I have never seen a German ghost. I'm sick of playing this piss poor game of searching for enemy soldiers disguised as Americans. This is the sixth time we have been on this ghost hunt and found nothing."

"I'm as tired as you," answered Rube.

"How many times have we stopped and delayed American troops to ask stupid questions?" blurted out Okie.

"Get ready, men, with your questions. The entire mess hall staff is heading toward us," announced Rube.

"We know all those suckers. Why go through the charade again?" questioned Okie.

"I agree," said Rube. "Why not have some fun with them."

"How would we do that?" asked Okie.

"Why don't we pull the Abbott and Costello routine of 'Who's on First' on them?" suggested Rube.

"They wouldn't fall for it," answered Okie.

"No one said these boys are Rhodes scholars," Rube said jokingly.

"Howdy, Boys! Ready for today's test?" asked Okie.

"Let's get this shit over with," answered one of the mess hall crew. "You see us every day. Why in the fuck are we still playing this bullshit game?"

"I fully understand, but don't blame me. I'm just following these ass-hole orders. If you have a beef, tell it to whoever is responsible for continuing this policy."

As Okie and the mess hall guy bantered over the time wasted by asking questions that everyone had answered many times, six heavily armed tanks pulled up to the checkpoint with a dozen soldiers riding atop each vehicle.

"Here we go again, slowing down the movement of troops, all because some idiot wants us to have a question-answer session," claimed the mess hall guy.

Rube started, "I hear you loud and clear, so I will make this as easy as possible. After I give you the name of the infield players on a team, all you have to do is repeat it back to me. I must warn you; these players have rather unusual names." Rube cleared his throat to get ready for his delivery. "Okay, Who's on first, What's on second, and I Don't Know is on third."

"Alright, give us the names," answered one of the cooks.

"We just did," said Rube. "Who's on first."

"Who's on first?" answered the cook.

"Correct. Now who's on second?"

"I don't know."

"No, I Don't Know is on third."

"Who?"

"No, Who's on first."

"What the hell are you talking about?"

"That's it. What's on second."

"I'm not talking about What. Who's on first?"

"Right again."

With laughter roaring from the guys on the tanks and Rube finally breaking down laughing, a lieutenant had to explain the play on words to the mess hall crew. After hearing the explanations, the head cook proudly announced, "May the bird of paradise continue to piss in all of your meals and don't expect me to remove the yellow yoke from your eggs." For that one moment, loud laughter drowned out the sounds of war.

PART III: THE DARK SIDE OF THE HOLIDAYS

With The Thrill now in a hospital in Le Mans, the three original crew members received a new Jeep and welcomed a new MP. Lloyd Bear could trace his heritage back to the Navajo Indian tribe, but almost from the start he showed contempt for the men in his Jeep. Even though he didn't talk much it was clear Bear would rather not work with White folks. Rube tried to explain that the generations of people who treated Indians badly, had passed away, and those Americans born after the Indian wars, or recent arrivals, shouldn't be blamed for the treatment of the native Americans. But Bear didn't care; he wanted only a professional relationship with his new partners.

As the search for the invisible enemy continued, despite very little results, the Pony Express crew again became part of "Operation Look Out." During a time out in their search for the elusive invaders, the Pony Express crew attempted to break the icy relationship with its new member by bestowing a nickname upon him. A couple of the guys thought they would call him Geronimo or maybe Sitting Bull because of his toughness. But Okie came up with the winner, "Why don't we give him a name opposite the character he claims to be? How about Teddy Bear?" Of course, when Bear heard his nickname, he hated it. The proud Navajo clarified he didn't want to be named after a warm and fuzzy stuffed animal. Chip gave him the history of how the stuffed animal, loved by kids worldwide, came about.

"Have you ever heard of Teddy Roosevelt?" asked Chip.

"Wasn't he president a while back?" answered Bear.

"Correct."

"You didn't think I knew that!" Bear responded with a little smile.

"Well, Teddy loved to spend time in the wilderness."

"That's why I remembered him."

"He liked to fish, hunt, and run in the woods around the Au Sable River in upstate New York, where he had a cabin."

"Too much information!"

"Anyway, when a president goes somewhere, he is followed by the press. On this occasion, Roosevelt and a few of his friends had gone hunting, and they discovered the hiding place of a bear. After quickly checking the cave, they found some cubs but not the mother. Someone from the entourage said, 'Are you going to kill them?' 'No,' said the president as he picked up one of the cubs."

Bear interrupted, "Sounds like something a White man would do."

Chip continued, "Now, back at the turn of the century, newspapers hadn't developed the technique of putting photographs into the daily edition. So, a cartoonist drew a picture of the event for a newspaper that showed a smiling Teddy holding up a cute cub. Someone from Texas saw the drawing and created a stuffed animal that he named after the president. That's how the name, Teddy Bear, came into existence."

"I didn't know that, but I know Roosevelt signed some bills that preserved wildlife areas around the country. But please don't call me Teddy Bear." That's where the conversation ended.

After a long day of searching for the unseen enemy and with darkness approaching, a radio announcement ordered the Pony Express crew back to base. Bear, behind the wheel, turned the Jeep around and headed for the camp. But in doing so, he almost crashed into two other Jeeps moving in the same direction. One of the occupants of the other Jeep screamed, "Watch where you're driving, you dumb asshole." How the soldiers used the word "dumb" reminded Rube of the German word *dummkopf*, which also meant stupid or dumb. For some reason, the word sounded the same to him.

Then Bear started an argument with that driver when he said, "Why weren't your lights on?"

"Why in the fuck would we be driving with our lights on if Nazis are in the area?" came an answer from one of the men from the two Jeeps.

Trying to ignore the remarks, Bear asked, "Are any of your men injured?"

"No, how about your team?"

"I was injured at Wounded Knee."

"We had a couple of our guys hit there."

"Where did they send you to recover?"

"... Paris."

"Me too.'"

"I'll be damned."

"Did you see General de Gaulle there?" asked Bear.

"Absolutely."

With that comment and realizing these were not American soldiers, Okie pulled out his Thompson machine gun and demanded all nine men get out of both Jeeps. As the soldiers departed their Jeeps, one fired at the headlights of Bear's vehicle, and he missed, but Okie didn't when he returned fire. One soldier fell to the ground, wounded.

"You must be the Germans we are looking for!" screamed Bear.

"You didn't have to shoot him," a voice cried out in the Jeep carrying the suspect German paratroopers.

"No more talking," said Chip. "Drop your weapons, or we will open fire in three seconds."

The Pony Express heard the weapons drop to the ground despite the darkness. Bear collected them and frisked each man for hidden weapons. Rube, while the nine soldiers lay stretched out on the ground, took his medical bag over to the wounded soldier. His wound wasn't life-threatening, but he lost much blood. Rube began working on the injury. "The bullet hit me in the upper part of my leg," the soldier replied in English.

The former medic made it easy for the Germans to understand when he said, "If you want me to save your life, identify the SS leader of your squad."

The wounded German said, "I can't."

"Then you will just bleed out."

With Rube preparing to leave, the kid, who looked about sixteen, said, "If you stop the bleeding, I will tell you." Still unsure, Rube fixed a tourniquet.

The young soldier whispered in Rube's ear, "The man second from the end of the line on the left."

After placing the wounded man in the Jeep, Rube told his three companions about the SS officer. Not wanting to reveal what the kid revealed, the MPs went down the line and asked questions to each prisoner, and no one answered. They made sure the SS officer was the last one to be questioned. Goldy and Bear took him to a deserted part of the woods. When he refused to talk, Rube managed to ask, in broken German, if he knew when and where the next parachute drop would occur. After repeating this question in English, and still no answer, Rube became frustrated.

"Do you know if he understands English?" asked Bear.

"I think so. That's what the Intel people keep telling us," responded Rube.

Speaking to Bear, Rube said, "It seems we have a proud German officer here. He would rather die than give out information. If the situation was reversed and I stood in his boots, I would do the same. We admire the officer's fortitude, so I will grant his wish. Bear, go get Okie and be sure he has his weapon with him."

When the Oklahoma kid appeared, Rube said, "We will execute this officer. I've given him a chance to save his life, but I'm sure he would rather die. So, both of you will be on the firing squad. I'll say, ready, aim and then you will fire on my command. Got it?"

Rube then turned to the German and spoke, "In these last few minutes of your life, let me tell you what will happen after we kill you. Do you see the MP whose helmet has a feather painted on it? He is a Navajo Indian. After battles, he goes around collecting soldiers' scalps. Once you're dead, he will go over to your body and cut off your scalp. Bear, why don't you show the officer your Bowie knife!" Bear showed off his golden tooth while placing the weapon in front of the officer's face with a smile. "Last time I went into Bear's tent, I saw two spears with twenty scalps."

"You're wrong," said Bear as he danced in a circle chanting. "This one will make twenty-five."

"After he's taken your scalp, we will leave your body here. I'm sure the insects and animals will have a great feast because of your unwillingness to answer my questions. So, gentlemen, check your weapons."

Rube moved away from the prisoner and began the count. "Ready, aim …." Before he could say "fire," he heard the officer mumble something. "What did you say?" questioned Rube.

"M … M … Mal … Malmedy," replied the SS officer.

"Have you ever heard of the place?" asked Okie.

"Hell yes," answered Goldy. "It's somewhere north of Bastogne, and I'm sure that's where the Germans executed eighty-four American Prisoners of War."

Okie asked the officer, "What is so important about that place?"

In broken English, he mumbled, "Paratroopers come."

As the three MPs and the German officer returned to the Jeep, another two Jeeps pulled off the road in front of the MPs. "Need some help?" one of the MPs shouted.

Unsure if this group might be part of the German infiltrators, with weapons drawn, Rube asked if they could tell him the name of the league in which the Chicago Cubs played baseball.

They answered, "National League."

The correct response allowed the crew to lower their weapons, and Rube remarked, "Yes, we can use some help."

After turning over the prisoners to Lieutenant Walt Rogers and his men, Rube learned about a nearby camp where a radio communication network was established and could reach Luxembourg. With the limited communication available in the Jeep, the information they learned from the German officer might never reach the proper authorities before an attack was underway.

After Bear received directions from Officer Rogers, he stepped on the gas pedal and accelerated the Jeep toward the camp. While driving, he spoke to Rube and admitted, "I like your style. Despite all the bullshit you fed that officer about me, you play the game rough."

"Glad to have you on my side."

"One other comment, would you have ordered us to fire if he didn't talk?"

"Hell, yes!"

Bear gave Rube the thumbs-up sign.

Twenty

All four men greeted Captain Holtz's voice with great relief. He had given the Pony Express crew the way to reach him if they needed immediate help.

"So, what's this intel you have for me?" asked Holtz.

Rube reported, "We think the Germans are planning another parachute jump in Malmedy."

"Where did you get this information?"

"From a German SS officer."

"Interesting, but it doesn't make sense."

"Why?"

"Well, you know what happened at Malmedy with our POWs?"

"Horrible, just horrible."

"So, if they already controlled the area around Malmedy, why would they need a parachute jump when they could just drive into the village?"

"That is an interesting point."

"I'll still pass along the information you obtained from the SS officer to the Intel section, located around the corner from my office," the captain pledged.

After talking with the captain, the team contacted headquarters in Le Mans and related for the first time all the events that transpired since their last communication. They were told to stand by, and they would obtain their new orders within a day or so.

About 1700 the next day, a messenger came to Rube's tent.

"Is there a Rube Goldfarb here?"

"Yes," the MP answered while sipping a beer with his crew at the

Army facility.

"Got a message and a letter for him and a Pony Express, whatever that might be," called out the message carrier.

"I'll take it," announced Goldy. "It's from Captain Holtz." The MP read the message as the three other men listened. "Just received a report from the Intel team on your message about Malmedy. Sorry to say your message was incorrect. The battle you talked about took place ten days prior. A few brave men, all under the age of twenty-one, were able to blunt the Germans from capturing the village and its strategic bridge. However, unaware that the Germans no longer occupied the village, U.S. planes mistakenly bombed the site and tragically killed more men than when the SS executed our POWs."

"Oh, my God," screamed Goldy.

"That SS officer conned us," said Okie.

"Son of a bitch," Chip could only muster.

"I'm sick, totally sick over this," a depressed Goldy mumbled.

The Bear only said, "That's how I always feel when American Indians get screwed."

Rube hated himself for not killing the SS officer. By evening, he was much calmer and became philosophical about "trust." He realized how critical trust becomes when dealing with his buddies on the battlefield, in playing with his teammates in a sporting event, and between a husband and wife, but the only trust with the enemy comes from verification.

The next day, Rube awoke, hearing the voice of a GI asking for volunteers for a mission. Upon hearing the word "volunteer," almost all GIs have one reaction — head for the exit. Rube couldn't get dressed fast enough. He zipped up his pants, buckled his belt, put on a pair of dry socks, flung a shirt over his shoulder, and headed out of the tent. Rube recalled that it had a satisfactory ending only once when he volunteered. Back in basic training, after volunteering, he was sent to the camp's bakery and was able to munch on cookies and cake.

Almost out of the tent, Rube heard the last remaining GI ask, "What's this all about?"

Rather apologetically, the soldier responded, "We are searching for volunteers to help transfer wounded GIs from the battle of Malmedy to another hospital location."

Rube stopped and said, "I might be able to do that."

The elated soldier stopped momentarily and asked, "Do you have any medical experience?"

Rube smiled when he stated, "I used to be a medic."

"Follow me," answered the GI.

Riding in the front seat of an ambulance, Rube relished the chance to discover the details of what happened during the Battle of Malmedy. It was necessary to move the less injured soldiers and those who had recovered sufficiently to a hospital in Noville due to an influx of newly arrived casualties. Filled with guilt about his blunder in providing the wrong information about Malmedy, Goldy was eager to talk to anyone about the battle. When he arrived at the hospital, one soldier who had suffered wounds while defending the town offered to tell Rube his version of what happened on December 21.

Brad Bickford vividly described the scenes from the battle of Malmedy. He said, "If there was such a thing as the battle of the ages, this had to be it. We could only muster thirty-three soldiers, most under the age of twenty, to confront the Nazis, and some of those arrived on the day of the battle. The day started with reports that German troops had assaulted Baugray, two and one-half miles from Malmedy. Once we heard our artillery launching a massive rocket response against the enemy, we felt confident the Nazis would retreat, which would end the fighting. That's what happened, but that's how the Germans planned it. This attack was a diversion, and the real attack had yet to be launched at Malmedy. As the fog lifted early in the day, we observed about 150 men and five tanks headed directly toward the town.

"At first sight, those approaching were wearing American uniforms and were supported by tanks. One looked like an M10 Sherman tank, but we recognized the shape as much like a German Panzer. As it came close, we saw the tank had been painted olive drab, with a white star on the side. One of the tanks struck a mine and exploded. The Germans continued to advance and screamed at the young troopers, 'Don't shoot; we are Americans.' We might have been young, but we weren't stupid enough to fall for the costume show.

"I was stationed in a window on the second floor of a brick building that stood next to a bridge and overlooked a prairie-like valley that stretched about 1500 yards in width. As 150 German soldiers approached, we had plenty of targets on which we used our BARS and 30 caliber machine guns to create holes in the enemy line. We moved from window to window, firing our weapons. That made the Germans think we had many GIs inside, but we only had a handful of soldiers. We still inflicted heavy casualties on the enemy."

An astonished Rube stated, "It's unbelievable how these young men adjusted so quickly to a war zone combat situation, with so little experience. Sorry I interrupted. Brad, continue with your story."

"Our biggest concerns, however, were the four tanks leading the charge. One tank was disabled when a shell struck its tracks. Two tanks made it through our defense, allowing German troops to attack our positions. Gunfire and exploding grenades ripped apart the interior of the building. That's when I felt shrapnel ripping into my back. The four other GIs in the room with me continued to fire at the enemy from their position. But one by one, each soldier sustained a combat injury, and all five of us lay helpless on the floor, near the windows, upstairs in the building, guarding the bridge.

"We could hear the Germans below and prepared for our demise, but this tall, slim kid charged into our building and cleared the Germans out of the first floor with his machine gun. He then secured a Bazooka and took out a tank. With very little ammo remaining, the young kid learned that additional weapons and ammo remained in an armored vehicle behind the building. Dodging bullets, he returned to the half-track and secured an M1 Garand, which could fire grenades. Shortly after, he launched a series of grenades at the enemy tank and eventually caused the tank to erupt in flames as the engine blew up and the soldiers inside retreated from the death trap. The last tank was taken care of by another trooper who attached a grenade to the rear of the tank and disabled its engine.

"The Germans no longer wished to launch a counterattack when the shooting stopped. Those U.S. soldiers who survived the battle returned to the brick building next to the bridge and found the casualties of both sides scattered amongst the debris on the first floor."

"Do you remember that young kid's name?" Goldy asked.

The injured man said, "I think they called him Frank … he had two last names … Sherman-Currey, that's it. But I tell you, he deserves some medal for forcing the Germans out of Malmedy."

"How many Germans were lost?"

"I'm not sure. But I would guess we killed over one hundred."

"I still have difficulty seeing how you knocked out those German tanks."

"I think because the tanks were only yards away from us, and our Bazooka shells and grenades were fired from point-blank range, we couldn't miss."

"Did you find out how many men we lost during the battle?"

"No," replied the injured GI. "I was lying on a stretcher attached to a Jeep after being hit in the back with shrapnel from a grenade. But I think our guys were incensed by what happened two weeks earlier, and we fought like demons."

"I hope you don't have any more bad news."

"I'm afraid I do."

"Oh, no," Rube said nervously.

"The bridge we defended had been wired with explosives in case such an attack occurred."

"So, why wasn't the bridge blown?"

"Because no one expected the Nazis to attack the town, they disconnected the wire to the explosives."

"I can't believe it."

"Believe it."

"Did you hear about the accidental bombing?"

"Yes, I did."

"I'm afraid that village will live in infamy as one of the great tragedies of World War II," concluded Bickford.

After talking with the wounded soldier, Rube assisted with the transport of the recovering GIs to the other hospital location.

Back at their base, it almost felt fitting, the new year less than a month old, resembled the past year, with a winter and war that never seemed it would end. For Rube and his buddies, being huddled around a trash can filled with burning wood, became the norm as the winter weather dragged on and more and more men departed the field of combat with frost bite. The entire Pony Express crew could only hope for a different ending in 1945 and that they would still be alive. At least for now, Rube had a chance to read a letter he had received from his pen pal.

After finding a quiet spot, Rube opened Roberta's letter.

December 18, 1944

Dear Rube,

Two new things to report. I have a temporary job working in a District post office, sorting mail. It's just for the holidays, but I will make some money that I can spend to buy gifts. Also, I received my first War Rationing Book.

How are things going? I guess you are starting to feel the first effects of winter. Hope you are inside somewhere instead of in a foxhole. I had wished you would be home for the holidays, but it seems the Germans messed up those plans.

I went downtown to see the Christmas windows at the Woodward and Lothrop store. It wasn't as good as last year, but the display had many moveable parts surrounding a fast-moving train.

Have you taken any real train rides since visiting Paris? One time in my life, I would like to travel by train, the route my grandparents took when they fled Eastern Europe.

Do you miss being a medic? I've arranged to meet Sylvia for lunch next week. She seems very busy since working at the Navy Yard. I hope this letter is delivered before the holidays. Let's hope you will return home next year, and we can exchange gifts at a party. Stay Safe.

Your pen pal,
Roberta

Then Rube took time to write his girlfriend Sylvia, his parents, and Roberta.

January 20, 1945

Dear Sylvia,

More than once, I wasn't sure if I could write another letter to you. When you go through my experiences, you thank God you're still alive. My heart bleeds for those who didn't make it and those who are wounded. I'm still in an area being contested by both sides. I'm supposed to be sent to another location, but I haven't received orders yet.

The weather has turned cold. You can't imagine how difficult it is to dig a foxhole into the frozen ground of winter.

As much as the soldiers have endured, the civilians in this part of Europe live in unbearable conditions.

I guess D.C. has seen its first snowfall this year. I still remember the snow fight at Fort Stevens and sitting by the fire at your house, waiting for our clothes to dry.

Let's hope the coming year will see the end of this terrible war, and we can return home and live in peace.

Love always,
Rube

January 20, 1945

Dear Pop and Mary,

Sorry for the mess up dealing with my status. Believe me, the army screws up many things, but this time, they were doing their job but had the wrong information. At least no one got killed this time.

The weather over here is bitterly cold. Despite the conditions, the war continues. At times, it seems we are fighting the enemy and the weather simultaneously. Life is tough for the soldier but even more difficult for the civilians. We see them all the time, wandering the streets and roads with little more than the clothes on their back. Some towns I've seen are no longer standing; the only thing left is piles of rubble.

Hope everything is well. Did the cat have any more kittens?

I received another letter from Roberta. I truly appreciate the letters from Sam's family. I can't explain how much a simple letter helps improve our spirit and provides hope that we will return home one day.

Love,

Your son, Rube

January 20, 1945

Dear Roberta,

I wish I were home watching a war movie in a movie theater, and the trouble is I'm in that war movie. Honestly, for a while, I didn't think I would ever write another letter, and I think I have escaped more danger than in a Hollywood movie.

How are things going back home? I guess the weather is playing havoc with your social plans. My social events are usually spent in a foxhole with a guy, and it's very lonely until the German rockets attempt to join us.

Being an MP is far different than when I was a medic. I still treat some guys with minor injuries, but we are guarding something most of the time. Do you know what's the most sought-after item over here? Cigarettes. Well, maybe one other. You guessed it, booze. Both are very scarce and expensive.

Fighting the Germans and the weather isn't easy, so let's hope the war will be over by the spring.
Fondly,
Your pen pal, Rube

Twenty-One

THE SOUNDS OF WAR NEVER CEASED as armies battled against each other when the calendar turned to February. One day, while Rube's team was providing traffic control on roads leading to combat areas, they observed a squad of fast-moving planes flying directly toward them. Rube ordered Okie to check if the planes were friends or foe. Okie, using his binoculars, spotted the markings of a red tail on the back of the planes. A much more relaxed Rube stated, "These must be the new P-51 Mustang planes used by the Tuskegee airmen."

An inquisitive Chip remarked, "Never heard of them."

"Here's what I know. All the pilots in this unit are Colored and they have been providing cover for our bombers who have been striking deep inside Germany. I understand the P-51 can carry 1000 pounds of bombs and rockets and has two 50 caliber guns on its nose and four 30 caliber machine guns in its wings."

"Man, that's a lot of firepower. Before Chip finished his thought, the quiet of the day suddenly erupted into a violent cameo of sounds that vibrated for less than ten minutes. As silence retuned to the area where the P-51s attacked, only flames and smoke could be seen.

"That was impressive, but I'm not sure if the rest of you guys noticed something unusual about what took place during the attack," stated Okie.

"What was that?" queried Rube.

"I never saw any enemy anti-aircraft fire against the attacking planes."

Late in the afternoon all four MPs drove to where they had heard the explosions. As they approached in their Jeep, they could still smell the bombs' residue. Passing through the smoke clouds and avoiding bomb craters, the crew found themselves in a graveyard of tanks, trucks, and other machinery. Damaged and destroyed military equipment, still smoldering, covered the field.

What made this scene so strange was the lack of casualties. They discovered only a few bodies. When checking for remains inside the tanks, they found only empty chambers and shell casings. With all the damage to the military hardware, it didn't seem possible that there were so few deaths. Chip suggested that the enemy received a warning before being attacked by the P-51s. But that didn't jibe with all the firepower the Germans had. They could have easily challenged the raiding planes. "So, what happened?" questioned Bear. "Maybe the Germans quit and just abandoned everything on the field."

"No way," said Rube. As the crew continued to look around, they came upon large empty gas cans. "That's it!" proclaimed Rube. "They ran out of gasoline. With all those war vehicles just sitting here, our planes had a field day targeting an armada of defenseless weaponry. Maybe this is the first sign that the Germans are preparing to surrender."

"That would be great, but don't bet on it yet," Chip answered.

Upon returning to camp, the Pony Express crew received their new orders.

Three GIs lit cigarettes in the back of a cargo plane as they lifted off for a flight to an airfield near Le Mans, France. Rube never paid for cigarettes, but when he received free packs from the homeland from a campaign known as "Smokes for the Yanks," he lit up. Bear was the only one not smoking cigarettes, and he indulged himself by smoking some strange stuff he called "weed in a pipe." Whatever Bear was smoking seemed to change his personality from nasty to someone funny. While on the plane ride, Bear asked the three MPs if they ever listened to the Lone Ranger on the radio.

"Of course," came back the answer.

Bear asked, "Do you remember the episode when the Lone Ranger and Tonto, his Navajo companion, were being chased by the Indians?"

"Can't say I do," stated Okie.

Bear continued, "Both were cornered in a canyon with Indians all around them, and the Ranger said to Tonto, 'We are in big trouble.' Then Tonto replied, 'What do you mean, WE are in trouble, White man?" Bear laughed his head off, but none of the others even chuckled.

Okie countered, "May a coyote come into your dwelling and eat your headdress."

Bear didn't laugh and said, "Coyote no good, just like your jokes."

Laughter and hand slapping broke out among the men in the cavernous interior of the airplane, and Rube said, "Touché, my buddy, touché."

When the team finally arrived at the central office in Le Mans, they were greeted with the usual insults. "Well, well, look what the wind blew in," a joking lieutenant offered as Rube, Okie, Bear, and Chip entered the military police headquarters. "I hope you all had a wonderful vacation at the French Riviera. Are you ready to become soldiers again?" Although the sarcastic remarks of the officer were made in jest, the staff greeted the four men with great admiration. Over coffee and a welcome home cake, the story of the Pony Express crew circulated from office to office. Surviving the battles of Bastogne, Marvie and Sibret and discovering a German parachute squad became interesting fodder for officers and enlisted men.

"I hate to break up this love fest, but your presence is required in Colonel Woody Wilson's office at 0900," said one of the office staff.

"Glad to have you back. I hear you had a rough time getting here," summarized the colonel.

"For a while, it was touch and go," answered Rube.

"Our situation here is as difficult. We are short of everything, especially MPs. We have been given three major objectives, which I doubt we can complete. Our first objective is to provide security for our military convoys that use certain bridges, ports, and military sites. We have been given a new assignment to house thousands of German prisoners and, most recently, have been tasked with preventing black marketeers from stealing supplies and goods and reselling them for a profit. The other day, a convoy of trucks carrying everything from food to cigarettes was attacked. That's where we lost five MPs. Our trains have been derailed and robbed, and our ships barely place their cargo on the wharf before it begins to disappear.

"The big question, of course, is who's responsible for and behind these lawless acts. We believe unlawful citizens from local communities are one group, followed by organized crime gangs, some pro-Nazi squads, and I'm sorry to say, some of our own GIs. Since we have so many hot spots and only a limited number of MPs, I have no choice but to split up your team. I realize you fellas have developed an excellent comradeship with each other, and your accomplishments are outstanding, but I need your combat experience to help us to increase our success with these new undertakings. You will go to a different war zone to perform a special assignment. I truly appreciate your efforts during the German offensive, but we now have a lot of new challenges."

Before leaving the colonel's office, all four men received new assignments.

Establishing temporary POW camps went to Okie. The Bear was headed to a secret company to send messages in code around the globe. Chip became part of a military group that provided security for and maintained the critical transportation network of military sites. Rube's assignment had him providing security for trains between Brussels, Antwerp, and elsewhere. The colonel concluded, "Each of you will have the power to arrest and, in some cases, to use force if necessary. Good luck."

Before departing, the four men did one last thing together. Chip discovered the hospital where Will The Thrill had been sent to recover from his wounds, and with their newest member, the Pony Express team visited a ward where injured soldiers were in the last stage of recovery. For that reason, the tone of the men was upbeat. As Rube and his buddies came upon The Thrill's bed, a moment of fear came upon them as it was empty. Okie fearfully asked a GI lying next to the vacant bed, "What happened to the guy in this bed?"

"Oh, he's still in rehab and will likely return in ten minutes."

Greatly relieved, Chip asked, "How's our buddy doing?"

"He had a tough time for a while, but once he overcame the depression that comes with being injured, your buddy has improved to a point the docs are thinking about releasing him," replied the roommate.

Rube introduced himself, Chip, Bear, and Okie to the inquisitive GI named Fred Tompkins, who was twenty-four years old and lived in Buffalo, New York. Fred inquired, "So, did you and your buddies share in any war experiences with Will?"

"There weren't many days we didn't engage the enemy."

As Rube began to relate a few stories, Fred stopped him when he said, "You must be the boys from the Pony Express who he talks about all the time."

After the three MPs shared some of their accounts of war, Rube came up with the question that all returning GIs would be asked by families, friends, and acquaintances, "What did you do in the war?"

Fred responded, "I'll tell you, but I will never mention anything about the war to my family."

"Why is that?"

"I fired flamethrowers during the war. Every time I tell GIs what I did, I get that look. Rube, I see that look on your face already."

Rube was speechless at first but said, "Tough and dangerous job."

"Now, let me answer the question you're about to ask me — how did I feel about using that weapon? Different than you might think. The damn thing weighs seventy pounds. And when I fire it, a mixture of napalm, gasoline, and diesel fuel travels a hundred feet to its target. One of the two tanks I carried would be empty in only eight seconds. With this weapon, I took out cement bunkers, pillboxes, caves, and tunnels."

Rube inquired, "Did you ever fear a bullet striking one of those tanks would cause an explosion that would engulf you?"

"All the time."

"I hate to ask this question. Wasn't it difficult to see the results?"

"I rarely saw the results, but the screams stayed with me."

"Is that why you are in the hospital, because of psychological effects?" asked Chip.

"No, shrapnel from an exploding bomb got me."

"How were you able to manage the psychological impact on yourself?"

"I think the hatred I had for the enemy kept me going. The horrors my weapon unleashed on the Nazis seemed to balance out the pain, suffering, and death that innocent citizens suffered due to the war and Nazi atrocities."

"So, you didn't feel sorry about what you were doing?"

"Maybe if I was a replacement, I might have had a different feeling, but after seeing the horrors created by the German military, I viewed what I was doing as payback. Another thing, I saved a lot of GI's lives by taking out death traps. Yes, by me squeezing the trigger of the flame thrower, I caused horrible deaths for the enemy, but how many millions of deaths did they cause around the globe!"

"I don't believe we have seen the worst of what Hitler's regime has inflicted upon innocent people," said Rube.

"I think both of us are on the same page."

"One last question, what did you do before the war?"

"I just finished my first year as a fireman," answered Fred.

Mercifully, The Thrill arrived, and with great joy, the Pony Express crew would meet for the last time. After the warm hugs and handshakes, Rube introduced Bear to The Thrill.

One of the first things the wounded MP said to his former teammates was, "Who put those damn bugs on my body?" Rube quickly pointed to Chip. "Thanks," said The Thrill. "The doctors told me those bloodsuckers might have saved my life."

The Pony Express crew chatted briefly, wondering what had happened to their original Jeep. No one had an answer. For men who fought and almost died together, saying goodbye was difficult. A sullen Rube and his three companions departed the hospital, somewhat dejected but relieved to see their old buddy had almost completely recovered from his wound.

While leaving the hospital, Okie, Bear, and Chip spotted an American Red Cross Clubmobile. Half truck and half bus, the Clubmobile brought a touch of home to the soldiers at the front. From a large open window, Red Cross women volunteers, nicknamed Donut Dollies, provided coffee, cigarettes, chewing gum, newspapers, and donuts to long lines of GIs.

While his three buddies *noshed* on donuts and coffee, Rube meandered to where their replacement Jeep was parked. As he approached the vehicle, a new sound struck his eardrums — the siren of an arriving ambulance, followed by two crews of MPs who parked their Jeeps near his vehicle. Rube passively watched as medics brought in two wounded soldiers on stretchers. Rube's mind, much like a newspaper, conjured up a headline that read, "When will it end?"

One of the newly arrived MPs caught Rube's eye and Rube immediately went to talk to the man. "Aren't you Lieutenant Walt Rogers? Didn't we transfer nine German prisoners into your custody?"

The soldier stared for a second and replied, "Oh! I remember you, Rube. I don't recall your last name, but yes, we delivered the prisoners to Intel headquarters."

"Good, so when did the execution take place?"

"I hate to bust your bubble Rube, but since the German contingent had no plans to perform sabotage but only to surrender, they were placed in a POW camp."

"Wait, do I hear you right? Those lying bastards are still alive?"

"As far as I know, all are still breathing."

"I don't get it. We finally caught that elusive group of German paratroopers operating in Allied territory disguised as GIs, and they're still alive. What's going on?"

"Here's what I learned from the Intel staff. First, the Germans were not paratroopers. They were regular soldiers from Malmedy. They were part of about 150 men sent by the enemy to recapture the village. After a vicious fight during which many German soldiers were killed, a small group managed to flee the combat scene in two American Jeeps they came upon during the battle. According to the Intel people, these nine soldiers decided they had enough and planned to surrender. But it wasn't that easy. Because of what happened at Malmedy several weeks before, U.S. forces stopped taking enemy prisoners, especially if an SS officer were present. So, if they surrendered in German uniforms, they could be shot on the spot. To keep this from happening, they devised a plan where they asked their officers, who were unaware of their plan to surrender, to send them behind enemy lines where they could launch attacks against the American troops.

"With official approval, they drove through Nazi lines in German uniforms and switched into U.S. Army gear before entering Allied territory. They hoped to find a small group of Americans and surrender. Instead, they found a group of MPs. Then some ambered-skin soldier with a feather painted on his helmet started an argument, and the rest is history. I also was told that the captured Germans gave valuable secret information to our guys regarding the strength of enemy troops, mechanized vehicles, and territorial positions. In addition, the SS officer you almost killed had just started taking English lessons from the soldier your men shot."

"I'll be damned. I screwed up. When the SS guy said, 'Malmedy paratroopers come,' I misunderstood because of a communication problem. He was trying to tell me that he wanted to surrender."

The rest of Rube's team arrived just as Lieutenant Rogers concluded his story. For the first time, Rube realized that the Pony Express crew used the same tactic when fleeing enemy territory disguised as Germans. As if the air in a balloon had just been released, a deflated and dehydrated Rube crumbled on the side of the Jeep.

The lieutenant then said, "Chin up, old man. Thanks to you, my men are about to receive medals."

Before a staggered Rube could end the conversation, a smiling Bear appeared to relish the moment when he said, with joy, "You fucked up, Rube."

Magically, a bottle of liquid refreshment appeared, and the soldiers and the lieutenant took a swig. When Rube was offered a drink, he shook it off and said, "I'm driving."

Rube had never been so wrong in dealing with a military matter. At least no one was killed by his mistake. Rube didn't like being wrong, but his mind compensated for the error by focusing on the men of the Pony Express. Over the last four months, his team had engaged in numerous combat missions.

Because of his leadership, all survived. Instead of being remorseful about what happened with the German paratroopers, Rube focused with pride on his role in the successes of those who rode with him on the Pony Express Jeep.

There were still miles of roads to travel, but Rube felt buoyant that, with a little luck, his entire team would make it home safely. Mistakes happen. No one is perfect, even generals. Rube would have to chalk the events in the first days of 1945 to a learning experience he would never forget. As Rube drove, he wondered if the men in the Jeep appreciated that each was a valuable piece of the puzzle that linked them together in the war as a band of brothers. The MP could only hope that the world's population would celebrate a lasting peace sometime in the new year.

Before departing, as a final sign of friendship, Bear gave Rube his Bowie knife. At first, the former quarterback from Roosevelt High thought Bear wanted to partake in a blood-brother ceremony. Again, Rube was incorrect. Because of his new assignment, the Native American felt the knife might be more valuable to his companion than a guy who would become a code talker.

Twenty-Two

Alone, with his Pony Express buddies gone, Rube had the opportunity to read a letter from his brother, Sam.

January 12, 1945

Dear Rube,

Your last letter scared the hell out of us. I can't imagine how fragile life can be on the battlefield. Let me make this clear as a sound of a bell. It is impossible to compare anything at home to what you deal with each day. In war, there is only one option, kill or be killed.

Nonetheless, I'm afraid life at the home front has become more dangerous. I'm not talking about my part-time security position as an air raid warden. Yes, my heart is racing when the alarm sounds at two or three in the morning. I grab my helmet and gas mask and race into the darkness of the street. So far, I've experienced only the silence of the night but constantly listen for the sound of explosions. There have been none. But I don't know how I would react if a bomb exploded on Missouri Avenue, 16th Street, or on the mall near the White House.

Now as a young lawyer, I must react to the shattering of the scale of justice that is taking place in this country. You are fighting to end the threat of Nazism and other isms that challenge our freedom. Yet here in the states, we have seen many examples of true justice being forgotten or neglected. Why are Japanese

Americans being held in camps? How come our military units are still segregated? I'm not sure if you heard about a recent race riot in the city of Los Angeles. American sailors and citizens attacked Mexican Americans and other minorities because they wore a Zoot suit. Many were injured, but strangely 600 Latinos were arrested, and they were the ones being attacked. How many arrests have been made after a lynching? Why are American Indians sequestered on reservations, not to mention all the restrictions and forms of antisemitism against Jews. There is a pattern here that can't be denied. America is a great country but not for all.

This isn't what you're fighting for. As a lawyer, how can I say justice is done when violent incidents go unpunished, separate but not equal is the norm, and people are incarcerated for not breaking the law, like in the case of the Zoot Suit riots.

I can only hope one day, when you come home, all Americans, regardless of skin color or religion, will be guaranteed the same rights stated in the Constitution. Only then can we say true justice has been restored. Hopefully, we can drink, eat, or watch a football game together in the future without worrying about who can sit next to us and enjoy the freedoms every GI fought to preserve.

I'll end my letter with a statement I heard on the radio from a military officer. He said, "A good soldier puts one foot in front of the other and continues to do so until reaching his or her destination. Carry on!"

One more thing. Marie has moments where she stresses out about the war, but thanks to her girlfriends and her two sisters, Rose and Ann, she has been able to handle the ebb and flow of the news cycles. However, I wonder what the four-year-old kid thinks. He listens to the news with us, but I'm sure he doesn't understand much. I see him playing war with the neighborhood kids. I guess it's a game for them; they fall as if they were shot. Then a girl who plays nurse fixes them up, and they charge into the battle within

PART III: THE DARK SIDE OF THE HOLIDAYS

seconds. Such is life as a kid in the 1940s.
Your brother, Sam

After reading his brother's provocative letter, Rube attempted to gather his thoughts into a response that could adequately address Sam's concerns.

January 28, 1945

Dear Sammy,
I hear you loud and clear. Sometimes I wonder why such policies exist in our country, but right now, all those freedoms that are supposed to be shared by all Americans are being threatened by the Nazis' attempt to rule the world. We must first defeat this terrible blight against humankind before any changes occur in our country. I don't know how long that will take, but all signs indicate that despite heavy casualties, the Allies are making great progress against the enemy.
When ...

As Rube continued, the arrival of a new replacement interrupted his letter-writing. Standing in the doorway of Rube's quarters, a young soldier dressed in full MP gear appeared. "Joe Green reporting for duty," he stated. Rube introduced himself and learned about the replacement's background. The corporal hailed from New Hampshire and could trace his family heritage to the Green Mountain Boys during the American Revolution. He had less than thirty credits to complete his degree at Dartmouth College. His family was actively involved in state politics, and he had a girlfriend.

Upon speaking to him, Rube could tell he was as green as a Green Mountain boy. "So, why did you enlist when you were so close to graduation?"

"Well, if I should ever enter the political arena, this would look great on my resume."

"Sounds good, but I wouldn't guarantee you will be able to add your military service to your resume."

"Why not?"

"Maybe you have forgotten, but a war is going on, and you could be killed."

After hearing Rube's remarks and war stories, the replacement seemed to realize he was in a new ballpark, and a major adjustment was necessary if he hoped to return home to pursue a political career.

Like a good politician, Green changed the subject and asked, "So, Rube, what's your story besides what has taken place on the battlefield?"

"If I make it out of here alive, I must decide between college and opening my own business. As a medic, I would have chosen to remain in the medical field."

"Wait a minute. You were a medic?"

"Yes, but because of bureaucracy, I had to join an MP unit."

"Too bad."

"That's what I thought at first, but I must admit the move might have saved my life."

"Do you have a girlfriend back home?" inquired Green.

"Sort of."

"What does that mean?"

"Well, you never know what Jody is doing while you are overseas."

"Jody, oh … you mean another guy."

"You got it."

"Does your girlfriend send you love letters?"

"Not for a while."

"That sure doesn't sound good."

"Do you still write her?"

"I do."

"Why?"

"Excellent question. I hope we can renew our relationship if I make it home, but it also lets her know I'm still alive."

"Any other reason?"

"I think she provides the outlet to vent my frustration and fears. In some ways, letters to Sylvia have become my journal."

"What the hell! If it helps you mentally, continue writing."

"Thanks for the advice. You never know when dreams come true," responded Rube.

Part IV:

The Light at the End of the Tunnel

Twenty-Three

A few days later, Rube, now part of the 381st MPs, was introduced to his new commanding officer. "Do you know anything about trains?" inquired Major Alvin Hooper.

"Not much. I rode a few and had a model set when I was a kid, but that's it."

"What about truck convoys?"

"That I have a lot of experience with."

"Good to hear. We just had an entire truck convoy wiped out, and we lost men and equipment, which is now becoming the norm."

Rube asked, "Where did that take place?"

Using the map on the table, the major pointed out exactly where the attack occurred. Rube looked over the map and offered, "It looks exactly like what I experienced in the bocage. Most likely, it's an operation planned by German soldiers or sympathizers, and they seem to have selected the same type of terrain they used to ambush convoys in the bocage."

The major continued, "On each occasion, the enemy launched strikes precisely when the convoy trucks slowed down to make a turn in the road. Those planning the operation timed it perfectly. The convoy was cut in half, and without visual contact with the head of the column, the ambushers within minutes had completed their objective."

Rube commented, "These guys are really good."

"I'm hopeful your experience in the bocage will help us devise a better plan to end these attacks. Have you met Colonel Benjamin Kay yet?"

"No sir, I haven't."

"He has been working on a plan so that we could challenge the strategies used by the black marketeers. Hopefully, you can give him some suggestions to combat this threat."

The next morning Rube met Benjamin Kay. Not quite six feet, the colonel had a long history with the military. Now in his thirties and heavier than the 140 pounds he weighed when he entered the service, the colonel spent time in the Philippines and Wake Island. On December 4, 1941, he traveled by plane to Henderson Field in Hawaii. On the day the Japanese attacked Pearl Harbor, he was walking on a tennis court and preparing to play a match with a cute nurse. As Benjamin's racket struck the tennis ball, Japanese planes began flying above the court and dropped bombs on the ships stationed in the harbor. He and his date ran to his military car and watched clouds of smoke rise from the harbor. Kay said that he never felt so helpless. Each bomb blast caused him to cringe, and he swore that America would get revenge for the unprovoked attack.

Less than a year later, he became part of the initial force that landed in Casablanca, Morocco. His first battle experience came as part of Operation Torch with the attack on Oran. Less than two years later, he landed at Anzio in Italy before being sent to London to begin work on the Allied invasion of Europe. He landed on the Normandy shore, D-day plus nine and took part in the battle at Saint Lo, where he was injured. Debris broke his left arm from a collapsing church steeple. For almost two months, he worked in headquarters with his broken wing. After that, he participated in the tail-end of the campaign against the Germans at Brest. He was attached to an engineering company that helped blast holes in the walls that protected the enemy positions.

After giving a brief report about his war experiences, which included combat at the Battle of Brest and Marvie during the Battle of the Bulge, Rube wanted more information about those responsible for the supply raids. According to the colonel, various groups actively participated in the operation of the black marketeers. Before the meeting ended, Rube and the colonel kicked around some ideas to combat the illegal activities occurring at railroad depots and transportation routes throughout the Antwerp-Brussels corridor.

Rube's first action came when assigned as part of a rotation of MPs who patrolled rail-line yards and stations. Compared to what Rube had been doing as a medic, this job became routine and boring until one night when Rube and two other MPs uncovered a plot to break into an unattended boxcar. Because of the danger involved, the MPs carried their revolvers, shotguns, and semi-automatic rifles.

At about 0230, a Jeep with an MP signature painted on it and a small truck, pulled up to a boxcar. Watching from the cabin of a train engine, three MPs waited until the uninvited guests used C-4 explosives to enter the boxcar. The MPs moved toward the invaders as they were entering. Their advance came to a quick halt as the intruders noticed the MPs and opened fire. Lying on the ground, the trio returned fire, and two invaders hit the ground. The truck driver stepped on the gas pedal and drove directly at the MPs. A wave of bullets fired by the MPs smashed the front windows of the truck as the driver and the truck crashed into a parked train engine. A blast from Rube's shotgun was enough for those still in the boxcar to surrender.

Soon the rail yard shined brightly from the lights of MP vehicles that flocked to the site. Besides the three prisoners taken, the MPs found C-4 explosives and all types of photographic and radio communication equipment in the attackers' truck. Inside their Jeep, the MPs recovered several pairs of binoculars and a briefcase filled with maps and pictures. Thankfully no one was hurt except the black marketeers. Rube's role in this incident was noted in Colonel Kay's report.

During the winter months, the supply chain couldn't meet the Allied demands, with railroad cars and road convoys running on abbreviated schedules because of weather conditions or mechanical failures. But the greatest danger to supply routes came from black marketeers and rogue Axis units.

Twenty-Four

During the winter months, Colonel Kay met with officers and enlisted men to work on a plan to combat hostile forces' attempts to hamper the military pipeline. Rube had become a team member after being recommended by the colonel. They discussed many suggestions and ideas, and Rube offered a plan to survey and build a series of new roads.

Rube's idea became one of the five strategies to be tested. On the Ides of March, Rube and some MPs were joined by an engineering team that explored the area near the main road for transporting men and supplies. After surveilling the terrain, they determined that the ground they examined was hard enough for heavy trucks to transport goods. The "go ahead" was given to begin construction of the new roadways.

The first truck convoy crossed the new roadways a few weeks later. Rube was part of the convoy, which encountered no German opposition or attacks from the black marketeers. Every other day, convoys of trucks journeyed between the two cities. Slowly the backlog of cargo began to shrink, and shortages no longer plagued the troops.

But right on schedule, the gang of thieves readjusted their battle plans, and a convoy came under fire but managed to escape before being stopped.

Rube's name appeared on a list accompanying the next truck convoy. The acting sergeant and the rest of the team would present to Colonel Kay an updated version of a plan to counter any offensive moves made by the pro-Nazi alliances. From reports of the previous attacks, Colonel Kay's team recommended the establishment of five new routes for the convoys. They hoped that these additional transportation avenues would complicate the effort of the marauders in their attacks against the convoys. Moving the convoy about 200 yards west to one of the new trails lessened the possibility of encountering minefields. Another new strategy agreed upon was to install large pieces of metal, maybe from a wing of a plane, aboard the trucks, allowing the MPs better protection in their vehicles. As soon as the first sound of gunfire erupted, the canopies of the trucks would be removed, giving the MPs a clear shot at the aggressors as they attacked in open spaces. The committee also recommended that the convoy, when attacked, form a circle much like the days when wagon trains in the Old West were attacked by Indians. By implementing such a maneuver this would allow guards on the trucks a clear line of fire against any frontal assault by the enemy.

Colonel Kay liked what he heard but asked, "How can you be so sure the marketeers will strike this convoy?"

Rube answered, "There is no guarantee, but we must admit the attackers always seem to be one step ahead of the Allies, mainly because some civilian drivers provided information.

An officer solved that problem; "This time, we will only allow Americans in the driver's seats."

The colonel countered, saying, "Wouldn't that alert the enemy?"

"That's what we want, exactly," answered the officer. "Having only U.S. drivers might indicate there was something valuable in the trucks. Maybe we should allow the civilian drivers to see us loading all types of boxes on the trucks, and when we depart, make sure they only see a few MPs aboard the trucks. The rest of the MPs could join the convoy several miles down the road."

The colonel then remarked, "What are we waiting for? Put your plan into action."

At 0900 on March 20, a large convoy of trucks with ten drivers and ten MPs left the base at Antwerp. Five miles outside of the city, twenty-five MPs joined the convoy. A practice session had been held the day before to work on forming a circle quickly. All boxes were loaded aboard the trucks; some were empty, and others carried items such as K-rations, shovels, and even

C-4, a putty-like substance used for explosions.

Once on the way, the MPs prepared their weapons for combat and relaxed if they could. After a ninety-minute ride, the line of trucks reached the old trail and quickly moved toward the new route. The convoy moved farther west and began crossing the frozen field but met no resistance from the enemy. Nothing happened until they were almost across the field. Several trucks, Jeeps, and armed vehicles came into sight. For a moment it looked like two trains racing down the same track that most certainly would collide. In an instant, the canopies on the trucks vanished, and between the ribs of the truck, the GIs stood behind large pieces of metal with their offensive weapons.

Before the first shots, the convoy had formed a circle, and the enemy seemed unsure how to respond. From the ribs of the trucks, blasts of gunfire tore apart the formations of the attackers. The circle of trucks appeared to invite the marketeers to attack, but they were caught in a web of fire.

The MPs in the vehicle only had to face one assault, and the battle ended. Around the circled trucks, many hostile combatants lay prone with their blood soaking the ground. The escapees ran toward the old dirt road. A few crossed into minefields planted by the enemy, which caused the entire field to explode.

Communicating with his troops from his Jeep nearby, Colonel Kay ordered them to follow those who escaped. Closely followed by American troops, the defeated rogue soldiers raced for the safety of an old castle about a mile from where the convoy had come under attack.

Rube, like most of the men, had never seen a real castle. This castle had all the features that they had read about in books and seen in pictures. Although it was dry, a moat surrounded the castle, and the walls were thick and had a lookout tower from which to spot the enemy. Like most castles, a thick wooden gate had just been closed as fleeing mercenary soldiers entered for safety. At the castle the most challenging feat was crossing a treeless area of about seventy feet between the woods and the fortress. If this could be accomplished without being detected, the advancing soldiers could hide in the moat before striking. With only a small group of enemy guards at the castle, eliminating the entire marketeer operation seemed plausible.

Colonel Kay quickly reacted when he heard the attackers were cornered at the castle and ordered two tanks to assist his MPs. While waiting for the tanks to arrive, the MPs began planning the attack on the castle. Two hours later, the sounds of the tanks were heard as they crashed through the woods. Before the attack could be launched, an order from headquarters arrived. All troops were to stand down. No one could understand, but a dejected Colonel Kay notified the MPs that the castle had been classified as a historic building and couldn't be destroyed. "Bullshit" was heard over and over again among the men. Rube recalled this was the same crap that cost thousands of Allied troops to become casualties at the Monte Cassino battle in Italy. Rube explained, "Because it was a religious shrine, even though it was being used as a fortress by the enemy, the Allies were not allowed to bomb it, but they could die fighting for it. Finally, after many casualties, the politicians gave the okay to bomb the monastery. Still, our troops never captured it, but Allied troops eventually ended the siege."

Not willing to move his troops at night, Colonel Kay's men spent a cold evening looking at the castle, knowing it wouldn't take much to capture it. Sitting in the back of trucks with the motor running and the canopies restored, the men tried to stay warm and talk about how politics stopped them from a big victory over the black marketeers. Rube seemed to act as the moderator in the discussion the soldiers had.

One soldier said, "I always thought being a knight was glamorous." Another soldier mentioned that the only knight he knew was on the chessboard.

"My only experience seeing knights was in the movies," answered another GI.

An officer who sat among the group related that the most he knew about castles came from books written by Shakespeare, and he couldn't remember in what country the story of Macbeth took place. Rube noted, "Scotland."

"A good distance from here," remarked a sergeant. A couple of medics entered the conversation and recalled the witch's prediction about Macbeth when the forest moved toward the castle.

"I never understood what that meant," another soldier related. Rube said his English teacher pointed out that the trees were disguises used by the forces challenging Macbeth. A strange silence emerged in the truck. Rube didn't know who said it, but everyone in the truck had the same idea.

About five soldiers asked permission to talk to the colonel.

After listening to the GIs, the perplexed colonel said, "What's this about dressing up as trees?"

Corporal Louie Pittman told the colonel that the idea came from Macbeth.

"I recall the story, but a plan like that would never work today," commented Colonel Kay.

Albert Miles, a second lieutenant, agreed that the account of a battle in the middle-ages went completely off the grid, but he commented, "At two or three in the morning, a tired guard might not recognize the movement of trees near the castle. If we could get a squad of men into the moat, they could plant bombs at the gate and within seconds, we could be inside the castle."

"There's no way we could carry bombs to the moat." said the colonel. Rube, who accompanied the group to the colonel's tent, said, "We have a crate of C-4 explosives in one of the trucks."

"I know this is crazy," said Miles, "but if it works, we could finish off this black-market group."

The colonel responded, "Let me get back to headquarters. Talk to you in a few."

A dozen men camouflaged with branches and twigs attached to their uniforms moved slowly across the empty area in front of the castle. At five in the morning, they were stationed against the castle wall. As the motors of the tanks barked at 0600 and the big vehicles moved away from the castle, C-4 explosives ripped the gate open, and the GIs streamed into the castle. The last shot was fired at 0627, and the castle no longer served as a military threat.

Colonel Kay expected to be on the hot seat for his decision to allow the troops to go after the black marketeers, but higher commanders gave their unconditional support when they learned that large quantities of weapons, valuable paintings, and a massive amount of U.S. property were discovered in the castle's dungeon.

Of course, a politician from the Belgian government was furious. The only real damage to the castle came when the gate collapsed. Outside of a few bullet holes, the castle remained intact. When the politician arrived, breathing fire, he smelled of corruption. Even when the colonel showed him the treasures found at the castle, he continued his outrage. While the colonel and government official toured the castle, a group of captured mercenaries walked past the two men, and an astonishing event occurred. One of the prisoners recognized the politician and shouted, "Help us." After hearing the prisoner's plea, the politician's tone quickly changed.

After ten laborious hours in the castle cellar identifying and tagging stolen merchandise and valuables, Rube had a few minutes to write Sylvia.

March 22, 1945

My dearest Sylvia,

Today I had the opportunity to tour a real castle. I was surprised at how small and cold it was inside the home built for kings and queens. The warmest spot in the castle was the room where the ruler sat on a throne. A series of steps, which now served as a resting place or a spot where GIs could sleep, led up to where a visitor or locals bowed before the ruler. For a moment, when I stood at the top of the steps, I felt like a king until I had to use the outhouse used by the peasants of the community. No doubt the watchtower, the solid walls, and the moat around the castle provided security for those inside but also made them captives to the inner sanctums of castle life that rarely expanded beyond the drawbridge.

There were ...

Before Rube could complete his letter, Private Bennett Mulligan sat beside him. Immediately, Rube recognized the soldier was dealing with some distress.

"Anything wrong?" asked Rube.

"I'm about to write a letter to my folks and girlfriend and tell them I just killed someone," answered Bennett.

"If you do that, I'm afraid you will always regret it," answered Rube.

"I don't understand!"

"By doing so, you place civilians in your boots. They don't understand what we face each day. To them, the life and death of a soldier is a number in a newspaper, telegram, or letter. They don't see the real person and can't have the same feeling about death that we endure on the battlefield."

"Have you ever killed anyone?"

Rube nodded yes, and said, "It isn't easy to deal with, but you're alive because of what you did. There were no other options."

"So, how do you cope with killing?"

"The best advice I can give you is to put it in your brain's lost and found section. Doing so allows you to lose the guilt, but occasionally, it finds you again. But your desire to survive will override any hesitation in pulling the trigger when involved in a life and death struggle."

"Thanks; I think I will take your advice."

It wasn't until Rube and his fellow soldiers returned to camp that an exhausted group of men could sleep for an extended period. Rube looked at his watch as he rose from his cot the following morning. He couldn't believe it indicated that, for the first time in almost six months, his body had the opportunity to sleep for ten straight hours. No bombing raid, no sergeant screaming at him to get out of bed, no one pleading for a medic. It was beautiful, but the question remained, how long would it last? After caring for personal needs, Rube wandered over to the mess hall area. If still in the states, people would say he was about to have brunch, a combination of breakfast and lunch.

Carrying his food to a table, he noticed one of the soldiers who had disguised himself as a tree at the castle. "Can I join your group?" Rube inquired.

"Sure, if you don't mind sitting next to a tree," said Roger Stillman. A couple of his buddies continued to rib him about his performance as a tree. One said he looked more like the scarecrow in *The Wizard of Oz*. Roger admitted that he was covered with so much wood he was afraid "Woody Woodpecker would come along and peck at my pecker." According to Stillman, one thing was sure, "Shakespeare never had a taste for clothes. That twig I was wearing was too tight in the crotch." As the men at the table broke out into laughter, Rube realized he hadn't had a good laugh for a long time. He would have to write his dad, the tailor, about the men in the wooden suits.

Thinking back to the shootout at the castle, Rube couldn't forget the sleazeball politician who had some association with the black marketeers. He also remembered his conversation with the private and how he urged him to forego the guilt of killing the enemy. Still, Rube questioned his own nonchalant feelings about killing. At the castle, he shot a man in the latrine without blinking. In another incident, he and another soldier fired a grenade from an M1 launcher into the watchtower at the castle, killing two marketeers. As Rube and the other soldier went up the steps to verify the results, droplets of blood dripped on his helmet and uniform. Sadly, the only thing that bothered the MP was he would have to change into a new uniform. Once again, Rube realized how the impact of war dominates the soul of every soldier and eventually overcomes all types of civilized behavior but becomes essential to keep the soldier alive and moving forward.

Twenty-Five

After the attack of the trees at the castle, the debriefing held in Colonel Kay's meeting room turned into a love fest. Everyone was happy, including lieutenants, captains, colonels, majors, and generals. The platitudes flowed unabated, but all the men present knew that such happiness in the army meant that something else would soon be added to their plates.

Colonel Kay played it cool when he asked, "I need the best of the best to be part of a massive assignment; would any of you wish to volunteer?"

In Rube's mind, a red flag appeared, and a printed line read, "Don't you dare." But instantly, like a line drive heading at your head in a baseball game, Rube's hand went up as did others. As the last hand from an enlisted man rose, the colonel said, "I knew I could count on you guys."

With that comment, the men in the room who had second thoughts about their quick decision could only listen to their next assignment.

"This assignment will be one to remember," said the colonel, "and if all goes well, there will be little danger from the enemy." Rube's gut reaction recalled that the Pony Express crew was told the same story when tasked with escorting the Ghost Army to Luxembourg.

"Here's what's going to happen," offered Colonel Kay. "You will take the train to Brussels, where you will meet another train with three heavily armed flatcars, two passenger cars, and about twenty-five flat cars which will carry a combination of tank bulldozers or armored bulldozers."

"May we ask where the trains will be going?" one of the soldiers questioned.

"The German border, where the Siegfried Line is located."

Another MP aimed a question at the colonel that wasn't as cordial. "Sir, you said we wouldn't have to worry about enemy action, yet you're sending us to the German border. Colonel, have you forgotten the war isn't over?"

"Question well taken. Do you know anything about the Siegfried Line?"

"Little."

"Let me paint you a picture. It is comprised of thousands of cement blocks, bunkers, tunnels, and tank traps stretching almost 390 miles. It was originally built opposite the French Maginot line but was extended further by Hitler. This massive defensive line was partially constructed by slave labor, mainly by kids between fourteen and sixteen. To be honest, these obstacles, and the persistence of the never-surrender Nazi troops, have for months delayed any movement of heavy firepower into Germany by the Allies. Beyond the difficulties I mentioned, another American problem that constantly had to be dealt with was the lack of fuel for our tanks. General Patton once said, 'My men can eat their belts, but my tanks gotta have gas.' As we speak, things have drastically changed, and we have overcome the logistic problems, and hundreds of tanks are sitting at the Siegfried Line, ready to move into Germany."

"Hold on, colonel," answered another GI. "Why are we escorting bulldozer tanks and armored bulldozers if our Sherman tanks failed to breach the line?"

"That's the type of questioning I expected when selecting this group for this assignment. Those bulldozers and tanks will provide the way to cross the Siegfried Line."

Rube offered, "Colonel, I'm confused. The bulldozers won't be able to remove the cement blocks. Am I correct?"

"You sure are. But they will be able to build a land bridge over the dragon teeth, the smaller cement obstacles, with the help of our engineering corps."

"I'm still puzzled," answered Rube. "Could you explain further?"

"Sure, they will dig out a massive amount of the earth near the Siegfried Line and place it on the top of the cement blocks and once completed, we will have a bridge into Germany."

"I have to see it, to believe it."

"You will, as your job will be to direct the bulldozers and tanks from point to point until a land bridge is constructed over a segment of the Siegfried Line. You will not be the only unit involved in this massive project. If you are successful, other units will continue the work, eventually allowing more land bridges to be built and finally allowing the Allies to penetrate deep into the enemy's bailiwick."

In less than a week, in total disbelief, the MPs watched American tank bulldozers and armored bulldozers build a bridge over the Siegfried Line from the earth's soil. "Unbelievable," remarked one of the MPs upon seeing an artificial miracle. All the MPs shared that same word, as no one suffered any serious injury, and no shots were fired at those who built the dirt trail over the barriers. With the completion of the first land bridge at the Siegfried Line, many others were built and used by the Allies to "leap-frog" into enemy territory. Despite Nazi resistance, Allied forces flooded the border into the German homeland.

Rube's MP unit, positioned only yards away from the German border, anxiously awaited the Army's next move. Would his company be sent back to Antwerp or across the border into Germany?

Not until the final land bridge was built, were the MPs given the mission of moving into Germany and escorting prisoners to a new location. Rube and his buddies would cherish seeing how this once-powerful army accepted defeat. Upon their arrival, the MPs' exhilaration instantly changed to disgust. Paraded before them were thousands of children in Nazi uniforms. David Osborne, one of the MPs, said to Rube, "It looks as if these kids range from age twelve to fifteen. Some aren't a decade out of kindergarten and now have experienced the horrors of war. I can't believe any government, even one like the Third Reich, would send its children off to war."

"I've seen some terrible things during this war, but this has to make the top ten list," answered the frustrated and angry MP. Rube could have never realized what might be at the top of that list.

Twenty-Six

As the winter months disappeared, Allied forces continued advancing over the Siegfried Line. Also, in 1945, U.S. forces stormed unabated toward the Rhine River. One by one, all the major bridges crossing the Rhine River were destroyed as the German high command attempted to delay the Allied offensive into Germany. Whether by luck or circumstance, the last passable bridge across the Rhine River, the Ludendorff Bridge, in Remagen, withstood an explosion. Although damaged, the bridge remained intact, which allowed thousands of tons of military hardware, vehicles of all types, and thousands of marching troops to cross into Germany before its frame collapsed, killing twenty-eight engineers and injuring sixty-three other GIs.

Despite the tragic ending, U.S. forces continued crossing the Rhine River after a series of pontoon bridges built by Lieutenant Colonel David Pergrin's engineers provided the highway into Germany. For the enemy, the last chapters in the rise and fall of an empire were about to take place. With caravans of U.S. troops in Germany, the Nazi forces, still positioned on the opposite side of the Rhine River, had to either surrender or fight to the end. Until the enemy made that choice, the melodrama of war would continue.

Back at the base, after a few days of R and R, Rube received a message to report to Colonel Kay's tent. Rube wasn't surprised as he expected to attend a debriefing about the events at the Siegfried Line, but the words in the last sentence, "at your convenience," baffled him.

Something was about to happen, and the sooner he found out, the better. An hour later, the colonel greeted Rube in front of his tent. Without a salute, the two men entered together. "Before we start, I have something for you."

Colonel Kay told Rube to place these items on his uniform. "You are no longer an acting sergeant, and from now on, when you are wearing these stripes, you will answer to sergeant." Rube gracefully accepted the sergeant stripes but knew something else was coming.

"Your team did some excellent work at the German border. Even I was surprised how quickly the land bridges allowed our tanks to maneuver over the cement obstacles," proclaimed the colonel.

Rube responded with this observation. "What surprised me was watching the 614th, an all-Colored unit, charge into Germany. It looks like the cavalry has finally arrived, and it's only a matter of time before the days of the Third Reich are over."

"I see what you're saying, but I don't want to get ahead of the game. There is plenty yet to do before that happens."

"Agreed," answered Rube. "What puzzles me is why the German soldier continues to fight when the war is lost."

"That's one of many unresolved issues the Allied high command has to consider in dealing with the unrelenting will of the enemy to continue fighting."

"I can't understand that the German soldiers refuse to quit despite being outnumbered, with limited supplies and ammunition, and not having enough gasoline to complete a major counteroffensive."

"Many theories were offered, but only one that seems to make any sense was told to me by a southern-born lieutenant named Simpson Delaney. He said, 'Back home, we have this old prophecy, and it goes something like this — the wild horse won't let you ride it until you show the horse you can.' The Germans will continue to fight for pride and glory and make sure their opponents pay a heavy price before giving up the fight. To the German soldier, it is not about losing; it's the way you fight."

"Do you feel the German allegiance to Hitler has much to do with this fanaticism?" asked Rube.

"Some, but the warrior mentality causes the enemy to fight when all is lost."

Rube responded, "I know this isn't a fair comparison, but my football coach used the same psychology when we were behind by three touchdowns to continue the fight until the last second."

Changing the subject, Colonel Kay stated, "Let's talk about the other reason why I asked you to come over. I'm sure you know Easter weekend is just less than a month away. Therefore, we will have a skeleton crew that weekend, but we will continue to ship supplies during this time. Since we want all our Christian soldiers who wish to attend church services to do so, I won't have the necessary human resources to guard our trains …. Aren't you Jewish?

"Yes, sir, I am."

"Is it possible for you to put together enough Jewish men to take over that duty just for that weekend?"

"If I had a list of the names of the soldiers, I certainly could accomplish that task."

The colonel handed a paper with twenty names on it to Rube. "I must add, this will not be a sightseeing tour. The train must travel through the Tunnel from Hell, which black marketeers used on three occasions to attack our supply trains. Granted, there hasn't been any such attack in over ten weeks because of the severe weather, but you never know when they will strike. I realize that most of your experience comes from convoy travel, but I think you can handle this assignment."

"I agree."

"Well, let's get to it. Any help or supplies you need, be sure to inform me."

"I will, sir."

Despite the efforts of the MPs and other military units to confront the theft of Allied material, the black market became an important economic source in Antwerp and most other cities throughout Europe. Even some U.S. military personnel found themselves caught in the web of the corrupt economic system. Most often, GIs, including MPs, sold their cartons of cigarettes which were given to them free, to supplement the meager amount of money they received each month. According to military records, the average soldier received between fifty and seventy-two dollars a month.

Another area of corruption in which some American soldiers dabbled happened to be with U.S. currency. Since the men overseas were paid in dollars, they had to convert their money into foreign currency. Unscrupulous financiers made extra money in the transfer of currency.

In addition, the scarcity of food and supplies caused costs to skyrocket, allowing some people who controlled the goods to resell them at a greater profit.

Although the MPs were unable to control the illegal sale of merchandise and goods, they continued their efforts to at least limit black marketeer activity.

Now in a position of authority, Rube realized the immense responsibility he faced in completing the Easter weekend mission. Most of all, the new sergeant needed time, energy, and supplies to execute this assignment, and by chance, if the train came under attack, he hoped luck was as on his side. To his credit, Rube understood his survival, along with that of the soldiers, depended on the training each MP received in the coming days. With mostly an inexperienced team, Rube used every resource he could find to prepare his men for what might lay ahead. This was serious business.

Twenty-Seven

Much like an assortment of different candies in a Russell Stover candy box, Rube's company represented an assortment of various Army job titles. Upon meeting with his team for the first time, Rube's opening remarks surprised his newly formed crew. "Warriors, welcome. I hope you are ready for a challenge. Thanks for volunteering to be part of the team assigned to confront the lawless gangs threatening our transportation network."

The word "warriors" brought smiles to the faces of sixteen Jewish soldiers and another ten volunteers who signed up for the mission. As Rube looked over his group of soldiers, he recognized a familiar face, Joe Green. For whatever reason, the soldier whose heritage linked him to Ethan Allen's Green Mountain Boys, upon seeing Rube's name as one of the leaders, decided to volunteer.

Rube continued, "Gentlemen, most of you don't think of yourselves as warriors. I can understand, as only three of you have any combat experience. But we wear the same uniform, and just because you share the job title of clerk, medical aide, engineer, lawyer, driver, chef, and information specialist doesn't mean you can't perform other duties. I don't care about your motive for volunteering for this assignment. Maybe you wanted twelve days away from your present specialty or to be part of another challenge. It doesn't matter. We are here to perform a task vital to the war effort. It's not only my job to keep the trains running over the Easter weekend but to have each of you return safely to your outfits. Since few of you have combat experience, we must alter our training to include self-defense, weapons use, and increasing your stamina, so that our unit can perform at a high level.

"Except for one day, we will train between 0900 and 1700. Be prepared for a lot of physical activity. Many of you wonder why we'll spend so much time training for something that lasts two days. I would agree if we didn't have to travel to a certain location. But we have a major danger zone to cross. Three trains have already been attacked, resulting in deaths, loss of property, and injury. You are correct if you heard there hadn't been an attack at the Tunnel from Hell for several months. But the weather is getting warmer, and they will strike again sooner or later. If we cooperate and work together, I promise we will be at our best when we finally board the train on Easter weekend."

Those who joined Rube's ragtag outfit never expected the training they would have to endure. So, they bitched about racing 200 yards while carrying a weapon. They cringed at the thought of jumping from a platform six feet above the ground. The soldiers complained about crawling under mess hall tables. Most of all, they hated spending hours at the firing range, shooting at targets that shot back at them with firecrackers. More than once, Rube heard comments like, "You give a man a little power, and he goes crazy." Rube quickly learned that being in a leadership role comes with a price. Being lonely is one thing but being hated takes a lot of discipline to understand.

Nonetheless, Rube's outfit continued to train, and four days before Easter, the entire unit visited the Tunnel from Hell. They walked the tunnel three times. Each GI darted in and out of the entrance to adjust to the darkness and light. All the soldiers' helmets could easily be recognized as they had glowing tape attached. None of the GIs realized Rube paid money out of his pocket to purchase the tape from a black marketeer.

The next day, Rube's soldiers played catch with a baseball, then with a lacrosse ball and finally with fake grenades. Those who had combat experience had the opportunity to work with M1 grenade launchers.

On March 28, the Jewish members of Rube's team celebrated the first night of the Passover holiday with a mini-*Seder*. Although they didn't have a Passover *Haggadah* to read about the exodus of the Jews from Egypt, the soldiers told the story they had heard so many times. They even chanted the four questions and discussed why this night differed from any they had observed. The one major part of the service the soldiers truly missed was a meal of turkey and brisket. Instead, the men munched on square pieces of *matzo* and slurped bland *matzo* ball soup around six picnic tables.

The guys appreciated the cook's efforts, but the *matzo* balls were so hard they could have been used when practicing throwing grenades. They also made Hillel sandwiches with *matzo* and horseradish. Thanks to the generosity of an unknown donor, the *Seder* ended when eight bottles of wine, not Manischewitz Concord grape, were offered to the men. Each soldier completed the ritual of having four cups of wine. With the wine in Elijah's cup gone, the men sang a song, called *Dayeinu*, paying tribute to God's generosity during the time of the exodus from Egypt. As the men departed, they were told not to mention anything about the wine, but their breath gave away a prominent part of the ceremony to celebrate the holiday of Passover. For Rube, it was a blessing to participate in a holiday that began thousands of years before and celebrate the freeing of the Jews from slavery.

What was so ironic to Rube was that America's system of slavery ended with President Lincoln's Emancipation Proclamation only eighty-two years earlier.

Two days before Easter, the twenty-seven-man team traveled to the armory and selected the weapons they would carry on the train. They then spent the afternoon calibrating and firing those weapons they hoped they would never have to use. On the last day, in a team meeting, everyone was given time to picture what might happen if an attack occurred. Rube's harping about quickly reacting seemed to pay off as soldiers related what they might do if attacked.

While soldiers prayed on Easter, Rube and his team boarded the train and shortly entered the outer rings of Dante's world. For a while, it looked like "Hell" was taking a nap. But as the train slowly approached the tunnel's exit, "Hell breathed fire."

Then, a no-longer ragtag outfit performed like a well-oiled machine. Upon hearing the first shots, U.S. soldiers jumped from boxcars to the ground, and with the glowing tape attached to their helmets and uniforms, the troops avoided shooting at each other. Knowing the terrain inside the tunnel, the newly formed company had no trouble finding the enemy. Others crawled under the train cars and pinpointed fire from the enemy's weapons. Within five minutes, the black marketeers began to retreat. As flashes of light and sounds of gunfire echoed through the tunnel chambers, the shadows of figures appeared on the tunnel walls, and much like in a movie, their images danced in slow motion around the railroad tracks.

Rube, with his shotgun, moved toward the exit with two other soldiers who carried grenade launchers. The sergeant heard a disturbance in the engineer's cab and pulled himself up, where he spotted a mercenary on top of the locomotive engineer. A struggle ensued, and with his shotgun, he struck the man with the butt of his rifle and forced him off the train. While Rube attended to the engineer, unexpected help came from the politician-to-be, Joe Green. Jumping into the cab, he covered Rube and the injured engineer. Seeing a machine gun nest at the mouth of the tunnel, Joe, with a flip of a grenade, took care of that armed weapon. Just then, the attacker Rube had kicked off the train, grabbed his weapon, and aimed it at Green. Joe was faster, and a blast from his rifle ended the threat. With the engineer on his feet, Rube gave him the order to move the train forward. As the train began to leave the tunnel's cover, a German grenade had been dropped at the feet of the three men in the cabin. A quick kick by Joe knocked it off the cabin floor, and it exploded harmlessly on the side of the train.

With the train moving, Rube jumped from the cabin and joined the two men carrying grenade launchers. Once outside the tunnel, they fired their weapons skyward at targets above it. As shots continued inside the tunnel, the last part of the train made its way through the exit. Those GIs trapped inside the tunnel managed to fight into a position where they could throw grenades at enemy positions blocking their path out of the tunnel.

As the battle continued, several GIs climbed aboard the top of train and aimed their rifles at targets overlooking the outside rim of the tunnel's exit, where enemy fighters prevented the egress of the remainder of Rube's volunteers. After an anguishing five minutes, where a dozen GIs under fire climbed a hill and silenced the enemy position, allowing almost all of Rube's team to flee the tunnel's darkness into sunlight. The opposition evaporated as the GIs aboard the train continued to pepper those above the tunnel with unrelenting fire. Suddenly it was over.

As the wounded escaped the tunnel with the help of other GIs, Rube expected the worst when he heard the casualty count. Four were wounded, one was missing, but no confirmed deaths yet. Rube led a few men back into the tunnel to search for the missing soldier. The floor of the tunnel was covered with enemy bodies. About a third of the way into the tunnel, they found the wounded GI. He had a knife stuck in his back but was still breathing. Rube noted that if the knife had hit his heart, he wouldn't be alive, but he determined the damage might be more to the lung area. After carrying the injured man to the train, the engineer nursed the locomotive back to life, and within twenty minutes, the train reached the safety of a small village where ambulances waited for the wounded. Messages were sent, and shortly a convoy of trucks arrived at the village, and civilians helped unload the train's contents.

Rube stood with a bloody uniform among his men. He couldn't pull the knife from the GI's back but did give him a shot of morphine to keep him from going into shock. Much like when he was a medic, Rube's uniform dictated that he played a key role in what had just happened. Sometime later, Rube addressed his men and congratulated them on their performance. He even speculated that many of his men would receive medals for their actions at the tunnel. One soldier Rube believed deserved commendations was Joe Green, whose actions in the tunnel were instrumental in escaping the black marketeers' trap.

On April 2, still at the village of Bruen, the remainder of Rube's warriors spent their time resting as an engineering company repaired damages around the tunnel, and another company removed the bodies of the enemy killed in the engagement. Rube had time to write letters home.

April 3, 1945

Dear Pop and Mary,

Just completed a major assignment. For the first time I was in a leadership role; my guys performed well.

The weather is starting to break here, and we can sometimes feel the sun's warmth. Can't wait until I feel the warmth of the sun in D.C. There are still some battles to win, but the Germans are in retreat and with Russian troops moving in on Hitler's army from the east, just maybe the war will be completed by the fall.

Maybe I'll be home in September for the Jewish New Year if all goes well. Did the family get together for Passover? A small group of Jewish GIs conducted a small Seder without a rabbi, and we even had wine, but I yearned for a taste of Mary's sponge cake the entire time. We did have some matzo and made bitter herb sandwiches.

Miss you and life back in D.C. dearly. Stay well.

Love,

Your son, Rube

April 3, 1945

Dear Sylvia,

I am surviving. Seen lots of action lately. Still in one piece, but the stress of war can sap your strength. But if my buddies can continue, so will I. Over here, a buddy means a lot more than back home. We must cover each other's backs all the time. We owe our life to the way our buddies perform. It's an unwritten oath that we don't leave our buddies behind. Moving along, what's happening in D.C.? I'm presently in Antwerp, Belgium. It's not Paris, but the girls seem more friendly, and the city has some charm. It's too bad; missiles sent by the Germans have destroyed parts of the city. I would compare the city to Baltimore, smaller but without the tumult we see in D.C.

Have a happy Passover. Say hello to your family for me.
Love,
Rube

April 3, 1945

Dear Roberta,

I'm still alive. Just finished a successful mission. Don't know where we will be sent next. But with the German attempt to recapture Antwerp a failure, and with their troops retreating from the areas they captured during the Battle of the Bulge, the outlook for them to continue the war becomes bleaker every day. I'm afraid they might fight to the last man. I hope I'm wrong.

Presently, I'm patrolling the streets of Antwerp and traveling aboard trains. Some of the scenes in Europe are beautiful. It's a shame that war has a way of destroying beauty. Yet, I believe what we are doing offers a chance for change, hopefully for the better.

We didn't have much time to celebrate Passover, but the guys had a small Seder. Hope your family had a wonderful time at the Seder. It was a good feeling to know that what we are doing overseas allowed Jews and Christians to celebrate religious holidays.

I truly appreciate your letters, and before long, I want to meet you instead of writing letters.

Much love,
Rube

Twenty-Eight

When Rube's tunnel fighters returned to base, they were given a heroes' welcome by many of the GIs from the various companies of the 381st. Rube couldn't believe how many soldiers now recognized him when he traveled around his home base. The former medic constantly heard congratulations aimed in his direction about the success at the tunnel. More than a couple of times when Rube visited the beer circuit that existed among the troops in the tent city, he was offered a drink or two. Thankfully, after a week, Rube's celebrity status faded as normalcy returned. Shortly, Rube would return to the mundane mission of providing security for trains traveling between Antwerp and Brussels, Belgium.

While on a security detail, riding a train somewhere between Belgium's two major cities, the MP heard his name called out as he sat behind a 50 caliber machine gun. Standing on the same flatbed car where Rube's guard post was located, a young soldier who Rube thought would be his replacement announced, "Joel Grove, a reporter for the *Stars and Stripes* newspaper."

Rube's first reaction shocked the reporter when he said, "I had nothing to do with that nude photo that appeared in your newspaper."

The newspaper reporter retorted, "I don't know what you're talking about. I'm here to interview you about the shootout in the Tunnel from Hell."

"Oh," said Rube, "I'll be glad to talk to you in ten minutes after I'm relieved of guard duty." For the next hour, Rube retold the reporter his story.

"Great story, and should make for an interesting article," stated the reporter.

Rube surprised the reporter when he asked, "Have you been involved in any noteworthy events lately?"

"Glad you asked. A few weeks ago, I had the opportunity to cover the meeting of the U.S. forces and the Russian troops on the Elbe River."

"It must have been thrilling to be part of that historical event."

"It was, and it wasn't for me. First, the trip took forever, even by train, and the Russian troops refused to speak to the reporters, while Russian officers glorified the feats of their soldiers."

"Did the U.S. and the Russian troops have time to mingle with each other?"

"Very little. Each group showed minimal comradeship. It seemed the Russian troops were told to subdue any form of celebration with the American side and acted aloof when talking with the American troops. So, I had very little to write about."

"Too bad."

"But I found a few U.S. soldiers who spoke Russian, and I managed a few nuggets. I learned that the Russians hated the Germans much more than the Americans."

"I can understand because of how the German troops invaded their country and systematically destroyed everything in their path. Certainly, that was a good enough reason for their hatred."

"I can't explain it, but I felt something else was behind the hatred. It was almost like the Russians wanted to replace the Nazis and control the land and countries the Nazis had just conquered."

"Sounds ominous. Only time will tell what role the Russians will play in Europe."

A week later, Rube read Grove's story about the tunnel in the *Stars and Stripes* newspaper. With great pride, he walked into Colonel Kay's office with the newspaper under his arm and with the other GIs, except the wounded, who had been with Rube in the Tunnel from Hell.

In the meeting with Rube's patchwork crew of band of brothers, Colonel Kay surprised all the soldiers when he said, "Sorry I haven't met with you sooner, but all I can say about the job you all performed deserves a big *mazel tov*; job well done." The colonel's remarks brought cheers and laughter from the entire team. "I have obtained your new orders. This affects all members of the 381st MPs. On April 6, you will have the opportunity to enjoy a seven-day pass. That means you must report back to camp by 2359 on the April 13. We don't care how you return. It could be by bus, train or Jeep or any other transportation. Just arrive back at camp before the calendar hits April 14. I don't want to send MPs looking for you. Understand?"

"Yes sir," the men shouted.

"Now, get out of here. Shower, shave, and pack. See you in seven days. Be safe and have fun."

For the members of the 381st MP company, a question remained. Should they visit Paris again or travel to some other location? For Rube, money would be the ultimate factor determining how he would spend his week away from military life.

Before making that decision, most Jewish soldiers attended a dinner given by French citizens on the evening of the last day of the Passover holiday. At the dinner, Rube happened to sit next to one of his crew who, disregarding his safety, had charged a boxcar filled with enemy soldiers and planted a satchel of explosives under it. Rolling beneath the boxcar, he dashed out the other side and was thrown forty feet by the explosion. Somehow, he only suffered scratches and bruises. "I wish I had your speed and courage," said Rube.

Jack Goldstein replied, "I wish I had your toughness and leadership abilities." The two spent most of the evening reviewing what happened several days before. After indulging in a delicious meal, both men agreed to travel to the local railroad station and check the arrival and departure of trains going to various locations.

At exactly 0630, an alarm clock awakened the two MPs from a restless sleep. Neither man knew where he would be when the evening arrived, and hopefully, there would be a passenger train that departed before noon to an interesting destination. Dressed in their MP uniforms and only carrying a small bag, with a change of clothes and personal items, the two GIs heard the horn of a Jeep and went outside to the transportation that would take them to the railroad station.

The station resembled a small-town U.S. railroad stop. In a large room, a massive clock was in the middle of the floor. On each side of the clock, benches filled with sleeping GIs awaited the arrival of trains. As Rube and Jack went over to view the arrival board, the newly appointed sergeant spotted Ron Maggio, his stalwart grenade launcher, at the recent battle at the tunnel. "Where are you headed, Ron?" asked Rube.

"A place called Brugge," replied Ron.

"What's there?"

"Something that used to be there."

"Come again?"

"There's a house of worship in Brugge called the Church of Our Lady, and it once was the location of the statue "Madonna and Child," sculpted by none other than Michelangelo."

"What happened to it?"

"The Nazis stole it."

"Bastards, but you don't expect to find it, do you?"

"Of course not, but maybe I would find some clue to help authorities recover it."

"So, you want to play detective for a few days."

"That's a good way to put it."

Jack, seeing both GIs talking, came over and entered the discussion.

"Find anything interesting, Jack?" asked Rube.

"Not really. Most trains leave around 11:00. What you got going on, Ron?"

"He's going to Brugge," answered Rube.

"Where's it located?" inquired Jack.

Ron responded, "It's a little over fifty miles from Antwerp, and the travel time by train should be less than two hours."

"Do you know anything about the town?"

"Well, it was built in the Middle Ages and still has cobbled streets, many restaurants and specialty stores. According to what I've read, it's very picturesque, and because the location is near the ocean, their main food source is fish."

"How much was your ticket?"

"I can't give you the exact amount in U.S. currency as we have to pay in Belgian money, but it's cheap by our standards."

"Great, do you know anything about the cost of housing?"

"All I know is if I can find a place to rent for a week, and if you wish to join me, we could split the cost among the three of us. How does that sound, guys?"

"Okay with me," replied Jack. "What about you, Rube?"

"I'm a little short on cash, but I have a carton of cigarettes. If I sell it, that should leave me with enough money. It might work."

Just then, an employee of the railroad station interrupted the threesome's conversation. "Are all of you riding the train to Brugge?" he asked.

"Actually, only one of us now," answered Rube.

"Well, if you decide to do so, we could use some security because we have had disturbances between civilians and former pro-Nazis. If you agree to serve in that role, all three of you could ride free, and I would refund the money for that one ticket."

It didn't take long for the GIs to accept the station man's offer, and two hours later, they arrived in Brugge.

Twenty-Nine

Fortunately, the threesome found an old, remodeled townhouse to rent for a week. The widow who owned the building, charged a little more than the MPs expected, but since it included a breakfast of eggs, bacon, Belgian waffles, fruits, and coffee, that was an offer they couldn't refuse.

The first two days, the GIs toured the city. They watched a cobbler make a pair of shoes, and Jack was fascinated with the art some locals painted. The MPs visited a museum that told the city's history and finished the first day by treating themselves to an excellent dinner.

On the second day, the guys piled into a horse-drawn carriage and traveled along the bumpy cobblestones through parts of the city. In the afternoon, they rented a small fishing craft, and the pilot found a spot where fishermen were having a lot of success. Each guy caught a fish and returned it to the widow, who made them a delicious meal.

On the third day, they visited the Church of Our Lady. Wearing their uniforms, the MPs immediately caught the eye of the brothers working at the building. A short time later, a deacon came out and welcomed them. "Is there anything I could help you with?"

"Yes, there is," answered Ron.

"Would any of you like to have a priest conduct a confession?" inquired the deacon.

"Maybe later, but we want to talk to a priest."

"What should I say is the topic?"

"The Madonna statue."

"Please wait. Father Marc will see you."

A few minutes later, Ron said, "Father, these are my buddies from my MP company, Rube and Jack. We would like in some way to help find the statue."

"We truly appreciate your willingness to help, but for months the church has cooperated with the authorities to no avail."

"I make no promise that we will find the holy statue, but maybe we could discover a clue that might help those trying to locate the Madonna."

"I can't stop you, but you're wasting your time."

"Our time is limited to three days."

"By all means, give it a go. If you find anything, and I mean anything, please notify us."

"Will do."

"Where do you want to start?"

"Right here at the church. The night it was stolen, was anyone at the church?"

"Yes, and they have been interviewed on four different occasions."

"Was anyone hurt?"

"No, all the religious leaders were forced into a room. The door was locked, and then once we were freed, the statue was gone."

"Did you recognize anyone who had locked you up?"

"No, but one was an officer who wore a white uniform and had the letters SS on his shirt collar."

"Is there anyone in the church who wasn't interviewed?"

"Only the altar boy."

"Is he around?"

"He only comes in on Thursday to help prepare for services the following Sunday."

"Okay, if we meet with him?"

"It's up to him."

After meeting with the church official, the three MPs began canvassing the homes on the same street as the church. With the help of Deacon Philippe, who spoke Flemish, they asked over fifty people, "Did anyone see what happened on the day the statue disappeared?"

The answer was "No," until a man said, "I saw the whole thing."

Standing in the doorway of his small apartment, a man over fifty, wearing a pink and brown pair of pajamas and a shabby-looking robe, startled those in the hall with his answer. Even before being invited into the apartment, all four men entered the man's living quarters. Although small, the place was neatly kept, with only a newspaper out of place. "Who might we be speaking to," asked Rube.

"Luc Peeters."

The deacon spoke to the older gentleman in Flemish and asked if the man spoke any English. He replied, "Some." The deacon then had the task of translating Flemish and English into coherent statements that all four men could understand.

Jack wanted to know his occupation, and it took several minutes before the deacon could complete his answer. According to Luc, he held three different jobs. One job was being a groundskeeper for three different soccer fields, and he worked as the "super" for this apartment complex. His other job consisted of delivering ice. That's why he was still in his pajamas at three in the afternoon. Luc reported that he sleeps from 7 a.m. until 3 p.m. because his job requires him to deliver ice all night.

After listening to Luc's work resume, Rube had questions about his character but thought his eyewitness account might be their best lead. Ron went right to the central issue, that is, where he was the night of the theft. While sitting on an old but comfortable couch, the ice man, with the deacon's help, created a picture of the events of that night while the four men intently listened as they sat on the only chairs left in the apartment. "I just finished delivering my first batch of ice. About 1:30 in the morning, I was in my truck, about to turn from an alley into the street where the church could be seen." Luc continued, "I hope you had a chance to go inside. It's truly beautiful, and once lit up outside, it is undoubtedly an elaborate site." Then, he returned to his story.

"Before I stepped on the gas pedal, I saw many fast-moving lights heading in my direction. So, I waited. First came a German automobile, then two troop carriers. That was followed by a flatbed truck that carried a pitchfork-type machine. At the convoy's end came a big truck that must have served as an ambulance as it had a Red Cross painted on it. I watched as they passed and was shocked when the convoy stopped before the church. I would say twenty or more men came out of the trucks, carrying different items. I could see a few men had heavy ropes over their shoulders. I hardly heard any noise from the men, but the sound of the motor from the forklift broke the silence. I prayed they weren't going to burn the house of worship. I waited about twenty minutes and listened for gunshots or anything loud, but everything remained quiet. I then left to complete my second run. I returned about forty-five minutes later, and the convoy of vehicles still stood in front of the church. I left again for my final run, and when I was finished, my curiosity got the best of me, and I returned to my spot near the church. This time a lot of men were gathering around something big. It was covered up, and the men seemed to have difficulty moving the object. I saw the forklift push toward it, but the ambulance blocked my view. It took almost fifteen minutes to put what we now know was the sculpture, wrapped with either mattresses or pads around it, into the ambulance. By 4:45 a.m., the convoy departed. I watched them drive northwest to the road that leads to a major artery that extends to the Belgian border. Obviously, they wanted to leave the country as quickly as possible. I can only guess what country they wanted to go to, but because of their white uniforms, it must be to a nation with a cold climate.

"I drove to the church and heard screams and shouts, and I wondered if the priest had been shot. Fearing for my own life, I departed but returned in the morning to discover what happened just a few hours before. Shocking ... I still don't know how they got that statue over seven feet tall and made of marble off its base and moved it out of the church to the ambulance. This whole operation was well planned out. So many things had to go right. They must have scoped out the church to be able to pull this off."

"Are you saying this could have been an inside job?" asked Jack.

"Can't say, but they were aware of the church layout. Whether they had the architectural plan or their version of the inside of the church, I don't know, but this heist needed a lot of planning."

"Any idea who might be responsible?" asked Rube.

"There's only one person you can blame, and he shares the responsibility for the millions of deaths in the last six years … Hitler."

"So, you're sure he had a hand in this?"

"Absolutely, he's been stealing priceless historical pieces for years. He probably thinks he will display them in a museum later or at his summer home in the Alps in Austria."

"I forgot about that. Anything else you can tell us?" asked Jack.

"I would concentrate on where he might store these stolen items."

"Good advice."

"Well, gentlemen, I would have loved to talk to you longer, but I must get dressed and prepare to work. My customers only care that the Ice Man cometh."

"I guess it's time for us to go, too," said Rube.

Once outside the building, the deacon seemed shattered by the thought of inside help. Jack said, "He never committed to that answer."

But the Ice Man had planted a seed in the deacon's mind, making him suspicious about why nothing was done for over three hours to alert the community. "At least someone could have pulled the ropes to the church bells, especially at that hour, and that would have certainly alerted the community that something was wrong," said Deacon Philippe.

"In times of severe crisis, sometimes people don't think rationally," commented Ron.

"I agree," stated Rube.

Jack asked Ron, "Have you seen the site where the Madonna was on display?"

"Yes," answered Ron.

"How could all these men take it down without making enough noise to alert the community?"

"Maybe they did hear it but were afraid to do anything about it."

"You could be right."

The four men returned to the site of the abduction. On each side of the space where the statue stood, were two other statues left untouched. Ron remarked, "Whoever took the Madonna knew something about art. This was the only creation by Michelangelo that departed Italy, and he created it and his famous sculpture of David during the same period between 1501 and 1504."

After an early breakfast on the fourth day, the three MPs interviewed the choir boy, Bernhard Quest, at the church. He told the men that from his hiding place in a vestibule in a church tower, it was impossible to understand what the men in the white uniforms were saying since he didn't understand German. But he did recognize one word, "Alps." He also remembered the route taken by the fleeing convoy. "The Nazis traveled in a northwest direction on their way out." Bernhard also noted that all the vehicles in the convoy had chains on their tires.

"We don't have much," claimed Jack.

But the deacon who attended the meeting stated, "We still have an avenue to travel."

"I don't get your point."

"We have pinpointed the route used to take the Madonna out of the country, which gives us a trail to follow."

"But I don't see any value in doing so, just because we know the exit trail doesn't give us any new leads."

"Correct, but the soldiers involved in the theft might leave a clue or two along the way."

"Please continue."

"We can assume wherever they are taking the statue, it will be far from Brugge. Who knows, arriving at the destination may take four or five days. The Germans didn't have enough food or drinks to last that long. We should travel their path for at least fifteen kilometers to see if they stopped."

"I doubt anyone would remember, with all the troop movement recently, seeing a group of soldiers stopped at a particular location almost nine months ago."

"I get your drift, but what if they broke up the place or stole items from that place? I'm sure those who survived would remember."

"I see what you mean. Maybe we should look for places that soldiers often visit on their way to different locations."

The rest of the day, the MPs and the deacon made many stops along the way to the Belgian border. Their efforts were rewarded at an outside farm market, a bar, and a gas station. The occupants and owners remembered having difficulties with a group of Nazis at each place. Each told stories of being forced to relinquish food, liquor, and gasoline at gunpoint. A few were even injured. They provided a few nuggets when asked if they could identify any significant features about the troopers. One recognized an insignia worn by one of the soldiers as being part of an infantry unit. Another questioned that soldiers had different patches on their uniforms, meaning not all were from the same unit. The gasoline station owner, who lost hundreds of dollars as he was forced to pump unpaid gallons of gas into the convoy's vehicles, noticed that each truck had extra cans of gasoline that he filled. He figured if the convoy used all the gasoline he had to give away, they could travel 800 kilometers. The victims provided little information about the ambulance, only saying the vehicle had a Red Cross on it, but they never saw any victims in it. However, one individual recalled how German soldiers put air into the tires.

An extremely tired group of GIs and an exhausted deacon called it a day and returned to Brugge before sunset.

Thirty

While eating breakfast the next day at the townhouse, the phone rang, and it was a call from the deacon. An excited deacon said to Rube, "Have you listened to the news on the radio today?"

"No, why?"

"There is a report, although unconfirmed, that at a place called Merkers-Kieselbach, a large amount of gold and valuable paintings stolen by the Nazis have been found in a salt mine.

"Really? Was the Madonna among the items recovered?"

"There is no confirmation about that, but this gives me hope that it might be found in some other hideaway."

"Great news. I'll tell the guys. Do you know how they found out about the cave?"

"The reporter said a couple of MPs had been driving a few women somewhere, and one showed them the mine."

"How about that!"

"Do you have plans for today?"

"Your phone call just changed everything. Are you aware of any caves or caverns around Brugge?"

"There are plenty of caves in Belgium but none near Brugge."

"Damn, I was hoping we could travel to Merkers or somewhere else that might be a hiding place for Nazis' stolen treasures. I wonder if there is a train to Merkers. I think we will check at the train station about such a trip. We will let you know what we find."

With the release of the news story, the deacon and his parishioners felt buoyant enough to predict that the missing statue, one day soon, would be returned to the church.

While inquiring about available train rides to Merkers, the three MPs found two other men interested in a train ride to Merkers. They were told none was available and that a six-hour car ride would be the best way to travel. Somewhat discouraged, the two men turned to the MPs and asked how they expected to make the trip. Ron remarked, "I think we are out of time. How about you?"

"At the moment, we are in limbo," said one of the men.

"Join the club."

"By the way, what organization do you fellows work with?"

"Doesn't the uniform tell the story?"

"No, do you work for the FBI or another government organization?"

"No, just the U.S. Army."

"Well, what organization do you represent?"

"We are part of a special government investigative team. We call ourselves, the Treasure Hunters who search for priceless stolen works of art and wealth that might be hidden in secret Nazi hideaways."

"Like the one in Merkers?"

"So, you are aware of that one?"

"We have spent time finding clues where the Madonna statue might be hidden."

"Have you any leads?"

"Yes, some."

After the men introduced themselves, they all decided to go to lunch. At a small bistro in the center of the medieval town, five men sat around a circular table with the same mission, finding the Madonna.

"Let's go around the table and see if we can piece together where the statue might be hidden," said Fred Baron, one of the two searching for the statue. His assistant, Ken Frankel, noted what each group had discovered.

Jack started first. "Without a doubt, the Madonna has been taken to some cold weather country. The uniforms of Germans and an eyewitness account provided the direction they used to transport the statue. Our sources also reported the trucks in the convoy all had chains on the tires, and the word "Alps" was used by the people who stole the Madonna. That seems to dictate its location. But where in the Alps, that's the big question."

Ron spoke next. "I guess it's located near Hitler's summer hideout in the Alps, certainly not in Berlin. His insanity might have reached the point where he thinks the woman in the statue is his mother, and since he considers himself a god, he is the child. I would draw a circle within a hundred-mile radius of his summer house. Somewhere in that area, I believe the Madonna will be found."

Rube spoke last. "I'm taking a little different approach. The Madonna and the recent discovery of paintings and gold make it clear it's Hitler's path to freedom. It's easy to say he loved art because he tried to enroll in an art school. But when his application was rejected, he hated those who felt he wasn't skilled enough to be at the school. One of those happened to be Jewish. I feel he arranged to steal art and then the Madonna, not for the love of the work, but to use as a hostage if his world collapsed. With the priceless art he has collected, he could pay off anyone who could safely move him to another part of the globe. I'm sure somewhere in Latin America, Africa, or because of his hate for Jews, he would be welcome even in an Arab country. I agree the Alps, as a prime area to search."

The Treasure Hunters said they were working on some leads which they hoped would bring the statue back to the Church of Our Lady.

After the group finished lunch, they prepared to leave the bistro but waited as a young couple entered the establishment. The five men shook hands and wished each other Godspeed and good hunting. On the sixth day, the three MPs shopped for gifts they would take home if they survived the war. Ron bought a watch for his girlfriend. Rube found a small model of a wooden Jeep he purchased for his nephew, and Jack fell in love with a puppet he had seen in a store window. When he went inside to purchase it, the store owner invited all the MPs to a puppet show that would start in twenty minutes. The tired GIs were delighted to stay. Just before the show started, the couple they had seen enter the bistro the day before, walked in with several other people and watched the puppet performance.

The next day the MPs had one last breakfast meal with the widow at the townhouse before leaving for the train station. After an hour's wait at the station, the three GIs boarded the train back to Le Mans.

Selecting one of the cabins found on European passenger trains, the GIs hoped to sleep most of the trip home. That never happened as Jack, coming back from the dining room car with three cups of coffee, entered the cabin with a bizarre statement, "I think we have a tail. Do you remember the couple who entered the bistro when we left and appeared at the puppet show? They're on the train."

"It could be a coincidence," said Ron.

"I don't believe in coincidences," answered Jack.

"Alright, no need to panic. Let's be on extra alert," Rube calmly stated. While two MPs tried to sleep, one would always remain vigilant. The train arrived on time at the Le Mans station. Since soldiers arrived at the station all day, a Jeep awaited the threesome. After storing their luggage in the Jeep and as the driver took off, Rube, out of the corner of his eye, saw the same couple jumping into a car and following the Jeep. "Our tail is moving behind us," Rube called out.

"Do you have any weapons on the Jeep?" Jack asked the driver.

"No, sir."

"Okay, step on the gas and call into headquarters that we are being followed." The chase was on, and both vehicles darted around other cars down the road toward the military base.

The radio cracked with a message saying, "Turn right at the next light. That will lead directly to the checkpoint." The driver stepped on the gas pedal as his vehicle headed straight toward the checkpoint. Following close behind came the thunderous sound of the speeding car. Within a minute, five vehicles merged at the American checkpoint, and the loud noise of metal and steel violently crashing into each other gave the impression of a demolition derby contest. The MPs managed to avoid major damage. Armed

MPs appeared with guns drawn and pointed them at the smoking car. The three members of the vehicle realized the hopelessness of trying to shoot their way out and, with hands held high, abandoned the car. What the MPs found in the car sent chills up the spines of the GIs. Two Thompson machine guns, several grenades and a Bazooka were in the backseat and the trunk.

After eight hours of interrogation, the captives confessed that they had been assigned to observe the three MPs asking questions about the whereabouts of the missing Madonna and Child statue. The captives also mentioned that as the MPs began to unravel where the Madonna was located, the pro-Nazi followers received new orders to eliminate those involved in the search for the missing statue. When asked if they knew the present location of the statue, they said, "It remains unknown to us." They also revealed that they came close to killing the threesome when the GIs traveled along the escape route, but heavy traffic prevented them from getting off a good shot. The two assailants and the driver then told how they followed their prey on the train and planned to eliminate them while traveling back to their base in a Jeep.

Later, the three MPs, somewhat shaken, reported to headquarters. A smart-ass corporal offered a greeting of contempt. "You guys sure know how to make an entrance. Even after getting a week of vacation time, you bring trouble to our door."

Rube said, "We never realized we were targets until we came to the train station."

"In your case, Rube Goldfarb, trouble seems to find you," the corporal stated.

Never had a statement been so true as Rube would find out in the next twenty-four hours.

PART V:

THE TRUTH BE TOLD

Thirty-One

After completing various forms about the events that ended in a five-vehicle crash, Rube collected the mail he received during his absence. Lying in his bed, Rube, unable to sleep with all the excitement of the day, began to read his mail. He saw a letter from his father and friend Roberta, and as usual, nothing from Sylvia. He received another letter with an unfamiliar address.

Rube opened Roberta's letter first.

March 22, 1945

Dear Rube,

You asked me in your last letter why Sylvia hasn't been writing. I am sorry to tell you; she's now dating a sailor. I know you will feel awful about this, especially since you wrote her many letters over the past months. I feel bad that I'm the one telling you this. That isn't a way to break up a relationship, without writing. Trying to understand why she chose this path is fruitless and upsetting. I can only suggest that you continue to be an outstanding soldier and look forward to coming home. Maybe this is for the best because if someone treats you this way, it might be what could happen if you were still together. No words can ease your pain. I think you are a great guy, and I'm looking forward to writing and hopefully seeing you when you come home. By the way, why don't you call me Bobbi?

Love,
Bobbi

Rube sat silently on his bed for a long time. He finally picked up the letter with the unknown address. He opened the letter with some apprehension as he recognized it came from Stuart's parents. It said, "Rube, I'm sorry to tell you, Stuart was killed in action a month ago." He couldn't read any further. In a few moments, he learned that he had lost his girlfriend and best friend.

Devastated beyond belief and oblivious to all other events, Rube struggled to make the 1100 meeting at Colonel Kay's office on April 14. Arriving five minutes early, he saw all the Jewish guys who were part of the mission at the tunnel, but none of the non-Jews were present. Another soldier noticed the same thing and questioned whether the meeting was a debriefing or a medal ceremony. One MP joked, "I wonder if Colonel Kay is waiting until we have a *minyan* (ten men) before he starts our conference." They didn't have long to wait, as the colonel's door opened exactly on time.

"Gentlemen, let's start with a good news story. Teddy Schwartz, the soldier who had been stabbed at the tunnel, and all the other wounded have recovered enough that they might be released from the hospital next week."

Taking a deep breath, the colonel continued, "Some of you have recognized that only the Jewish soldiers are present at this meeting. There is a reason for this, and I feel horrible that I must inform you of one of the worst events ever. I'm sure you have heard the rumors of Jews being placed in work, prison, or concentration camps. All that is pure bullshit. They were death camps. Just a week ago, American troops came upon a small concentration camp. It's hard for me even to describe the survivors' conditions. I'm afraid there might be hundreds of these camps, maybe even more, where millions of Jews were slaughtered."

Among the moans, groans, and cries of the Jewish soldiers, the colonel suddenly stopped, and emotion took over. "I understand the Russian forces came upon such a camp in July 1944, but their discovery wasn't revealed to any of the Allies. So, here we are, almost a year later, when our forces come upon a concentration camp for the first time. I don't know if our military was complicit in the cover-up, but I understand why Joseph Stalin, the ruler of Russia, wanted to keep it a secret. Much like Hitler, the dictator eliminated many foes in the same way as the Nazis by death camps or execution. But that doesn't excuse any U.S. government officials who knew about these camps and failed to notify the public about their existence. It wouldn't surprise me that high-ranking officers were aware of the camps and told not to reveal the discovery. The only excuse I could give to those who were responsible for this decision is that it might have caused a change in America's air attack on Germany.

"I pray for the souls who lost their lives. I can't imagine how distraught and angry you must feel, so I'm giving orders to restrict Jewish soldiers from visiting the camps. Once this becomes known, I'm sure you will see the horrible pictures and films that make you sick. You have my greatest sympathies. I have arranged at the mess hall for you to have coffee and to commiserate together if you wish to remain there. For the next few days, I am putting all of you on light duty. I have also called for a rabbi to offer prayers if you so wish. Otherwise, you may pay homage to those who perished in your own way."

"Are we dismissed, sir?" one GI called out.

"No, I have one other piece of bad news. In case you haven't heard the news, our president, Franklin D. Roosevelt, has died, and Vice President Harry Truman, is now president."

Stunned, shocked and delirious with hate, fifteen Jewish soldiers made their way to the mess hall. Some sat in silence; others cried, and a few screamed. As each minute passed, they tried to comprehend what they just heard. Rube was a basket case and searched for answers but found none.

"I feel I've been raped," proclaimed one GI.

"You mean violated," announced another soldier.

"Yes, violated. I risk my life daily and do so willingly, but I can't understand why my country neglected to reveal this horrible crime against humanity."

"Why, why I can't understand," pleaded another GI.

No one offered any explanation. Another soldier angrily pointed out, "They had to know these death camps had existed for some time as the various branches of our military have photos of every piece of land in Europe."

Rube noted when he was in the bocage, he saw planes conduct flyovers, not to drop bombs, but to take photographs of the terrain.

"Still," someone else retorted, "with so many death camps, it might have been difficult to spot one of these places if it was located, like in Poland."

"Who cares," said Private Levi Apple. "Why didn't they drop bombs on these places? I'm sure the excuse was that innocent people would be killed, yet, the Germans killed defenseless Jews daily."

Corporal Nathan Epstein mentioned, "Look at all the innocent civilians we killed in bombing missions and what about all those GIs killed accidentally when we mistakenly hit the wrong targets? Even if some Jews had died in the bombing raids, the death camps would have been eliminated."

Phil Cohen, filled with anger, screamed, "If we heard the rumors, and I'm sure government officials knew about it, they share in the responsibility for possibly millions being slaughtered."

The outrage against the government and the military continued before the lone voice of Corporal Leonard Plotnik spoke out, "I can't deny what you guys have concluded, but one thing you forgot to include is politics. President Roosevelt, who barely got the Lend-Lease bill through Congress, had to deal with our nation where antisemitism was part of the American fabric. He had to use all his cards to fight the war, so maybe he had to bend to those he disagreed with and forgo attacks on the death camps."

"I don't buy it," another soldier remarked. Sergeant Irv Luckman stated, "I don't believe that powerful government employees who might have been antisemitic were in positions that had enough authority to stop any presidential attempt to wipe out the concentration camps."

Another soldier said, "The government gave tacit approval to what was happening to the Jews by being silent." Another GI offered that the government feared reprisals from Hitler if it released information about his final solution. He noted that maybe the dictator had more powerful weapons than the V-2 rockets pounding European cities.

The desperate sounds of pain and suffering from the mess hall continued unabated, which caused one of the grievers to say, "Our cries of sadness and anger resemble those who once prayed at the Wailing Wall in Jerusalem."

Colonel Kay then entered the room and attempted to comfort his men by proclaiming, "Gentlemen, excuses are not enough. This is a failure of humankind to address the threat Hitler posed since 1933 when he took control of the German government. His book, *Mein Kampf*, and antisemitic events warned the world but were neglected. Now not only have the Jews suffered unimaginable torture from this madman, but the entire world is now experiencing the ravages of hate gone wild."

After two hours of self-flagellation, one of the soldiers had the men form a circle and asked if they could recite the *Kaddish* prayer together. In a ghostly tone, the group repeated the words of the prayer of remembrance to those who had died, "*Yisgadal v'yiskadash* …." Tears flowed as the Hebrew words were spoken, and cries of anguish were heard. Then one soldier said after the prayer was finished, "Can we say aloud the names of fellow soldiers who died fighting this terrible curse?" Rube was the first to mention Stuart's name. Others followed.

While the group huddled in the middle of the mess hall, and tears dropped to the floor, the soldiers who arrived for lunch questioned what all this was about. One of the mess hall people said, "They are calling out the names of buddies they lost in the war." Soon other GIs joined the huddle, and as it expanded, the names of others were shouted to the rafters. Hundreds of names followed as more and more men joined the huddle. For the first time, Rube felt the comradeship that only the band of brothers could share. He knew that those who died in combat would not die in vain. For Rube and all the men crowded in the mess hall, one day, Hitler and his world of hate would soon end. The former medic and now MP only hoped he would be alive to witness it.

Thirty-Two

Later in the day, when the men in his company began discussing the new President, Harry Truman, Rube who had already endured so much grief in the last twenty-four hours, felt like a bowling pin. However, he gathered his strength and shouted, "Enough about Truman. Yes, we don't know much about him. But he fought in World War I, and I heard he's a tough guy who wouldn't back down from a fight. I have no fear that Harry will continue the war to its conclusion. Look, he stood up to a gang of Klansmen, and even though he was backed by a corrupt political group known as the Pendergast gang, the guy's a winner."

Rube's harangue seemed to stem the tide of negative comments about the new president. Certainly, it would be tough to follow a president who served longer than any other chief executive. But many tough decisions remained, all of which would impact not only Rube's life but every citizen in the United States. No one would question Roosevelt's leadership carrying the nation through the Great Depression or his determination to defeat the Axis alliance, but Rube figured it was too early to give up on the new president.

After giving his opinion about Harry Truman, Rube thought about himself. He realized that many words he said about Truman could be applied to himself. Even with all his losses, it was too early to give up on life. Despite trying to convince himself that was the proper course to follow, he felt empty and without a purpose.

The lonely nights seemed to fit him perfectly, riding solo in a Jeep patrolling the deserted streets of Antwerp. This way, he could avoid the pain of losing other friends and commiserate with himself about his misfortune and future. This he hoped would keep him from spiraling even further into depression.

After a week of despair, Rube, in his Jeep, drove past an old building filled with numerous bullet holes in its exterior. Rube noticed the sounds of music coming from somewhere. After he slowed the Jeep to a crawl, Rube heard the sound again. Rube thought, *damn, this sounds like the music from Benny Goodman's band.* He pulled the Jeep to a stop and departed toward the music. He wasn't sure if it might be a trap to lure GIs to its location as he gripped his forty-five pistol and moved toward the sound of music.

As Rube approached the site, he saw flashes of light coming from a basement, and then the music died. Staying motionless for several minutes, he heard music from another band. This time he found the steps to the basement of the building. Slowly, he moved to the door where the music came from and pushed it open. There was a mixture of young men and women dancing. As he entered, everything stopped. The twenty or so people stared at this man in a military uniform holding a revolver.

Rube was speechless. One young woman spoke English and said, "All we were doing was dancing." Rube putting his pistol away, said, "Can I watch …? Put on another record!" Everyone seemed to relax as the MP watched the dancers, who appeared to be about eighteen-to-twenty-two years old, move to the beat of the music. When the music stopped, Rube clapped. He realized that the partygoers might fear returning to the same place if he departed without saying another word. So, he said, "Can you play 'Sing, Sing, Sing' again?" He then pointed to a girl he thought was a good dancer, and once the music started, he reached for her hand, swung her around, and from that moment, the MP felt alive again.

Everyone went wild as they saw an MP swing and sway to the music of the big band sound. He charmed the "kids" for the next half-hour, and all the girls wanted to dance with him. He found out that when the Germans controlled the city, the young people met at secret places to listen to and dance to music from America. Rube found out this group met three days a week, Tuesday, Thursday, and Saturday, at this same venue at the corner of

36th and Wine. Rube told them, "I will try to come as often as possible." As he returned to his Jeep, Rube had a big smile. Just maybe, dancing would provide relief from the war, and one day, he could dance again in D.C.

An excited MP couldn't wait to write Bobbi about his discovery of the dance hideout. Rube's happiness, however, was tempered by the sadness about other events in his life.

April 18, 1945

Dear Bobbi,

I can't make any predictions about the war, but with the Russians on the outskirts of Berlin and our forces across the Rhine River, time is short for Hitler. Presently, my home base is in the city of Antwerp, Belgium. It can't compare to Paris, but it has some charm, and the girls are very friendly.

You wouldn't believe I found a place to dance. And the other day, I went to an ice cream parlor that would rival our own back home.

I have had some bad news lately. My best friend Stuart was killed in action. Then we were told about the rumors we had heard about the killing of Jews in death camps. It made me sick but more determined to end this terrible war. Of course, the death of President Roosevelt was a shock. How are the folks back home dealing with it?

I'm still upset with Sylvia's behavior. She didn't have the common courtesy to write me about her new friend. Thank you for telling me. I truly hope Sylvia will be happy with her new boyfriend.

Don't worry about your brother coming over here. Things are a lot better now than when I first arrived.

We are feeling the warmth of spring more and more, and I hope the temperature continues its upward climb.

Wish I was home to enjoy the coming summer. Can't wait to

see a Washington Senators baseball game and see you.
Congratulations on losing 23 pounds.
Stay well and safe.
Love,
Rube

The next time Rube returned to the dance site in the basement, the young people were in an uproar. One of the girls told him that the supposed owner of the property, who supported the Nazis when they controlled the city, wanted them to leave his property.

Rube said, "Let me talk to him."

"He will be in later," said the girl.

"I'll hang around the neighborhood," answered Rube.

Around 9:00 p.m., a car approached the bombed-out neighborhood, and the building owner walked menacingly toward the basement. Before any disturbances occurred, Rube arrived. The owner, Maxim Janssens, threatened to go to the municipal building where his property had been registered and to bring the police next time to evict them. One of the dancers revealed that both buildings had been destroyed by V-2 rockets sent by those the owner supported.

Rube thought the best action was to remove the owner and take him for a ride. The owner refused, but Rube didn't accept "no" for an answer. He drove the owner through the devastated areas of the city. Then he asked, "Are you proud of this?" In a tirade, the owner blamed everything on the people of Antwerp, Jews, and Americans for the destruction. Seeing his efforts were useless, Rube drove the man to his car and warned him not to return until he could show evidence about his claims.

The owner cursed Rube, and the MP needed all his patience not to put a bullet in him. As Rube drove away, he heard several shots. Reacting instantly, the MP drove toward where the shots came from. Unable to spot any movement or individuals, he turned his Jeep around and returned to where he had left the so-called owner.

The headlights of his Jeep focused on the real target of the shots, a body lying in the street. Rube immediately recognized the owner, who had been shot while entering his car. The MP quickly examined the body and found two bullet holes in his chest. Rube automatically reached for his walkie-talkie, and within minutes four Jeeps arrived. The MPs tried to canvass the area, but darkness covered those who committed the act. Two shell casings were found the next morning, with the help of two dogs who sniffed the spot where the assassin had waited.

Because Rube was the last person to see the owner alive, he became an instant hero to the dancers, even though the bullets taken from the deceased didn't match Rube's weapon. Both bullets came from an M1 rifle. The owner's demise didn't even create a ripple of concern for a city that had seen so much death. The city's inhabitants had their problems to deal with, and certainly, the death of a supporter of the Nazis only drew the comment, "Oh, well."

Thirty-Three

For those dancing in the basement, it was a great relief. Two days later, when Rube returned, he was so popular that a girl named Yvonne asked if he would give her private dance lessons. Rube, somewhat surprised by Yvonne's request, rejected the idea. But the thought of dancing with a regular partner offered another way to isolate the demons of war that plagued him. Further, he thought, *what harm could come from an innocent dance relationship?* And for the first time in months, Rube envisioned himself back home, dancing with Bobbi and being the best dance couple on the floor.

Rube's attempt at being a dance instructor ended before the first lesson as he was told to report to Colonel Kay's office by 1900 on April 24. Upon hearing about the urgency of the meeting, the MP had a bad feeling about what to expect. The captain wasted no time informing Rube that he was to become part of a desperate mission.

"What's going on?"

"We are in deep shit," said Kay.

"You mean me?"

"No, the entire MP corps. I can't tell you the whole story. But the Germans or black marketeers have captured a boxcar carrying something top secret."

"Can you tell me what we are looking for?"

"No can do, but we must find the boxcar to prevent a major disaster."

"Are those involved aware of what they have taken?"

"Not yet, because it's hidden, but once back in Germany, they will surely discover its contents."

"How can we identify the boxcar?"

"The number 1098 was painted on the side of the boxcar. I presume it's painted over, but I am unsure."

"What has been done to find the boxcar?"

"I have sent five troop carriers with twenty men each to hunt down the boxcar."

"Have they had any success?"

"Not yet, but time is running out. So, Lieutenant Willie McNutty will join you and twenty other troopers to search for that missing freight car. Prepare to leave tomorrow at 0600."

The colonel's assistant provided the lieutenant with a series of maps and photos that he hoped would be useful in finding where the box car could be hidden. The next day, Sergeant Goldfarb and the lieutenant reported to the motor pool, where a large troop carrier waited for the GIs who would be sent on this impossible mission. Even Lieutenant McNutty, who stood at five-foot-eleven and was a recent graduate of West Point, seemed perplexed as to what to do next.

After traveling for two days to several different rail lines looking for the boxcar, the operation stopped when the truck broke down. Stranded in unknown territory, the MPs had a choice of waiting a couple of days for a replacement truck or marching eastward toward another rail line. The major concern for the lieutenant was that they might run into a pocket of German soldiers still occupying captured territory.

At least the weather was warmer as the men covered several miles. The grumbling among the troops, who felt the whole mission was doomed from the start, halted as they heard tires spinning. Not knowing if the noise was from an enemy vehicle, the group of GIs carefully approached the area where the sound source resonated. To their surprise, the contingent of MPs discovered a large troop carrier stuck in the mud. As the MPs approached, one of the two Black drivers said, "I've been trying for hours to get out of this mudhole."

With the help of the MPs, who gathered tree limbs and branches and placed them on top of the ruts created by the tires, and with the human resources of fifteen men pulling on ropes, they freed the vehicle.

Lieutenant McNutty then informed the driver about his own mission and claimed he had the authority to take over the vehicle that had been stuck in the mud. The drivers, Louis Walters and Leroy Willis, who had driven for the Red Ball Express, urged the officer to forego the use of this vehicle to transport his troops.

"Why?" demanded McNutty.

Walters responded, "It's loaded with ammo and weapons. One accurate shot from the enemy and all of us will be heaven bound."

The new lieutenant had to make his first major decision about whether to place himself and his men in danger. The lieutenant overriding all the concerns, felt it was more important to complete the mission. He ordered his men to board the truck. Louis, and Leroy made it clear they didn't want the responsibility of carrying all the lieutenant's men in the truck with such dangerous cargo aboard. McNutty told them they could remain in the woods and wait to be rescued or join the crew. Both chose to join the mission. Rube and Louis communicated well, but Rube never understood some slang words when the two drivers spoke together. Nonetheless, the MPs were impressed at how skillfully the two drivers maneuvered the vehicle.

While driving toward an unknown destination, the lieutenant received a message that an unscheduled train and the missing boxcar had been located by air surveillance about five hours away. McNutty answered, "We are basically out of the loop since there is no way our troops could catch up with the train." Another message came over his radio informing all units that the air corps had planned a bombing raid which most likely would delay the train's movement for a day.

After receiving the coordinates where the train was located, Rube and the lieutenant calculated their position and found it possible to meet the train if any future obstacles didn't delay them. Much to the officer's displeasure, his troops would soon be challenged by a major problem. In the distance, they heard gunfire from a firefight underway.

Pulling the truck behind where they found American vehicles parked,

Rube and the MPs moved toward the combat.

For the American troops engaged in the hostilities, the sight of additional soldiers acted as a stimulus and relieved their exhausted bodies. That was not the case for the officer in charge. "Are you all my replacements? And do you have my tanks?" questioned Captain Richard Sneed.

"Neither," replied McNutty.

"So, why are you here?"

"Is it too much to ask what the fuck is happening here?" Captain Sneed responded sarcastically. "Can't you see we are in a confrontation with an enemy force that controls the high ground of this major transportation crossroad?"

"I thought German forces were long gone from this area."

"True, but not exactly," replied Sneed.

"Would you mind elaborating on your answer?" commented McNutty.

"A combination of pro-Nazi supporters, a special operation company of German soldiers, and several groups of black marketeers managed to overtake the crossroads before us," Captain Sneed responded.

"What's so important about this shit-hole piece of land?"

"It has provided the escape route for enemy troops and sympathizers fleeing back to Germany."

"I don't understand. There's enough Allied firepower to overtake this obstacle within an hour, so why are you having so much difficulty?" queried the lieutenant."

"With Allied forces moving into Germany, most of our heavy weapons and equipment are on the German border. I've been waiting for a pair of tanks to arrive."

The lieutenant insisted, "I don't have time to wait. We need to get to the road on the other side of this wooded area immediately."

"I've been trying to do that for the last few days. Every time we attempt to cross the field, we get blasted by mortars and machine guns from the woods. I can't take many more casualties," offered the captain.

"We are on a special mission and must advance beyond the crossroads," pleaded the lieutenant.

"Lots of luck. You see those men lying in the field? They were trying to do just that, and now I'll have to remove the bodies."

While the two officers talked, Louis came over to Rube and mentioned he had driven in this area before and found a natural path between the trees in the woods, wide enough so that his truck, despite its size, could squeeze through. Rube, overlooking the battlefield, spotted an area near the tree line that offered some cover for half a dozen soldiers. He then asked Louis if the path he discussed was near the alcove, and Louis said, "Yes."

The sun was setting when Rube went to the lieutenant with a plan to attack the enemy. With Captain Sneed present, he outlined his plans. Under the gun to advance, the captain offered, "I don't think it will work, but nothing has, so let's go for it."

After an hour or so, a cease-fire was arranged to allow for the removal of the dead and wounded. Rube gathered the twenty MPs and spoke, "Listen closely; if we're going to try to pull this off, everyone must be on the same page. First, I want each of you to use this tape I'm giving you and make a cross on your helmet. This will identify you as part of the Red Cross team. I will use my medic helmet liner, so you can locate me if you have any problems. Captain Sneed has at least ten stretchers available. I want you to move those brave soldiers who didn't make it to that alcove." Rube pointed to the location.

"Then, remove the wounded back to our lines. Just remember you can't carry any weapon on your person. The only thing you should carry is the stretcher. Each stretcher will have a blanket. Under each blanket will be a weapon, either an M1 rifle, machine gun or a Bazooka, which must be covered completely. Screw this up, and we are all dead. As you return to the alcove, leave the weapons there and return to the field of combat to collect the deceased and wounded soldiers. I will be out there helping the wounded. Please signal me when you have taken all our weapons to the alcove. Once it darkens, we will continue removing the bodies from our lines. That's when the critical phase of our plan begins. I have selected eight GIs, including myself, to carry four stretchers back to the alcove. When we all return to the alcove, Louis will drive his truck through the woods and onto the main road where the mortars are. He will abandon the vehicle after pressing on the gas pedal. The rest of us in the nook will charge behind the vehicle and prepare to fire a Bazooka shell into the truck. The explosions from the ammo in the truck will alert Sneed to begin his charge across the field. If everything works, Sneed and his troops will join us as we meet the train."

Nothing usually works as planned, but the arrangement for the attack came close. The pro-German forces enjoyed watching the stretcher-bearers, including Leroy, pick up the wounded and dead. The team performed like real medics, and the stretcher carriers were outstanding. Just before darkness took over the sky and all the wounded and dead had been collected, Louis began the dash through the woods in the truck. As he passed the alcove, eight well-armed MPs ran behind the vehicle as the Bazooka launcher positioned the weapon on his shoulder and prepared to fire a shell directly into the back of the truck as it came close to the hidden position of the enemy's mortars. Seconds after Louis abandoned the vehicle, a thunderous blast erupted from the firing site of the mortars, signaling Sneed's men to charge across the field. With the woods on fire and smoke covering the advancing soldiers, the combination of pro-German forces broke, and the fighting was over after an hour of combat.

Rube, Leroy, and six other MPs ran to where Louis leaped from the truck. He was dazed but unhurt. Leroy, who was first to arrive, noticed that Louis was covered with munition residue and dust, which caused his face to look quite unusual. "What are you looking at?" asked Louis as Leroy stared at him.

"I'm not hurt," said the driver.

"But your face looks white," answered Leroy.

"What are you talkin' about, Leroy?"

"We don't have time to wait for this chameleon to turn to a different color," insisted Rube. "Let's get out of here because we have to catch a train."

They heard a familiar sound as the GIs fought through the maze of trees into the road leading to the railroad tracks. Captain Sneed shouted, "I think my tanks finally arrived."

Thirty-Four

Around 0530 the next morning, the train carrying the stolen boxcar chugged down the tracks. The engineer suddenly had to stop as two tanks blocked the passageway. As the train slowed, GIs stormed the two passenger cars. Gunshots were heard as flashes of light ripped across the glass windows. The movement of shadows within the car created the sensation of a frame-by-frame motion picture. The picture frame images turned into real figures as the occupants fled the passenger car only to run into a volley of fire from the soldiers waiting alongside the railroad tracks. Hands quickly rose as a dozen men surrendered to the well-positioned troops. Included among the prisoners, the train's operator confessed he had no idea what type of cargo had been placed on the train but understood every item aboard would be removed at a stop near Brussels and taken to a warehouse near the historic town of Waterloo.

A few hours later, much like a scene from a science fiction movie, men in all-white coveralls were seen moving toward a poorly painted boxcar that revealed the number 1098.

The entire army of GIs witnessed the scene from over 300 yards away. Still, no one knew what was in the boxcar, but it must have been very secret as the white-uniformed men erected a tent that covered most of boxcar 1098. Hundreds of GIs gathered most of the day as if at a frat party picnic. Guys took off their shirts and lay down relaxing as if on a beach with the sun's rays infusing their bodies. A few even tossed a baseball around. The only thing missing were girls and cases of beer.

By 1600, the tent came down, and the respite ended.

Rube and his team boarded the train, still with many dead black marketeers in the passenger cars. It didn't take long for the train's locomotive to arrive at a small village on the outskirts of Brussels, where a dozen trucks sat waiting to deliver stolen merchandise to a central storage facility. Before the unloading could occur, GIs jumped from the train, surprising the members of various gangs. Gun action settled all hostilities. Rube, along with Lieutenant McNutty, entered one of the trucks. With guns aimed at the driver behind the wheel, it only took moments before a convoy of trucks now occupied by GIs rambled toward the main warehouse.

With the lieutenant and Rube squeezing into the truck's cabin and leading the convoy, the seven-mile trip took less than fifteen minutes. While traveling, Rube asked the driver if Waterloo was where Napoleon lost his most important battle.

The driver responded, "You got that right, Yank."

How ironic, Rube thought, *here I am about to engage in a combat situation in the shadow of a battlefield that ended Napoleon's reign. With the Russian forces surrounding Berlin, would it be possible for the city to become Hitler's Waterloo?* Rube could only hope that history would repeat itself with the abrupt ending of the reign of the Third Reich. The sight of the warehouse brought Rube back to the moment's reality.

Much like the scene from a liquor raid in the 1920s and 1930s by FBI agents, the MPs crashed their vehicles through the warehouse's main entrance, where they were met with gunfire. Hiding behind their vehicles, Rube aimed his shotgun skyward as three men on a ramp above the warehouse floor kept the troops from advancing. One of the men dropped from the ramp after being hit with a sniper's bullet. Both Rube and McNutty dashed to the steps leading to the ramp. At the base of the steps, the officer fired his weapon and took down the second man as Rube climbed up the steps to finish the third. But it was almost impossible to get a clear shot from his position.

As the lieutenant raced up the steps, the assailant moved to obtain a better view for a shot. Rube, using his belt to reposition himself, aimed and fired both barrels at the armed assailant. Knocking the shooter down, Rube slipped in another round when the man rose to take another shot. Rube fired again, causing the man to fall from the ramp into the boxes stacked below. No further gunshots sounded. Rube pulled himself back onto the ramp and lowered himself to one of the large piles of boxes. Slowly he jumped from pile to pile until he came close enough to the floor to finally jump. He heard the lieutenant say, "Be careful; there's a metal piece creating some light near you. It might be a gun from the guy you just shot down." Rube turned the corner and saw the dead gangster. About twenty feet away was a piece of metal sticking out of a crate. Cautiously, Rube moved closer. Thinking it might be a booby trap, Rube looked for wires near the wooden shipping container but found none.

McNutty arrived, looked at the metal piece, and said, "It has strange letters."

Rube checked it out and uttered, "My God." He then opened the front of the crate with his Bowie knife and stared at a dirty cover that fits over the most sacred religious artifact for the Jewish people, a scroll containing the five books of Moses. Paralyzed for several moments, Rube could only stare. His first reaction was uncontained anger at the condition of the *Torah*, but somehow, he managed to appreciate the importance of his discovery and reached into his shirt pocket, where he kept a small bible, the Old Testament, and removed it. He noted how its pages were no longer crisp and clear, but even though the good book had gone through a lot of sweat, blood, and tears, it remained intact. Holding the Bible, Rube slowly moved it toward the *Torah*, then softly touched the *Torah* with the edge of the Bible and gently kissed the outer edge of the book. From that moment, Rube's mind went blank. He remembered chills rushing through his body, but the MP recalled little else until riding home with his buddies on the train. As Rube returned from his out-of-world experience, he worried about the *Torah. Where was it?* When he asked Lieutenant McNutty if he knew its location, the officer said, "Don't you remember? You placed it on this train in a boxcar."

———•———

Thirty-Five

For almost eleven months, Rube had attempted to block out from his mind the unforgettable scenes from the war, but on this occasion, these visions came back with a vengeance. It was easy to explain why he awoke in a cold sweat after reliving scenes from the war, but he couldn't explain why he blacked out everything after finding the *Torah*.

Early the next morning, Rube stirred after hearing someone calling his name. Still aching and recovering from the past day's events, the MP sergeant wondered if some new disaster had occurred on his day off.

"Hey, Rube," one of the MPs uttered. "There's a fellow out here named Rebbe West who wants to see you."

"I don't know any Rebbe. Oh … is it Rabbi Avi Vest? That's who they told me might come."

Rube quickly exited his tent and hugged the rabbi, and he reciprocated. "Please come in."

Once inside Rube's tent, the MP introduced the rabbi to his two tent mates, Charles and Kevin.

"I hope you're not offended by their dress," mentioned Rube. Charles was wearing only his boxer shorts and T-shirt, and Kevin was bare-chested with only his pants on.

"I've seen a lot worse."

"Thank you so much for coming."

"What would you like me to perform — a prayer for someone who is sick, someone who recently died, or has recently been injured in combat? Or is someone near death at home? Maybe you are lonely and need someone to talk with?"

"None of the above."

"So, why am I here?"

"I want to show you something special."

The rabbi was heard to mumble, "*Oy gevalt.*"

Rube commented, "I think it's a miracle!"

"Miracles I like, especially if it comes from the hand of God."

Rube moved over to the crate that stood next to his cot in the tent.

"So?" said the rabbi in a questioning way.

Rube then asked Charles and Kevin to stand next to the rabbi. "Sometimes, when you witness a miracle, you don't know how the body will react."

Rube, using his Bowie knife, slowly pulled back the front of the crate and watched the knees of the rabbi buckle.

"Oh, my, oh, my! I don't believe it. Where … where did you get it?" It took some time before the rabbi regained his composure. He called his aide, "Stephen, get your ass in here."

Charles and Kevin seemed surprised to hear the rabbi say "ass." The assistant flew into the tent and skidded to a halt when he saw the *Torah*.

"Oh, my God. Where, how did you get it?" questioned the assistant.

"We found it in a warehouse with other stolen goods," responded Rube.

"Can we touch it?" asked the rabbi.

"Sure, go ahead, but the cloth cover over the *Torah* needs a cleaning."

"What a wonderful discovery!" declared Stephen.

The three MPs watched as the rabbi placed the silver plate over the two wooden poles that held the *Torah* together. They then attached the two jiggly silver pieces to each pole. The rabbi said a short prayer in Hebrew and gently caressed the *Torah*. Rube thought his prayer was known as the "*Shehechayanu*," which is said after a first-time event or when holidays begin.

The rabbi lifted the *Torah*, and the MPs placed pillowcases on each end of the scroll. They then covered this cherished religious item with a sheet and handled it as if it were a masterpiece made by an unknown hand, but for the rabbi and the Jewish people, its words came from God.

The aide then took the *Torah* into the Jeep and carefully placed it in the back seat. As Rabbi Vest prepared to leave, he asked Rube if there was anything he could do for him besides saying thank you.

"I do have a question."

After telling the rabbi how he blacked out mentally after finding the *Torah*, Rube wondered if the rabbi had an explanation for what had happened.

"For a rabbi, the easy answer would be, you had a religious experience that caused a spiritual awakening with God, which might be true. But there is another answer. Rube, did you see a lot of combat during the war?"

"Far too much, I'm afraid."

"That might be critical in determining the reason for your mental blackout. GIs, Jewish or not, have told me the same story. Although each story was different, they all had one thing in common, the stress of war. The best way I can explain it is like a balloon filled with air; your mind simultaneously releases the tension coming from war. Much like if the air in a balloon is released, causing it to crumble and lose its form. I can't say if this is the correct answer, but upon seeing the *Torah*, your mind triggered an avalanche of war visions that temporarily escaped your brain, causing a blackout. So, it's up to you to select whether you may have had a religious experience or a reaction from the stress of your war experiences, or maybe neither is a satisfactory answer for you, but that's the best I can do."

Before the rabbi departed, he gave Rube a big hug and kissed him. Then, with a hop, skip and jump, the rabbi dove into the Jeep as his assistant started the engine. Rube viewed the dust from the departing Jeep fly into the rays of the sunshine, creating a sparkling effect as the dirt slowly drifted back to earth. Rube knew he had done more than a *mitzvah* by returning the *Torah* to the rabbi.

As Rube turned to reenter the tent, he saw Charles and Kevin give him a stink eye and immediately predicted what would come next. Charles gleefully asked, "How was the kiss?"

Kevin giggled and said, "Was it the best you ever had?"

Rube answered with a story. "When I was about ten or eleven years old, we had an Australian Shepherd dog named Sparky. She was beautiful and smart. When she was young, her back legs were so strong that she could jump over three or four-feet tall fences. One day I was walking her, or she was walking me down Allison Street, toward Roosevelt High School in my hometown. As we ambled down the sidewalk, we saw a woman approaching us. Sparky sat down and waited until the lady was next to us. Then she jumped up and gave her a wet kiss on the lips. I was so shocked I didn't know what to do or say. I tried to apologize, but no words came out. Then the woman said, 'Don't worry, that's the best kiss I've had in years.' So, to answer your question," as Rube winked, "with the amount of emotion that went with the rabbi's kiss, it was one of the best kisses I've ever had."

The two guys continued to mess with Rube when Charles asked, "Do you have any plans to chase down any trains today?"

"No, I'm relaxing today. For me, April 30 is much like all the other days, nothing special or different, except we are still alive."

Rube could have never been so wrong with his remarks, as, at 2309, a reporter on the radio announced, "Adolf Hitler is dead." The excited reporter explained that the world's most hated man had died in a mass suicide with his newlywed wife and some of his officers in a bunker beneath the streets of Berlin.

Corporal Jay Nelson, the first to hear the report, while holding a beer bottle, remarked, "I will believe it when I see his dead body." Several hours later, radio accounts and newspaper stories told of Russian soldiers finding Hitler's remains in a shallow grave outside his underground sanctuary.

Thirty-Six

May 12, 1945

Dear Bobbi,

We partied for four days when we heard about Hitler's death. It took me another three days to get over the hangover, and less than twenty-four hours later, we celebrated V-E Day (Victory in Europe). I'm so happy the war is over, but true peace will take much longer. We have already begun to see revenge killings, and those invested in black marketeering are still involved in everyday criminal activity.

My situation is also unsettled. We have been told my unit will be dissolved, but those with combat experience will soon become part of the 399th MPs. The others get a trip home, and we might take a trip to Asia if the war continues. So, I have no idea when I will be home. Hopefully, if we are sent to Asia, I will get a pass for at least a week around the Jewish holidays in the fall. Before I go off to war again, I must see my folks, friends, and you.

In the meantime, we have been involved in clerical-type work. Getting GIs on boats going home and identifying items recovered from black marketeers has been difficult. Occasionally, I ride the trains to provide security for merchandise shipped to different locations, but most of my time is spent in Antwerp.

I guess you had a big celebration back home. I spent the entire day and night at the dance place celebrating. I danced so much that my legs felt as if I had just marched twenty miles. My liver has had a lot of work in the last few days, to say the least.

No one knows how long the Japanese will hold out, but I don't see a quick end to the war with how they fought at Iwo Jima and battling at Okinawa. So, please keep writing. Even though the days go by quickly with all the work we do, it's still lonely, and I never thought I would say this, but I miss life in D.C.

Europe is a beautiful place, especially when the guns are silent. I hope to return to Allison Street one day and begin a new life. I will never be able to match what I've seen and done over here, but it will be time for me to settle down and be thankful that I was able to return home alive and well. Next time I write, I'll outline where I've been and tell you about some battles.

Enjoy the summer fun.

Yours always,

Rube

After sealing the envelope, Rube carried the letter to the main tent. As he prepared to leave, a GI who dealt with sending mail back to the states, asked Rube if he could do him a favor. "We are so short of men. Could you carry the newly arrived mail back to the headquarters of the 381st?"

"Absolutely," Rube replied. "I used to deliver mail to GIs when I rode in a Jeep called the Pony Express."

This time Rube carried the mail over his shoulder in a bag about the size newspaper boys use to deliver papers like the *Evening Star* and the *Washington Post*. Upon arriving at headquarters, Rube couldn't believe how quickly word spread that mail from home had arrived. Normally, mail calls turned into a mob scene. This mail delivery was no different, as for the first time since the war ended, the GIs would have the opportunity to read about how the folks back home celebrated Germany's surrender.

Since Rube served as the division mail carrier on this occasion, he became the first soldier to receive mail. Somewhat disappointed, he was only given one envelope, which wasn't from Bobbi or his family. On the front, in bold print, was the U.S. War Department logo. At first, Rube feared what might be inside. Then he became very excited as this could be his order to return home. With shaky hands, Rube opened the envelope and searched for the date that would send him across the ocean. Indeed, he found a date, but it wasn't what he expected.

May 13, 1945

Sergeant Rube Goldfarb, for your action in late April during the firefight at the crossroads and the capture of a stolen vehicle at a railroad junction, you are to be given a medal, along with Private Steve Morgan, Corporal Norman Blumberg, and Private Butch Ringo at a ceremony to be held on June 6, the first anniversary of D-Day. You will be notified of the time and place by your company commander.

Congratulations.

Completely shocked, Rube wasn't sure if he should be angry or proud. Sure, he was dissatisfied about not returning home, but he rejoiced that the Army would honor him with a medal.

For the rest of the day, Rube felt unsettled about the letter's contents. Something was missing, but he couldn't tell what. On two occasions, Rube reread the letter and still couldn't identify the reason for being uneasy. It wasn't the tension that came with the medal ceremony; it was something else that caused him to be so uncomfortable.

While Rube contemplated his predicament, a large convoy of trucks entered the campsite. Bingo, it hit him. The name of Louis Walter was missing. The former Red Ball Express driver, who risked his life by taking his truck filled with explosives into enemy lines, whether by mistake or deliberately, was not among the recipients of those honored with a medal.

Over the next week, the four medal winners met and discussed what they believed was a miscarriage of justice. They all agreed that the color of his skin was a factor in Louis being left off the list to receive a medal. "I can't think of another reason," concluded Steve Morgan. The other men agreed and felt that there should be an inquiry as to whether the Army had made an error or whether it was part of an undeclared policy that existed not only in the military but everywhere else in society. Shortly, the four MPs began to ask some questions that upset many of those wearing silver on their shoulders. They heard the can being kicked down the road wherever they went, and no one knew anything but suggested they should ask an officer up the chain of command. After cutting through many red tapes, the quartet obtained an audience with General Titus Montgomery from Mobile, Alabama.

"I can't see how a general from the deep south will provide us with any information about Louis," predicted Ringo.

"I think the Army set the whole thing up, and they expect us to melt away after talking to the general," remarked Morgan.

Butch Ringo went even further by saying, "From where the general comes from, we will be lucky if he acknowledges race was a factor in Louis not receiving a medal."

The conference lasted twenty minutes, and the group left with a different outlook. The general admitted he knew very little about what had transpired. But after listening to the men's details, he felt that Louis should have been included in the medal ceremony. He offered a legitimate reason why Louis' actions might have been overlooked. He said that because Louis belonged to the Red Ball Express, which had been disbanded, the Army possibly couldn't find the location of his new unit. The other possibility could be that he had died in a combat mission. To Rube and his men, the general's comments seemed sincere as he offered to investigate the matter personally.

"You might think I approve of a segregated military because of my birthplace, and that couldn't be further from the truth. During the war, I have had the highest respect for the actions performed by the Colored troops, and I would gladly fight alongside our Negro officers like, Benjamin O. Davis and others who, in my eyes, have no color but are only true patriots. You will hear from me well before the medal ceremony," stated the general.

Rube and his men saluted, did an about-face, and exited the general's office.

"I still don't believe what I heard," stated Joe.

"Believe it," answered Rube. "He proved to be my type of officer, strong enough to buck the system but going beyond the book to do the right thing."

Two days before the men received their medals, Louis appeared in camp!

———◆———

Thirty-Seven

To break the monotony of his job and when he wasn't providing security for a train, Rube continued to dance with the Antwerp kids in the basement of the damaged house. The question remained about being sent to Asia, but as the days passed in Europe and the guns remained silent, Rube had the time to pursue one of his favorite activities. The MP admitted that dancing helped him reenergize his body and mind and when a girl named Yvonne asked him again about dance lessons, he agreed. What impressed Rube the most about his pupil, was her flexibility. Barely over five feet, with Yvonne's cute face, blue eyes, and tight skin, Rube became attached to her, but he tried desperately not to make her a sex object.

For someone who had just passed her teen years, she showed the maturity of a young adult. Maybe the war had something to do with her advanced maturation. This feature and Yvonne's ability to speak three languages, including English, allowed her to learn difficult dance steps easily. With Yvonne slightly over ninety pounds, Rube could easily lift her as they practiced dips, throws, and carries. At first, the couple departed the rehearsals sweating, breathing hard, and with aching muscles but without any sexual feelings involved. Then after a while, as they danced, there was some playful touching, some accidentally occurring. The innocent scene soon changed to erotic moments. The sight of Rube's bare chest and her shaved legs brought the first kiss. It wasn't long afterward that other sexual responses became routine. The way Yvonne combed her wet hair, and the way Rube lit a cigarette and placed it in her mouth or as they toweled off after dancing, brought them to another stage.

Neither ignored what could happen with such an affair, and each tried to set boundaries on how far they would take their relationship. Rube was different than Yvonne as he feared where the eventual outcome could lead, while Yvonne seemed more in tune to allow their relationship to advance to the point of whatever will be, will be.

So, each had concerns about the future, and each had a vision of love but continued to embrace their romantic relationship as they danced to American swing and sway music. As Rube spent his off-days dancing with Yvonne, and their relationship continued to grow, many of the GIs wanted to know how serious he was about her, and he gave them a *facockta* (crazy) answer. "I like her very much, but I think her relations with me are 'play tonic'."

"You mean platonic," said another soldier.

"No, her relationship with me is play tonic. She can tell her friends she dances with a big, strong U.S. military police officer. So, it's 'play' for her, and my dancing with Yvonne has become a 'tonic.' Now when you dance together, there is a lot of touching and feeling. I don't know who made this quote, 'Never the twain shall meet.' We met and engaged in all types of sex, but one, which caused her to get angry with me. She would say, 'You don't love me.' I would tell her, 'I'm doing this because I love you and don't want to leave you with a child after I sail home. I would feel nothing but guilt being unable to care for my child and you.'

"She would say, 'There are safety measures we can take.'" This unsettled issue continued until the needle of a borrowed Victrola nestled into the groove on a record that played the song by Marilyn Beau, "Hot Fever."

Even with the withdrawal of German troops from Belgium, the men who wore the cross-pistol insignia on their lapels continued to be challenged by pro-Nazi forces. Rogue German units remained in parts of Belgium, and the continuous assaults against law-abiding citizens by radical groups persisted. As a military force, the MPs in Antwerp supported the burgeoning local police as they reestablished order in the city.

Rube, now part of the 399th MP division, didn't have to make many new adjustments as he alternated providing security for trains traveling between Antwerp and Brussels. But for at least three days a week, Rube still managed to dance with Yvonne at the basement dance hideaway. Despite his objections, Yvonne entered them in a dance contest. Both individuals had developed a chemistry together that made them excellent dancers. The same could be said about Rube's main team, the MPs who guarded the train lines. Using a system of teamwork that included surveillance, military action if needed, and information provided by government officials, robbing trains almost became obsolete.

The MPs' success on the rails failed to be transferred to reduce crime in the city.

Usually, when Colonel Kay called Rube to his office, he thought something bad would happen. He expected the worst but was surprised when the captain greeted him with a smile.

"I hear you now are known as the dancing MP."

"Any problem with that?"

"No. We want you to keep dancing."

"How did you find out?"

"Many of the kids you dance with are the children of families at the top of this city's economic and political scale. They feel you offer security for their kids, and they like you. In turn, this has helped us maintain better relationships with the community. However, there's one other thing we would like you to do. Be a listening post for our Intel people. We want you to be aware of any information you hear about radical groups planning activities through loose lips."

"You want me to be a spy?"

"I won't go that far. Just keep your ears open. We are hearing rumors that revenge killings are coming."

"Against us?"

"No, I don't think so, but the pro-German elements complain that they always receive death threats."

"Aren't these folks the same people who shot at us when we first arrived?"

"Yes, but if something happened to them, and they start defending themselves, we could find ourselves in the middle of a civil war."

"Hopefully, this won't happen, but if it does, we'd better get our butts out of town fast."

"That's why I want to keep a lid on things until we can get our people home."

"How does that affect me?"

"I'm assigning you to Antwerp for the next month so you can help lower the tension between the different groups."

"How can I do that?"

"Just be seen by people, visit restaurants, bars, and local events. If you hear anything, I mean anything, rumors included, get in touch with us."

"On another subject, can I get an answer about the future of the 399th?"

"Unchanged at present. I expect something will come down by July."

"One other thing, I'll be entering a dance contest in three weeks. The girl I dance with is very poor, and we need a dance contest costume for her."

"Sorry, I'm not a tailor. What about your dad?"

"I thought about that but don't think we have enough time."

"What type of costume were you thinking about?"

"Since I'm going to wear my Army fatigues, I thought she could be dressed as a WAC."

"So, I'm getting the picture; you would want to see if the Army could provide her with an outfit. With all the problems I deal with daily, this might be the easiest. I'll personally call the supply depot and arrange for her to be fitted with a uniform, but also get yourself some new threads."

"I didn't think you were hip, colonel!"

"Break a leg, not really; give it your best shot. If I have time, I might come to watch."

Yvonne looked cute in her new outfit, but a major problem remained. Her skirt was too tight for her to be able to perform the type of dancing necessary for the show. Rube sent a V-mail letter to his dad, hopeful he had a solution to the dress problem. Rube's brother Sam assisted with reading the letter and responding to it.

PART V: THE TRUTH BE TOLD

May 15, 1945

Dear Pop and Mary,
  I need an answer quickly on this problem. A friend of mine, a young lady, needs more space in her skirt to make it possible to dance in a contest. What would you recommend for increasing her mobility to dance in her skirt?
  Rube

May 23, 1945

Dear Son,
  Grab a scissors and cut a slit on the side of her skirt. She will have more than enough room to dance. Are you dancing with her? Is she pretty? Is she Jewish?
  Pop

Over the next two weeks, Rube and Yvonne choreographed a dance that fits nicely with the music of "Boogie Woogie Bugle Boy." There was only one major thing missing from their dance — a dramatic ending. One night when the GI returned to his tent, Private Alex Rodman was sitting on Rube's cot looking at pictures he had just developed. Rube had forgotten that he borrowed Alex's black rectangle camera and then clicked two pictures of Yvonne. She wore her regular clothes in one, and in the other, she wore military attire. Alex showed him both photos, and Rube offered him some money, but he just gave Rube the photos. Alex then showed other pictures of his family, and Rube politely looked at them. One of the last pictures showed his niece bouncing on her parents' bed. "That's it," said Rube.

"What?" retorted Alex.

"The end of our dance routine."

By the time the next dance session occurred, Rube had assembled a series of empty wooden crates that became the essential prop in their dance routine. Because of Yvonne's slight build, she could easily stand on the large squares used to transport U.S. supplies. Rube then arranged the boxes into half of a triangle, with the top box reaching about four feet high.

Yvonne loved jumping from one box higher than another until she reached the top box and dropped four feet onto a small bouncy spring mattress which flung her into the air.

When the night of the contest arrived, the moon and stars illuminated the lobby of a building that no longer had a roof. A standing-room-only crowd eagerly awaited to see the best dancers in the city perform. Rube had that feeling in his stomach, much like he did the night before going into combat. Yvonne couldn't wait to perform.

As expected, most of the dancers were outstanding. Selected ninth out of the twelve to perform, Rube and Yvonne had the opportunity to view the other dancers. They felt they could receive a prize if they performed at their best. Dance group members helped arrange the boxes and the spring mattress when their turn came. As the music started, the smiling couple did their stuff. No major mistakes interrupted their performance as they came to the last part of the dance. Then Yvonne twirled over to the edge of the room and began running toward the boxes. After weeks of practice, Yvonne hit each box perfectly as she jumped on one after another, and then when hitting the top box, she dropped down to a mattress that sprang her into the air. Rube timed his slide perfectly as Yvonne flew in the air. With one leg bent, sliding on the floor and the other pushing upward, Rube, with both hands raised, grabbed his dance partner around the hips and locked his arms while lifting Yvonne over his head. Like a statue, while the crowd applauded, Yvonne kept her head, chest, and legs up and her arms spread out as if she was about to fly. After about ten seconds, Rube dropped his left arm and gently rolled Yvonne down to his bent knee. With one hand extended and her head bent, almost striking the floor, the music ended. The crowd went wild. Applause and cheers seemed to last a long time. Rube saluted the crowd, and Yvonne threw kisses while she posed, exposing her leg where the split in her skirt stopped just below her thigh.

When awards were given out, Rube and Yvonne came in third. There were some boos in the crowd, but both were happy. Yvonne received a bottle of cognac and the Jewish soldier a crucifix as a prize. Yvonne told Rube, "I think they meant to give me the crucifix and you the cognac, as I'm barely old enough to drink." So, they switched and reveled in the support of their performance.

Several days later, Colonel Kay congratulated Rube on his performance.

"I thought I might be scared, but I remembered my friend Stuart and dedicated the dance to him. He was killed a couple of months before," said Rube.

"Sorry to hear that about your buddy, but that's common around here. You did a great job at the dance contest, and since you're in the entertainment business now, I thought you might be interested in being part of a security team for a USO show that will be coming to perform for the GIs."

"Now that sounds exciting. Who are the headliners?"

"How does Dinah Shore, Bob Hope, the Andrews Sisters, Jerry Colonna, and Frank Sinatra sound?"

"When do I start?"

Thirty-Eight

With the arrival of USO entertainers less than two weeks away, a certain amount of tension greeted the MP volunteers, even before the welcome speech. Captain Andrew Story's opening remarks added to the uneasy atmosphere when he said, "The next thirteen days will be a new experience for everyone in this room."

As Rube looked around the lecture hall, he noticed about a dozen WACs seated in the back row for the first time. The captain continued, "Our security team for the USO show will consist of vets, replacements, and WACs, and as a unit, we will train together, eat together, and, if necessary, fight together. Training is training. It's a time to learn. I don't care about how we trained in the past. But from this moment on, we will be a team. I don't want to hear a lot of bitching. We have a job to do, and we will fulfill our obligations. Any questions?"

All the MPs seemed surprised by the openness of the captain. The Army wanted to show off its best to the entertainers and press that would follow.

Most vets viewed the training with a jaundiced eye but seemed generally excited about hand-to-hand combat training against the WACs. Many men hadn't touched a woman's skin for months and couldn't wait for the battle of the sexes. After learning self-defense maneuvers, the games began. A few MPs were embarrassed as they landed on their butts after wrestling with some WACs. In other training sessions, Rube was surprised by the WACs' accuracy when firing weapons on the rifle range.

After a grueling day of physical exercise, Rube dragged his tired body back to the barracks. While walking, he heard a female voice shout, "You have a minute, Sergeant Goldfarb?" Turning around, Rube saw Sergeant Madison Belanger walking toward him. Rube had to admit she was the best-looking sergeant he had seen in the military.

"Sure," he answered. The answer would have been the same if she asked for an hour of his time. With her hair cut short, the proper Army-length skirt, and her five foot seven frame, the sergeant seemed more than confident in her abilities.

"How did my WACs do today?" she asked.

Rube thought briefly, saying, "I wouldn't want to meet any of them in a dark alley."

"You mean socially or militarily?"

"Neither!"

Rube's comment brought laughter from both sergeants. "Your squad performed quite well, and I was impressed," stated Rube. That brought a big smile to Sergeant Belanger's face. "The only negative came from my men, who seemed a little uneasy about training with women."

"Maybe one day in the future, this won't be a rare event but will be normal."

Rube hoped not but changed the subject by asking if Madison had been in any hot spots.

"Sergeant Goldfarb, you don't care about my answer. You want to know if I've ever been in any combat action, correct?"

"Well, yes."

"Okay, I didn't arrive in Europe until the end of March 1945. The war ended in early May, so I never endured any combat action. But after fighting ceased, I engaged in a combat situation."

"What happened?"

"I was with eighteen WACs escorting about forty female prisoners to a POW camp. Most of those in captivity were former Nazi supporters, concentration camp guards, and black marketeers. We traveled in a convoy of two troop carriers and three Jeeps. We were also transporting two fully armed GIs to a new location. As we came into a small village, our progress was blocked by a mob of over twenty men who attempted to free the prisoners. I was riding in a troop carrier when a Molotov cocktail hit the front windows, causing a fire to erupt.

"Shots were fired at those in the Jeeps. Each WAC had a pistol and a club, but I had what was known as a grease submachine gun. By the time my squad made it to the second troop carrier, the prisoners were escaping, and the WACs in the vehicles were being overwhelmed by the prisoners. The GIs halted the mob by hurling grenades into the crowd, but gunshots continued to be aimed at my squad. I had no choice but to open fire with my machine gun, as did the GIs. Three of my WACs were badly beaten, and I noticed one being carried away by a guy who had her slung over his shoulder. I managed a lucky shot that found its way between legs that struck the ground and bounced into the guy's Achilles heel. As the man stumbled to the ground, I rescued my WAC. While this was taking place, another convoy with about a hundred GIs appeared, and for the next half hour, it was a scene of hand-to-hand combat. It had to be the scariest time in my life."

"I had a similar experience during my first combat mission," admitted Rube.

Madison continued, "With the help of the GIs from the other convoy, my squad of WACs held firm until the rioters were subdued."

"Did you get all the prisoners back?"

"All but six, who were killed. The prisoners and the members of the mob suffered so many additional casualties that another convoy of trucks had to be sent to transport the wounded to medical centers. But three members of my squad suffered broken bones, two had concussions, one was cut with a knife, and another lost three teeth when hit with a rock in the face. Our worst casualties came from gunshots fired by those in the mob. Thankfully, the few who were hit escaped serious life-threatening injuries. Besides bumps and bruises, the rest of the WACs completed the mission, but seeing the enemy combatants receive the same medical treatment as my girls, made me cringe. It just didn't seem right since many of the POWs watched and were accomplices to what transpired in the concentration camps. I'm sure none showed remorse for the calamity the Nazis created worldwide."

"One hell of a story."

"After that experience, I was a perfect candidate for crowd control. How about you? Did you see much action?"

"Too much, but I don't want to talk about it now."

"I understand."

"But I do have a personal question for you. Don't take this wrong, but your body looks like you must have been a dancer or did a lot of dancing."

"Excellent observation. Before the war, I danced with the Rockettes in New York City."

"You were a Rockette? So, why did you join the military?"

"When my brother enlisted, I did the same."

"I give you a lot of credit."

"Since you asked me about dancing, do you dance?"

"While in Antwerp, I found a place to dance, and if I'm not on duty, I dance at least three times a week with my partner."

"Really!"

"It would be great if the singers in the show would allow some GIs to dance to their music, and I hope to ask them if that would be possible when they arrive."

"If you get a positive response, let me know, and I'm sure most of my girls would be more than happy to join you on stage."

"Are you aware there will be two shows, one at night and the next day in the afternoon; would that be a problem for you and your WACs?"

"Not to my knowledge unless some disaster takes place."

"I have a problem with the show in the afternoon; my partner needs to work and won't be available."

"I think I know where you can find a temporary partner."

"Are you talking about yourself? Do you know how to dance to swing music?"

"Does a Rockette kick high during a chorus line? I think this can work, partner."

———•———

Thirty-Nine

The next day, with twenty-five MPs under the command of Wendell Pike, the team began planning security arrangements for the show. All GIs placed their names next to three specific security duties they would like to perform. Rube selected crowd control, guest security, and transportation supervision.

Major Pike gave a brief speech to the MPs and WACs, emphasizing the importance of protecting the entertainers. He spoke further about the proper behavior displayed while circulating with the guests. His last words dealt with the MPs' appearance and willingness to answer to the needs of the performers.

Twenty-four hours later, the names of those selected for various security positions were posted on a board outside of headquarters. Rube couldn't be happier, as he found his name next to the protection of guests and transportation security. He didn't have much to learn since he had experience in convoy security. But he never expected the detailed training he received in guest protection. Included was everything from dealing with hostage situations to negotiating with kidnappers. He also spent several hours learning self-defense. Even firing his pistol at the target range came into play. The final piece of the training consisted of learning about the entertainers. The Army left no stone unturned to satisfy and protect those Americans who volunteered to travel thousands of miles to be with the troops.

A few days before the tour's arrival, the MPs and WACs assigned to escort each performer were taken into the facilities where they would stay and to the dressing rooms. For security reasons, they also took a tour of the area where the show would be held.

A crowd had gathered to watch the flight carrying the guests land at the airstrip near Antwerp. His first glance at the guests left Rube somewhat let down. Like anyone else who traveled, they waited for their luggage to be delivered. Immediately, six MPs rushed to their assistance. When the bags arrived, Rube carried Dinah Shore's luggage to his Jeep. Her agent and make-up specialist joined them. Rube expected Dinah to sing a song while they were driving back to camp, but she just talked about the flight over, much like any ordinary traveler on a trip.

Dinah was delighted and asked Rube if he had a girl back home. The MP announced with a sigh, "No, Jody got her." Then Rube had to explain the meaning of Jody. But he added, "I have a gal here who is my dance partner, and we just won a prize in a dance contest."

"Did you dance to one of my songs?" questioned Dinah.

"No, ma'am, but we danced to the song by the Andrews Sisters, "Bugle Boy."

"Let me ask the sisters if they might let you dance when they sing it at the show." Rube was thrilled about that!

Once at headquarters, reporters surrounded the touring group. With officers and those sneaking a peek at the stars having encircled performers, the MPs had to rescue them from the chaotic scene and escort the group to the mess hall. They were served a wonderful meal because they hadn't eaten since leaving the United States. Even the cooks were dressed to perfection. On one occasion, Rube observed a server politely say, "Yes, ma'am, I can get you another plate and heat your meal." Rube remembered that man saying to a GI, "You want what? This isn't a five-star restaurant. Get your ass outta here." Rube realized the regular GIs would never receive the same service as the VIP guests, but it sure would be a welcome change.

Moving the performers to their rooms was another adventure, as autograph seekers blocked their departure. Rube bumped into Frank Sinatra as he tried to plow through the crowd with Dinah's suitcases. Once settled, Rube knocked on Bob Hope's door and asked, "Do you need anything, sir?"

Bob said with a chuckle, "Two new knees!"

In the lobby, the Andrew Sisters were surrounded by WACs. Rube interrupted and said, "Ladies, please follow me to your room."

As two MPs carried their luggage, one of the Andrew Sisters said, "Thanks for rescuing us. I need a bathroom break."

At night after dinner, the performers went to the stage where they would perform two shows, with about 8,000 GIs at each.

The entire cast came to the stage area at sunrise and rehearsed for the night show.

While rehearsing, Rube spotted the Andrew Sisters and told them how he danced to their song, "Bugle Boy."

"Oh, you must be the dancer Dinah told us about?"

Somewhat bashful, Rube answered, "Yes."

"You're up," called a stage crewman to the musical trio.

One of the sisters said, "Rube, when we start to sing "Bugle Boy," come out and dance with me." Rube's knees wobbled a bit, but he pulled himself together, and when Patty Andrews waved to him, he joined her as the girls started the song. Rube found she could dance and easily followed his lead.

When they finished, both were *schvitzing* (sweating). Rube told Patty, "There's nothing better than a good dance to bring out the sweat."

The show's top performer, Frank Sinatra, practiced a few songs and left to visit men in the hospital. Dinah Shore blasted the song "My Mama Done Told Me." And Bob Hope practiced delivering one-liner jokes.

Just before a new shift of MPs and WACs arrived for duty at the USO compound building, Rube heard someone shout, "MP, I need to talk to you."

As Rube turned toward the direction of the voice, he recognized Frank Sinatra. Rube replied, "How can I help you?"

"Why don't you step into my room so we can talk." Inside a spacious room with a small bar, record player, and a king-size bed, the teen idol flopped on a cushiony sofa and lit a smoke. "Do you want one?"

"Not at this moment, but thanks for offering," answered Rube.

"I'm glad to come here to perform for the troops, but it gets lonely out here."

"You need not tell me about it; I've been there many times."

"Now you see that bar over there. It's empty except for a few glasses. You wouldn't know a place where I could purchase some liquid refreshments?"

"I understand. I know a place, but it's guarded."

"Come again?"

"We had confiscated a lot of liquor and wine from black marketeers. It's in a storage facility on the base, but a guard is always stationed at the entrance."

"Do you think you might be able to acquire a few bottles?" inquired Sinatra.

"I doubt it; I know a few officers and a few sergeants visit the place, and I'm sure they don't leave empty-handed, but you have to know the right people to get inside."

"Aren't you a sergeant?"

"Yes, but as I said, you need the right connections before permission is granted to obtain a few bottles."

"Would money help?"

"Doubtful."

"How about my name?"

"That might work, but those with the authority to issue the requests have left the base for the evening."

"Damn, you don't know anyone else?"

"Not really."

"I was hoping to find a few people who could come over and spend the evening with me and have a drink."

"Why not invite the cast members of the USO?"

"I see them all the time."

"Well, I wish we had a bunch of starlets over here, but our cast only includes grunts and a few WACs."

"I saw a few of those WACs. I guess I'll spend the evening alone."

"Hold it; I might find a way. I'm supposed to practice for the show with my dance partner in ten minutes. She's the sergeant in charge of the WACs and used to be a professional dancer with the Rockettes."

"Really?"

"Let me talk to her, and maybe we can work something out."

Several minutes later, Rube met up with the WAC sergeant. "Madison, I have a problem."

"You always have a problem."

"That's true," said Rube with a chuckle. "This one could be solved but involves some adventure."

"Are you including me in your adventure? Most men tell me the same story that ends up in the same place, in their bedroom."

"Well … I must admit the same is true this time, but it's much different."

"How's that?"

"Well, I'm involved, and another guy is in the picture."

"Are we talking about a *ménage à trois*?"

"I wouldn't go that far, but the other guy might have participated in a few."

"Who is the other guy?"

"Frank Sinatra."

"What?"

"Yes, the singer."

"Frank Sinatra wants me to come into his room?"

"Yes, but there's more to the story."

"This does sound like an adventure. Continue, this is getting interesting."

"Well, he told me it's lonely at the base, and he would like to have some guests over during the evening."

"What are we waiting for?"

"Well, there is a catch."

"There's always a catch. Is sex involved?"

"I'm unsure, but he wants me to bring some alcohol."

"Where could you get that?"

"I know some of the guys have a stash somewhere, but if they find out their booze is going to Frank Sinatra, we'll have a mob scene …. There is another option. Are you aware of a cellar in a storage facility on the base filled with wine and liquor confiscated from black marketeers?"

"I heard the girls talking about it. They say it's guarded day and night."

"That's correct."

"Rube, I see that look in your eye. You must be working on a plan to steal some hooch."

"I wouldn't say steal. Acquire is the right word."

"You know if we're caught, we could get busted."

"I know that, so let me ask you again, are you still in?"

"Hell, yes!"

At 2100, a Jeep carrying two sergeants stopped about fifty yards from the storage facility. Sergeant Madison Belanger, fully dressed in her WAC uniform, departed the Jeep while Rube parked it behind a dumpster.

From a distance, Rube watched a very tense guard relax as Madison used her charm, and he eventually escorted her into the storage building. About ten minutes later, she reappeared carrying a cardboard box filled with half a dozen bottles. Before she left, she gave the guard a big hug and a kiss. While Madison and the guard said goodbye, Rube drove the Jeep to the front of the storage building. Saluting Madison, Rube shouted to the guard that the general would be quite gratified for the help he provided at this time. The guard smiled and saluted. Madison placed the box into the Jeep, and it was off to see Frank Sinatra.

"How did you pull that off?" asked Rube.

"I told him the truth."

"I don't buy it."

"I told him that this order came from the general, but it was to be kept quiet and then told him who would be given the booze. He knew about the show and Frank Sinatra being in it, and I told him he could be my security since I would also be in the show. I also promised him a signed photograph of Frank Sinatra that he could send to his girlfriend back home."

Returning to Sinatra's room was easy, but both had no idea what to expect. Frank greeted them with open arms, and the party commenced.

After Rube introduced Madison to the singer, the MP used his Bowie knife to wiggle the corks from the bottles. Like dogs waiting for their meal to be placed in a dish, the threesome salivated as the liquor inside the bottles jiggled. Both sergeants drank from different wine bottles, and Frank claimed a bottle of champagne for himself. After the first gulp, the faces of the group of three resembled a child tasting ice cream for the first time. By 2200, several empty bottles lay on the floor, and Frank turned on the record player and listened to the music of Bessie Smith. The music seemed to create an atmosphere conducive for Frank to sing a few of his songs. He then asked Rube and Madison to show him the dance they were performing in the show. Removing the bottles from the floor, Frank found some swing music, allowing Rube and Madison to practice their routine. Rube noticed Madison's balance wasn't the greatest, and she seemed to brush against him more than usual. He wasn't sure if it was the booze or if Madison deliberately caused the extra contact. Frank asked if he could swing some with Madison after they danced. Frank attempted to twirl her around playfully, but his balance was also lopsided. With limited mobility, both held each other up and danced as if slow music were playing in the background. Frank's hands seemed to slip on a few occasions, but Madison didn't seem upset as her hands also slipped.

After a few more drinks and another empty bottle, Frank recalled playing spin the bottle at parties when he was young. In a somewhat drunken state, he announced, "Why don't we play that game tonight?" Neither Rube nor Madison objected, and all three sat on the floor and began spinning the bottle. Since Madison was the only girl, kisses came from both men, and she also kissed each man. After a dozen spins, Frank's evening came to an end. Frank passed out because of the booze, the trip flying across the Atlantic Ocean, or a combination of both. It took about ten minutes for Rube and Madison to tuck him into bed. With two bottles unopened, the MP and WAC took one each, and the inebriated male sergeant drove cautiously back to the barracks where Madison's security team resided.

Before leaving the Jeep, Madison leaned over and gave Rube a big kiss and said, "That was one hell of an adventure. I loved every second. See you in the morning."

As she entered the barracks, Rube heard her holler, "What the hell is going on here? You ladies should have been in bed an hour ago, and we have a big day scheduled tomorrow."

Another voice shouted, "How you look, you must have had one hell of an adventure tonight."

"I beg your pardon. Why would you say that?"

Before Madison could utter another word, Rube appeared in the barracks holding a bottle of cognac. Totally oblivious to his surroundings, Rube proclaimed, "You left this in the Jeep." Instantly, laughter consumed the entire barracks.

Thinking quickly, Madison took the bottle from Rube and shouted, "Ladies, I brought this home for you." Cheers erupted among the WACs as Madison winked toward Rube, and he reciprocated with a wink and quickly exited the barracks.

Recovered from his late evening adventure, the next day, Rube brought Yvonne to the early evening show, where they danced to the songs of the Andrews Sisters with other GIs dancing with some of Madison's WACs. Both shows went on without a hitch, and in the afternoon show, Rube danced with his new partner. All the acts were great, but the pin-up girl, Margaret Stewart, received the most whistles.

At the after party, the night of the last performance, with Yvonne at his side, Rube had a chance to talk to some stars. All seemed thrilled at the reception they received. The women entertainers approved of Yvonne's sexy dress, and Dinah gave her a pair of nylon hose. Each performer handed out photos with their signatures to the lucky guys who provided the security for the last two days.

The only person unhappy about the show was Yvonne; she seemed upset because Rube danced with the Rockette and felt he no longer would want to dance with her. Rube assured her that couldn't be further from the truth. He explained that he had greater chemistry with her than the Rockette. But she said the Rockette was prettier. Rube replied, "A make-up artist can make you just as pretty."

"Rube, do you think I could become a Rockette?"
"Why not? Just keep working; you have the skills and talent."

Part VI:

Homeward Bound

Forty

The entertainers and the USO became a distant memory as the rush to "Bring the boys back home" reached a crescendo. Most soldiers would see the U.S. mainland very soon, but Rube was not in that category.

Rube was chosen for another assignment. The Belgian population had provided the Third Reich with thousands of volunteers. Now that the war was over, no one could predict how those who survived would respond to the new order when they returned.

It didn't take long before bodies began to pile up on the streets of Antwerp. It was as if Al Capone and Bugsy Siegel were staging a gang war, and Rube and the MPs were in the middle. Revenge killings became the norm, not the exception.

Rube happened to uncover one of the worst incidents. When riding in his Jeep, he noticed a crowd of people in an indoor parking area. As he approached, the crowd dispersed, and he became sick. A string of lifeless bodies oozing blood lay in contorted positions along a wall. As Rube attempted to regain his composure, he noticed a line of bullet holes on the wall behind the victims, resembling the size and form of bullets fired from a machine gun. One thing he could compare with what he had just seen was pictures of the Valentine's Day massacre in Chicago. Because this mass murder occurred in Antwerp on October 31, it became known as the Halloween Massacre.

Almost all MPs from Antwerp spent time at the scene of the crime. Over a dozen Jeeps stretched around the block. Even a general visited. Rube, who reported the massacre, had time to investigate before the rush of local police and MPs arrived. Walking between the bodies, he counted eight, including two women. They had undoubtedly been mowed down by at least one or two machine guns. Yet he found no cartridges. He almost stumbled when his foot hit a body. By chance, a shell rolled out from under one of the dead. He picked it up and placed it in his pocket. Then he followed a blood trail leading to another victim outside the garage. He figured it must have taken less than a minute to gun down these people. But so far, no one had told him they heard the shots. The parking lot was in a commercial area but not far from a series of apartments.

After interviewing a few people, he obtained enough information to believe those murdered were pro-Nazi supporters. Other MPs canvassed the neighborhood without much success. One piece of evidence discovered at the scene was footprints, some covered in blood.

As for the MPs, local officials, and police, they hoped this wasn't the start of a new war.

Rube had difficulty falling asleep as the day's events kept flashing in his mind. It reminded him of when he entered a pillbox filled with broken bodies. It took almost two months before he placed the horrible scene in the back of his mind. After glancing at the clock, which read after midnight, Rube realized that he would have to report to a group of officers in ten hours. He still hadn't completed the outline of what he would tell them before sleep finally ended this horrible day.

At 0900, Rube walked into Colonel Kay's office and immediately focused on the sullen faces of several officers. Colonel Kay initiated the meeting, commenting, "What do you have besides many dead bodies?"

Rube reached into his pocket and rolled a 30-caliber cartridge across the table surrounded by officers. Each picked up the cartridge and agreed it could have been fired from several weapons. Rube began, "That's our first piece of evidence. Now how many groups legally possess these weapons? I can only think of one, the local police. I'm not saying they're responsible for this criminal act, so let's move on. Second, as all of you know, in the last two months, there have been fifteen incidents of murder involving nearly three dozen people. To my knowledge, there hasn't been one arrest. Either the police are incompetent or don't want to make any arrests. Still, I'm not sure they are behind what is happening.

"Next, we must look at the church, where opposing groups pray and hate each other. The divide between the Flemish people and other Catholic parishioners is great, and only if the community leaders can walk the fine line between them can a healthy atmosphere be maintained. If the balance is broken by a leader who seems to favor only one side, violence becomes possible.

"Add to the mix the return of pro-Nazi people who joined Hitler's army, and you have a pot about to explode. It doesn't mean this is the only reason for the rise in crime and murders."

Colonel Kay interrupted, "With all the potential predators among the local population we can see the difficulty in finding the culprits. Do you have anything more specific to report?"

"Sir, our most visible clues, in this case, are the bloody footprints left at the crime scene. We could ascertain that at least three people participated in the massacre. There were three footprints, specifically two larger and a smaller one. We believe at least two males and one female were at the crime scene. At this point, we're unsure if all three fired weapons. But at least three individuals in the city have blood stains on the bottom of their shoes.

"Finally, families who have been enemies for years continue to battle for power. At a time when it's possible to kill without being prosecuted, the opportunity to eliminate the opposition is great."

"So, what we have are a lot of dead bodies. Does anyone else have anything to add, except let's get the hell out of here?" asked Colonel Kay.

"What options do we have?" questioned one of the officers.

"Little, but maybe if we start a campaign that explains why revenge killing is not the answer, that might help some," said Rube.

"But most people don't care about reasoning," offered another officer.

Rube responded, "Exactly, but we must try. Maybe we can limit the number of murders until we depart, whenever that happens."

Colonel Kay asked, "Does anyone besides Rube have any other suggestions about how to deal with the investigation?" No one could offer any new ideas. Rube pleaded for a few more days to conclude the investigation, and it was granted.

Unknown to Rube, a meeting of officers was held later that night. It was the consensus of those at the meeting that time spent investigating the massacre would only hamper and slow down the withdrawal of troops. It was decided that officers wouldn't lead the investigation but would oversee its findings. After a short discussion they decided to search for someone who could devote more time and energy to the investigation. "How about the young man who gave the report to us?" called out an officer.

"If he is successful great. If not, so be it," responded another officer.

The next day, Rube was informed he would be the lead investigator in the Halloween Massacre.

Rube's first attempt to discover any link to the crime came when he talked to his dancers.

On a cold Sunday night, he addressed the group and assured them that MPs would be stationed in front of the entrance to the basement while the group danced. He then spent fifteen minutes informing them to avoid being caught in the web of revenge killings. While talking, Rube tried to identify any signs of blood stains on their shoes that might implicate them at the scene of the crime but drew a blank.

In an attempt to find blood-covered shoes or boots, Rube and other MPs continued interviewing cobblers who sold new or repaired old shoes. Only three cobblers were able to provide some information about the gruesome murders. The first had sold and repaired shoes for three people, but all were senior citizens. The second repaired three sets of shoes, but all had extensive damage, meaning any footprint could be easily identified. The footprints discovered at the crime scene had no sign of shoe damage.

The third sold a half dozen shoes after the massacre but discarded the old shoes in a trash bin, which had been taken to a city dump two days before. For Rube and the MPs, the shoe trail vanished.

PART VI: HOMEWARD BOUND

A few days later, "Not enough," said Colonel Kay. "According to you, other people were in the garage when you arrived, correct?" Rube nodded yes. "At that time, you didn't see them carrying any weapons; is that correct?" Rube nodded again. "Even if we had more evidence and could legally take their shoes, it would take months for an agency like the FBI to determine if the marks on the bottom of their shoes were blood and matched those people who were murdered. I feel it's best to keep our relationship with the community positive and that we shouldn't attempt to arrest anyone but allow the local police to investigate further and let them make the final call if an arrest should be made."

"No argument from me. I agree," said Rube.

Forty-One

Some call the hot summer month of August, the dog days. Despite the heat, work continued to facilitate bringing U.S. troops and war equipment back home across the Atlantic. The decision on whether to send Rube's MP battalion from Europe to Asia remained a mystery until August 6, 1945.

Much like all days since V-E Day, the soldiers remaining in parts of Europe waited for clarification as to their status. A radio report changed everything when it announced that the U.S. had dropped a bomb on Hiroshima in Japan.

"So, what's the big deal? Millions of bombs have been dropped during the war," remarked an MP in Rube's unit.

"Not like this one, and it destroyed the whole city," responded Rube.

"Holy hell, I didn't know we had a bomb that powerful," called out a sergeant.

On August 9, 1945, another one of these bombs was dropped on Nagasaki, and two days later, Japan surrendered.

No one could believe the war was over. No one was going to Asia. Instead, most of the troops were going home. GIs celebrated day and night. It wouldn't take long before most of the GIs began the long trip back to America. However, some had to remain to help with the final removal of troops from Europe. Rube stayed.

As fall approached, revenge killings subsided. It's hard to determine if the efforts of the MPs, local police, and the church were responsible for the decline. Still, working with the community officials did seem to lessen the tension throughout the city. Another positive came with the rebuilding that had begun from the ashes left behind by the war.

Rube spent the next few months working to provide passage back to the states for thousands of GIs. As Thanksgiving approached, the remaining MP staff planned a big dinner for military personnel and invited some local citizens and friends of the soldiers.

Yvonne stood next to Rube as everyone in the military wore their best uniforms. Even though Yvonne couldn't match the attire displayed by the other women, she looked pretty.

The dinner had all the trimmings. The turkey tasted wonderful, and in Rube's own words, "There was plenty of champagne and more champagne that my cup overflowed." The couple even had time to dance as D. D. Davis, a corporal from the 333rd, played some hot jazz music on the piano.

After celebrating the holiday, Rube returned to work, and learned the meaning of the slogan "The air at the top is much different than from below." Since Rube had been made lead investigator in the Halloween Massacre, the new sergeant had taken plenty of criticism for not having a plan of action for stopping the violence. True, the murder rate in the city had skyrocketed just after the war's conclusion but had declined until the massacre. No one seemed to blame the crime wave on the return of former Nazi supporters or the shortage of all types of items or food. People were trying to survive any way they could, and despite the efforts of community leaders, the church, and MPs, crime became a big part of the recovery. Rube never mentioned it, but he felt some in the city made him the scapegoat. In other words, being Jewish made him the perfect target, just like the Nazis blamed the Jews for all of Germany's difficulties.

Forty-Two

During World War II, the American military faced many problems dealing with numbers. It had to deal with the number of supplies, casualties, or replacement troops, but for those serving, there was only one number every GI wanted to hear, and that was the number of points each GI had to have before being eligible to return to the states. For Rube, that number was fifty-six. A soldier could acquire points from success in past performances, completing a mission, or showing proficiency in a particular area. Rube was close to that number, but something always happened, leaving him just short of accumulating the necessary points.

When Rube heard that Colonel Kay wanted to see him in his office at 1300, he knew that trouble would soon be part of his future. Promptly, at the appropriate time, he entered the colonel's office. "Nice to see you again, Rube. I know you have been busting your ass sending GIs home, and you probably wonder when your time will come. I've just been handed this new assignment and immediately thought about you. Aren't you a few points away from heading home?"

"You're right about that, sir," answered Rube.

"For that reason, I'm moving you temporarily from your present duties of returning GIs home to finding who is responsible for recent thefts of very valuable items. You will have enough points to return home when you complete this assignment. Crystal Sylk, short a few points, will join you. Crystal has served as a WAC for four years, and she will be able to provide valuable assistance in solving this mystery."

At first glance, Rube was amazed at the figure of this woman, and she looked more like a football linebacker than a woman who measured five foot six. To Rube, she had more muscles than he did with her 180-pound frame.

"I know both of you are looking for points to go home. If you complete this assignment, you should be home before Christmas. Here's what's going on. A gang of black marketeers has stolen, on two separate occasions, dozens of crates of women's stockings that could be worth thousands of dollars. We want you to track where these items are going and who is responsible for stealing them off the trains. So, I will send you to Brussels to check out a few department stores and women's lingerie businesses to see if any stolen merchandise has appeared in those markets. I expect a report in a week. You will each have a room in a building in Brussels to work and sleep. Good hunting."

Rube had some misgivings about this assignment, especially working with a woman as his partner. On the last day of November, the two investigators moved into their quarters after a train ride from Antwerp to Brussels. Everything the colonel had expressed proved accurate except the word, sleep. Rube, whose room was next to Corporal Sylk's, had his sleep constantly interrupted by Crystal performing exercises throughout the evening. He heard her lifting and dropping weights. Then came the sounds of grunts and swearing, and finally, his room shook as she did her jumping jacks.

Most of the people Rube and Crystal interviewed seemed eager to provide information about the missing silk stockings. The appearance of Rube and Crystal seemed to heighten each person's desire to talk. They discovered the stolen merchandise began arriving in stores just days after the robbery. When asked to identify the distributors, all mentioned the same characteristics. After learning about the facial features and size of the individual, Rube and Crystal had a clear picture of the culprit. Upon further interviews with other storekeepers, especially those in women's apparel, the two MPs were provided with an additional lead as another accomplice emerged — a woman.

When meeting in Colonel Kay's office a week later, both investigators gave an incomplete picture of what they had uncovered.

"I'm not happy," insisted the colonel.

"Neither am I," retorted Rube.

"I hope you have something else to tell me," the colonel impatiently commented.

"I do."

"Let's hear it."

"I would like the Army to provide a security team for the next shipment."

"I thought about that. Not on my watch. Can you imagine what would happen if some reporter discovered that the Army was using its workforce to guard a stash of silk stockings? I'm on my way out of the Army within minutes of its publication."

"I fully understand. That's why we will unload the hose directly from the train and leave them at the warehouse, but our well-armed convoy will move on to Antwerp with only empty crates. So, if we are attacked, the headlines would only report an attack on an American convoy."

"That's not bad, but what about the stockings that remain at the warehouse?"

"That's the best part. We have buyers make the transactions in the warehouse under our supervision, and no more stolen goods."

"I like it. Let's do it."

Despite the colonel's approval, Rube wasn't sure about his plan. His biggest concern dealt with loose lips. In this case, someone could easily rip a hole in the "hose" by revealing the plan to those who supported the black marketeers. Nonetheless, a security patrol of six vehicles would make the trip between Brussels and Antwerp, including a half-track, four Jeeps filled with MPs, and a truck carrying nothing but empty boxes.

Once again, the MPs realized they were the pawns in the operation, which most likely would come under attack by the ambushers. Thanks to Crystal, the plans for the decoy convoy took only hours to develop instead of days. Like a hurricane speeding through a small eastern shore town, she bulldozed past the red tape, and except for a few items, she was ready to start the mission to Antwerp. Rube heard an exhausted GI who helped Crystal arrange all the necessary supplies and time schedules say, "That's one crazy woman."

While Crystal was assembling the convoy, Rube watched where the crates of hosiery were being stored in the warehouse. In addition, he observed an Army photographer taking pictures of the serial numbers of each crate. As the photographer completed his job and retreated from the darkness of the warehouse, Rube recognized Jason Wiley. The two had met on another occasion, and his photograph in the *Stars and Stripes* newspaper had caused Rube some anguish. The first thing Rube said to Jason was, "Planning to do any more partially nude photos?"

Jason, who always had a comment, stated with a smile, "Times were tough, and I had to give the GIs something to look at besides war footage."

"I understand, but you owe me one," said Rube. The two conversed for about twenty minutes, and Jason agreed to be Rube's lookout. He would spend the night on the top floor of the warehouse and photograph any unusual activities. If any suspicious activity occurred, he would contact Rube from a radio that the MP secured for him.

Two hours into the trip, Rube's radio came to life, and Jason's loud and clear voice punctured the air. "Are you aware of a Major Steinhorn?"

"I've heard of the name …. Sure, the major died in the battle of Brest."

"Well, someone by that name signed orders to remove your precious cargo to another depot."

"What? How far has this gone?"

"They are loading three trucks right now and should depart in ten minutes."

"Any way to stop them?"

"I see about fifteen armed men."

"Alright, watch what direction they take. Thanks!" Rube turned to Crystal and said, "Find those maps we took. Unless there is a shortcut somewhere, they will travel on roads parallel to ours."

Jason confirmed Rube's prediction, and Rube and his team crisscrossed country roads and splashed over small creeks to intercept the black marketeers. Even when the convoy ran into a stretch without a road, the half-track created one. The race to stop the heist of the silk stockings concluded at a crossroads about ten miles from Antwerp.

Rube's team, having arrived early, waited patiently for the illegal convoy to arrive. Rube and Crystal each took grenades and gave four to MPs riding in Jeeps. Others, well-armed, would remain hidden along the road and wait for the signal to move.

The signal would be the explosive sounds of grenades thrown by Rube, Crystal, and the other GIs in front of the escaping vehicles. As the trucks carrying silk stockings came into view and approached Rube's position in a syncopated motion, five arms released the grenades, and within eight seconds, the explosion stopped the convoy in its tracks. Before the black marketeers could react, the MPs surrounded them, and fifteen smugglers surrendered after a short firefight. Among those prisoners now held were thirteen men and two women. One of the men fit the description given to Rube and Crystal of the distributor of the stolen items. Also among the captives was a woman who matched the description given by other witnesses of the female involved. A second woman turned out to be a buyer from one of the department stores.

After all the prisoners had been secured and guarded, Rube conducted a roll call of all his team. All answered, "Here, sir," except one, Crystal Sylk. This started a panic search for her body or remains. After a half-hour search which found nothing, Rube and Corporal Ronald Simpkins walked back to the team's radio and prepared to send a missing-in-action report to headquarters; as they passed the driver's cabin of one of the trucks, they saw a face appear in the window. Reaching for their weapons, they suddenly stopped as they identified the face of Crystal in the window.

"Where in the hell have you been?" a frustrated Rube shouted.

"Well, when the shooting started, I left," Crystal answered sheepishly.

"You what ...? You left?"

"Yes, I didn't even throw my grenade. I couldn't do it."

"I'll be damned," answered Rube.

Those were the same words used by Colonel Kay. He continued, "I have no answers for you, sergeant, and I'm just stunned."

Rube said, "Here's my take. I'm sure all guys dream about going on a date with a beautiful girl with everything, looks, charm, and a great body, and when she accepts your invitation, you go bonkers. But for whatever reason, it doesn't click. Instead of what you hoped, it is far less than you expected. I'll let your mind deal with that last part. Crystal was the perfect match for an assignment with the MPs. She was strong, tough, and aggressive, making witnesses so uncomfortable that they didn't have to be coerced to talk. But when things got hot, she bailed."

"I couldn't have said it any better myself," said the colonel. "But as you know, many soldiers freeze on the battlefield."

"But with her scary demeanor, she would be the last one I would expect to bolt. To be honest she scared the hell out of me," said Rube.

"That makes two of us."

Rube then saw a big smile on the colonel's face and then came something that Rube never heard before. The colonel laughed, as did Rube.

Even though the silk stockings mission came to a successful conclusion, Rube only secured one point because of the near disaster that was only avoided by the photographer's action. Again, like so many times in the past, it seemed to Rube that every time he accumulated enough points to be eligible to return to the United States an unfortunate event took place.

At first, Rube thought it was due to the massacre; then, he suspected it had something to do with antisemitism. He even scheduled a meeting with Colonel Kay and presented his theory. The colonel disagreed and said, "Any reason for not sending you home is complicated by the good work you are doing and the need to transport many GIs home before the holidays. I believe none of this has to do with acts of antisemitism against you." Rube accepted the colonel's rationale.

After meeting with the colonel, Rube wrote Bobbi.

December 6, 1945

Dear Bobbi,
I just completed a mission and was supposed to receive three

points. Now I'm being told that since the mission was not a total success, I'm only getting one point which still leaves me short of qualifying to come home. I can't help bitching. I'm sure my time will come, but I don't know when I will return. We are still sending thousands of GIs home weekly.

How are things back home? Have you lost any more weight? Can't wait to see you.

I'm still dancing when I can. Life as a sergeant sometimes is more demanding than when I was a corporal. You always put out fires, and the men aren't as friendly. For all the extra time I'm putting in, even the additional pay doesn't afford me any more glory.

Stay well!
Always,
Rube

Forty-Three

Little has been written or revealed about one of the greatest missions of World War II, the return of American troops from Europe. The massive operation would last until the latter part of 1946 and beyond. Thousands of men and women who were part of this massive operation received very little press or accolades for safely bringing millions of troops home. Their job sounded simple — place a GI on a boat, plane, or train, and all that remained were the welcome home parades and parties for those returning.

Overlooked were the hundreds of hours spent by those working to complete the tasks. First, they had to find the vehicles needed to transport the troops. Second, they had to arrange the final destinations for those returning to their hometowns in America. Third, they had to complete the paper trail that covered everything from orders to arrival time. Finally, they had to provide all the personal items necessary for the trip home. For those working in "Operation Hometown," every day became a mind-blowing experience, as burnouts limited the time of those working on the project. Workers were often on the job for twelve to fifteen hours, and no labor union in America would accept such conditions for its employees. Another more sinister variable muddied the waters — many working in this operation used their position to become rich and powerful.

All these factors would land on the desk of Rube Goldfarb, now wearing a symbol of staff sergeant on his sleeve. Although still a member of the 399th MP regiment, he volunteered to be part of the massive return home project when the Army realized the magnitude of completing such a task. Rube took pride in his new job, even though it meant working long hours.

To him, bringing the troops safely home became his reward and exceeded some of his accomplishments on the battlefield. Once an armada of ships and planes was acquired to transport the troops home, getting the men back home accelerated.

As Rube's office hours began to expand, his time dancing with Yvonne greatly decreased. Everyday thousands of names of troops arrived at his department. His staff of over fifty people rarely had time for a break, as the rush home became a stampede. One thing that Rube noticed about his position was that he had become extremely powerful, which caused others to seek him out to use his newly acquired authority. There wasn't a day he didn't receive letters, calls, or telegrams from people of authority, urging him to approve sending home a certain individual. He often thought about how one in his position could become quite wealthy and powerful. Rube's premonition proved true when he began to receive letters that offered him a gift or a stipend for his assistance if he could bring home a certain soldier early. After accumulating dozens of this type of letter, Rube would always send back the letter with a note, notifying the sender he would do his best to bring their loved one home as soon as possible. As part of the letter, Rube clearly stated that he could not accept any type of gifts but a thank you response would be welcomed. Many times, Rube thought he was one stupid fool, but he always returned to doing what was right. Rube, however, wondered about those who didn't think the same way.

While Americans prepared for holiday shopping at home, the Antwerp contingent, in the rush to send the GIs state side had reached the breaking point. After working a twelve-hour day, Rube decided to stop at a local cafe for a drink. While having a mixture of Coke and rum, he heard a voice ask, "May I join you?"

"Absolutely," answered Rube to Sergeant Madison Belanger. Over the next fifteen minutes, the two sergeants dealt with an untold consequence of the war. Each tempered their dialogue to focus on how the end of the war would impact their lives.

"Rube, please don't think I'm not grateful; in fact, I'm delirious the war is over, but I'm somewhat scared."

"Why is that?"

"Everything we did during the war is now obsolete."

"I don't understand."

"The war changed everything in our lives. It took us away from our families, relatives and friends and brought us into an environment totally different. No longer secure, we feared for our lives and did things beyond anything we could imagine. We established our own rules of law and in a sense had enormous freedom. We met a whole new group of people and adjusted to a new way of life. Everyday there was no normal. Who would have thought there is now a bomb that can destroy a whole city. Time is moving so fast it's going to be hard to return to the old normal. In a few months we will encounter what used to be normal even though we have changed and the world around us has changed."

"I thought I was the only one who had a similar viewpoint."

"It's hard to imagine becoming a civilian again."

"Well at least you will have a job when you go home."

"Not true, Rube. All the Rockettes must be between the age of 18 and 23 years old, I'm about to turn 22. I love dancing but there is no way in less than a year I will be able to perform at the level needed to be a Rockette. How about you Rube, where do you stand?"

"I hate to say it. I have no job, no career or business awaiting me when I return home. I would like to open a dry-cleaning business but at this time I don't have the money."

"Are you and Yvonne planning to continue your relationship when you return home?"

"No, as you can see my future is somewhat cloudy. I have a lot of things to figure out."

"I understand."

"Our situation is like an athlete whose talent has diminished and he realizes it's time to return to a different lifestyle."

"So true, but athletes at the end of the road have money."

"Maybe, but we have the rest of our lives to achieve our dreams."

"I like that," responded Madison.

Looking at his watch, Rube remarked, "Damn I'm late for a meeting. I've got to go."

"Me too, we are still in the Army and obligated to complete our duties at least until we receive our discharge papers."

"Well, Madison, if we don't meet again, all the best to you."

"Same to you Rube."

Both sergeants rose to their feet and instead of saluting, they hugged.

Returning to his job of bringing the American troops safely home across the Atlantic Ocean, Rube's next crisis materialized in mid-December when his secretary, Mindy Wilson, made him aware of a sinister plot. Extremely upset, Mindy, a twenty-four-year-old college graduate, recently hired by the U.S. State Department to oversee visas and all activities related to the transportation of the troops, lashed out at Rube.

"Some high-ranking political official asked about placing a civilian on the list of troops returning to the U.S. and I don't know what to do about it."

Rube asked, "Does he have a visa?"

"Not sure. It's a request."

"Do we have a name or picture?"

"A name … let's see … John Smith."

"That's it?"

"That's all."

"I don't like it."

"Maybe he's one of our spies we used against the Nazis during the war."

"Could be. I'll check with Captain Wells and see what he thinks."

Calling the captain did nothing more than kick the can down the road. With so little concern shown by the officer, Rube approved the request.

Five days later, another request arrived asking for the prompt departure of two men. This time Rube went to see Colonel Leeds, and he told Rube to deal with his duties and not to worry about the job of others. Reluctantly, Rube approved the request.

Within twenty-four hours, a new request arrived, this time with three names on the list. It became obvious to Rube that the high officials who wanted these individuals to be brought to the "land of the free" had been using him as a conduit to establish a route where a chosen few individuals would be allowed to flee Europe. Rube decided to explain his situation to an officer he could trust, Colonel Kay.

"Nice to see you again, Rube," stated the colonel.

"Likewise."

"We haven't talked in quite a while."

"Sorry, I've been really busy with this new job."

"I understand."

"I have a problem."

"You usually do when you come to see me."

"That's true."

"So, what is it this time?"

Rube told him the story and waited for the usual answer, but it never came. The colonel surprised Rube when he asked, "Do you think I look older than the last time you saw me?"

The colonel's observation made Rube uneasy but replied, "All of us look older."

"You're right about that. Believe me when I tell you I know what you were talking about. I haven't been able to sleep lately because I'm positive there are forces in the military, government, and financial centers that will spend millions of dollars helping former Nazis escape to other countries. I can't sit and watch this happen."

"That's how I feel, but what can we do?"

Let me ask, "Do you have pictures of those seeking to leave the country?"

"No, none were included."

"That's our first objective. I just was able to have General Sandy Rothman sign off on requiring all individuals, including soldiers, to have a photo of themselves to return to the United States."

"I think that's an excellent idea, but we know it's easy to forge IDs, and kids do that all the time to buy beer before the legal age."

"Well, let's not worry about that part.

"So, what's my next move?"

"I will assign a photographer to you who will take pictures of these three seeking to leave Europe."

"That might not be enough. The people who are protecting those fleeing, I can almost predict, will stop us from taking their picture, and I'll be back in your office tomorrow."

"I understand. Is your old MP unit still active?"

"Absolutely."

"I'll have five MPs join you in your visit to where these men are staying. Be sure not to call them before you arrive. Once you get the photos, bring them to our lab, and we can print them."

A few hours later, Rube knocked on the door. No one answered at first. Then a voice answered, "Who is it?"

"We are here to take pictures of the three men seeking to leave on a boat for America."

"No pictures allowed."

"Then no trip on the ship."

The door then opened. Two large men stood in the doorway. Their threatening tone became less when they saw the MPs.

"We don't know anything about pictures."

Rube handed them a number they could call to confirm the new regulations. Rube asked, "Can we come in while you make the call?"

Without fanfare, the group moved into the room. The three men weren't present. One of the thugs went to the bedroom, and Rube heard the man talking to someone in German. After ten minutes, the man returned and said, "Take your pictures."

During the photoshoot, no one talked.

Late the following day, Rube received a call and was told to report to the colonel's office at 2100. When he arrived, several men were looking over the photos taken of the three men.

Seeing Rube, the colonel introduced him to the other men in his office. Rube learned the men were lawyers and were preparing evidence for trials to be held in Nuremberg against those who committed "crimes against humanity" while operating concentration camps. It was pointed out to Rube that all three men in the photos were associates of the men on trial.

Before the meeting ended, a plan was drawn to arrest the threesome. At 0700 the next day, the street in front of the apartment would be blocked off, and MPs would make the arrest. Rube asked to be present at the arrest, and his wishes were granted. The next day, with the sun rising, a convoy of Jeeps silently moved toward the building only to see two individuals dart into a car filled with other occupants and dash away. Half the convoy followed. The other soldiers in the convoy checked out the apartment and found it empty. "Someone must have tipped off the Nazis before we could arrest them," one MP shouted.

With the streets vacant, the screeching sound of vehicles speeding through Antwerp could be heard. As the cars and Jeeps raced toward an unknown location, Rube watched the competing vehicles take an ominous turn when both parties tried to speed toward a traffic crossing as a train approached. Rube couldn't believe his eyes. In a sequence, within a few seconds, the fleeing car carrying the Nazis and the train collided in a massive explosion.

The entire incident covered the front page of the newspapers for days. Rube spent hours on the phone answering calls from high-ranking officials in Washington. Blame came from all circles. Some blamed the military for what happened; others wondered why these men were being brought to the United States. Rube seemed stuck in the crossfire. Such was life in the Army as winter and Christmas were about to begin. But a letter from Bobbi gave him some hope for the future.

December 12, 1945

Dear Rube,
I am looking for a date to go to a holiday party. Too bad you are still in Europe because if you were home, I would ask you.

I have finished my bookkeeping class. I thought I would continue taking classes but found a full-time job. I work for a company that conducts surveys for department stores in Washington. I'm working in the Jelleff building in an office above the store. We tally comments made by customers who shop at Hechts, Kanns, Lansburghs, Woodward and Lothrop, Garfinkles, and other stores. Then, we write a report and circulate it to the various department heads. This report also reveals what the public is buying and how they view the service at the store. So far, I have enjoyed the work. The girls I work with are friendly, and it's only a short ride on the streetcar to get to work.

Have you been given any date for your return home?

I went to a movie the other day and became sick when the newsreels showed what happened in the concentration camps. I hope those who were involved are brought to justice. It won't bring back those killed, but it will show the civilized world won't tolerate regimes like the Nazi regime.

I'm unsure if any parades are scheduled for returning troops, but our new president, Harry Truman, expressed his desire to provide financial assistance to returning GIs who want to start a business or attend college.

Stay safe. Maybe in your next letter, you will have some good news.

Your Pen Pal, who can't wait to see you!
Much love,
Bobbi

Forty-Four

Just as the furor of the tragic chase incident began to subside, a new volcano would soon erupt in the city. Being transferred to a public relations position offered Rube some relief from the daily grind of sending troops back to the states. But only a few days into his new job, Rube found himself going "out of the frying pan into the fire." He became aware of a simmering dispute between a Jewish family, whose home was now occupied by an Antwerp family.

Minus a mother, two sons, and a daughter, who had died in a concentration camp, the Jewish family arrived in October to reclaim their former home. In the house's backyard, the father, one daughter, and two sons recovered from a hole, the metal box which contained the deeds and ownership papers to their property which they had hidden before being arrested by the Nazis. They then confronted the people living in their homes, and they were threatened with bodily harm and went to the authorities. Despite showing all the legal documents to prove they owned the property, the family met resistance when attempting to move into their former home. After engaging legal services offered by the American military, the "volcano began to rumble."

The Jewish family accepted an offer to live in a Quonset hut until the legal issues could be settled. After ten days of intense negotiating, the local authorities agreed that the house belonged to the Jewish family. Still, the Flemish family, who occupied the house, refused to accept living in another location free of charge until the summer. One last attempt was made to find a peaceful solution, but it failed, which caused the government and the military forces to remove them from their home as Christmas approached.

The Jewish family moved inside, and the city teetered into two armed camps for the next few days. Legally the Jewish family had every right to return to their property, but the same hate that began with the rise of Hitler quickly returned as some wanted to use force to drive the Jews out.

The Jewish family became prisoners in their own home. Daily, windows were broken, and threats were made against the family. "This is going to blow up," said Rube at a meeting of military officers. Several officers inquired about who seemed to be responsible for agitating the situation.

One GI helped answer the question. "Former Nazis who operate Firehouse number 116 are responsible for most of the trouble. Those firemen inside the building only answer calls to extinguish fires if it happens to be in a particular area where their supporters live. They use threats and intimidation to force those who disagree with them to sell or leave their homes and go to another area. Sometimes they even have set fires which they refused to extinguish."

"Why doesn't the city offer to do something?" asked another MP.

"They don't want to rock the boat. In addition, certain members of the clergy have given them their support," reported the colonel.

"So, there is little we can do?" promoted another officer.

"Well, if we want to take a stand, we can certainly reduce or eliminate their power, but it could cause an increase in hostility toward our troops," said Colonel Kay.

Rube said, "One of the reasons we fought this war was to stop this type of ruthless aggression against innocent people."

Lieutenant George Summers noted, "If nothing less, those in Firehouse 116 should be fired for not performing their duties."

"Something has to be done, but what are our other options?" asked Captain Randy Turner.

"We will try to find a solution, but let's keep a close watch on the house of the Jewish family," said Kay.

On a visit to Yvonne's house, Rube regrettably found his girlfriend wasn't home, but he had the opportunity to meet her father who said, "I heard you both make a nice dance couple. Sorry I missed the show you danced at, but I had to work."

As they talked, Rube felt Yvonne's father wanted to tell him something, but he didn't dare to spit it out. So, Rube tried to ease his fears and told him he would be leaving in a few months, and he wished him and the family and Yvonne the best. "Also, if you have something to say, please speak. I can help you with anything but money."

"I'm hesitant because I don't want anyone in my family to be hurt."

"I have the entire military behind me. We did one hell of a job removing the Third Reich."

"You must not reveal where you got this information."

"Ask your daughter. When I give my word, I keep a promise."

"There is a plan to firebomb the Jewish home, which will happen shortly."

"Who's going to bomb the home?"

"People, that's all I know."

"Where did you hear this?"

"From someone at work who heard it from a person at the firehouse."

"You mean at Firehouse Number 116?"

"That's all I'm going to say."

"I understand. Look, I must go. Please give Yvonne this gift."

"But Christmas is a few days away."

"Well, put it under your tree."

"We won't have a tree this year, but I'll keep it until Christmas."

"Thanks."

The war room, which hadn't been used since the cessation of fighting, was placed back into operation as the central communication site for all types of activity. It was at this location where high-ranking military officers signed off on a plan to prevent pro-Nazi gangs from destroying the property of the rightful owner.

Three days before Christmas, someone called a city official and said, "Antwerp will burn tonight." No one could be sure if it were a crank call or an actual threat, but the MPs decided to initiate operation "Bright Star." If it was a fake call, at least they would have the opportunity to practice the strategy for thwarting any possible attack.

Rube volunteered to be one of the guards that would stand on the steps of the house for an hour with his shotgun. He would be replaced at 0100. A crowd of fifteen men appeared in front of the home a little after midnight, carrying Molotov cocktails.

"Get out of my way," shouted the leader.

Using his strongest voice, Rube responded, "It would be best for all concerned that you and your gang disperse."

"We ain't going nowhere, *Jude*, but you are."

Rube insisted, "We wish you and your gang no harm. We have people sleeping in this building that they own. No one is threatening you; it's time for you to move on."

The spokesman then pulled out a lighter and lit the rag covering the bottle filled with gasoline.

"I urge you not to throw that bottle."

"Men, light up."

"If you attempt to throw a single bottle at the house, I'll have to arrest you."

"Fuck you."

The leader then tossed the firebomb at Rube, who easily ducked, but the bottle struck the front of the house and started a fire. In the next few seconds, everything seemed to explode in rapid fire. First, a blast from Rube's shotgun blew the assailant's body parts all over the street. Instantly, lights placed along the rooftops of buildings turned the night into day. MPs appeared on the rooftops and windows from out of nowhere and came out of the house's cellar. Suddenly the mob below heard the clicking sound of forty rifles being prepared to fire.

"I'm not fucking around," Rube screamed. "I don't think any of you want to join the guy laying in the street, so please put your bottles on the ground and have a seat."

At first, no one moved, maybe because some didn't understand English, but finally, one of the gang members sat down, and others followed.

Meanwhile, the fire continued to burn in the front of the house. Several calls were made to Firehouse 116, but each time the person at the firehouse answered, he replied, "The trucks are out fighting a fire someplace else."

Stationed near the firehouse were two MPs who took pictures of the dormant engines inside the building. A city official who joined the MPs went into the firehouse and ordered the firefighters to depart immediately to assist in extinguishing the fire at the house occupied by the Jewish family. They refused. By the time an engine from another fire station arrived, more than enough damage had been done to the house that the family had to flee for that night. The rest of the night and into the early morning, Rube worked with many other GIs, arraigning those arrested in the incident.

The sun had just appeared as an exhausted and happy Rube prepared to depart Army headquarters. His mood instantly changed when a church official wearing a long robe and a crucifix around his waist entered the building. Immediately, Rube realized his hope for a peaceful Christmas day in Antwerp was at risk. Much like a pot of boiling water, Rube's blood pressure rose as he understood justice was in jeopardy.

The next few days were filled with accusations, mostly untrue, but it allowed the church to enter the now legal conflicts. The church official requested that all those with Molotov cocktails not be charged with having deadly weapons because none had been thrown. Those representing the firefighters requested only a charge of dereliction of duty be placed against them. The priests representing the now-jailed thugs asked that all the men be released to the custody of the church, especially since they wouldn't be able to celebrate Christmas if they were incarcerated.

Arguments broke out among the city's population about what should be done. Rube and the MPs remained steadfast that the law had been broken and these men should not be released. But as expected, the church won out. The city administrators approved a plan that all those who attempted to burn the home of the Jewish family would sign a document that pledged that if arrested again for breaking the law, they would face the more serious charge of arson. This legally binding document would be in effect for five years. All the firefighters were released without being charged, but all lost their jobs and could never rejoin the fire department in Antwerp.

A despondent Rube, once again alone in his Jeep, decided to visit the concentration camp survivors' home. At least he could offer condolences to the family and explain why the mob who threatened them and wanted to destroy their home, would not be charged with any crime.

When Rube arrived at the home, he climbed the steps to the entrance and found a sign attached to the door. Unable to read what was written, the MP asked a passerby who spoke English to translate the message on the sign. After hearing what was stated, Rube remarked, "I don't understand. How can the home be condemned when there was only minor damage to the outside? Are you sure?"

"Absolutely," said the man. "And the entire family seemed eager to leave after a meeting was held inside their home."

"Do you know who the meeting was with?"

"No, but they left last night after dark."

A stunned Rube gathered his thoughts as he leaned against the locked door. Using his back to propel him toward the steps, Rube noticed a bronze cylinder about three inches long, somewhat battered, and attached to the doorpost with a Hebrew letter. Rube immediately identified the object as a *mezuzah*. As mentioned in an important prayer during religious services, Jewish families place them on the doorpost to bring blessings to those who live and visit under the house's roof. Inside the *mezuzah* is a slot for inserting a *klaf*, a prayer that appears on a small piece of parchment. The family who owned the house failed to remove it. Taking the Bowie knife given to him by Teddy Bear, Rube pried the religious symbol off the doorpost. As he walked down the steps, Rube stopped and placed the *mezuzah* in his pocket. Raising his arms and hands skyward, he shouted, "Dear God, I must surrender and admit that the spear of antisemitism and racism has once again pierced my soul. I accept the fact that in my lifetime, it will never end. I can only hope this curse will be greatly minimized sometime soon."

Forty-Five

Rube couldn't believe what had taken place. He told everyone who would listen, "We just fought a war to prevent this situation. Millions died, yet the proper authorities failed to perform their duties to allow justice to prevail. Have we already forgotten the horrors of World War II?"

Although there was talk of an investigation into whether a conspiracy between the government, church, and military officials had taken place, no one of authority recommended that such an inquiry should occur as the house had been sold.

Rube's pleas and anger didn't go unnoticed as a week later, he received word that he now had fifty-six points and had to leave Antwerp by January 30.

It seemed strange to Rube that his attempts to return home were delayed because he failed to have enough points in the past. But now, when he stood up for something that would challenge those in power, he was sent home.

A conflicted Rube tried to relish that he was going home, but in some ways he felt betrayed. He knew the war was a dirty game, but politics might be worse because appearance seemed more important than choosing what was right. Unlike politics, where timing is critical, life decisions encompass many other factors which are often forgotten by those in power. Maybe, that's why Rube cherished breathing the air that swirled around the Statue of Liberty rather than having to adjust to the limited air at the top of a mountain. He had his moment in the sun and was blessed to come home to America.

One last meeting with a military official made Rube thankful he would be leaving Antwerp. At his meeting with Major Tom Miller, he found out that the priests wanted to charge him for the murder of one of his parishioners even though Rube fired in self-defense. "Just be glad you're going home," said the major.

Rube inquired, "What about the Jewish family?"

"Why should you care?"

"So, the Jewish family becomes like a "fiddler on a roof," without a family, home and country?"

"I don't know what you are talking about. The house was sold in one day, and the family received a good price. That's the way it works sometimes."

"Who was the buyer?"

"Unknown."

"In one guess, I bet I could name the buyer."

"It doesn't matter, and everything is copacetic now. Is there anything else?"

Rube responded, "I guess the devil came down to Antwerp and won."

"What does that mean?"

Rube shrugged and said, "Have a good night's sleep, major."

Rube saluted, did an about-face, and as he was leaving the major's office, the staff sergeant faintly heard someone say, "God damn Jews." Upon shutting the major's door, Rube turned around and reached for the handle but stopped when he heard an officer inside remark, "Who do these Jews think they are, the conscience of the nation?" Rube then placed his right foot forward and made a ninety-degree turn, and as he departed, Rube hoped the major understood the full meaning of the remarks about conscience. As strange as it seemed, Rube remembered reading an article by Mark Twain, where the famous author came to a similar conclusion about the Jews being the nation's conscience.

The next week began with well-wishers coming to Rube's office. Rube was overwhelmed by the thoughtful Antwerp community. A few even gave him gifts to take back home. This show of kindness left Rube speechless at times, especially when the couple he had paid to make his pen pal a pair of shoes graciously gave Rube a free pair. The dance gang surprised him when they showed him a sign that would be attached above the dance room, which read, "Rube's Place."

The toughest goodbye, no doubt for Rube, came when he met Yvonne for the last time. Playing the adult role proved increasingly difficult as neither knew how to end a relationship properly. Rube and Yvonne agreed to write to each other, and they would always share the memories of growing into adulthood together.

With only four days left on his tour of duty in Belgium, a woman and young child came to visit Rube. He expected to hear the gracious comments other civilians and citizens of Antwerp bestowed upon him. Instead, another can of worms cracked open in front of him. The woman, with swollen eyes, in broken English, told her story. Rube had to bring an interpreter to his office to hear her son's story. He listened to a horrible story told between outbursts of tears. Rube, unable to control his emotions, called Lieutenant Carlson to come into his office. Captains, colonels, and a major then followed him. Within an hour, numerous officers had listened to the woman's story.

As the mother continued her narrative, Rube became aware of a name that he had heard many times recently. The same priest that worked so diligently to free members of the mob that threatened the Jewish family seemed to be mentioned on many occasions by the mother. After more than three hours of compelling testimony, the woman, her son, and Rube were told they were excused. Before she left, she gave Colonel Kay an envelope with a list of young boys' names. When Rube departed for home, the officers were still in his office discussing what should be the next move.

The next day, every officer that passed by him seemed to give Rube the stink eye. Something was about to happen, but the MP was kept out of the loop until he learned Cardinal Benedict was rumored to be on his way to headquarters.

The following day Rube was restricted to his office, giving the retiring staff sergeant the time to write Bobbi.

January 9, 1946

Dear Bobbi,

I'm coming home. I should be leaving by January 30. I thought it would never happen. Hopefully, I'll be able to see you shortly after I come home. I have so much to tell you. I will call you from New York when I arrive, around February 14. We will be traveling, not on a luxury liner like when we arrived, but on a Liberty Ship. I expect more than 250 soldiers will be aboard. Happy New Year. For me coming home is a great way to start the year.

Love,
Rube

Around noon, Officer Bart Gerson brought lunch to Rube's office. Both soldiers spent a lot of time talking about baseball. The two had a great conversation about Gerson's hometown team, the St. Louis Cardinals. As Bart prepared to leave, Rube said, "I guess if I'm to see the Cardinals play ball, it will mean taking a road trip to Brooklyn, New York, to watch a game at Ebbets Field."

Just then, another officer passed Rube's door and suddenly stopped, like when a film splits and the frame freezes. "You ain't going anywhere near the cardinal," the officer shouted angrily.

"What the hell are you talking about? I'm referring to the St. Louis Cardinals," Rube pointed out.

"Oh. I'm sorry," replied the officer.

"In this place, at times it's better not to listen too hard because it can cause a lot of misunderstandings," stated Gerson.

Near 1700 hours, Colonel Kay thrust his head into Rube's office. "Father, may I come out of my corner. I'll be a good boy," said Rube.

"Yes. I think you've been in time-out long enough!" answered the colonel. "How did it go?"

"Well, when the cardinal arrived, I would say he rated a nine on a scale of ten for anger. It must have gone past the limit when he departed and hit twelve. We will see what takes place shortly."

Forty-Six

In his last full day, tension at the headquarters appeared to decline. Those remaining arranged a goodbye luncheon for Rube. After several speeches by different individuals offering farewells, they asked Rube to say a few words. Not normally a great speaker, Rube delivered a home run with his farewell speech. Without notes, his words perfectly fit as he summarized his thoughts by offering these remarks.

"Don't ever forget what we did here. Together we formed a union of Americans from Hicksville to the big cities. The little people came and used their resources, skills, and energy to defeat an evil enemy. God forbid this should happen again in the future. If so, the next generation must stand as one, like we did, because a divided nation cannot prevail. Combined with the desire to live in freedom, we showed our allegiance not to political parties, giant corporations or nefarious organizations but to our families, country, and God. Nothing should be cherished more than our way of life. So, let me salute and honor those who fought for freedom. We can only hope future generations will show the courage and fortitude necessary to protect our established rights and offer all citizens equal opportunities to live the American dream."

Rube woke up at 0500 on January 29, 1946 and within a half hour stood waiting for the tram that stopped near the Army camp. The MP saw a paperboy while looking down the road for the tram. He heard the boy shout something about the cardinal and priests. The paperboy approached Rube, showed him the front page, and asked if he wanted to purchase the paper. Upon seeing the picture but unable to understand the headlines, he asked the boy if he could translate it into English.

"I think I can. I'm learning it in school."

"Could you read the headlines for me?"

"I already read the story."

"What did it say?"

"Just that the cardinal praised the priest for doing a wonderful job in Antwerp, and he was being sent to another assignment to continue his work."

"I guess you're surprised and upset he's leaving," remarked Rube.

"Not really."

"Why is that?"

"I'm glad he's leaving," He then asked Rube to bend down so he could whisper into Rube's ear.

"Oh, my, that's horrible!"

"It's been known for a long time, but no one did anything to prevent it."

"I'm so sorry."

"GI, are you buying the paper?"

Rube pulled a dollar from his wallet and gave it to the boy. With a smile, he said, "No change necessary."

"Thank you, GI. Have a good trip home."

Finally, the tram arrived, and Rube placed his duffel bag and suitcase aboard and sat in front of two ladies with identification badges which most likely meant they were interpreters working at the American embassy. In ten minutes, the tram arrived at the wharf, and Rube had to tell the driver to wait as he gathered up his luggage. One of the ladies asked, "Going home?"

"Yes, ma'am."

The other lady said, "Please tell your President Truman thanks for ending this horrible war."

"I sure will, ma'am."

As Rube approached the plank of the ship with the duffel over his shoulder and a suitcase in hand, aides took his luggage, and he walked the final steps before boarding. Rube spoke the words he so often dreamed about, "Permission to come aboard, sir?"

PART VI: HOMEWARD BOUND

The Albert M Boe, the last of 2,710 Liberty Ships built during World War II, departed from its shipyard on October 30, 1945. Over eighteen shipyards produced vessels that carried two-thirds of all American cargo during the war. The Bethlehem-Fairfield shipyard in Baltimore built 384 Liberty Ships. It was estimated that twenty percent of all ships produced were made by "Rosie the Riveter," the nickname given to women who worked in war plants during WWII. During the conflict, about 200 Liberty vessels were sunk by German aircraft and submarines, and almost 7,000 American Merchant Mariners and 1,800 Naval Armed Guards lost their lives. The ships had a crew of about forty-five and could transport 450 soldiers. Rube would travel home aboard the Liberty Ship *Matthew Lyon*.

The trip across the Atlantic moved at a slow and laborious pace, and because of the weather, Rube had few chances to stand on deck, but on a day when the ship came closest to the equator, he enjoyed the sun's warmth. While observing the beautiful ocean scene, he ruminated about the last eighteen months of his life. In his mind, Rube envisioned he had just played the key role in a Shakespearean tragedy as he contemplated all his losses since leaving American shores. Death, destruction, and deprivation seemed to highlight his war experience. How many buddies had he lost? How many times did he see men suffer from battle injuries? How could he forget the buildings and homes destroyed by Allied and enemy fire? What about the sights of the homeless refugees walking into an unknown future? How difficult was it for those who went hungry and had to deal with the pain of being unable to feed their children? What would happen to all those who survived the concentration camps? As all of this built up in Rube's mind, he recognized his losses — losing two girlfriends; his best friend Stuart dying on the battlefield, as did many of his buddies; the death of Captain Lytton; and his initial disappointment of being transferred from the medics to the MPs.

However, to Rube, the greatest loss was the emptiness of not having the opportunity to grow into a young man without the stress of war. In less than three months, Rube became much like the injured patient Mo whom he cared for when he wore the red cross of a medic. No longer a naive kid from Allison Street, he had morphed into an angry, hateful, and unforgiving combatant who became a killer without a conscience. Yet without that attitude, he likely would have never survived the war.

At last, his long and difficult journey was coming to an end. Thankfully, unlike those who paid the full price of war, he would make the trip home, without a major injury, except for the mental images that refused to leave his mind.

The two-week trip gave him time to reflect, meet other returning GIs, and listen to their depictions of the war. Of the different stories Rube heard on the trip, the one he remembered most came from Martin Snyderman. He claimed to be General Eisenhower's private cook. Martin told Rube how he suffered from flat feet. Despite this handicap, he was placed in the infantry after joining the military. He became a pain in the ass, not because of his flat feet, but due to his big mouth, as he always complained about the food. One day his sergeant said, "Let's see if YOU could do any better!" and sent him to the kitchen. He never returned to the field again. The food he made not only tasted good, but he presented it in a manner, not slopped together but proportionally measured in each tin meal plate used by the GIs. Rube never understood how he became Ike's top cook, but he believed in Snyderman's desire to work in a campaign to have the general run for president.

The Forever trip finally docked in New York City on February 14 at 11:11 a.m. Going to Grand Central Station became the first item on Rube's agenda.

After paying for a ticket on a train leaving for D.C. at 2:00 that afternoon, he called Bobbi. She was thrilled to hear his voice, which made Rube extremely happy. Bobbi then told him that after work she would meet him at Union Station. While Rube waited for the departure of the train, he listened to a radio broadcast as he was eating lunch at a counter at the railroad station. Precisely at noon, the station's human traffic paused as the National Anthem music filtered through the main hall. Rube recalled being at the Kennedy movie theatre in Washington to watch a matinee before enlisting, and as the curtain opened, he listened to the "Star-Spangled Banner." Only now, the song's impact had a far different meaning to him and all those who fought under the colors of the American flag.

Tired of waiting, Rube went outside the station to look around. The city seemed to bloom as people rushed from street to street. Cars piled up at lights, and the cash registers were clanking. People were working; money was being made; cabs with passengers arrived at hotels; and invisible radio waves crossed through the city without being noticed. America had changed since he left, hopefully for the better. Time would only tell, but he wanted to be a part of it.

Besides reading the newspaper, Rube slept most of the trip to D.C. As the train pulled into Union Station, his excitement had reached such a point that his duffel bag felt more like a pillow after he lifted his suitcase.

Forty-Seven

Standing on the walkway between the trains, he searched for Bobbi. At first, crowds of people blocked his vision, but as the platform began to empty, he saw a girl about twenty years old standing beside a pillar. She wore a stylish open overcoat, revealing a vest, white blouse, and neutral skirt stretching above the knee. She didn't look familiar, so Rube slowly walked toward her and spoke, "Are you, Bobbi?"

She responded, "Are you, Rube?" Both smiled, then lunged at each other. First, a huge hug and then a kiss that lasted much longer than a welcome kiss.

"I made it!" exclaimed Rube.

"Yes, you did."

"You look great, Bobbi."

"You ain't that bad either, Rube."

For a moment, they just stared at each other without saying anything. Rube broke the silence and said, "Have you eaten?"

"No, not yet."

"I'm sure there's a good restaurant nearby."

The two adults took a cab to the Willard Hotel and had a wonderful dinner. Rube said, "From here, I'll take the streetcar home, and we can travel together until you need to transfer to another car."

"I can't go with you."

"Why?"

"Well, the girls in my office collected money and reserved a room downtown for me in case you would be delayed. They didn't want me to stay here alone, so they paid for a room. But you're welcome to stay with me overnight if you wish, and that's why I brought my valise along."

Rube stammered briefly and said, "I told my folks I would come home right after arriving in D.C."

"Well, you can tell them you're late coming from New York, and it would be better to see them tomorrow afternoon."

Rube thought momentarily and realized he was now the adult in charge, so he said, "Why not!" with a broad smile.

While talking to his happy parents, he told them he was exhausted since he arrived very late in D.C. and that he planned to stay at a hotel and would see them tomorrow afternoon. He further asked them to tell Sam's family to join in the celebration.

Rube hadn't seen or been in a room like the one at the Willard. When he saw the bed, he felt like a kid who wanted to jump up and down on it. Instead, he just flopped onto it. Bobbi followed. It was soft and clean and fresh, much like Bobbi. Not in his wildest dreams could Rube have imagined a homecoming where he hugged and kissed his pen pal on a bed in the Willard Hotel. After the embrace, they both lay their heads on the soft pillows. Almost immediately, Rube's eyes began to shut. The fifteen-ton gorilla following him through the war suddenly vanished, and at last, he was free.

As the evening grew later, Bobbi, still playing somewhat innocently, went to the bathroom to change. Rube quickly called Stuart's parents and told them how sorry he was about their son's death. They graciously accepted his heartfelt sympathies and invited him to dinner sometime, which he accepted. As he hung up, the door to the bathroom opened, and Bobbi stepped out wearing a beautiful silky nightgown. In the light of the only lit lamp in the room, Rube could see the outline of parts of her body. Her appearance almost took his breath away.

He felt almost embarrassed as he lay in his sweaty GI skivvies and undershirt. Certainly, he couldn't match the aura created by Bobbi, but Rube's attire didn't matter. Soon they were locked together, and the war, at least for a while, was a distant memory. Relaxed and extremely happy, Rube closed his eyes, held Bobbi's hand and went to sleep. It was about 10:00 a.m. when he woke up. Bobbi had breakfast brought to the room. This time she wore a short sexy robe that, when open, revealed a tight pair of black panties and a bra. Both had a breakfast of eggs, bacon and fruit, including bananas and grapefruit. Their eyes told what was coming next.

After enjoying one of life's best experiences, the couple cuddled so close together that Bobbi's perfume tickled Rube's nostrils. Looking directly into Bobbi's turquoise eyes, Rube thanked her for writing him during the dark days of the war. With their lips a fraction of an inch apart, they melted together, and as they parted, Rube's heart rate achieved a different rhythm than when he kissed Sylvia goodbye at the train station. For a moment, they just stared at each other and whether by women's intuition or for some other reason, Bobbi felt Rube wanted to say something else to her. She was correct, but what surprised her was the content. "Bobbi, I have been thinking about this for a long time, and I must ask you a question. It's not meant to be derogatory, but a necessary trust factor in our relationship."

"Rube, it's been such a wonderful night and morning. I don't want to answer any questions."

"I understand, but I want you to listen to the question, and if you don't want to answer it now, that's fine."

"Go ahead."

"Did you know Sylvia had a boyfriend when you started writing me?"

"Well, I knew Sylvia was dating different men, mainly sailors. You know she was very pretty and worked at the Navy Yard. I couldn't hold that against her as all of us were uncertain about your future and our own. Since Sylvia was dating other men, I felt it was alright for me to write you. I remembered seeing you from our snowball fight and being at Sylvia's house waiting for our clothes to dry. I thought you were cute then; now you're one big hunk. I'm so glad I became your pen pal. The letter I wrote telling you Sylvia had a steady boyfriend is when she informed me that her relationship with you was over. But she never asked me to write you as a fill-in for her. My letters were my letters, and I'm so happy to have written you."

"Thanks for being so honest. This has been an unreal homecoming, and I only hope this isn't a one-night stand."

"Rube Goldfarb, you don't have to worry about that."

Once again, the two were locked together in each other's arms, feeling safe and secure. The next few hours only became a memory as both dressed for the day ahead. Rube would leave the hotel at noon and take a streetcar home. As Rube prepared to leave, he pulled from his duffel bag a pair of shoes. As Bobbi sat on the bed, Rube, with one knee on the floor, gently placed the shoes on one foot, then the other. For a moment, Bobbi felt like Cinderella. Her *mensch* rose after seeing the shoes fit perfectly. He stood and kissed her softly on the cheek. Rube told her the shoes were hand-made and came directly from Antwerp. Bobbi, overcome with emotion, could only hope when the clock struck twelve, everything didn't disappear. At noon, Rube departed for Allison Street. Bobbi waited another hour before she left and prepared to follow Rube to his parents' home.

Lugging his duffel bag and suitcase on the streetcar, Rube spotted a soldier in uniform seated near the front of the coach.

"Mind if I sit next to you?"

"My pleasure … just returning?"

"You bet. Haven't seen my folks in almost two years."

"Where were you stationed?"

"Basically everywhere, France, Belgium, Luxembourg, England and numerous cities like Antwerp and Brussels and several battlefields. What about you?"

"Man, you must have seen a lot of action. I spent most of my time right here near D.C."

"At Walter Reed?"

"No, at Fort Hunt."

"Never heard of it."

"Very few people know about it."

"What did you do there?"

"We interrogated German officers, soldiers and scientists."

"Really? Were you alone when you did the interrogations?"

"No, believe it or not, we had many German Jews, who the Nazis had attempted to destroy, now subjecting the top echelon of the 'superhuman race' to a series of interrogations."

"If I were there, they would never have finished the interview. They would be dead."

"No, we didn't kill anyone, but a couple tried to kill themselves."

"Any notables you interrogated?"

"A fellow named Wernher von Braun. He was involved in the V-2 rocket assault against England and citizens in Belgium."

"I saw some of his work in Antwerp."

"By the way, who are you?"

"Rube Goldfarb."

"I'm Stanley Goodman. Nice talking to you. Here's my stop."

Stanley departed the streetcar where Georgia Avenue and Sherman Avenue converge.

At this stop on Georgia Avenue, someone who worked in something like a foxhole under the street switched a piece of equipment under the car, which allowed it to continue. While the streetcar remained motionless, Rube noticed that the old steel water trough where horses used to drink, had yet to be removed and remained attached to the sidewalk. On his left, he recognized the old firehouse and the bowling alley where he, Sylvia, and Stuart had tried to knock down some pins.

Once the streetcar moved, it wasn't far from his Pop's synagogue at Eighth and Shepherd. Then the Petworth library appeared on the left, with Roosevelt High School in the background. As the streetcar passed Webster Street, it began to slow. Suddenly emotion took over Rube, as the cavity under his eyes began to fill with tears. Rube couldn't believe everything that had happened and he was coming home alive. For a second, he thought he was dreaming.

Jumping down on the same cement island where his journey began almost two years ago, Rube dashed across the southbound streetcar tracks onto the awaiting sidewalk with his duffel bag on his shoulders and a suitcase in his hand. As if walking on air, Rube turned the corner into Allison Street. Everything looked much like before he left, but the returning GI realized how much his life had changed.

Rube climbed the seven steps to the porch and threw his duffel bag and suitcase next to the metal rocking chairs. He then opened the old storm door. Immediately, he noticed that his folks had bought a new front door. He squeezed the handle, and the door opened. Leaping three steps at a time, he flew into the dining room amongst screams, shouts, tears, and lots of love. For a while, the family hugged, danced and cried. Bernie stopped crying when Rube offered to take him next door to buy comic books. The homecoming couldn't be complete without a toast. Sam and Marie spoke about how much they missed Rube and couldn't wait to hear some of his stories. Sam said, "At least Rube could shower in a bathroom instead of a creek!" Everyone laughed.

After everything calmed down, Rube and Bernie went to the variety store connected to Rube's house. Bernie picked out Superman and Batman comics while Rube hugged some of the workers he remembered before leaving. He also picked out a GI Joe comic that the store owner gave him for free. Back at the house, Rube watched the four-year-old struggle up the steps with his short legs. When he reached the top of the steps, Bernie shouted, "Uncle Rube bought me a Superman and a Batman comic, and he got a GI Joe comic for himself!"

Before returning to his family, Rube looked to see if Bobbi had arrived. Bobbi wasn't drop-dead beautiful, but many guys standing in a corner watching all the girls go by would say, "Not bad."

Momentarily, Rube noticed her turn the corner, and they waved at each other. Rube came down the steps, and they embraced. Slowly their lips parted, and Rube said, "Ready?"

Bobbi answered, "Ready," and they walked up to the porch together. Before going inside, Rube rummaged through his duffel bag and found a wooden Jeep he bought in Brugge and wanted to give to his nephew. He opened the new door and closed the old storm door as Bobbi entered. Once inside, she asked Rube if there was a spot where she could place her valise. He checked where his father stored customers' dirty clothes under the counter. It was vacant. Together, hand in hand, Rubin and Bobbi cautiously walked up the steps to meet his family. As they reached the top of the steps, Bobbi stopped and said to Rube, "I feel anxious about meeting your family."

Rube looked into Bobbi's eyes and remarked, "No need to worry, my lovely pen pal; they are just ordinary folk."

Epilogue

Here is what became of some of the ordinary folk you've just met.

RUBE GOLDFARB

Less than a year after returning from Europe, Rube and his nephew Bernie attended a Theodore Roosevelt High School football game. As Rube watched those playing on the field, his mind wandered back to when he wore the school's Rough Riders football uniform. So much had transpired since high school; it made him wonder how he adjusted to many life-changing events. Almost twenty-five-years-old, his boots had landed in five foreign countries. He had fought in two major World War II battles and numerous smaller engagements. He sustained a war wound and saved numerous lives while being a medic. He traveled to many towns and cities in Europe and flew in the sky over the land that ancient armies had conquered. He had driven a vehicle, known as a Jeep, hundreds of miles and rode trains even farther. Along the way, he fought with a band of brothers who defeated a powerful enemy, and regrettably, he had to kill to remain alive. He witnessed historical sites and endured the ravaged remains of towns and cities. He had looked into the eyes of the dead and living and worked to send home the members of the greatest generation.

A year after Rube returned home, he married his pen pal Roberta. Shortly after, he opened the first of three dry-cleaning stores in Northwest Washington with his dad as the tailor. As the population in Washington expanded, Rube's business ventures also grew with stores being established in Silver Spring, and Takoma Park, Maryland.

One of his customers was the manager of the Washington Senators baseball team, Sam Mele. When Rube told him about playing catch with Warren Spahn during the war, Mele, who had been in the Marines during World War II, arranged to have three tickets available for Rube, Bobbi, and Bernie to watch the Boston Braves pitcher when he played in Philadelphia. After the game, the threesome took pictures with Warren.

On the way home, Rube drove to the Gettysburg battlefield in Pennsylvania. After parking the car on a narrow road, the trio trudged up a hill and stood on a rock-filled overlook. They could see the beautiful valley scenes below from this high hilltop. Rube turned toward Bernie and said, "It's hard to believe a major battle in the Civil War was fought here." Bernie waited for more information from his uncle, but Rube seemed fixated on something far away. An awkward moment passed as Bernie waited for a response, but there was none. Finally, Roberta spoke and told Bernie that the site of Little Round Top was a critical point in the Battle of Gettysburg. She also mentioned that Rube had fought in a major battle during World War II, the Battle of the Bulge. Something seemed to click as Bernie mentioned, "Is this the Civil War battlefield where President Lincoln gave his famous speech?"

"Yes indeed," Bobbi responded.

Bernie also wondered what visions pulsed through his uncle's mind as he stood on the ground of this famous battlefield.

Rube made a major shift later in life. After twenty years, he sold his dry-cleaning business and accepted a job as an administrator for a management company that operated hotels and apartments. With Rube traveling to Washington to work in his new job, the couple moved into an apartment complex recently built on property that once served as the home for a large Afro-American community. This whistle-stop community just west of Georgia Avenue in the D.C. suburbs was built along a railroad line in 1853 and remained almost unchanged until the 1950s. As the Washington suburbs began to expand, much of the property was sold off, and new landmarks appeared, like the Walter Reed Hospital extension, a school for women, and the apartment building where Rube and Bobbi resided. For Rube, every time he wrote his new address, it caused him to think back to the days of World War II when he fought with brave men in France and Belgium. Whenever Rube finished addressing an envelope from his new location in Lyttonsville, Maryland, he was reminded of Captain Lytton, who had fought with him and died in combat.

Another relic from the past that stirred Rube's passion was connected to the doorpost of his new apartment. The *mezuzah* he took from the Jewish home in Antwerp reminded him that wars only bring limited success as the winners often fail to take advantage of the magnitude of their victory. Unlike the famous slogan offers, "To the victors go the spoils," politics often denies the winners what was won on the battlefield. According to the Army veteran, because of the outcome of World War II, the next generation of Americans will have the best opportunity to institute changes in the political, economic, and social arenas.

Bobbi and Rube had no children but remained married for over forty years.

COLONEL BENJAMIN KAY

Colonel Benjamin Kay became a career Army officer. He served in the Korean conflict and eventually received an assignment at the Pentagon. He married and had a daughter. After retiring from the military, he joined a "think tank," which provided Congress with information about funding military operations against adversaries. By chance, he and his wife met Rube and Bobbi at an Army birthday celebration dance in Washington. They had an enjoyable evening reminiscing about their days in Antwerp. Finally, the two wives cajoled their husbands to dance. After seeing Rube dance, the colonel stated, "Rube, you still got it." Of course, he failed to mention anything about Rube's dance partner in Antwerp, Yvonne.

COLONEL RON GILMORE

Colonel Ron Gilmore never received fame or glory for commanding the Ghost Army. Despite being involved in twenty missions that saved the lives of thousands of GIs between June 1944 and March 1945, the exploits of the secret unit remained unknown until 1996. The 23rd Headquarters Special Troops, mainly artists, designers, and engineers, made Europe their stage. They performed in cafés, gave out disinformation, fought fake battles, and built phony planes and tanks. Their radio show and broadcast stories seemed more realistic than what U.S. citizens listened to back home.

Finally, in 2022, the nine surviving members of the Ghost Army were awarded the Congressional Gold Medal.

LLOYD BEAR

Bear was transferred from the Military Police and sent for a month of training at Fort Elliott, near San Diego. He was one of 420 Navajo soldiers and other Native American tribe members that sent thousands of coded messages between 1942 and 1945. Arriving just before the Marines landed at Iwo Jima, Bear, along with other Navajos, sent over 800 messages without the Japanese being able to decipher any of the coded Navajo languages during the battles. On one occasion, while Bear was in a cave sending misinformation, a Japanese soldier wielding a large sword attacked Bear. Several Marines who protected the code talkers saved Bear from severe injury.

As the fear that paralyzed his body began to recede from his near-death encounter, Lloyd asked his saviors a question. "If you White boys knew I was an American Indian, would you have still rescued me?"

One of the Marines answered, "Hell yes, as long as you were wearing the uniform you have on, we are a band of brothers in combat."

"I wasn't sure, but now I understand. It's about the uniform and what it represents."

Lloyd Bear passed away in 2000, but the efforts of the code talkers were finally recognized when twenty-seven surviving members were presented with Congressional Gold Medals.

JORDAN TURNER (KNOWN AS OKIE)

After being released from the Army in 1946, Jordan returned to Oklahoma.

It didn't take long before Okie became restless and decided farming wouldn't be his life-long ambition. After seeing Paris, he wanted more adventure. For a while, he worked on a farm, training horses. This led to a job at a racing stable. Soon, he was the most sought-after trainer and held jobs at different racing venues. But because of various recessions that impacted his profession and made financial conditions unpredictable, he pursued another interest. When one of the horse farms where he had worked filed for bankruptcy, he took his life savings, borrowed a large sum from the bank, and started a dude ranch. With all the cowboy shows on television in the 1950s and '60s, going to a dude ranch became popular among vacationers. Although not massive, his ranch offered picturesque scenic views of nearby mountains, streams, and woods. He even constructed an area for those who wished to fire their weapons. With success, he added a barn used for dancing and shows, and a pool and spa for those who were sore from riding horses and walking the trails around the facility. He arranged small cattle drives with neighboring owners to make the ranch more realistic. He also set up a pony express ride, where some guests delivered mail to a small nearby town. One of his guests, a very attractive woman, visited the ranch for a ten-day vacation and never left as she became Okie's wife and the bearer of two children. Okie lived until age eighty-one.

WILL RAMSEY (KNOWN AS WILL THE THRILL)

After leaving the service, Will Ramsey came home with a problem. Where many soldiers returned with symptoms of shell shock, The Thrill came home with a drinking problem. No longer able to perform the duties of a regular cop because of his injuries, he was assigned to desk work which he despised. Between the drinking and the job he hated, Will's first marriage fell apart. He then found part-time work at a bar he liked, but all the booze was too much to handle. When a friend of his, who played in a band, sought help for his addiction, the two began attending meetings and "Went on the wagon." Meeting a new woman friend who didn't drink and finding a new job at a security company changed The Thrill's life forever. Later, he became a partner in a new security firm that expanded into two big cities. Will and his wife had a son and adopted a daughter. He died in 1991.

AL WISE (KNOWN AS CHIP)

Al Wise remained a bachelor until his early thirties. He returned to college, completed his Ph.D., and taught biology at Marshall University in West Virginia. For fun, he began writing mystery stories, and when one of his stories made it to the best sellers' list, writing became his main occupation. He met his wife at a book signing. He lived in Seattle, Washington and had three children. Until he died in 2001, he always attended Veterans of Foreign Wars meetings.

CAPTAIN NOAH HOLTZ

Even though World War II had ended, Captain Holtz remained in Germany. The captain became part of the Army's integral team that oversaw the transformation of the German government from an authoritarian dictatorship to a democracy. Complicating the captain's mission was the attempt by the Soviet Union to establish a satellite state that Russia could control.

Berlin, the capital of Hitler's empire, had been divided between the Soviets and the other allies. Two drastically different governments ruled in the confines of the city. What made the operation extremely difficult on the democratic side of the city was its location. Since Russian troops were permitted to enter Berlin first, they assumed control of territory well beyond the capital. Eventually, Soviet troops encircled the portion of the city controlled by the Allies, and only a few highways connected the capital to the western part of the country. German citizens and Allied forces living in Berlin were at the mercy of Russian aggression tactics. While Captain Holtz and his team worked to rebuild the shattered city, the Russians closed off the Allied highways leading to the city, leaving West Berlin without food or supplies. Harry Truman, President of the United States, countered the Soviet action by ordering an American airlift to the city. The United

States gambled that the Russians wouldn't shoot at U.S. planes and start a war. Truman's prediction proved correct as the Russians backed down. For almost a year, American planes continued to fly daily. Captain Holtz's team administered the distribution of supplies until the Russians allowed the highways to reopen.

After the Berlin crisis ended, Captain Holtz was sent to another hot spot, Korea. He landed with American and United Nations forces at Inchon, crippled the invasion of North Korean troops, and forced them to retreat. Before a cease-fire eventually ended the conflict in Korea, Captain Holtz commanded units that fought against Chinese forces along the thirty-eighth parallel that separated both armies.

Having survived two wars, Captain Holtz left the military before a third war broke out. Seeking a calmer environment where he could raise a family, he moved near Milwaukee, where he joined a major beer company and eventually became an executive.

Fred Baron and Ken Frankel

The Treasure Hunters and other military units eventually discovered the Madonna statue in a cave in the Alps mountains. The return of this religious shrine to Brugge brought great joy to the church leaders, worshippers, and Christians everywhere.

Lieutenant Rick Parker

After the firefight near Sibret, Lieutenant Parker and most of his men were captured and spent over five months in a German prison. While in prison, Parker wrote about his experiences in a diary given to him by a soldier who didn't make it. After being released at the war's end, he used the diary to help deal with nightmares, and the reorganization of his lifestyle. Even though the diary was filled with sadness and despair, Parker once laughed at something he had written about an incident in prison. He could not believe he had laughed at something so dark as life in a prison camp. This event sent him in another direction as he wrote a book highlighting the comic relationships between German and American characters within the POW camp. Somehow Parker's book caught the eye of a television producer, who made his war time experience into a popular television show.

Louis Walters

With a medal hanging from his uniform, the former Red Ball Express driver became emotional after the ceremony. As a youngster, he remembered being chased by a White mob who wanted to hang him. Another time, he recalled helping an old White woman across the street, which resulted in his arrest. Still, the grandson of a formerly enslaved person felt that just maybe, in the future, race relations would improve.

But after the war, Louis became disillusioned as segregation remained part of the American scene. Even when he applied for the GI bill that helped veterans return to school, Louis met resistance and red tape before being admitted to a Black college. There he studied journalism and eventually obtained a job with a newspaper in Baltimore.

Louis had the opportunity to witness two major civil rights events. One took place in a baseball stadium in Brooklyn, New York. The other came when President Truman repealed segregation in the military. As a reporter, Louis wrote stories about famous Black entertainers like Billie Holiday, who campaigned for equal justice. The singer made a major impact with her songs, especially "Strange Fruit." This song and a horrifying picture of Black men hanging from a tree caused many White groups to join the struggle against hate and prejudice.

Articles written by Louis followed the Civil Rights movement's successes and failures for over three decades. His greatest moment came when he received one of the pens President Lyndon Johnson used to sign the Civil Rights Act of 1964.

Francis (Frank) Sherman Curry

For his actions on December 21, 1944, at the battle of Malmedy, Belgium, Curry received the first of many medals. Later Frank, wounded three times in combat, earned the nation's greatest honor, the Congressional Medal of Honor.

TERRY KEYS (WOUNDED MEMBER OF THE 333RD ARTILLERY UNIT)

Terry Keys suffered another wound the same day General Patton's Third Army broke the German blockade at Bastogne. Corporal Keys received the Bronze Medal and a second Purple Heart for his actions during the battle. A month after the battle, Terry returned to the states.

As a war hero, he was interviewed by several Black radio stations in his hometown of Birmingham, Alabama. One station offered him a job which he accepted. When a disc jockey was fired, Terry took over the spot and began playing records that had a new sound. Rock and Roll music became popular, and after ten years at the station, Terry moved to a DJ job at a Black radio station in Philadelphia. In the mid 1950s, when Black and White singers began performing together at Rock and Roll shows, he was instrumental in having many Black entertainers and bands appear on Dick Clark's televised American Bandstand show. Terry would not only wake up the city with popular records but would actively participate in the civil rights movement.

Keys' greatest thrill came when he announced from a small radio studio on July 26, 1948, that President Harry S. Truman had issued Executive Order 9981, abolishing discrimination based on race, color, religion, and national origin in all branches of the armed forces.

CRYSTAL SYLK (MP WHO WORKED WITH RUBE ON A CASE)

Rube, while reading the sports section in the *Washington Post*, found a picture and story that piqued his interest. He even asked his wife, Bobbi, to glance at the picture. After seeing the picture, she questioned what was important about a woman wrestler.

Rube's response shocked her. "That wrestler once was my partner."

"Rube Goldfarb, you better have a good answer for this one. You worked with a wrestler?"

"When I was with the MPs, she worked with me on a case. At that time, she wasn't a wrestler."

"What was the case about?"

"Stolen women's stockings."

"Now, this is getting interesting."

Rube then told Bobbi the whole story. Together they read and talked about the article.

As written in the newspaper, the article revealed a story about a World War II vet who began searching for a new career upon her return to the United States. In the early 1950s, professional wrestling became popular. Thanks to the advent of television, unknowns became known. It didn't take long before Crystal Sylk became the Sylky Lady and remained champ for almost two years. On one occasion, her opponent left the ring before the match started after seeing all her muscles. Anyone who challenged the Sylky Lady feared her crunching back-breaking move that sent all opponents to the dressing room defeated. More than once, she floored an opponent with a forearm shiver.

One of her admirers, after several tries, managed to arrange a date with his favorite wrestler. Shortly afterward, they became a couple. After wrestling for six years, Sylky Lady retired and married her boyfriend. The couple had three children, two girls and a boy. Years later, her son would make the all-state high school football team as a linebacker.

Bobbi summed up the article when she told Rube, "Good for her. I wish other occupations would hire women. You can't deny we showed that we could handle the workplace when you guys were overseas fighting. Maybe one day you will see lots more women doctors, lawyers, and politicians."

"I will believe that when I see it."

YVONNE

Yvonne never became a Rockette. Some years later, she, her husband, and two daughters traveled to New York City for a vacation. The first place they stopped was The Radio City Music Hall, and with four tickets bought by Rube and Bobbi, they watched the Rockettes perform.

THE LEGLESS BEGGAR AND HIS MONKEY (REFERRED TO BY RUBE)

In 1936, Eddie Bernstein appeared on the streets of Washington, D.C. Due to a railroad accident in Pensacola, Florida, he lost both of his legs. Because of the injury, his parents sued the railroad company and won $12,000. However, Eddie had to beg for his supper. At first, Bernstein attracted people to his location at the 1200 block of F Street, Northwest, in front of Reeves Tea Room, by using a dog named Snowball. There he sold newspapers and pencils and asked for donations. After the white Spitz dog died, he was given a Capuchin Monkey by one of Washington's richest persons. The owner of the *Washington Post* and Hope Diamond, Evelyn Walsh McLean, helped Eddie survive with the gift of the monkey. Eddie named the monkey Gypsy.

When Gypsy died a few years later, he acquired another Capuchin Monkey, which he also called Gypsy. Eddie only worked the F Street site for half a year and spent the rest of the time in Florida, where his parents lived. While leaving Washington, he paid the Washington National Zoo to care for the monkey.

During his early years of panhandling, Eddie encountered difficulty with the local authorities, who would accept his dog but rejected the monkey as a wild animal and refused to permit Eddie to bring Gypsy to his spot on F street. However, after protests from Bernstein and others, they allowed him to keep the animal if he paid $1.00 daily. Eddie objected to the fee and said he would be bankrupt if it were implemented. Eventually, the fee was removed.

By 1959, rumors spread that Bernstein was worth much more money than he claimed. While in the hospital after passing out in his bleak apartment, a plastic bag was discovered in his clothing containing $2,350 in cash. In 1960, Eddie gave Gypsy permanently to the National Zoo. While in Europe for a vacation, he was told the zoo couldn't continue caring for the monkey as the other monkeys couldn't get along with Gypsy. When Bernstein returned, he wrote a letter to President Lyndon Johnson, who assured Eddie that the monkey would stay at the zoo until its death. Eddie continued to visit

Gypsy at the zoo, and after thirty-nine years of friendship, the monkey died in 1976. Gypsy was buried at the Aspen Hill Cemetery in Montgomery County, Maryland.

Bernstein's wealth became an issue thanks to another beggar, Wilbur Davis. The man with the monkey denied having much money, but when he died in 1979, his estate was worth $691,676. It was also noted that while Eddie was begging on the streets of D.C., he collected an average of about a hundred dollars daily. Also, part of his estate showed he owned a topless bar, a delicatessen, a house, a Cadillac, and a pair of artificial legs.

JOE GREEN

Joe never became a politician nor desired to pursue a political career. Upon returning to the States and completing his degree, Joe, with a couple of his wealthy classmates, started a shoe company that produced sneakers. Over the years, their business expanded into all types of athletic footwear. Joe married and had four children. He lived to age ninety.

DAN SILVERSTEIN

Dan Silverstein returned home after the war to find his wife had departed. It took a while for Dan to realize his marriage was based on his insurance policy rather than anything to do with love. After having his marriage annulled, Dan returned to work at the National Archives in Washington.

While attending a conference on World War II, Dan was introduced to a female employee who had helped arrange the three-day meeting. Although there were many interesting speakers, Dan became more interested in the conference planner. She invited him to speak about his WWII experiences at her next conference. Upon receiving an invitation from Dan, Rube went to hear his talk. Afterward, Dan introduced him to his new girlfriend, Lynn Glass. A year later, Rube and Bobbi attended their wedding. For the next thirty years, Dan became a fixture at the Archives. After he retired, Dan gave talks to various senior and veterans groups on WWII and taught the same subject in classes at junior colleges. When the United States Holocaust

Museum opened in 1993, he volunteered as a docent. Dan and his wife had three children.

JERRY GRAYSON (FORMER HIGH SCHOOL QUARTERBACK AND MP)

With the celebration of V-E Day in May of 1945, Jerry Grayson's commitment to the military ended. As one of the early service members returning from Europe, Grayson had a head start in searching for a new career. Instead of searching for a new career opportunity, the former MP sought a job in the sport he used to watch and play — football. With his knowledge of the game, he secured a job as an assistant football coach at his old high school.

Grayson attended a football conference at the University of Maryland during the football season. The main speaker was a young, first-time football coach. Paul (Bear) Bryant related his experiences in the Navy to training on the football field. In the question-and-answer session, Grayson asked where Bryant had been stationed in World War II. While serving in North Africa, Bryant claimed he was nothing but an errand boy and never came under fire. During the Battle of the Bulge, Grayson revealed his combat missions while part of General Patton's Third Army. After the conference, Bryant invited Grayson to an after-party where the two talked about military matters and football.

Thus, started a long-time friendship between the two men. Bear even came to scout players from Grayson's football team. After the season ended, Bryant accepted a job at the University of Kentucky. Grayson was shocked when Bryant asked him to join his staff in Kentucky. With glee, he answered, "Yes." While in Kentucky, Grayson married, and the couple had their first child. Eight years later, Bryant moved to Texas to coach the Texas A & M football team, and the Grayson family joined the coach's staff. After a four-year stint in Texas, Bryant moved to the University of Alabama, where he became one of the great college coaches of all time. This time Grayson remained in Texas. Now with two sons, Grayson ended his coaching career and opened a Texas-style barbecue restaurant near the college campus.

Grayson operated the business for thirty years and then turned it over to his sons when he retired.

Madison Belanger

While in the military, the Army sergeant and the former Rockette dancer worked with Rube at a USO show. After the war, she returned to the states in search of the perfect partner. It didn't matter what city she chose, men rushed to meet her. But most of the men only wanted one-night stands.

After accepting a job as a model, she met a photographer who was interested in photographing rather than sleeping with her. One of his photos of her landed in *Life* magazine. It showed Madison in a pilot's uniform standing next to a P-51 aircraft, with the scribe below stating, "What's next?" The *Life* photo sent her across the country to Hollywood. In her only picture, a horror movie, she was a knife attack victim. Her movie career might have continued, but she refused to go along with the program of some of those at the studio. With her Hollywood career over, she tried a new medium, television, and became a regular on *The Ernie Kovacs Show*. When the *Kovacs* show ended, Madison became part of an award-winning sitcom. At an Emmy Awards ceremony honoring Madison, Rube and Bobbi had the opportunity to meet the television star. Madison immediately recognized Rube. His first words to her were, "You sure had one hell of an adventure." They both laughed.

Petra Mylosh (the homeless and destitute refugee with her mother at Reims)

Almost two decades later, Petra Mylosh arrived in College Park, Maryland, after a long flight across the Atlantic Ocean. She was about to complete her final class before receiving a business degree from the University of Maryland University College. This educational institution was originally established for American military personnel, but later expanded to include foreign students who wanted the opportunity to obtain degrees in numerous academic categories.

EPILOGUE

For Petra, a very long and arduous journey was about to conclude with completing a business survey class. As she sat among ten other students, many of whom were older, Petra waited for her name to be called by the instructor. After answering, "Here," Petra listened as the teacher finished reading off the list of students. One name in the class drew her attention. After the session ended, she went over to an older woman who was about to leave the room. "Is your last name Goldfarb?"

"Yes."

"Are you married?"

"Why do you ask?"

"Is your husband's name Rube?"

After listening to Petra's story, Bobbi remarked, "No words can adequately describe my complete astonishment. What a small world we live in."

"There is a lot more to tell, but I must return to the motel where I am staying," remarked Petra.

"Don't you dare," insisted Bobbi. "Rube should be in the parking lot waiting for me, and we will drive you back to the motel."

Rube, who had gone to see a Maryland lacrosse match while Bobbi was in the class, turned on his headlights when he spotted Bobbi walking with another student. "Rube, come out of the car. I want to introduce you to someone," requested Bobbi. In the light of the headlights, Bobbi questioned whether Rube recognized the student, whose name was Petra. Rube thought for a few seconds but couldn't remember meeting her.

"Well, maybe this will help," an excited Petra stated. Moving her arm closer to Rube's face, he saw the bracelet Sylvia had given him so long ago.

"Oh, my God. Oh, my God. I don't believe it," an astonished Rube proclaimed.

As Rube drove Petra to her motel, the Goldfarbs listened to a voice from the past who related an amazing story. Upon arriving at the motel, Petra asked Bobbi and her savior to remain in the lobby while she went upstairs to put her books away. In less than five minutes, she returned with her mother. The foursome hugged, kissed, laughed and cried as they heard a story of survival. The desk clerk, hearing intermittently crying moments, inquired if anything was wrong. "No," answered the group. "Everything is perfect."

———•———

Suggested Readings

Balkoski, Joseph. *Beyond The Beachhead: The 29th Infantry Division in Normandy*. Harrisburg: Stackpole Books, 1989.

_____. *From Beachhead to Brittany: The 29th Infantry Division at Brest*. Mechanicsburg: Stackpole Books, 2008.

Beevor, Antony. *Ardennes 1944: The Battle of the Bulge*. New York: Penguin Books Random House LLC, 2016.

Connor, Joseph. "Butcher of Bataan." *World War II.* 37 no. 1 (2022): 38–47.

_____. "Trigger Point." *World War II.* 36 no. 4 (2021): 54–63.

Franssen, Theo. *The Battle of Antwerp: City of Sudden Death*. Translated by Lt. David Arenstein. Antwerp: De Sleutel, 1945.

Fratus, Matt. "The Story of Francis Currey: World War II Medal of Honor Recipient, One-Man Army, G.I. Joe." *Coffee or Die Magazine*. October 11, 2019. https://coffeeordie.com/wwii-medal-of-honor-recipient-francis-currey-dies.

Hambucken, Denis. *A GI In the Ardennes: The Battle of The Bulge*. Yorkshire — Philadelphia: Pen and Sword Books Limited, 2019.

History.com editors. "How Did the Treaty of Versailles Lead to World War II?" Treaty of Versailles, updated April 24, 2023. https://www.history.com/topics/world-war-i/treaty-of-versailles-1.

Hymel, Kevin M. "Patton's Dual Drives." *World War II History.* 22 no. 4 (2023): 36–43/74.

Imperial Society of Teachers of Dancing. "Queering History: Josephine Baker's iconic legacy," February 11, 2022. https://www.istd.org/discover/news/queering-history-josephine-bakers-iconic-legacy.

Lengel, Edward G. "Crossing the Rhine at Remagen." March 6, 2020. https://www.nationalww2museum.org/war/articles/crossing-rhine-remagen; loc.gov/collections/veterans-history-project-collection/serving-our-voices/world-war-ii/jewish-veterans-of-world-war-ii.

MacDonald, Charles B. *The Siegfried Line Campaign*. Washington, DC: The U.S. Army Center of Military History, 1993. https://history.army.mil/html/books/007/7-7-1/CMH_Pub_7-7-1.pdf.

Macdonald, John. *Great Battles of World War II*. New York: Macmillan, 1986.

Petcemeterystories.net. "Eddie 'The Monkey Man' Bernstein: A Rags to Riches Story." August 13, 2018. Update September 3, 2020. https://petcemeterystories.net/2018/08/13/eddie-the-monkey-man-bernstein-a-rags-to-riches-story.

Project Liberty Ship. "The Liberty Ship John W. Brown Marks the Anniversary of her Participation in The Invasion of Southern France 'Operation Dragoon.'" *LIVE*. Baltimore: Project Liberty Ship. 2014.

Shawyer, Katrina. "Letters from Oblivion: Auschwitz and Buchenwald." *World War II History*. 22 no. 2 (2023): 54–61.

Sugihara, Chiune. "The Japanese Schindler." LIFE — *Heroes of World War II: Men and Women Who Put Their Lives on the Line*. (2022): 44–47.

Syken, Bill, ed. "Iwo Jima's Navajo: The Code Talkers." *LIFE — Heroes of World War II: Men And Women Who Put Their Lives on the Line*. (2022): 39–43.

The Anti-Defamation League of B'nai B'rith and The National Council for the Social Studies. "The Holocaust in History, 1933–1945." *The Record*. An Advertising Section of *The Washington Star*. April 16, 1978.

Tuskegee Airmen. https://en.wikipedia.org/wiki/Tuskegee_Airmen.

Zablocki, Peter. "Generation Yank." *Military History*. 38 no. 5 (2022): 24–31.

Acknowledgments

THERE AREN'T ENOUGH WORDS TO THANK those who helped make these books a reality.

My wife Harriet, acting as my first editor, devoted many hours reviewing the books. Her positive reinforcement and ability to find grammatical errors were critical in the completion of the historical novels. Beyond the stories, Harriet's suggestions and fingerprints are visible throughout the books. Many thanks.

Ron Bruno, an expert on World War II vehicles, and his military knowledge provided an invaluable source of material for writing both books. His conversations with me about his visit to Normandy and his discussions with WWII vets enhanced the content of the books.

Thanks to Alice Heiserman of Write Books Right, for her hard work on these books.

Two very important sources of information came from Joseph Balkowski's books, *From Beachhead to Brittany* and *Beyond the Beachhead*. The outstanding research on the day-to-day operation of the 29th division from D-Day to the Battle of Brest supplied the background for the character of Rube Goldfarb and other characters to appear in the books. For anyone interested in studying World War II, Mr. Balkowski's are important books in recounting battles that impacted the European theater.

Dr. Bill Mugleston, a lifelong friend and graduate of Johns Hopkins University, spent many years teaching American history at several universities. His comments, suggestions, and encouragement were extremely valuable in completing the books.

The books would have never materialized without the positive feedback from Nat Brown, who taught history at a high school in Washington, D.C., for many years.

To Jason Weil, of Jason Weil Photography, in Rockville, Maryland, much gratitude for his pictures depicting a war scene using model WWII vehicles and soldiers and for taking the photo of me.

Not enough kind words can be said about the assistance provided by Jain Lemos for both volumes of *The War of Ordinary Folk*. Her expert guidance in every stage of the publishing process were critical in completing the books.

Special recognition goes to the staff of The National World War II Museum in New Orleans, Louisiana, especially Rebecca Poole, Historical Research Specialist, who sought information about the military service of my uncle.

Brandon Weil, graphic designer, offered invaluable information on the presentation of the books.

Many thanks to other people who served as readers and provided helpful comments.

Of course, perhaps most important was the inspiration and information from my Uncle Rubin, who wrote letters back home during World War II.

About the Author

Jason Weil Photography

SAUL LEBOW, BUILDING ON HIS MASTER'S degree in history from the University of Maryland, and inspired by World War II events and personal letters from a soldier, creates two historical novels.

For twenty-eight years, Saul shaped young minds as a social studies teacher in the public schools. He donned the uniform of the D.C. National Guard during a turbulent time and became a member of the first staff of the National Portrait Gallery. As part of an internship, Saul participated in the restoration of classic planes for display at the new National Air and Space Museum. He also served as principal of a local religious school.

In his novels, Saul includes a unique love story, but none could have been better than his own special relationship with his wife Harriet, that is spanning more than fifty years. They live near Washington, D.C. and have two daughters and two grandsons.

Don't Miss Volume I in *The War of Ordinary Folk*

VOLUME I
Exploits of a World War II Medic

THE WAR OF
ORDINARY
FOLK

SAUL LEBOW

Made in the USA
Middletown, DE
01 May 2024

53694819R00205